SAILORS

&

SPIES

THE INTELLIGENCERS  BOOK THREE

BY

JANE GLATT

Sailors & Spies

The Intelligencers ⚓ Book Three

By

Jane Glatt

TYCHE BOOKS LTD.

Published by Tyche Books Ltd.
Calgary, Alberta, Canada
www.TycheBooks.com

Cover Design by Indigo Chick Designs
Interior Layout by Ryah Deines
Editorial by Karley Hauser

First Tyche Books Ltd Edition 2020
Print ISBN: 978-1-989407-12-7
Ebook ISBN: 978-1-989407-13-4

Author photograph: Eugene Choi
Echo1 Photography

This book was funded in part by a grant from the Alberta Media Fund.

Chapter 1

"WE'RE READY."

Dag looked up to find Calder hovering in the open doorway.

"I separated the twelve Pilalians," he continued. "Four will go with Captain Eklund on the *Tazeyar*. I'm sending Jaak with them as well. The rest we'll need to help get us through the Teeth."

"All right." She pushed her hair from her eyes and nodded at Nadez, who was seated behind what used to be Joosep's desk. "Is there anything else?" She and the new Master Intelligencer had been comparing notes about all of the Intelligencers and students along with their Traits. Additional observations were scrawled beside some of the names on the list Dag and Gustav had compiled while hiding with Joosep and Arnor.

"This should be enough for me to decide which Intelligencer's and student's Traits will be the most useful," Nadez replied. "So I know who to try to track down. Thank you, and safe journey."

Dag nodded and joined Calder.

"How's your mother?" she asked as they headed through the hallways.

"Furious," he replied and then grinned. "But she'll do it, even though she spent much of her life avoiding this kind of responsibility."

"Then she shouldn't have bought so much land." They rounded a corner and exited the Hall, and she had to shade her eyes against the afternoon sun.

Dag had been shocked to learn that Calder's mother was the largest landowner in the Three. She held vast tracts of land in Byholt: everything north of Langin and all the way to the White Wood belonged to Lauma Strauskas. The only reason she had never been elected Grand Freeholder was because she didn't want the role. She'd even appointed Calder's brother Yakop as Clan Freeholder, so she didn't have to deal with the responsibilities that came with land ownership.

"My father kept sending her money," Calder said. "And my mother isn't one to spend on luxuries. Even though people offer to help her, she still catches and dries fish and chops her own firewood."

Dag shook her head; Tarmo Holt was willing to do anything to gain and keep power while Calder's mother had no desire for it. How much better off would the Fair Seas Treaty Alliance countries have been if Lauma Strauskas had exercised her rights as a landowner? Or would power have corrupted her and made her more like Holt?

Once they reached the harbour, they were intercepted by people looking for direction from Calder. Dag left him to deal with the last-minute instructions and walked out to the edge of the dock. A ship in full sail was heading out of Tarklee Harbour: the *Tazeyar* on its way north to the Frozen Pass.

A second ship, the only other vessel in the Three that could sail to the Sapphire Sea, waited just offshore. Like the *Tazeyar*, the *Atlaine* had been listed on the second, secret set of titles as belonging to Tarmo Holt. Now, both ships had been commandeered to help bring in supplies before winter set in.

"Let's go aboard," Calder said when he joined her. He led the way along the dock to where a sailor waited, the painter of a dinghy in his hand. Dag stepped into the boat and crawled past the rowers to sit in the bow. Calder joined her, and the dinghy left the dock and headed out towards the ship. A dozen minutes later, they reached the *Atlaine*. A rope ladder was lowered, and she clambered up it and onto the deck of the ship.

"Stow the dinghy," Calder said once all the rowers were on board. "First Mate, take us out." He joined a huddle of people on a slightly raised deck near the rear of the ship.

Dag dodged the rowers who were now hauling the dinghy up and over the gunwale and joined Calder. Beside him, a woman called out orders, sending sailors scrambling up the mast. The sail was unrolled, and the ship lurched when the wind caught and filled the canvas. In less time than she'd expected, they were heading away from the city.

Her only experience being on a moving ship was when she'd stowed away on Margit Ansdottir's *Vassan*, although at the time, she hadn't known it belonged to a pirate. And like now, that ship had headed to the Serpent's Teeth. But this time it would be up to her to get them safely through the jagged spires.

Dag caught Calder's eye, and he turned to her.

"Will we make the Teeth in time to go through before dark?" she asked.

Calder looked up at the sky. "With Luck."

"Is there somewhere I can rest?" she asked. "Until we get there."

"Of course. Rafael!" Calder called. A young Pilalian man hurried over. "This is Dagrun Lund. She'll be navigating us through the Teeth, and she needs some rest before she does that. Take her below to the Captain's cabin and get her anything she needs." Calder turned to her. "Rafael is Second Mate."

"It's very good to meet you," Rafael said. "Please, this way." He escorted her to a door that led below the raised deck.

Dag followed Rafael down a set of steep stairs and along a lamp-lit corridor. Half a dozen narrow doors lined the wooden walls.

"Do all the sailors sleep here?" Dag asked.

"Just the officers and most senior crew," Rafael replied. He stopped at a door at the end of the corridor. "The regular crew bunk down in the hold. Here you are." He opened the door and entered the room.

The layout of the room she stepped into was oddly familiar: then she realized that it was much like Tarmo Holt's cabin on his ship the *Neas*.

A table that likely did double duty for dining and meetings took up most of the space. She assumed that the wall lined with cupboards and shelves separated this room from a sleeping chamber. She peered through the half open door at a bed that was suspended from the ceiling by ropes. A bundle of bedding had been placed on the bed.

"There's a privy through there," Rafael said, pointing towards what Dag had assumed was a cupboard. "I'll have someone make the bed and bring you a meal if you want."

"No, thank you. I'm sure everyone has real work to do. I'll be fine."

Rafael nodded and left, and Dag sighed once the door was closed.

The past few days had been full of frantic action followed by meetings and decisions and far too little sleep. She shook out the bedding and quickly dressed the bed. After a quick trip to the privy, she tugged off her clothes and slipped between the covers.

GUSTAV CRAMMED THE roll into his mouth and chewed quickly as he hurried after Nadez. That had been his first meal—although he couldn't really call a bun with cheese a real meal—in twelve hours and he was still hungry. He couldn't believe just how much there was to do. He'd thought that once Nadez, Calder, and Dagrun had figured out a plan that things would be easier.

How wrong he'd been.

He'd spent the hours since Calder and Dagrun had sailed away running errands as Nadez sought out information about Intelligencers, students, and instructors. So far, he'd left messages for three people who were thought to still be in the city. Only one had responded, but thankfully, it had been Kaja, who had taken over the actual running part of running errands. That left Gustav free to take on other duties that probably used to be performed by poor Arnor.

Now Nadez wanted to make sure that Calder's mother wasn't coming up against any obstacles as she filled the vacancy left by Tarmo Holt.

"Good, you're here," Lauma Strauskas said as soon as he and Nadez stepped into the Grand Freeholder's outer office. "Holt's assistant has barricaded himself inside." She gestured to the closed door in front of her. "I was just deciding between finding an axe and breaking through the door myself or calling for reinforcements." She frowned and stepped over to the door. "You won't like me when I have an axe in my hand!" she yelled.

"Lauma," Nadez said. "We need diplomacy, not threats."

"I might be able to help," Gustav said. "I know Mykol a little."

"Go ahead." Lauma crossed her arms and stepped away from the door. "But if you fail, I *will* find that axe. And I do know how to use one."

Gustav met Nadez's eyes and she nodded. He squared his shoulders and stepped up to the door and leaned his cheek against the wood.

"Mykol, it's me, Gustav. I know you don't trust me, but you need to know that Tarmo Holt has left Tarklee. We think he's heading to the Sapphire Sea."

"He wouldn't leave me behind." Mykol's voice was quiet, and Gustav thought he sounded worried and maybe a little scared.

"Maybe he didn't mean to," Gustav said. "It all happened so quickly. I don't think he's coming back. Saulia and Asla went with him."

"No! He wouldn't just leave me!"

"I am sorry," Gustav said, trying to infuse his words with Charisma. "But it seems that he has. You need to open the door so that the business of the Grand Freeholder can continue."

"So that Timonis can be named Grand Freeholder without a vote? I won't let that happen. Tarmo Holt didn't trust him and neither do I."

"Not Timonis," Nadez called out. "Mykol, this is Nadez Norup. I've assumed leadership of the Intelligencers."

"Where's Joosep?"

"Joosep is dead," Gustav said. "I think you know that Holt had him tortured."

"Grand Freeholder Holt shouldn't have done that," Mykol replied, "but he wouldn't have had to if Joosep had just told him what he wanted to know."

Nadez looked like she was about to say something, but Gustav signalled her to stop.

"Intelligencers have to be neutral," Gustav said. "You know that. We can't align with any single Clan Freeholder, even one who is the Grand Freeholder." He paused. "Nadez Norup, the new Master Intelligencer, recommended that an Interim Grand Freeholder be appointed. Someone without any political ambitions who can fulfil all of the important and needed duties of the Grand Freeholder until the elections can be held. And we'd like your help."

Nadez frowned at him and he shrugged. Mykol knew where everything was: they should use him as much as they could. But they shouldn't trust him.

"Who is it?" Mykol asked. "Your Interim Grand Freeholder?" He sounded resigned now, which Gustav thought was a good sign.

"Lauma Strauskas," Lauma said. "The woman you've been keeping out of that office for the past hour. I don't even want this position and here you are, making it difficult for me to even get started."

The lock clicked and the door opened a few inches. Gustav stepped back as a dishevelled Mykol peered out.

"Lauma Strauskas, the largest landowner in the Three?" he asked.

"The same," Lauma replied. "If you know who I am, then you know that I have never wanted this office or the responsibilities that go with it. But someone has to do it, and Nadez here," she gestured with her chin, "has persuaded me that I'm the perfect choice." She sighed. "But if I can't convince *you*, then I have no chance of convincing the Clan Freeholders."

"No, she's right," Mykol said. "You *are* the perfect choice. A brilliant choice, actually."

"Will you help me?" Lauma asked. "I'll be terrible at the politics."

"She will," Gustav agreed, ignoring Lauma's glare. "She was ready to use an axe on the door. She needs your help. The Fair Seas Treaty Alliance needs your help."

"What about this?" Mykol gestured to the door. "Me locking you out?"

"You were just doing what you thought best," Nadez replied. "Trying to safeguard this office against the wrong people."

"I was," Mykol agreed. He nodded. "I will help. For the sake of the Three, I will help."

"Excellent," Lauma said. "Can you start helping me right away? Because I need to contact every single Clan Freeholder in all three countries and let them know that I want to hold a vote to allow me to take temporary control over this office." She sent a curt nod Nadez's way before entering the main office. "But this has been a real shock, so if you need to take some time first, Mykol, I will understand. Maybe you want to clean up and get something to eat and some sleep? I fear that we have a lot of work ahead of us."

"Yes, Freeholder," Mykol replied. "But if I can have an hour, I think that should do."

"If you're certain you don't need more time," Lauma replied. "What do you suggest I tackle first?"

Mykol pulled a sheaf of papers from a cubbyhole and placed them on the large desk. "These are all the complaints Clan Freeholders have made to this office that have yet to be resolved," he said.

Lauma smiled. "So, the answer to how to guarantee enough support lies here? Very good. I'll see you in an hour."

Mykol hesitated for a moment before he nodded and left.

"And you too," Lauma said, turning to Gustav. "Be back here in an hour."

"Me? I'm an Intelligencer."

"Now assigned to me," Lauma said. "Nadez?"

"Agreed. Gustav, you are now assigned to Lauma Strauskas, but as an Intelligencer, not as her assistant. You still report to me."

"Can I ask why?"

"I don't trust Mykol," Lauma said. "I was watching him when you said that the Fair Seas Treaty Alliance needed his help. He doesn't care about the Three, not really. His loyalty is to Tarmo Holt; and maybe to this office. But it's not to the Three. I need help keeping an eye on him."

"Your Trait will be useful too," Nadez said. "Charisma," she said to Lauma. "Take him with you when you meet with reluctant Clan Freeholders. At the very least Gustav will win over their staff."

Lauma sighed. "I really do hate politics."

CALDER LOOKED OUT across the bow; the jagged spires of the Teeth spread across the sea ahead of them.

The Pilalian pirates had given him coordinates for where Margit Ansdottir entered the Teeth, and he hoped they hadn't lied to him. It was entirely possible that the pirates didn't want him to catch up to Holt and they might assume that there would be no consequences for lying. It was also possible that none of them knew the coordinates but weren't willing to tell him that, thinking that if he had no use for them, he would leave them in Tarklee.

He'd ask Dag where she thought they should enter anyway.

He'd hoped to get the ship to a reasonably close point of entry before he had to disturb her. It would be up to her to see them through the Teeth and she'd said she needed some rest.

He also wanted Dag to speak to the pirates just in case they were hiding anything. He was certain that they all wanted to go home to Pilalia. He was also certain that they understood that this ship, navigated through the Teeth by Dag, was their best chance of getting there before next spring or summer. But did that include helping the *Atlaine* get ahead of Holt?

"Do we go in now, Captain?"

He turned to First Mate Darya Demer. "What do you think?" he asked her. He'd crewed with her a few years ago, before she'd joined the *Atlaine*. She'd always struck him as an extremely competent sailor and even better, she always put the safety of the crew first. Even if it meant going against the direction of the ship's captain or owner.

"We have a few hours before we lose the light," she replied. "So, if we can get through in that time, then we should go immediately."

"My thoughts too," he said. "I'll find our special navigator and see what she says. You have the bridge."

"Yes, sir."

Calder left her in command of the ship and headed below. To be honest, he wasn't sure Dag even needed light in order to get them through the Teeth, but the crew did.

He knocked on the door to the Captain's cabin, his cabin for this journey, before entering.

Dag was sitting at the table, a map spread out before her.

"I hope you're rested," he said as he joined her. He placed a finger on the map. "We're here."

"I got a few hours of sleep," Dag replied. "And some much-needed peace and quiet. Thank you." She stared at the map for a moment before placing her hand on top of his. He ignored the frisson of electricity as she moved his finger a little north. "We need to be here."

He leaned over her shoulder for a better look. "I'll get us there," he said. "In the meantime, I'd like you to talk to the pirates. I need to know if they're hiding anything."

"All right."

He stepped back to allow her to rise. "I'll have Rafael translate for you."

She grimaced. "Thanks. As much as I'd like to practice my Pilalian, I'm far from fluent and I know we can't afford any misunderstandings," she said. "Your mother speaks Pilalian very well."

"My mother was motivated to learn it," Calder said. "She wanted, no she *needed* to make sure that my father could never say that he didn't understand her."

"Did your father teach you?" Dag asked.

Calder held the door for her and followed her out into the passageway.

"Yes. When I was very young and he was around," he replied. "At the Hall it was just part of my studies, although I was better than most. I always thought that early exposure made it easier for me to become fluent."

Up on deck, he waved Rafael over.

"I'd like you to translate while Dagrun speaks with the pirates," he said. "I've asked her to make sure they don't have secrets that could be dangerous to us."

"Follow me," Rafael said to Dag. She gave Calder a nod before trailing Rafael towards the bow. Calder watched them for a moment before turning and making his way to the bridge.

"We need to be a little farther north," he said to Darya. He held out his hand for the compass. "Head west northwest."

"Yes, sir," Darya shifted the wheel slightly. "Now heading west northwest."

NADEZ LEFT JOOSEP'S office, what was now her office, by the small door. She was feeling forced into the role of Master Intelligencer and wanted, *needed*, to ease into the position as slowly as possible.

Instead of staying in her apartment in the Hall where she could easily be found by anyone and everyone with a request or a question, for the next few days she planned on being harder to track down. Within reason, of course; she did have a role to fill and there were tasks and meetings and decisions that only she could deal with.

But she didn't want to be predictable. Not when that might compromise her safety or even the integrity of the Fair Seas Treaty Alliance. Holt had fled and Ansdottir was dead, but she had no idea if there were any other, as yet unknown threats to the

Alliance.

She sighed. Joosep had been predictable; something she thought had contributed to his failure and ultimately to his death.

She'd never agreed with his practice of handing the information he'd gathered to the Grand Freeholder for direction instead of making his own determination about what the intelligence meant. And what should be done about it. He'd also, in her opinion, had an over reliance on Traits.

Joosep had accused her of being jealous because she had no Trait of her own when the reality was that she thought that some Traits just didn't seem very useful. And *nothing* replaced solid skills.

That was one of the reasons why she was so fond of Calder: he had a Trait and he used it, but it complemented his skills, it didn't replace them.

At least Joosep had allowed her to develop much of the training. Because of her input, every student learned statecraft, weapons and hand-to-hand combat, languages, history, and geography. Because of her, every Intelligencer graduated with a vast amount of knowledge they could utilize in their roles.

She paused at the door that led outside, debating which of her bolt-holes she would sleep in tonight.

"Are you coming out?" a voice whispered from the other side of the door. "We have things to discuss, and even if you don't need to sleep soon, I do."

"Lauma," Nadez said as she opened the small door. "Did Gustav tell you where to find me?"

"Yes," she grinned, her teeth gleaming in the light of the lamp she held. "He is rather delightful with that Trait of his. Although I pretend that it doesn't affect me."

"Does that concern him?" She liked Gustav; he'd proven to be very effective for someone only partially trained, but she worried about any Intelligencer relying too much on their Trait.

"I think he blinked twice but then got on with the task," Lauma replied. "I got the feeling he has experience with his Trait not working on someone. Where shall we go for a discussion?"

"Blow out your lamp and follow me," Nadez replied, her decision about where to go decided for her. "And Gustav's Trait *doesn't* work on everyone. He was poisoned not long ago by someone in Tarmo Holt's household."

She led the way to her little stable.

"I didn't think you were much for extra trappings and frills," Lauma said when the lamps had been lit, casting shadows over the small space. "It reminds me of my cabin: enough here to be comfortable but not so much that I couldn't replace it if I had to abandon it."

"Yes, exactly," Nadez said, upgrading her opinion of Lauma Strauskas. "But that's not something I expected to hear from the largest landowner in the Three." She gestured to the table and chairs. "Please, sit."

Lauma sat down and pulled a flask from a pocket. "I brought some mead, if you care to join me. Tarmo Holt has very expensive tastes. I may not surround myself with luxury, but I do appreciate the odd one when appropriate."

Nadez found a couple of cups and set them on the table before sitting down across from Lauma. The other woman poured a deep golden liquid into each glass.

"To the Three," Nadez said and lifted her glass. She gulped the sweet liquid and set her cup down.

"We have much in common," Lauma said as she refilled the cups. "Since we have both been pressed into roles that we never wanted. At least I assume that's why you weren't already Master Intelligencer."

"In part," Nadez replied. "Like you, I don't seem able to say no when my refusal could doom the place I love."

"That's good," Lauma replied, "to know that you love something. I love my children. I also love my community of Byholters. And making sure that no one from my family or community starves this winter is my priority. What's your priority?"

"Keeping the Three safe from internal and external threats," Nadez said. "Which includes starvation."

"I thought we would agree," Lauma said. "Calder doesn't talk much about his life, but he has spoken very highly of you."

"He's said hardly anything about you."

"He tends not to mention that I own a good amount of land. My other son Yakop holds the title and position of Grand Freeholder because I was never interested in having that responsibility. Although I have always understood that someone needs to do it well. That's one reason why I bought so much land."

She shrugged. "The other reason is that I have no desire for . . . things, and frankly, what is the point of coin if you don't put it to good use?"

"That's not an issue I've ever struggled with," Nadez replied. She'd grown up on the streets of Tarklee; her father had been around just enough that she wasn't considered an orphan.

"Yes well, I suppose there must be some compensation for an absent husband," Lauma said. She drank her mead and set the cup down on the table. "Now this is not a social call. I need to know what you think is the most urgent threat and how we can work together to nullify it."

"Making sure that we really do have the authority of our positions," Nadez said. "Otherwise anything we do could be undone."

"Yes, but how? I will be meeting with every Clan Freeholder I can; I've already instructed Mykol to notify them that they need to come here."

"How do you know the ones working against you will come?" Nadez asked. "I wouldn't."

"I told them that we were meeting to appoint an Interim Grand Freeholder." Lauma smiled. "Those itching for power won't be able miss an opportunity to acquire it legitimately. Don't worry. I am already well on the way to having the backing of enough Clan Freeholders to secure my appointment."

"Can I know who and how?" Nadez wanted to believe Lauma; she seemed intelligent and confident. But was she too confident?

"I'll tell you as soon as I have confirmation from a couple of people," Lauma said. "But I won't risk writing any of this down. I won't leave a permanent record of who I have spoken to and what I've promised them. We'll need to meet again in secret."

"No," Nadez replied. "I agree with not creating a record, but I would feel better if we keep all of our meetings formal and meet in the Hall. We can't assume that any secret meetings won't be discovered, and if they are, that could be used against us. I do realize that we can't discuss everything in either of our offices. I'll send Kaja to you. She trained with Gustav. Whatever you tell her she will relay to me word for word."

"A Trait?" Lauma asked. Nadez nodded. "And is there a specific threat you are worried about? Someone I should know about?"

"No." Nadez shook her head. "But I don't trust. It has always seemed safer that way."

"I see," Lauma said, and Nadez wondered what it was she saw.

"I look forward to meeting Kaja, and I'll see you in the Hall." The other woman nodded and left.

Nadez blew out the lamps and sat in the dark for a while. She wanted to believe Lauma Strauskas—wanted to believe that she could help figure out who might be plotting against the Three. But as she'd told her, she didn't trust.

Half an hour later she left the small stable. Only after she was sure she wasn't being spied on did she make her way to another of her safe places.

CHAPTER 2

DAG STARED AT the Teeth. Belmina, one of the Pilalian pirates, stood on her left and Calder was on her right.

"Captain Ansdottir used to stand here," Belmina said. "And give directions. The rest of us belayed her instructions to the First Mate at the wheel."

Belmina was the pirate with the most experience navigating through the Teeth; she claimed to have done it more than a dozen times with Margit Ansdottir. Dag knew she was lying. She was certain that Belmina had been through the Teeth many more times than that but was trying to minimize her past loyalty to the dead pirate captain.

With Rafael translating, she'd spoken to the pirates. Her Pilalian was so poor that she'd understood very little of what was said, but nothing had triggered her Trait. A few of them, like Belmina, were portraying themselves as recent converts to the pirate life, telling Rafael that they'd been with Ansdottir for a few months or a year when Dag was certain many had been with her for many years.

But they all desperately wanted to go home and knew that this ship was their best chance of that.

Dag and Calder had decided to trust the pirates to help them get through the Teeth. Once they reached Strongrock, they'd reevaluate. If they thought they were deliberately misleading them, they could set them ashore on the island.

"That's what we'll do then," Dag said, turning to Calder. "I'll need someone to translate my directions into something that allows you to steer this ship." They'd already decided that Calder would be at the wheel: if something Dag said was somehow misinterpreted, they wanted Luck on their side.

"Rafael will do that," Calder replied. "Along with Belmina."

"How long did it usually take Ansdottir to get through the Teeth?" Dag had asked this question before, but she wanted to make sure they all knew what they were in for.

"Two or three hours," Belmina replied.

"We should have time to get through before we lose the light," Calder said. "Are we ready?"

Dag squared her shoulders. "Yes."

"All right," Calder said. He smiled. "I'd wish you Luck, but we know that you rely on skill."

"I'll take the Luck too," Dag replied. Something ahead caught her eye. "Is that a whale?" She stared for a moment before she saw a plume of spray off amongst the spires.

"That's a good omen," Belmina said.

"I agree," Calder said. "If whales can get through, then so can we."

"Then let's go," Dag said, with more enthusiasm than she'd had a moment ago.

Calder squeezed her shoulder before leaving for the bridge.

The whale had lifted Dag's spirits and chased away some of her apprehension. She *knew* she could do this: she'd navigated a boat through the Teeth once already. Except it had been a small sailboat and the risk had been to just her and Calder. The weight of being responsible for the safety of the entire crew was something she hadn't expected. Calder didn't seem to be bothered by it, but perhaps that was because he'd captained a ship before.

"Captain is ready," Rafael said when he joined her. "First thing we need to figure out is speed, then he'll get some sail up."

"Slow," Dag said. "I think. Belmina?"

"Ansdottir usually started off at two knots," the pirate replied. "And then went faster or slower as needed."

"Two knots it is," Dag said. "And we need to head straight for about half a mile."

"Make course dead ahead at two knots," Rafael called. He

paused as the order was repeated behind them. "Hold steady for half a league."

Once that had been belayed back to Calder, Dag heard orders for the mainsail to be hoisted. She looked over her shoulder to see the largest sail being untied. It dropped and the ship lurched forward when the wind caught it.

She turned to study what was in front of them. The ship was in the Teeth now: there was no going back. She stared ahead, trying to let her Trait show her the hidden path. She saw another whale spout off in the distance and the itch started between her shoulders. That was where they needed to turn.

"I know where we need to go left," she said to Rafael. "See that really tall spire?" she pointed. "We turn left a dozen yards past it."

"Aye," Rafael said. A few moments later he called out. "Easy to starboard in a count of ten."

Dag stared ahead as the ship slowly turned left around a cluster of rocky spires. "Turn left again, hurry," she said.

"Hard starboard, now!" Rafael called.

"Straight for a quarter of a mile," Dag said.

The next two hours passed in a blur. The sun was going down and it reflected off the sea, forcing her to squint. Every few minutes she gave a new direction and Rafael's calls were echoed back to the stern of the ship.

"We're through the worst," Belmina said, and Dag pulled her gaze from the small patch of sea in front of them to scan the horizon. The pirate was right: the Teeth here were smaller and farther apart. Up ahead was open water.

She gave one more direction to Rafael before closing her eyes for a moment.

"We can go faster now," she said. "We're out."

"Full speed," Rafael shouted. "We're through!"

Cheers rose up, and in moments, sailors were climbing up the mast. The top two sails were unfurled; they billowed when the wind caught in them. Dag dragged a hand through her hair and rolled her shoulders, trying to ease the tension.

"As good as Captain Ansdottir herself," Belmina said.

"Thank you," Dag said. This might be the only time she would appreciate being compared to the pirate captain. "And thank you for your help as well." She turned to Rafael. "And to you too. We wouldn't have made it through without your excellent navigational translating. I'm going to find Calder."

"First Mate," Calder said. "You have the bridge. Set course for Strongrock."

"Yes, sir," Darya replied. She grabbed the wheel, and Calder stretched, trying to relax muscles that had been clenched since they entered the Teeth.

He headed towards the bow and met Dag and Rafael on their way aft.

"Well done, both of you," he said. "And thank you. We should reach Strongrock in a few hours." He turned to Rafael. "Take some time to rest and eat and then join Darya on the bridge."

"Yes, sir," Rafael nodded and left.

"Come on," he said to Dag. "Let's find the mess hall." He led the way to the door.

"Will we land at Strongrock while it's dark?" Dag asked as she followed him down a short set of stairs. "Or wait until morning?"

"That depends on what we find when we arrive," Calder said. He headed down a corridor. "Here we are." A moment after he entered the mess he was noticed, and the usual din subsided.

A sailor, a cook's helper from the apron he was wearing, came over.

"Captain, sir. If you tell me what you'd like I can have a tray sent to your quarters."

"I'd just as soon eat here," Calder said. He leaned closer to the sailor. "Unless you think that's a bad idea. We're just looking for a quick meal, not to disrupt meal service."

"Of course, you're both welcome," the sailor said. "There's a clean table right over there." He pointed to a table that was pushed up against the far wall. "I can have Cook make up some fish cakes. It won't take him but a minute."

"Thank you," Calder said. "Tell him not to rush since I think we'll both be happy to start with stew." He looked at Dag.

"If that's the fastest thing then yes, stew would be welcome," Dag said. "And lots of water."

"Right away," the sailor said and hurried off.

Calder followed Dag to the table and sighed when he sat down across from her.

"You don't really want fish cakes," she said to him. "Why

didn't you tell him?"

"Because it's my first meal on board and Cook wants to make me something special," he replied. "But I'm famished, and my guess is that you are too, so a special dish would be wasted on me when I shovel it down."

Dag laughed and he grinned at her. The sailor returned with a jug of water and two cups. He filled the cups before heading back to the kitchen.

Dag gulped her water and poured a second cup before he'd even finished his first.

"I didn't realize how thirsty I was," she said. "Between the sun and the wind and having to concentrate for so long . . ." She sighed and sipped more water.

"Here you go, Captain," the sailor said as he placed bowls of stew in front of him and Dag. A second sailor, a young woman, placed a plate of bread and a crock of butter in the middle of the table, along with eating utensils.

"Thank you," Calder said. "For the excellent service."

"Yes, thanks," Dag said.

The two sailors smiled and left.

"I take it no one else gets served?" Dag asked.

"Not usually," Calder said. He sniffed the stew and smiled. By the scent, Cook had some Pilalian cooking skills.

"It's really good," Dag said as she ate.

"You seem surprised." Calder spooned some stew into his mouth and smiled at the burst of heat and flavour. "Ships run on their crews and the crews run on their stomachs."

They ate quickly. Calder grabbed the last slice of bread and swiped it across his empty bowl, sopping up the last few drops of gravy.

"I'm tempted to ask for another bowl of stew," Dag said. She popped a crust of bread into her mouth.

"Don't," Calder warned. "We still have fish cakes coming, along with whatever else Cook decides to treat us to."

"All right." Dag refilled both of their cups and looked around. "I hope we didn't scare everyone away."

Calder looked up at the almost empty mess hall and shook his head. "Crews eat fast and we came near the end of the mealtime," he said. "That's one reason why I said that Cook didn't need to rush the fish cakes. Ship kitchens are small, and when it's mealtime, there isn't a lot of room to prep something else."

"You've spent a lot of time in ship kitchens?" Dag asked.

"That's how I followed you to Strongrock," he replied. "Peeling potatoes and serving up stew."

"And here you are in charge of the ship."

"It's just a different aspect of sailing," he replied with a shrug. "I think I've done pretty much every job there is."

"And you love it," Dag said. "Life at sea."

Calder had the feeling their conversation was about something else now. "I do love it," he agreed. "But I also love Cutterstown, where my brother lives."

"But that's not the life you chose to live."

"I never really had a choice," he said. "I was sent to the Hall when I was six. Later, when I finished my training, Joosep decided to send me to sea. The fact that I love it doesn't mean it was my choice. Or that I would have chosen it, or would choose it now, if I were given other options."

"Fair enough," Dag replied. "Oh, no. It's a very good thing I didn't ask for more stew. It looks like our fishcakes have arrived."

Calder turned to see one of the sailors who had served them heading towards them, plates draped across both of his arms.

"Cook sends his compliments," he said. "Fishcakes, fried potatoes, roasted beet salad, and smoked trout." The younger sailor hurried over and set down fresh plates and utensils before gathering up the stew bowls.

"It all looks delicious," Calder said. "Give Cook my thanks."

"Yes, sir. I'll tell him." The sailor headed back to the kitchen.

Calder grinned at Dag, who was already spooning beet salad onto her plate.

"What about you?" he asked. "You were older than I was when you arrived at the Hall. Was it a choice?"

"Yes," she replied. "I was so grateful when Joosep came and offered to train me. My mother had just remarried, and my new stepfather did not like the idea of feeding and clothing Inger and I, not when he had three motherless children of his own."

He slid a slice of smoked trout onto his plate. "And you convinced Joosep to allow Inger to come too."

"I wasn't going to leave her behind," Dag said. "My mother was doing her best, but she struggled after our father died. When she met Andrus, I think she thought it was her last chance at a stable life. He had a good-sized farm near Falkis, and I think to her that sounded secure. She found out later that his farm has poor soil and barely yields enough to keep them fed through the winter. If Inger had stayed there, she would have been married off for some sort of advantage for my stepfather. She was better off with me." She paused. "And even after all that's happened, I still believe that. Inger would have been no match for Andrus's scheming."

"Do you see her often?" he asked. "Your mother?"

Dag shook her head. "I haven't seen her in years. I write to her every few months, but I rarely receive an answer. I am in touch with a local Freeholder, so I know she's still alive and in relatively good health." Dag sighed and pushed her plate away. "I wrote to her just before we left. I didn't want her to hear the news from a stranger that one of her daughters was now an enemy of the Three."

"I'm sorry," Calder said.

"So am I," Dag said.

"If you're finished eating, I'll ask for some tea to be sent to the Captain's quarters," he said. "We need to discuss our options for when we reach Strongrock."

"Yes," Dag agreed. "You said that it depends on what we find when we arrive."

"It does. If the *Neas* isn't at anchor, we need to find out if we've arrived there before or after her."

"What if the *Neas* is there?" Dag asked.

"Yes," Calder replied. "Exactly. What if the *Neas* is there?"

GUSTAV BALANCED THE tray of jugs as he followed Mykol into the meeting room. Four tables were set in a square, all of the chairs on the outside facing in.

"A water jug goes in the middle of each table," Mykol said.

Gustav squeezed into the centre area, set his tray down, and moved a jug onto the table. Mykol carried a tray of glasses, enough for him to place one in front of each chair: four on three of the tables for the Clan Freeholders who represented each country and a single glass on the fourth table for the Grand Freeholder.

They were preparing for the meeting of all of the Clan Freeholders. It had been called with very short notice, so they didn't expect everyone to attend, but Mykol said that they had to have a seat for each of the twelve Clan Freeholders. Anything else would be seen as a sign of disrespect at best or, at worst, an attempt to interfere with the process and give one country or Freeholder an advantage at the expense of the others.

Lauma Strauskas claimed to have enough votes to confirm her appointment as Interim Grand Freeholder, but she wasn't going to sit in that chair until the vote. And since her son was the Clan Freeholder for her holdings, she didn't have a seat at the Byholt table either.

Gustav placed jugs of water on the other three tables before edging his way out of the square of tables. He left the tray on a sideboard and exited through the small door that was along the back wall. He stood just outside of the room and peered back into it through the open door. He was going to act as Lauma's assistant while Mykol received the Clan Freeholders.

Two men stood just inside the main door and Mykol headed over to greet them.

"Oh good, my son Yakop is here," Lauma said from Gustav's side. "The other Freeholder is Noak Carlsen. He's been a friend of my family for decades. They will have brought proxies for the other two Byholt Freeholders."

"Are you certain of the Swyford contingent?" he asked. "Timonis is next in line. Won't he see this as his turn to be Grand Freeholder?"

"This is still Nordmere's time to fill the position," Lauma replied. "Timonis will not want Ottosen to be named Grand Freeholder even for a few months. Are there any rifts in the Swyford camp? I don't expect anyone from Nordmere to vote for me, but will anyone from Swyford side with them?"

"You don't think so."

"I've done my best to ensure they don't, but that doesn't mean I can't be surprised." She patted a sheaf of papers that were tucked under one arm. "I have promised that as soon as I am elected Interim Grand Freeholder, I will use this meeting to resolve some of their long-standing issues."

A woman and two men arrived and were seated at the Swyford table. A few minutes later, Timonis joined them.

"They look like they're all getting along," Lauma said. "Go see if you can tell if they're having any arguments about me."

Gustav headed out into the meeting room and stepped back into the centre of the tables.

"Can I pour you some water?" he asked, lifting the jug that was in front of Clan Freeholder Timonis. He smiled, trying to exude Charisma.

"Yes," Timonis said. He didn't even look up from his conversation with the woman beside him. Gustav took his time filling all four water glasses but even he couldn't stretch the task out indefinitely. He put the jug down and prepared to move to the next table. Nothing he'd heard, neither in words nor in tone indicated that the Swyfordians were having any disagreements.

"Water, Clan Freeholder?" he said to Lauma Strauskas' son.

"Yes, please," Yakop replied. "I take it my mother is planning a dramatic entrance?" He raised his hand and signalled: *are you an Intelligencer*?

Gustav was so surprised that he spilled some water on the table.

"I'll take that as a yes," Yakop said softly. "Calder is my brother."

"Yes, of course," Gustav said, but he *had* forgotten.

He filled two glasses before setting the water jug down and moving to the next table. The Nordmere contingent had just arrived. From what he knew they had already been in the city, so arriving last was deliberate. Did they think it made them seem more powerful? And was that why Lauma was planning, as her son suggested, a dramatic entrance?

"Shall I pour you some water?" he asked a grey-haired man he thought was Clan Freeholder Ottosen. The man sitting beside Ottosen looked familiar even though Gustav was positive he'd never seen him before.

"No," Ottosen replied. "I don't trust any of you. Heikki?" he said. He leaned over and fixed his gaze on the woman who sat on the other side of the familiar-looking man.

"I don't trust anyone either," she said. "I will not be eating or drinking anything during this meeting."

Gustav shrugged and returned to the side door. He'd been poisoned by someone from Nordmere. Maybe it was a common thing for Nordmerians to do.

"Well?" Lauma asked as soon as he closed the door.

"Swyford is relaxed," he said. "No one seemed nervous, and

there were no raised voices or whispered conversations while I was at their table. But Nordmere? They are not happy."

"I'm not surprised about Nordmere," she replied. "Freeholder Seppa is the brother of Tarmo Holt's wife. But it's good to hear that Swyford isn't fighting amongst themselves."

"Asla's brother? I thought he looked familiar."

"How do you know what Asla Holt looks like?" Lauma asked.

"Sorry, I shouldn't have said anything." He closed his eyes, embarrassed that he'd thoughtlessly divulged a secret. He could discuss his past assignment with Nadez of course, but he wasn't sure Lauma was privy to Intelligencer assignments and reports.

"Never mind," Lauma said. "Do you think anyone will recognize you?"

"No one here has met me before," Gustav said.

"Good," Lauma said. Then she stepped past him and into the meeting room. She paused just inside the doorway and waited until she was noticed. Eventually the room quieted and Lauma walked over to stand behind the single chair at the Grand Freeholder's table.

Gustav slipped into the room. He closed the door and stood with his back against it. Ostensibly he was there in case any of the Clan Freeholders needed anything. In reality he was there to watch and listen and then report anything he found odd or out of place. His challenge would be what to report and to whom. He'd report everything he noticed to Nadez Norup, of course, but he thought that Lauma also expected to hear his thoughts.

He spent the first half hour watching the expressions of each Clan Freeholder as Lauma directed the discussions. No single person stood out as particularly defensive but the Nordmerians said little and Ottosen scowled the whole time.

The quick call for a vote surprised him. Seppa raised an objection, stating that there was already a Grand Freeholder, but Yakop reminded everyone that his brother-in-law Tarmo Holt had unilaterally tried to postpone the fall election and that now he'd fled the city.

Both actions made Holt seem guilty of *something*, and the Alliance needed an Interim Grand Freeholder to discover what, if any, transgressions Holt had committed. Even one of his fellow Nordmerians abandoned him then.

The votes were cast and Lauma accepted the appointment as

Interim Grand Freeholder. She sat down in the single chair and nodded to Mykol, who set a stack of documents on her table.

Mykol was in his element, and Gustav watched with interest as the assistant kept the meeting organized. He handed out documents as the topic of discussion changed while each of the matters contained in the papers beside Lauma was discussed and dealt with.

"All right," Lauma finally said. "That concludes the existing issues at hand. Now we need to talk about another, more urgent threat. We are facing starvation this winter *and* immediate trade disruptions caused by the loss of so many ships. The destruction of the Lavais shipyard means we have no easy way to resolve either issue."

"Starvation? Surely you are being overly dramatic," Seppa said. "There are warehouses across the city that are full to bursting. Besides, I'm sure that ships are due back from the Sapphire Sea before the Frozen Pass closes."

"Two," Lauma said. "Out of all of the ships registered with the Merchant Adventurers, there are only two ships left that can make the journey to the Sapphire Sea. Both have already been sent, but I fear that those two ships will not keep us fed until spring." She fixed her gaze on Seppa. "These warehouses you mentioned. Are they yours? Can you guarantee that they are full? Because the Intelligencers tell me that dozens of warehouses across the city are *not* full: at least the ones owned by Tarmo Holt are not. Clan Freeholder Strauskas, what steps are you taking?"

Gustav wondered who she was speaking to until her son replied. He'd thought Yakop would be named Rahmson, like his brother Calder. The same way Gustav was named after his father Gunnar.

"We've increased the number of people fishing," Yakop said. "By pairing woodcutters with fishermen. Others have been sent into the forest to hunt for game and schooling has been halted in order to free the children for foraging. Berries, mushrooms, and tree nuts are all being collected and stored communally. The same goes for all the dried fish and game. Each community has appointed two people to oversee the food storage and distribution in order to get everyone to spring alive."

"You gave your food stores to the community?" Seppa sneered.

"Yes," Yakop replied. "As did every single person in my Freehold."

"Mine too," Noak Carlsen said.

"No one is taking my food," Seppa said. "Not as long as I'm alive to protect it."

"You live in the city, don't you?" Noak asked. "Were you not here during the food riots? I truly hope that desperate people do not come for you and your supplies, but if your plan is to ignore what's happening, what has already happened, then Byholt will not save you. Not even if you are at physical risk from your own starving people."

"Is anyone else planning on hoarding their food for themselves?" Lauma asked.

No one spoke out, and Gustav watched Seppa, wishing he had Dagrun Lund's Unseen Trait. Was Seppa truly oblivious, or was he hiding something? How did he think to escape the city if starving people rioted?

And because he was watching Seppa, he caught the look that was shared by two of his fellow Nordmerian Clan Freeholders. A momentary glance, that was all, something he would have missed if he hadn't been focussed on the man who sat in between them. Ottosen turned towards Heikki and their eyes met before his focus returned to Karl Seppa. Neither one changed expression, nor did they speak. But that one short, shared look had Gustav trying to recall what he knew about the families.

Because that one look changed everything. Karl Seppa wasn't conspiring against the Three: Ottosen and Heikki were.

He let his gaze wander around the table and met Yakop's eyes. The Freeholder raised his eyebrows and flashed a sign. Gustav nodded. Calder's brother knew he'd discovered something; there was no sense denying it.

With a vow to learn how to better control his expressions, Gustav watched as the meeting dissolved into petty squabbling between the Clan Freeholders.

Eventually, Lauma ended the meeting and Gustav followed her through the door along the back wall.

"Well, that went about as expected," she said to him. "Off you go, I know you need to report to Nadez. I will be having supper with my son anyway. Find me once Nadez tells you what you can share with me."

CHAPTER 3

RAFAEL MADE HIS way around the table, pouring tea. Dag picked up her mug and sipped. It was no longer piping hot, but it was welcome nonetheless.

She, Calder, and Rafael were in the Captain's cabin. A map of Strongrock Island and the strait that led to the Sapphire Sea covered the table in front of them.

"We could take a dinghy and land here," Dag said, pointing to the spot on the map where a couple of abandoned huts stood. "We know it's easy to get to the harbour by land from here."

"I think it's too dangerous when we don't know what we're walking into," Calder said. "Landing here would put us ashore before we've seen what ships are in port."

"If Holt isn't at anchor, there's no way to know if we're ahead or behind him *without* landing."

"I volunteer to go," Rafael said. He'd set the teapot on a side table and returned to stare at the map. "Tell me where the paths are, and I'll scout the tavern and find out if Holt is there or has already been and gone."

"I'm the one who should go," Dag said.

"No. Maybe," Calder said and then sighed. "Yes. But not until we know whether or not the *Neas* is in the harbour. With good weather they would have had enough time to make it through the Frozen Pass. We'll sail past the harbour, and if there's no sign of Holt or the *Neas*, we'll land you between the town and the beach where the children live. That way the *Atlaine* can head off the *Neas* if we see it approaching Strongrock from the north. I won't risk stranding you unprotected on the island if Holt arrives after we do."

"That will work too," Dag replied. She was glad she didn't have to spend time convincing him that she should be the one to land. She knew Calder wanted to keep her safe, but that wasn't his responsibility. Nor was it his job to stop her from doing hers. But she wouldn't be foolhardy. "I'll take Rafael with me. If we can't overhear what we need to know, he can talk to someone; too many people on that island know Inger and have seen me. Pretending to be Inger might bring more scrutiny than Rafael's presence will."

"I agree," Calder said. "Rafael, ask Belmina if she can find you some clothing that will make you and Dag look like you belong."

"Yes, sir," Rafael said. He gathered up the teapot and cups and left the cabin.

Dag turned to Calder. "I know you want to keep me safe, but I hope this plan isn't more complicated than it needs to be. Someone on Strongrock, or on a ship in the harbour, might see us as we sail past."

"It's a slight risk," Calder said. "As the captain of this ship I'm responsible for the safety of every single person aboard." He paused. "But I can't lie, I especially want you to be safe."

"I know," Dag said softly. And she did know, although it was nice to hear him say it. She stepped closer and put her arm around him and leaned her head on his shoulder. "I feel the same way about you, but I also know that you have skills and talents and a Trait that we need to use if we're going to stop Holt and recover Inger."

"Yes, I—"

"Captain!" someone called from the corridor and then knocked on the door. "Strongrock Harbour is coming into view. First Mate has ordered all lights extinguished and requests your presence on the bridge."

"Let's go," Calder said. He blew out the three lamps and headed for the door.

Dag followed him out of the cabin, feeling a combination of excitement and nervousness.

The deck was dark and silent as they made their way to the

bridge. Dag peered out across the water: a few lights shone in the distance. Was it the Broken Mast? Was Ursa in her tavern serving Tarmo Holt?

Her gaze shifted to the harbour and she felt an itch between her shoulder blades. Concentrating as she stared out at the harbour, a darker shadow became clear.

"I see a single ship in the harbour," she said to Calder. "Without lights. How do I tell if it's the *Neas* or Ansdottir's ship?" Ansdottir had gone down with the *Bright Breeze*, and they all assumed her own ship was still in Strongrock. News of Ansdottir's death wouldn't reach the island until Holt did.

"If it's a single ship, I think we can assume that it's the *Vassan*," Calder said. "No one on Strongrock is going to sail that ship without Ansdottir's permission. Are you sure there's only one?"

"I'll check from the bow," Dag said. "In case Holt and the *Neas* are hiding somewhere." She walked along the ship's gunwale, staring out, trying to see if anything else was anchored off the island. She paused at the bow; they were closer to the harbour now, and she could hear shouts coming from the normally subdued tavern. Had the influence the pirate captain's Traits had over their behaviour died with her?

Or had Holt already visited, bringing news of Ansdottir's death?

She made her way back to Calder on the bridge.

"I didn't see another ship, but the tavern is louder than usual," she said. "I think something has happened."

"You think Holt has been and gone?" Calder asked.

"Or Ansdottir's death was felt here," she leaned in closer, "because when she died so did the hold her Traits had on her people."

"Interesting," Calder said. "And impossible to know if that is good or bad for us."

"The pirates will be less disciplined," Dag replied. "But will they become reckless or, like the Pilalians, will they just want to go home?"

"Let's hope they're just drunk and not reckless. Here." Calder grabbed a bundle from behind him. "Rafael was able to find you something to wear that will make you look a little more like a pirate. It will take about ten minutes to sail around the harbour and find a place to set you ashore."

"I'll be back before then," Dag said. She took the bundle and made her way back to Calder's cabin.

"It *was* the *Vassan*," Calder said when she rejoined him. "I got a look as we went past. I don't think anyone was on board, or if they were, they didn't see us. No one raised an alarm."

"Is that usual for Ansdottir's crew?" Dag asked.

"Not according to Belmina. If Ansdottir's death has removed some sort of control or discipline she had over the pirates, then we need to be extra careful."

"Agreed," Dag said. She took a deep breath. Inger was with Tarmo Holt: had he been influenced by Ansdottir's Trait? Even if he had, she didn't think he would suddenly become undisciplined or rash. The Pilalian pirates hadn't.

"Where are Belmina and the rest of the pirates?" she asked Calder. When she'd spoken to them earlier, she hadn't thought they'd been affected by Ansdottir's death, but now she was wondering if they had been. They were all single-mindedly determined to return to Pilalia. Was that something that Ansdottir's Trait had suppressed?

"They're below," Calder said. "They're being watched but not locked up. I don't think they'll want to ruin their chance to get home, but they have former shipmates on shore. It's possible they would want to help some of them get home too."

Dag nodded even though she wasn't sure Calder could see her. "Do you need me to keep watch for anything hidden?"

"We should be fine," Calder replied. "The sea approaches here are deep and clear. That's why the pirates like it so much. But you can let me know when you see that rock ledge we crossed. We should be able to set you ashore just south of it."

"All right." Dag walked over to the right to the starboard gunwale and stared out into the night, looking for anything familiar. She'd travelled this shoreline by foot a couple of times and expected to recognize some landmarks. And she did. They were coming up to the beach that led up to the ledge. The beach she and Calder had raced across while being chased by Ansdottir's pirates.

"We're here," she said when she returned to Calder's side. "The beach just north of here is where the children live." If they *were* still there. Teacher had likely been under the influence of

Ansdottir's Trait. What had happened when that influence disappeared? She couldn't imagine Teacher abandoning the children.

"We'll get a dinghy in the water for you and Rafael." He paused and leaned close. "Are you sure you don't want anyone else going ashore with you?"

"No, more people won't make us safer." More people would make them more likely to be discovered. She knew her Trait would allow her to keep one person Unseen, but she wasn't sure she could conceal more than that. Besides, this was an island where even one new face might be too many.

The crew was eerily quiet as they lowered the dinghy. They launched it from the side of the ship that wasn't facing the shore, hiding the smaller boat from anyone who might be watching from land.

Dag followed Rafael down into the dinghy and sat in the bow while he set the oars in place. A few moments later he was rowing them past the stern of the *Atlaine*. Dag peered through the dark towards land; she didn't see anyone, but that didn't mean the beach they were heading to was empty.

She looked over her shoulder at the ship. The night had closed in, and all she could see was a faint outline against the slightly lighter sky.

Calder would keep the ship where it was for half an hour and then travel north, in case Tarmo Holt was on his way south to Strongrock Harbour. By that time Dag planned on being close enough to the town to get answers. If they didn't overhear a conversation about Tarmo Holt's whereabouts, Rafael would have to find someone to talk to.

Once they had news, they would return here and wait for Calder.

The dinghy scraped sand and the surf pushed them farther into shore. Dag jumped out and was joined by Rafael, and together they tugged the small craft up onto the beach. Rafael stashed the oars in the dinghy, and Dag grabbed his arm and pointed to the path that led south to the settlement.

With one last look out towards the *Atlaine*, she ducked into the forest, Rafael a step behind.

SOMEONE KNOCKED ON her office door and Nadez looked up from

the report she was staring at. It was early evening, and she was alone in the office of the Master Intelligencer; she pursed her lips. It had been difficult to stop calling it Joosep's office but even more difficult to call it *hers*.

"Enter," she said.

The door opened, and Gustav poked his head in. "Is it too late to give my report?" he asked.

"No. Come in," she put the paper down face down on the desk. "I was hoping you would come by tonight."

Gustav closed the door and sat down.

"I expected the meeting to go for hours," Nadez continued. "Does that mean it went extremely well or extremely badly?"

"It started off fine," Gustav said. "Lauma was elected Interim Grand Freeholder and only two of the Nordmerians objected: Clan Freeholders Seppa and Ottosen."

"Heikki didn't vote with them? That is interesting." Nadez frowned. "Did Lauma get through her list?" Nadez had helped her decide which issues to promise to resolve in order to secure the votes, but she hadn't been able to add any insight. Despite never bearing the title of Clan Freeholder, Lauma Strauskas had never shirked the responsibilities that came with owning the land. She knew more about her fellow Freeholders' personalities and politics than Nadez did: maybe even more than Tarmo Holt had, and he'd become Grand Freeholder because of his ability to wield that knowledge.

"Yes," Gustav replied. He gave a thorough accounting of the discussions: all of it more or less what she'd expected.

"And how did Mykol act?" Nadez asked.

"He was in his element," Gustav replied. "He made special efforts with the Nordmerian Clan Freeholders."

"I suppose that's to be expected," Nadez said. "He's been in Holt's employ for years." They knew they couldn't completely trust Mykol. She'd have a chat with Lauma about him: Mykol might be too useful, or too dangerous, to let go.

"Where did the meeting break down?" she asked.

"When the topic of food collection and distribution started," Gustav said.

"Not surprising," Nadez said. "I assume that it was Nordmere who rejected the plan for handling food?"

"Yes," Gustav said. "Clan Freeholder Seppa was the most

vocal."

"No doubt he has Tarmo Holt's interests in mind," Nadez said. "Did you know that he is the brother of Asla Holt? Tarmo Holt's wife?"

"Lauma mentioned it," Gustav said. He sighed and looked away. "I'm afraid I made a couple of mistakes tonight, Master Intelligencer." He met her eyes. "I mentioned to Lauma that I thought Seppa looked like Asla. She asked how I knew what Asla Holt looked like. I didn't tell her," he quickly added, "that it was because Joosep assigned me to get close to Tarmo Holt's family, and so I befriended his daughter. She was fine once I assured her that no one at the meeting would recognize me."

"It's safe to tell Lauma about your assignment with the Holts," Nadez said. "It might even help her. You said you made a couple of mistakes? Do they all pertain to Lauma Strauskas?"

"No, the others have to do with her son, Yakop." Gustav paused. "When I greeted him, he used Intelligencer hand signals to ask if I was an Intelligencer. I didn't answer him, but I didn't have to. He knew by how I reacted."

"Hmm." Nadez was less concerned about the fact that Calder had taught his brother hand signalling and more interested in how she might be able to use that knowledge. "I wouldn't worry too much about that. I don't think Calder's family would do anything to harm the Three."

"Oh, good," Gustav said, obviously relieved. "Because Yakop knows I learned something really important during that meeting. I'm not sure he knows what it is, but he and Lauma are having dinner, and between them they might be able to figure it out."

"Are you confirming that Seppa is still working against the Alliance on Tarmo Holt's behalf?" It was what they'd all expected, so why did Gustav think it was such a revelation?

"No," Gustav said. "It's not Seppa: the Nordmerian Clan Freeholders we need to worry about are Ottosen and Heikki."

Calder stared out at the beach. He could see the dinghy that Dag and Rafael had pulled up onto the sand, but they were nowhere in sight.

"It's time," Darya said from his side. "Shall I have the anchor raised?"

"Yes," he turned to her. "Keep a quarter mile offshore and sail dark." He looked up at the sky; it was still mostly clouded over. It made it harder to navigate but easier to sail undetected.

Darya dispatched a couple of sailors to silently relay her orders by visiting the on-duty crew members. It took a little longer than usual, but soon the main sail was filled with wind and the ship was skimming across the water.

Calder kept watch at the starboard rail as they rounded the next point to the beach where the children lived. The huts should . . .

The small beach was ablaze with torches and lamps, and a ship was anchored just off the beach. A single dinghy sat in the shadow of the ship.

It was the *Neas*: Tarmo Holt was here.

Calder hurried over to Darya, noting that she'd pulled in the sails and dropped the anchor in order to slow them down. But even without lights, there was little chance of remaining undetected.

"*Skit!*" he swore. The *Atlaine* didn't carry a cannon, but he could see one at the stern of the *Neas*.

Lights waved furiously from the other ship, signalling that they'd been seen.

"Should we engage?" Darya asked, and Calder knew that what she was really asking was should they try to ram or board the other ship.

"No. Try to pass along their port side," he replied. "And stay out of their cannon's line of fire. We can't risk boarding unless there is no chance of damaging or losing this ship. And we can't ram them for the same reason." They couldn't afford to lose the *Atlaine*: the food it needed to deliver from the Sapphire Sea would mean life and death for too many people.

"Yes, sir," Darya said.

"I'll break out the long guns." Calder headed to the gun locker. He heard Darya call the crew to arms and was ready when eight sailors arrived. The rest of the on-duty crew was busy raising sails and hauling in the anchor.

He handed out the guns, powder, and shot.

"Port side and be ready," he said before grabbing a gun for himself.

He stared out at the *Neas*: sailors were climbing the rigging, letting the sails out, and as they passed the stern, he saw four people dragging the cannon into position. Abandoned now, the dinghy was being swept away from the beach towards the rocky shore.

"Ready," Calder called, and his sailors brought their weapons up. "Aim." They were alongside the *Neas* now, coming alongside their bridge. Would Holt be there or was he safe down below?

Then he saw her: blonde hair shining in the light of a nearby lamp. For a moment he thought it was Dag, thought that somehow she'd been captured and that he and his crew were pointing guns at her, prepared to kill her.

He paused just long enough that they sailed past her. And he knew that it wasn't Dag: it was Inger.

"Shoot!" he called, hoping that Inger was out of range while realizing that he might have missed their only opportunity to kill Tarmo Holt or the captain of his ship.

Shots rang out and the smell of powder filled the air. He heard cries of pain from across the gap between the two ships.

"Take cover!" he called and ducked below the gunwale, fumbling as he re-loaded his long gun.

A volley of shots rang out from the *Neas*, but they were already out of range. His gun reloaded, he returned to the bridge.

As he joined Darya, a couple of sailors ran up to her.

"No damage to report aft," one said.

"No damage fore," the other said.

"Captain?" Darya asked. "Do we approach again or see if they chase us?"

The *Neas* was making a wide turn in order to point its cannon at them.

"Go out to sea and try to flank them and head them off," he replied. "We need to keep them from reaching the town and harbour." Dag's destination.

At full sail, Darya sent the ship speeding away from the island, the *Neas* following close behind them.

"Now take us back into shore," he said to Darya. "Keep the *Atlaine* between the *Neas* and the town."

"She's not following," Darya called.

Calder pulled his gaze from the island and looked out to sea. The *Neas* was in full sail moving away from them.

"Should we chase them?" Darya asked.

"Those *skits* left them behind," Belmina said from beside him.

"Sent them ashore and then just left them!"

Calder frowned. She was right: crew from the *Neas* had been left on Strongrock, and the empty dinghy they'd been ferried over in was now foundering on rocks.

And the very thing he'd wanted to prevent had happened: Dag was on shore and stuck between Holt's people and the pirates of Strongrock. He turned to Darya.

"Let them go," he said. "We have our crew members to find."

DAG HEARD THE guns and instinctively ducked before realizing that the shots came from too far away to be directed at them. She looked out through the trees to the sea. In front of them the sea was calm: no ships or sailboats or dinghies that could carry pirates and their guns.

The gunfire had come from behind them, not from someone on the path ahead. So, the guns were either directed at or coming from the *Atlaine*.

"We need to find out what happened," she said. She slipped past Rafael and hurried back the way they'd come, leaving him to negotiate the dark path by himself.

A second volley of gunfire echoed across the water and she stared out to sea again, but there was nothing there.

A few minutes later, Rafael caught up to her.

"They must have met up with the *Neas*," she said, turning to him. "Unless you can think of another reason for gunfire?"

"The only other reason for gunfire would be if the Pilalian pirates mutinied and tried to take over the *Atlaine*," Rafael said. "Which I think unlikely."

"Me too," Dag agreed. "Belmina and her people have already been promised what they want: to go home." Gunfire had been exchanged; had anyone been injured?

Both ships carried people she cared about. Unless her sister had been set ashore. Now that Ansdottir was gone, would Holt still have a use for Inger? Or would he want to be rid of her?

Other than where she and Rafael had landed, the only other place along this coast where the *Neas* could set someone ashore was the beach where the children lived.

"We need to get back to where we landed," she said. "The *Atlaine* must have exchanged gun shots with the *Neas*, which means we have our answer: Holt is not in Strongrock and he's unlikely to go there now." She'd leave Rafael with their dinghy and make her way to where the children lived. In case Inger was there.

Dag led Rafael along the dark trail, stopping a few minutes later at the edge of the beach. She dropped to her knees and stared out. Cloud cover meant that there was no moonlight, but she was able to distinguish the dark shape of their dinghy, pulled up on the beach right where they had left it.

"If the *Atlaine* is out there they're still sailing without lights," Rafael said from behind her. He was about to step past her when she reached a hand out, barring his way.

"Someone is on the beach," she said. Was it Teacher? Why wouldn't she take the sailboat?

Dag closed her eyes, concentrating on her Trait. When she opened them, her gaze went straight to a group of adults trudging along the sand, coming their way.

"Eight people," she said to Rafael. "I don't see any way they will miss seeing our dinghy." Or the two of them if they kept on the trail.

"I can pretend to be a pirate," he said. "And say that my dinghy started taking on water while I was on my way to see the children."

Dag looked around and frowned. There was no place to hide where she thought she could keep both her and Rafael Unseen. They had two choices: one was to stay ahead of Holt's crew and make their way to the Strongrock settlement and the second was to do what Rafael suggested. She didn't like either option.

"Hey," someone called out from the beach, and Dag froze, thinking that they'd been seen.

"There's a dinghy here."

Half of the sailors huddled around the dinghy while the rest looked around, probably searching for whoever owned the boat.

Rafael rose to his feet, but Dag pulled him back down. One sailor hauled the oars out of the dinghy.

"We got ourselves a better way to get to the tavern," the woman said, holding the oars up. "A replacement for the one that never came back for us. Let's get this boat into the water. I'll even offer to row. Anything is better than walking."

"I want a drink," a second pirate said. "Or ten, now that I got no ship to return to."

"I told you Holt didn't really think of us as his crew," a third one said. "Ansdottir would never have left us like this. Skit Freeholder."

The sailors, Strongrock pirates according to that last comment, dragged the dinghy into the surf and climbed in, giving Dag and Rafael a third option. It meant that she and Rafael lost their way back to the *Atlaine*, but she knew what she needed to know: Inger was not among the sailors abandoned by Holt.

Her sister must still be on the *Neas*. Did that mean Tarmo Holt still had some use for her? She had to hope it meant he'd keep her twin alive.

"They're out of sight," Rafael said. "Should we start a fire and signal the *Atlaine*?"

"Unless we see the ship, I think we should wait for dawn," she said. "In case those pirates are wrong about the *Neas* being gone."

Dag stepped out onto the beach and sat down facing the sea.

She still didn't know what had caused the gunfire or if anyone had been hurt: if Calder and Inger were alive. Dawn was only a few hours off, but she knew it would seem much longer.

GUSTAV PAUSED WHEN he saw the light in the office. Was Mykol here already? It was still an hour before dawn, and he'd wanted to arrive before Lauma's assistant. Nadez had told him to go ahead and tell Lauma about his thoughts on the Nordmerian Freeholders, and he'd wanted to speak with her without worrying Mykol would overhear him.

"Good morning." He put all his Charisma into his greeting as he pushed the door opened and entered the Grand Freeholder's outer office.

"Good morning to you too."

It wasn't Mykol smiling up at him from his desk; instead it was Yakop Strauskas.

"My mother is in there," he gestured to the door that led to the main office. "She asked me to take a look and see if anything out here looks . . . unusual." He turned his head. "Mother, I've been caught."

"*Skit*," someone said from inside the office, followed by the sound of a chair scraping across the floor. Yakop grinned at Gustav as the door to the office was flung open.

"Don't any of you people sleep around here?" Lauma

Strauskas stood in the doorway, her dark hair piled in a loose bun. "Gustav, just the person I want to see. My son says that you have information. Can you share it?"

"Nadez says that I can share everything with you," Gustav said. "Even before I have a chance to tell her." He'd been the one to push the Master Intelligencer on that point, and eventually she'd agreed after acknowledging that it took time for him to get away from his duties here and meet her. Time that might make a difference. No one wanted Lauma to make decisions with incomplete information.

"Did she?" Lauma said. "Are you worried about divided loyalties?"

"No, Freeholder," Gustav said. "My loyalty is to the Fair Seas Treaty Alliance. I also have the discretion to withhold information if I think you are working against the Three."

"Fair enough, young Gustav." She turned to Yakop. "Did you find anything?"

"No," he replied. "If Mykol is still working for Holt he isn't keeping any evidence here."

"Good, then let's all have a chat." Lauma stepped back into her office and Gustav followed her. Yakop joined them, closing the door.

"I was right, wasn't I?" Yakop asked as he sat in the chair beside him. "You discovered something important at yesterday's meeting."

"I did," Gustav agreed. "Nordmerian Freeholders are still working against the Three."

"Seppa? We already assumed that," Lauma said.

"Seppa is being used as a distraction," Gustav said. "Since he's related to Holt, it would be obvious that he would side with him. Too obvious. The two to watch out for are Henrik Ottosen and Daina Heikki."

"Interesting," Lauma said. "Their families have been arguing about land claims for decades."

"They didn't even vote the same yesterday," Yakop said. "What makes you think they are working together?"

"Nothing more than a gut feeling," he admitted. "They shared a look. Just after Seppa said that no one was taking his food as long as he was alive to protect it." Gustav paused. "And then Noak said that Byholt wouldn't help him if his own starving people threatened him. That's when they shared a look."

"What do you think they are planning?" Yakop asked.

"I think they might try to use a riot as a distraction and then have Seppa murdered," Gustav replied. "They could even create a riot in order to do it."

"You think that these two Nordmerian Clan Freeholders are now actively plotting against one of their own." Yakop looked like he'd eaten something bitter. "Based on a single look you say they shared."

Gustav shrugged. Nadez hadn't quite believed him either but he *knew* that this was something they were thinking of. This was another reason why Nadez had agreed that he could take what he learned to Lauma Strauskas. As a Freeholder, Lauma understood the other Freeholders in a way that a Master Intelligencer never could: she could validate Gustav's concerns better than anyone else could.

"It makes sense," Lauma said. "In the context of what Heikki and Ottosen have always been after: land. It makes perfect sense."

"How does this help them get land?" Gustav asked. This was what he hadn't understood. Why would these two Freeholders turn against Tarmo Holt and his brother-in-law?

"Yakop, you tell him," Lauma said to her son.

"They are assuming that now that Holt has fled, he will never be allowed to return," Yakop said.

"He might be captured," Gustav replied. "Calder and Dagrun have gone after him."

"Yes. I am confident that my brother and Dagrun will find Holt. But if they do bring him back, he will face charges. My guess is that Heikki and Ottosen have proof that he committed treason."

"Which they can use to strip him of his lands," Lauma interjected.

"In which case the land goes to his heir," Yakop continued. "Or his closest kin."

"Would that be Karl Seppa?" Gustav asked.

"Yes, if Holt's wife Asla and daughter Saulia are also found guilty," Yakop said. "That's why Seppa has to die. So he can't inherit Holt's property."

"Whether Holt returns or not," Lauma said. "His property

could be settled on Seppa, minus some fines if Holt and his wife and daughter are all found guilty of treason. If Seppa dies before that judgment, then his heir only inherits Seppa's lands. Holt's properties would be divided amongst the three remaining Nordmerian Freeholders."

"Seppa's heir would still get some land," Gustav said.

"True," Lauma said. "But they would all have similar wealth. No single Freeholder would control the majority of the land in Nordmere. And because the Nordmerian Clan Freeholders hold a hundred percent of the land, they would be reduced to three and not the usual four Clan Freeholders."

"For Ottosen and Heikki it would be a more equitable division than it is currently," Yakop said. "Right now, Holt and Seppa control about sixty percent of the land. Holt owns about forty-five percent: by far the largest share of the Nordmerian Freeholders, and Seppa fifteen percent. This split would redistribute that: Ottosen and Heikki would then each control about thirty-five percent of the land leaving Seppa's heir with the remaining thirty percent."

"They would each have more land and wealth and power than they do now," Lauma said. "Together they would effectively make all of the decisions for Nordmere."

"Much like Tarmo Holt has been doing since he married Asla," Yakop said. "And Seppa became his most loyal ally."

"Eventually either Ottosen or Heikki would try to ally with Seppa's heir and cut the other out of the decision making," Lauma said. "Perhaps one of them already has a plan for that."

"What about Saulia?" Gustav asked. "I can see how Asla might be charged along with her husband, but how would they make anyone believe Saulia was involved?" He'd only befriended her as part of a mission but still, she'd been nice to him.

"She did flee with her father," Lauma said. "Many would just assume she was guilty. She'd need some very strong allies in order to not be seen as complicit in his treason." She smiled. "Thank you, Gustav. If the family is returned, it might make sense to ensure that Saulia Holt has those strong allies."

"You mean you," Yakop said.

"The girl might be entitled to forty-five percent of Nordmere," she said. "It might be worth it."

"What about Karl Seppa?" Gustav said. "I think we should try to keep him alive, don't you?"

"Of course," Lauma agreed. "I will help in any way I can, but frankly, I see that as an Intelligencer matter. Yakop? You have to get home. Don't forget I need you to talk to Berna."

"Yes, Mother." Yakop rose and Gustav followed him out. When they reached the door that led from the outer office to the hall, Gustav paused.

"How much of Byholt does your mother control?" he asked.

"Seventy percent," Yakop replied and grinned. "And yes, that means that she has the power to make all of the decisions in Byholt. She never misses giving me her opinion," he said more seriously, "but she has never once forced her will on the people of Byholt."

"But she could if she wanted to," Gustav said.

Yakop sighed. "Yes, she could if she wanted to."

Chapter 4

Calder paced the deck, stopping every few minutes to stare across at the settlement. Hoping that Dag and Rafael had been able to stay ahead of the crew Holt had left behind, he'd had Darya sail them to Strongrock Harbour. They'd been sitting offshore behind the *Vassan*, dark and quiet, for almost an hour.

Despite the approaching dawn, the tavern was still noisy. To his ears it sounded like nothing more than rowdy drunks and not a group of angry pirates with prisoners. There were no signs that Dag and Rafael had been caught. But there also were no signs that they'd safely arrived at the settlement as planned.

"There's a dinghy," Belmina whispered. "Rounding that point."

Calder followed her to the bow and peered out into the dark. The small craft sat low in the water, battered by waves as it hugged the shore. Voices from the dinghy drifted across to him. He looked up: the cloud cover was still thick enough that the risk of moonlight exposing them was low. As long as the crew of the *Atlaine* kept quiet and whoever was in the dinghy didn't look too hard.

He counted six, seven, no eight people in the dinghy, but there was only a single set of oars. No one had blonde hair: Dag was not in the little boat.

"I think it's *our* dinghy," he said to Belmina, "but not our people." Had they overpowered Dag and Rafael in order to acquire the boat?

"I recognize a couple of them even from this far away," she replied. "They were part of Ansdottir's crew."

"So, they're pirates and not Holt's sailors," Calder said. "It makes sense that he would be willing to leave them behind."

"Still shouldn't have left them," Belmina said.

"No, he shouldn't have," Calder agreed. "Do any of them look hurt?" Dag wouldn't fight unless she had to, but he knew her training: she wouldn't be captured without inflicting damage on at least some of her opponents.

"I don't think so," she replied. "If Edur was hurt he'd be wailing and whining. I think they came across the dinghy and took it."

"Good." Calder felt the tension leave his shoulders. "That means that Dag and Rafael are still out there." He returned to the bridge.

"Dag and Rafael aren't in the dinghy," he said to Darya. "If they don't turn up by dawn, we'll make our way back to the beach where we set them ashore." He had hope that Dag's Trait had kept them safe.

"Yes, sir," she said. "We'll be ready to move when you say."

Calder nodded and headed back to the bow to watch for Dag.

The pirates made plenty of noise as they tied up and scrambled out onto the dock. A few people from the tavern wandered over, and even from this far away, Calder could hear Tarmo Holt being cursed.

Then they started shouting about Ansdottir's death and more pirates rushed from the tavern. Calder held his breath when he heard the name *Vassan* but although a couple of pirates peered out towards them, no one raised an alarm. A few moments later they all left the dock and set out in the direction of the tavern.

"There was no talk of a fight," Belmina said.

"Wouldn't the news of Ansdottir's death be more significant?" Calder asked.

"A fight in the last hour would be mentioned first," she replied. "Especially if one of them was hurt. Ansdottir's death is more important but not top of mind."

"You know them better than I do," Calder said. He blew out a breath. Dag and Rafael hadn't been discovered. So, where were they? He stared at the settlement. Maybe they were there, hiding.

He shook his head: if Dag was close, she'd see the *Atlaine*. And she'd send a signal or use the dinghy to row out to the ship.

After a burst of noise and activity, the noise from tavern eventually subsided. Calder made his way to the bridge and Darya. Dag and Rafael weren't here: it was time to go find them.

A few minutes later they were on their way back to the beach where they'd set the two of them ashore.

"Light half the lamps," he said once they were out of sight of the Strongrock settlement. He didn't want too many lights in case the *Neas* returned, but he wanted Dag and Rafael to be able to see them.

The sky was starting to lighten by the time they rounded the point. Two figures on the beach stood up and waved, and he closed his eyes in relief.

"Launch a dinghy," Darya called, and Calder went to help. As much as he wanted to make sure Dag was all right, he didn't join the sailors in the boat. Instead he waited at the gunwale, watching as the dinghy made it to shore. Dag and Rafael waded out into the surf and climbed in and the boat headed back to the *Atlaine*.

"We heard gunfire," Dag said as soon as she joined him on deck. "Are you all right?"

"No injuries," he said. He wanted to ask her the same question; he wanted to take her in his arms. Instead he leaned close. "I saw Inger on the deck of the *Neas*. I don't think she was hurt."

Dag blew out a big breath. "I was hoping she'd been left behind," she said. "When we heard the gunfire, it seemed pretty obvious that Holt wasn't at Strongrock." She paused. "So we came back here. Then the pirates came along the trail complaining about being stranded by Holt." She met his eyes. "Is it true? He left?"

"Yes. We drew the *Neas* out to sea and it kept going east. We waited at the settlement to make sure you hadn't been captured. Come on. You too, Rafael. We need to get you warm and fed and then I'll hear your report."

Dag and Rafael went to change out of their disguises while Calder went to the mess. By the time they joined him, Cook had porridge and tea on the table.

"The only thing we don't know is why Holt was at the beach

with the children," Dag said.

Calder looked up at her. She and Rafael had eaten and given him their report: other than almost encountering the pirates, there wasn't anything that would help them track down Holt.

"You think that something's Hidden?" he asked, wondering if her Trait had been activated.

"Must be," she replied.

"Then we need to go there," Calder said.

NADEZ OPENED THE door to the outer office and sighed in relief. Kaja wasn't here yet: that meant she would have some time to herself. It wasn't that she didn't appreciate having an assistant, but she was used to being alone. And anonymous.

She unlocked the door to her office, quickly lit a couple of lamps, sat down behind the desk, and pulled out the sheet of paper that she'd tucked into the waistband of her trousers.

It was the list that she and Dagrun Lund had worked on: the list of Intelligencers, students and instructors, including everyone's Traits.

A few names had notes beside them: people that she'd already learned had left the city as well as some strange rumours that had surfaced. She needed to follow up on even the tiniest bit of information and make sure she knew where people were. Once she knew they were safe she would select a few to come back and help her.

She knew already which rumour she was going to track down first: an odd report that seemed unlikely unless you knew about Traits. And this Trait was one they needed now. She folded the list and tucked it away before leaving her office and locking the door.

Kaja had still not arrived in the outer office, and although she'd been grateful earlier, now she was annoyed. It was possible the girl could recall some little bit of information she'd heard that would help Nadez determine if she was walking into danger.

With a frown, she left the office and headed down the hall. She wasn't about to become a Master Intelligencer like Joosep: she wasn't going to be desk bound and rely completely on the opinions of others. Especially since she had the most experience of any Intelligencer still in service.

Just before noon, on the North Tarklee side of the river, Nadez paused outside of a grimy door. A man she'd spoken to had assured her that this was a tavern. A poor one, by the looks of it, which meant it could be dangerous. But it was also where she'd been told she could get anything fixed.

She tried the door and when it opened, she carefully pushed it all the way open. A patch of daylight illuminated the wooden floor and a path worn in the dirt that covered it. She took a step inside and stopped just on the threshold.

"Heard this is the place to get a drink," she called out. "Any time of day or night."

"You heard right," said a voice on her left. "You got coin?"

Nadez reached into her pocket and pulled out some coins. "I also have something I need mended," she said. "I heard I can get that here too."

"Yep. Close the door."

Nadez did as she was asked, closing the door and taking a few steps into the room. It took a few moments for her eyes to adjust to the gloom. She nodded at the man who was standing behind a dilapidated bar, staring at her.

Shaggy grey hair hung limp to his shoulders and his apron was covered in what she hoped was just food stains.

"Whatcha got that needs fixing?" The question seemed innocent enough, but his right hand clenched an ugly-looking spiked club that was resting on the bar in front of him.

"It's personal," she said. "I'll only show it to the person doing the fixing. Is that you?" She was certain that it wasn't; that was why she was here, but she didn't want this man to know that she knew anything about the person who was able to fix things.

"I gotta check for weapons," he said. "Before I send you in."

Nadez walked forward, lifting her jacket away from her body. She turned around slowly, keeping her breathing steady even as she worried about a blow that might come.

"I have no weapons," she said as she faced him.

"Coin," he said. "On the counter."

Nadez placed the handful of coins on the scarred wood and stepped back. The man grunted and scooped them up.

"Through there," he said, gesturing to the small door behind him. "And down the stairs. And don't start thinking you can steal from me. There's no way out of that room except through me."

Nadez nodded and went to the door. When she turned to close

it behind her the man was standing in front of the door, club in hand, watching her.

She closed the door and followed a faint light down four rough stairs to a cellar. Ale kegs were stacked along one wall, the smell of spilled beer masking anything else.

Until she stepped into a tiny space at the end of the corridor: then the stench of human shit and vomit assaulted her.

"Janni?" she called softly. "Jarri?" Something moved and then a pale arm reached out from under a pile of what she'd thought was rags.

"Who's there?" a soft voice called. "Jarri, is that you?"

"Janni." Nadez knelt down, doing her best to ignore the stench surrounding them. "It's Nadez. Where's your brother?" Janni pushed the hair from her eyes and stared up at her.

"Nadez? You can't be here," she said. "He'll kill Jarri if he finds out."

"That man upstairs is dead," she said. "He just doesn't know it yet. What has he done to you? Can you sit up?"

"I can't leave," Janni said. "He'll kill Jarri."

"How do you know your brother isn't already dead?" Nadez cursed Joosep for trying to make these two into Intelligencers. They were twins and had strong Traits: Janni could Make and Remake and Jarri could Unmake. But neither of them had the instincts needed for spying. If it wasn't for Joosep these two would be living in the village they were born into, using their Traits to help their family and neighbours. Instead, they'd been forced to try to learn Intelligencer craft and had been dismal failures at it. That had stripped them of their confidence.

And now this; somehow just a few weeks after leaving the Hall, they'd been kidnapped and were being preyed upon.

"They bring him back every day," Janni said. "They give him terrible drugs, so I do what they ask and every afternoon they bring him here and I help him survive the night." A sob escaped her, and she clamped a dirty hand over her mouth. "Then it starts again the next morning when they take him away and I have to Remake things for them."

"All right." Nadez pulled a broken compass from beneath her shirt. "I have to ask you to fix this for me." She was worried that Janni's captor would somehow know if she hadn't used her Trait, although he hadn't seemed to care what Nadez had brought, only that she had the coin to pay him.

"That was simple," Janni said, handing the compass back to her. She gripped her hand. "Please don't do anything. They'll kill Jarri, I know they will. They almost have already."

Nadez nodded and slipped the compass back beneath her shirt. Based on the smells in this hole, Jarri had very little time left. So, she would do as she was asked and leave: but she would be back.

She wanted every last person involved in this unconscionable enterprise to be found and punished. And she didn't care if that meant they ended up dead, although she'd prefer to make them suffer; the way they were making poor Janni and Jarri suffer.

She didn't tell Janni that she'd be back; she didn't think she had to. It did take all of her self-control to walk calmly up the stairs and be pleasant to the monster behind the bar.

He's a dead man, she told herself as she left the dingy tavern. It was just a matter of time before she made that a reality.

Kaja was at her desk when she got back to the Hall. She sent her to fetch Gustav before she entered her office, closed the door, and sat down. It took her a few minutes to get her anger under enough control; at least enough that she could harness it.

By the time she heard a knock on her door she was calm. She opened the door and gestured for Gustav to come in.

They had plans to make.

Dag stared at the beach: it was quiet, too quiet. A trail of smoke rose up from one of the two buildings suggesting that someone was there but there were no signs of children: no shouts or giggles and no youngsters scampering on the beach.

"I don't see anyone," she said to Calder. "But I doubt the *Neas* took them with them."

"I agree," Calder said. "I don't see Tarmo Holt rescuing orphans. I think it's time we went ashore to confirm it."

Dag nodded and followed him to the side of the boat opposite the beach. The dinghy that had been used to rescue her and Rafael earlier had been towed behind the *Atlaine*. Now it was ready to take them ashore.

Dag climbed into the dinghy and waited while Calder, Rafael, and Belmina joined her. Belmina claimed to know Teacher: she said she'd brought supplies to her a few times. The hope was that

Teacher and the children would recognize her and realize that they'd come to help.

And they had: it was just that none of them knew what help to give them.

While Rafael rowed, Calder steered them toward the dock. Dag sat in the prow, staring at the buildings. Now even the smoke had disappeared. Were they being watched?

A curtain fluttered in a window and she itched between her shoulder blades. But when she stared at the window, her gaze was drawn past the building to the surrounding forest.

"They're in the woods," she said softly. "Behind the buildings." She didn't see anyone, but her Trait was telling her that someone, or something, was there.

Belmina jumped onto the dock and tied them up. Dag stepped out, still focusing on the woods behind the buildings.

"Belmina should go first," Calder said. "And I'll be right behind. Rafael and Dag will stay here with the dinghy."

"No," Dag said. "I need to be in front. I'll see any traps that might have been set."

"Does Teacher have a pistol?" Calder asked Belmina.

"I've never seen one," the pirate replied. "But that doesn't mean she doesn't have one." She took Dag's arm. "We'll go together. Jebris knows I have no desire to walk into a trap."

Dag looked over the other woman's head at Calder, who nodded.

"Rafael, you stay with the dinghy," Calder said. "Keep your weapon ready. I'd prefer not to lose two dinghies on one day."

"Let's go," Dag said as she and Belmina made their way along the pier to the beach.

"Teacher," Belmina called. "I expect you're scared, but we mean you no harm. It's Belmina: we've met a few times in the past when I helped bring supplies here."

"Don't trust you privateers anymore," a woman's voice called out from the forest. "Not after coming in the middle of the night and scaring the children." There was a pause and then the voice came from a part of the forest. "We don't have what you're looking for."

Dag exchanged a look with Belmina, who shrugged. "If something was hidden here, I don't know what it is."

"All right," Dag replied. Her Trait hadn't sensed any secrets when she'd been here before, but then, she'd assumed that the children *were* the secret.

"Will you come and talk to us?" Dag called. "We've meet before, when I arrived on your beach hungry and thirsty after walking around the island. I'm Dagrun."

"Inger's sister? What are you doing with privateers?"

"We're taking them home," Dag replied. "To Pilalia. And looking for Inger. Tarmo Holt has abducted her. He's the one who was here last night."

"Is it true?" the voice was closer now. Dag put a hand on Belmina's arm when she took a step forward.

"Is Margit Ansdottir really dead?"

"Yes," Dag replied. She looked over her shoulder at Calder. "There is someone here who saw her go down with her ship. I think that when she died the hold she had over the pirates, the privateers, died with her."

Dag resisted the urge to scratch between her shoulder blades as she waited for Teacher's response. Her Trait triggered a moment before Teacher emerged from the forest, the pistol in her hand pointed at them.

"When," Teacher said. "When did she die?"

Calder stepped forward. "Just after dawn two days ago," he said. "I saw it myself."

"You claiming that it took just over a day to get here from Tarklee?" Teacher frowned.

"Ansdottir did that all the time," Dag said. "That's how most of the children were brought here."

"True enough," Teacher said. "But that was *Captain Ansdottir*. No one else did that. Ever."

"Until now," Dag said. "I navigated through the Teeth with help from Ansdottir's old crew." She gestured to Belmina.

"She did," Belmina said. "Just like the captain."

Teacher stared at them for a few moments. Finally, her shoulders sagged. "Two days ago at dawn," she said, lowering the gun to her side. "The little ones felt it too: woke up whimpering, some of them did. You say Captain Ansdottir had some kind of hold on us all?"

"I think so," Dag replied. "And it's safe to call the children back to the beach. We mean you no harm."

"No choice anyway," Teacher said. "Ansdottir was the one who made sure we had food. Without her, we'll all starve. Come on, children," she called out. By the time Teacher stood in front of Dag, over a dozen children had crept out of the woods and crowded around her.

Teacher sighed again. "They came in the middle of the night," she said. "Used to think Ansdottir's crew were friends, but the ones who came ashore last night weren't friendly." She frowned. "Then they threatened us. Me, a lone woman trying to protect a group of children. *Despicable*. That's when we heard the gunfire, and thank Jebris they left before they hurt anyone. Took off down the trail to find out what was happening to the ship that brought them."

"They were looking for something," Dag said. "Weren't they?"

Teacher didn't reply, but she pursed her lips.

Dag met Calder's eyes and nodded. "Whatever it is, I'll be able to find it."

GUSTAV PULLED HIS hat down over his eyes. He was watching the scarred door of the ratty tavern and had seen all the patrons leave, despite it being only late afternoon. They'd been chased out half an hour ago by a man who fit Nadez's description of the barkeep. Something he didn't want his patrons seeing must be about to happen.

Gustav leaned against his cart and casually looked around. Nadez was somewhere nearby but he didn't see her; for someone without a Trait she was very good at not being noticed.

He assumed that her own ability to fade from sight was one of the reasons why she was so angry that Joosep only trained people with Traits to be Intelligencers. And he had to agree with her. When she'd told him about Janni and Jarri Breck he'd been angry at Joosep too.

Janni couldn't walk: she could Make anything, repair anything, except herself. Her legs had accidentally been Unmade and horribly twisted by her twin when their Traits manifested.

Janni Made herself a chair so that she could get around, and Jarri did everything he could to help her. And then Joosep had recruited them as Intelligencers.

This was yet another thing Nadez and Joosep had argued about. Nadez hadn't told Gustav that, but she hadn't had to. She *had* said that Janni and Jarri should never have been recruited, that they didn't have the temperament for the job, which made Gustav wonder who else had a Trait but didn't have the temperament. He was pretty sure that described Vilis.

A couple came into view, the woman, her face obscured by a scarf, was being hugged tight by the man. At least that was what he thought until he saw Nadez step out from behind a building and slowly start to follow them.

Gustav tilted his hat higher on his head: he needed to be able to see Nadez's signal. Yes, there it was. He pushed himself away from his cart and out into the middle of the street. He bumped into the man and, for a moment, looked into the face of his companion. It wasn't a woman, it was another man, slightly built and unshaven. His eyes were unfocussed and glassy, and Gustav had to stop himself from retching at the stench.

"Apologies," Gustav said, tearing his gaze away from one man to look at the other. He grinned, putting as much Charisma into it as he could. "Had a touch too much ale and lost my balance," he said, brushing dust from the other man's jacket. "Can I buy you a tankard?"

"Get off me," the other man said, pushing at Gustav with his free arm.

"Sorry," Gustav said. Then he pulled on the man's arm and yanked him off balance. Nadez grabbed his companion so only the captor tumbled to the ground.

"I'll kill you for that," the man said.

"You'll have to catch me first." Gustav took off down the street. He paused to look behind him. The man looked at Nadez, seemed to discount her as a threat, and started after Gustav.

Gustav rounded a corner and dashed through the line of guards waiting there. As soon as his pursuer appeared, they grabbed him and pushed him to the ground.

"Give us a few minutes head start," Gustav said. A guard nodded and Gustav jogged back to Nadez.

"Jarri's in worse condition than I had hoped," she said. "But he is alive." She'd taken Jarri to the cart, and now the two of them helped him up onto it and wrapped him in blankets.

"He's been drugged, hasn't he?" Gustav asked.

"Yes, but at least we know Janni can help him." Nadez met his eyes, her face grim. "Time to go save her."

Gustav nodded and started across the street to the tavern. The door didn't open so he pounded on it. "Need a drink," he called out. "Heard you were always open, so open up."

"We're closed now," a man shouted from inside. "Be off."

"Open up," Gustav repeated. He kept pounding on the door despite the shouts from inside telling him to go away.

Finally, he heard what sounded like a wooden bar being lifted and the door was flung open. Gustav took a quick step back as a club was waved in his face, the spikes embedded in it coming way too close for comfort.

"I said go away," the man yelled.

"Just one drink," Gustav said. "Then I'll gladly be on my way." He took another half step back until he was in the road. Would this man follow him? Yes. He raised the club over his head, ready to strike.

"Go away or I'll make you," he said.

Nadez whistled and Gustav lifted his arms in a wide shrug. "Is that any way to treat a customer?" He grinned as the man's face clouded with anger and the club started on a downward arc. Then a guard grabbed him from behind, and another two stepped in front of Gustav and tackled the man.

"You got no right," the man yelled.

"Yes, we do," Nadez said as she joined Gustav. "You have been holding two Fair Seas Treaty agents captive. The minimum punishment for that is prison and the maximum is death."

"You won't be able to do anything to me," the man sneered. "I have powerful friends."

"Not more powerful than mine," Nadez said. "Take him and his friend to the prison. I'll deal with them once I've seen to my agents."

"Yes, Master Intelligencer," one guard replied.

The man looked at Nadez in surprise, and Gustav suppressed a grin. Then all desire to laugh fled: this man probably did have powerful friends. They needed to find out who and stop them from doing more terrible things.

"You stay with Jarri," Nadez said. "I'll go get Janni." She led two guards into the tavern.

"I'm Gustav," he said to Jarri when he returned to the cart. "An Intelligencer, like you."

He looked up at him with watery blue eyes. "Janni?"

"Nadez is getting her," he said. "You're both safe."

"I told her to let me die," he said with a sob. "I told her that if she let me die then they wouldn't have a hold on her. But she wouldn't. She just kept Remaking me."

"I've come across people like the ones holding you before," Gustav said, thinking about the men he'd saved Vilis from. "They would have just started hurting *her*. You kept them from doing that."

"Did I?" Jarri asked. "I've only ever caused her harm. Do you really think I helped?"

"I know you did," Gustav replied. "I know you did."

Nadez came out of the tavern, followed by a guard carrying a woman wrapped in filthy blankets. Nadez nodded, and Gustav blew out the breath he'd been unconsciously holding.

"There she is," he said to Jarri. "Your sister is safe now too. We'll get you both back to the Hall and get you some help."

The guards loaded the siblings into Gustav's cart, and Nadez hurried ahead to warn the infirmary. As he followed his cart through the streets, Gustav had to agree with Nadez's comment that the Brecks should never have been recruited as Intelligencers. Jarri's pain was old: Joosep must have been aware of it. And yet he'd chosen to train them anyway.

Janni was the one who couldn't walk, but it seemed to him that Jarri was the one who was broken.

CHAPTER 5

Calder silently handed a bowl of porridge to Dag. She took it and absently spooned it up using her fingers. When she was done, she handed the empty bowl back to him and wiped her hands on her trousers.

She'd been up and down the beach half a dozen times since Teacher and the children had emerged from the forest, and she still hadn't given any sign that she'd found what was hidden.

Calder stepped away to return the bowl to the cooking hut. He was on his way back to Dag and glanced out to sea when his focus narrowed. Almost at the same time as he saw it, the bell on the *Atlaine* rang out.

"It's the *Tazeyar*," he said when he rejoined Dag. "They made it around the Frozen Pass. I'll have Rafael go and greet them." He left her studying the forest and returned to the dinghy.

"I'd like Jaak to come ashore," he said quietly to Rafael. "Can you go and get him?"

"Aye." Rafael jumped into the dinghy and settled the oars while Calder untied the painter and tossed it into the bow. With a shove, he sent Rafael out into the little bay.

"Sending for reinforcements?"

Calder turned to find Teacher behind him. "Yes. One of your former charges. You remember Jaak? He was brought here to live before joining the pirates."

"I know Jaak," Teacher said. "He was always a trustworthy

lad."

"He still is," Calder replied. "That's why he's now one of my crew." He thought Teacher paled slightly: she knew more than she'd admitted. Was she hoping to keep whatever was hidden for herself?

"I thought Dagrun was supposed to be able to find anything," Teacher said, looking towards Dag.

"That's right." He didn't say anything more because it *was* right: he had no idea why Dag hadn't been able to find anything. Unless there were no secrets to be found on this beach. "If it's here, she'll find it." And if it wasn't, he was hoping Jaak might know where to look.

He turned and headed back to Dag. Holt had the pirates land here for a reason.

"I'm not finding anything," Dag said, her frustration evident in her voice. "No matter how many times I scan the beach and forest, my Trait is not activating." She met his eyes. "Sorry."

"I asked Rafael to bring Jaak ashore," he said. "He might be able to help."

"More than my Trait?"

"I don't think there's anything wrong with your Trait," he replied. "I don't think anything is hidden on this beach. But the pirates landed here for a reason."

"You think that there's some sort of map or directions here telling us where to look?"

"Or Teacher knows where to look," he replied. "With the sailboat, she had access to every bay on this side of the island. I think the pirates were here for her."

"I'll talk to Teacher," Dag said. "See if she's hiding anything."

"Yes," Calder agreed. Dag turned, and he followed her to the cooking hut, where Teacher was supervising half a dozen children cleaning up after their meal.

"It's not here," Dag said as she reached Teacher.

Teacher didn't react that Calder could see but Dag smiled.

"I wasn't sure until just now," Dag said to Teacher. "Why won't you tell us where to look?"

Teacher grimaced and then sighed. "How will I look after these children?" she asked. "If you take everything from us? Margit Ansdottir made sure we were safe and fed. Now that she's gone, these children have nothing. Again. They've all been abandoned, one way or another, but not by me. *Never* by me. So, find it if you must, but I won't help you."

"You refused to help the pirates," Calder said. "Is that why their dinghy was going back to the *Neas*? Were they going to bring someone here to try to convince you?"

"Said they would bring Charis," Teacher replied. "As if him being second to Captain Ansdottir means I'd trust him like I trusted her." She shook her head. "You won't find it with my help."

"At least we know it's not on this beach," Dag said. "I need the dinghy. I don't think Teacher has ever been much for walking along the coastline." She turned and left, and Calder studied Teacher, who looked defeated.

"She *will* find it," he said softly.

"I won't help," Teacher said. "Not when it means we're left with nothing."

"I'll make sure that you and the children are looked after," Calder said. "But you can't stay here. Our other ship has arrived: we'll send you back to Tarklee." He sighed. "My mother will get you sorted and safe."

"I'm not leaving," Teacher said, but Calder could tell that she knew she couldn't stay, not without support from Strongrock settlement.

"You know that the pirates who landed here will eventually sober up and come back," he said. "Now that Ansdottir's hold on them is gone they will be meaner. You know that."

Teacher glared at him. "All right. We'll leave on this ship. I'll get the children ready." She paused. "But I'm still not going to help you find what's hidden. It's a promise I made to the captain, and it's one I mean to keep. Along with keeping the young ones safe."

"Fair enough," Calder replied.

THE SMILE FELL from Nadez's face as soon as she was out of the infirmary. She leaned against a wall and took a deep breath.

Jarri Breck was in very rough condition. Janni seemed reasonably well, other than being worried sick about her brother, and she rightly refused to leave his side. Especially since her Trait could help him.

Kalvia. According to the healer, that was what Jarri had been given and in large enough doses to almost kill him, over and over. Every day for two weeks Jarri had been brought to Janni near death and she had used her Trait to Make him better. And every day they took him away and gave him another near-deadly dose of drugs. All so their captors could profit off Janni's Trait.

Nadez squared her shoulders and stepped away from the wall. There was nothing she could do here that wasn't already being done, and she had a meeting with Lauma.

It took her only a few minutes to reach the Grand Freeholder's offices. Mykol looked up and smiled.

"She's expecting you, Master Intelligencer," he said. "Go right through."

"Thank you," she said and opened the door. Lauma Strauskas was looking out the window and she turned and nodded a greeting. Nadez joined her.

The sun shone down on the harbour and the calm and empty docks. But no matter how lovely the day looked, the lack of activity was dangerous. This late into the fall the docks should have been teeming with ships being unloaded, their goods transferred to wagons or barges to be distributed throughout the city.

"I heard some rumours that you rescued a couple of Intelligencers," Lauma said. She turned to her. "Are they well?"

"They're safe," Nadez replied. "But one is not well, although there is reason to hope."

"Who was behind it?" Lauma asked. "This abduction. It does not seem random."

"Not to me either," Nadez agreed. "Someone knew enough about Traits to know who to target and then how to exploit one. I've asked Gustav to try to find out if there is a connection between the people who did this and either Holt or Ottosen and Heikki."

"You." Lauma paused. "We *all* seem to be relying on Gustav quite a lot. He's not fully trained, so is that wise?"

Nadez laughed but not from amusement. "Wise no, required, yes. Besides, he's the same age as Calder was when he became an active Intelligencer." She looked over at Lauma. "I see many of the same things in Gustav that I saw in your son at that age."

Lauma nodded. "I see them too. I just want to be sure that we are both aware that we are putting young Gustav at risk."

"I understand the risks far too well," Nadez replied. She worried every time she sent Gustav out for information. The problem was that he had become far too useful, and at the moment, she had no one else.

"I'm sure you do," Lauma said. "So, what was it about these rescued Intelligencers that made you go after them yourself? Made you risk yourself?"

"Perhaps I don't want to fall into the trap my predecessor did," she replied. "And let my skills deteriorate without even noticing."

"I believe that's part of it," Lauma said. "But that doesn't tell me why they were important enough for you to make them your personal mission. Your very first mission as Master Intelligencer." She turned away from the window and sat in one of a pair of chairs beside a small table. "Sit down and you can tell me."

Nadez sat down with her hands in her lap and stared at them. "I have a vague plan," she said finally. "But I needed Janni and Jarri for it." She looked up and met Lauma's eyes. "Even though I always felt that they were never good candidates to become Intelligencers." She looked away. "And I still don't. Now more than ever."

"But we need them," Lauma said. "You think that we need their Traits even if they are not well enough for the task."

"Yes," Nadez said simply. She'd been concerned about this before trying to find the Breck twins, but now that she had found them, she was really worried. The Brecks were fragile. And their Traits were desperately needed.

"What is it you think they can do?" Lauma asked. "What is it you think *only* they can do?"

"Repair the shipyards," Nadez replied. "Between them they can repair the shipyards faster than anyone else will be able to."

"*Skit*, that was not what I was expecting," Lauma said. "How? My reports tell me that it will take much of the winter just to clear out the damage."

"Jarri can Unmake anything," Nadez said. "He will be able break down everything that was burned and save even the smallest pieces. Janni can use them when she Remakes the equipment those pieces came from. It will save weeks, maybe even months of work. If Janni and Jarri are healthy, it's possible the shipyards could be operational before spring."

"*Nyorden.*" Lauma sat back. "That is months ahead of what we'd thought. That means new ships sailing to the Sapphire Sea as early as next summer. When can we send them to Lavais?"

"I said if they are healthy," Nadez said. "Which Jarri is not. And even then, I'm not sure I should send them on this mission."

"I'm sure," Lauma said. "We have to. We will give them all the support that they need so that all they have to do is concentrate on using their Traits."

"Are you going to go with them?" Nadez asked. "Because that's what it might take: the Grand Freeholder there in person, removing any barriers."

"Something like that," Lauma agreed. "If that's what it takes. But it will be my representative: I'll send my daughter. Berna should already be on her way here. We should also send someone who is local, don't you think? There must be an Intelligencer who is from Lavais. Send them."

"There is one," Nadez replied. "Gustav Gunnarson comes from a shipbuilding family."

"Perfect. We trust him, he has good sense, and it should keep him relatively safe."

"Yes," Nadez agreed, although she wondered how she and Lauma would be able to manage without him.

DAG SHIFTED IN her seat in the bow of the dinghy and, with a hand shading her eyes, stared out at the rocky shore. Trees lined the cliff that rose above the surf. There were very few areas where flat land reached out into the sea.

"You're sure that this is the place?" she asked.

"Unless Teacher moved it," Jaak replied from the seat behind her. "I sailed her over here a couple of times, back before she learned to manage the boat by herself."

"Then we keep looking." At the very least she should be able to find where it had been even if it was no longer there.

Coins, was what Jaak said when he'd arrived from the *Tazeyar*. Coins that filled half a dozen small, wooden boxes. Teacher had glared at him, so Dag assumed that they really were looking for pirate treasure and not something like the cache of weapons she'd found during her walk around the island.

"Do you want me to take us in to shore?" Calder said over his shoulder. "Maybe you'll find it on foot."

"Yes," Dag agreed. "I'll find us a place to land." Calder's oars dug deeper into the water and the dinghy surged towards land.

Dag scanned the shoreline, looking for a safe place to land. Suddenly the itch between her shoulder blades started.

"Found it," she said. "A place to land and where the treasure is. Or was, if it's since been moved." She pointed to a sharp ridge of rock. "There's a shallow inlet just behind that rock there."

"Huh," Jaak said. "I missed that, but now that you point it out, it does look familiar. I think there's a tree we can tie up to."

In a few moments, the small boat swung past the rocks and into a tiny inlet. There was a tree: years ago, a storm had knocked it down from the cliff above. Silvered branches stretched out across the rocks and into the water.

Jaak grabbed a branch and held it as Calder used a single oar to turn the boat around. Once the bow was pointing back out to sea, Jaak tied them to the dead tree.

With the oars pulled in, Calder climbed to the stern and stepped out into knee-deep water. With a hand on the tree trunk, he waded to shore.

Dag followed Jaak, ignoring the itch between her shoulder blades.

"It's close," she said when she joined the others on shore.

She glanced up at the cliff. She must have passed close to this area when she'd walked around Strongrock Island, but it was possible she'd been too far inland for her Trait to be triggered. Had she missed other, important secrets?

"There," she pointed. A few steps up a large, flat rock leaned against a pile of smaller rocks. She climbed up and pulled the rock away from the rest. Someone—Teacher, she guessed—had created a small hollow, and nestled in it were weathered wooden boxes.

"That's them," Jaak said from right behind her. "That's what I remember." He picked one up and pried open the lid. Coins, some of them green with oxidation, filled the box. Jaak snapped it shut. "More money than I ever thought to see," he said.

"Pass them down to me," Calder called out. "And we can get back to the ships."

"Here." Dag handed another box up to Jaak. "We need those children off that beach before the sailors return looking for this."

"Yeah," Jaak replied. "If they knew how much was here, they'd never have left." He turned and handed the boxes down to Calder. "Most of 'em would kill for this much coin."

"They've probably killed for less," Dag agreed. She brushed the sand off another two boxes and handed them to Jaak before digging more boxes out of the hollow.

In all there were seven boxes: each one weighing about five pounds. Once they were loaded into the dinghy, both Jaak and Calder picked up oars.

Dag navigated them out of the small inlet and back out to sea. A few minutes later they'd travelled far enough to see both the *Atlaine* and *Tazeyar* anchored off the beach where the children lived.

Had lived, Dag amended. By now they should all be aboard the *Tazeyar*, ready to be taken to Tarklee.

Calder and Jaak rowed them directly to the *Tazeyar*. Dag stayed in the dinghy while Jaak and Calder carried four boxes of coins on board.

She stared out at the now-empty buildings and small dock. It was a little sad to think that so many children had grown up here with few choices and fewer opportunities. People like Jaak, who'd become a pirate because he didn't really see another life for himself.

The rope ladder bucked, and she looked up to see Calder climbing down.

"Jaak stayed on board," Calder said. "Captain Eklund doesn't trust Teacher, and Jaak knows her better than anyone else. Eklund also doesn't think the delay caused by returning to Tarklee will hurt his chances of filling the *Tazeyar*'s hold with food." Calder sat down at the oars. "The extra coin will make sure he gets the best anyway."

"Good," Dag replied. "The coin will help us buy food too." It might also buy information that helped them find Inger and Tarmo Holt. If she felt comfortable spending coin for that.

"It will. As soon as we make it to the Sapphire Sea." Calder pushed off from the *Tazeyar* and pointed the dinghy towards the *Atlaine*.

THE RATTY TAVERN was empty. Gustav had watched from across the street as rough-looking men descended on it and stripped it of anything of value. Ale barrels had been carted off first, followed by what looked like everything that wasn't fixed to the building: furniture, bedding, tankards, and pots.

A couple of men who came late even dragged three wooden doors out the front.

That had been almost an hour ago, and he was wondering if that was it: if no one was going to come and search the building.

Nadez thought that a man like the one who'd imprisoned Janni and Jarri probably had a secret or two: something hidden that he hoped gave him leverage over the important friend he claimed to have. She'd said that someone would come for whatever it was. And that he'd know them as soon as they saw them.

So, when the girl seemed to dawdle in front of the open door to the tavern, he wasn't surprised that he did *know*.

She was dressed in rough clothes, much like anyone else in this part of town, but underneath a surface layer of dirt, she was clean and healthy. She had white teeth, clear skin, and although she was thin, she didn't have the gaunt look of the chronically underfed. He'd spent enough time in the poor parts of town to know that she did not belong here.

She casually looked around, her gaze slipping past Gustav and his cart, before entering the tavern.

Gustav rose and followed her, crossing the threshold into the interior. He stopped, knowing that his outline would be visible in the doorway. He was here to ask questions, not take her by surprise.

"Think all the good stuff is already gone," he said cheerfully. "I had a good view of it all from my cart."

"Was there ever any good stuff?" a voice asked from the gloom. "Didn't ever look like it from the outside."

As she walked towards him Gustav recognized the way she held her body. He'd learned to carry himself the same way in hand-to-hand combat classes. He deliberately stood slightly off balance to make it look like he had not been trained to fight.

"You know someone who used to come here," he said.

She was older than he'd first thought: fourteen, or fifteen maybe, but small for her age, with shoulder-length light brown hair and blue eyes.

"My Da," she said. "Spent all our money here." She frowned. "Meant I had to scrounge for food all the time. I was curious about the hold this place had on him."

"Pretty sure it was the drink and not the place," Gustav said.

"I guess," she said. "Sometimes he'd stay here all night playing ludus and drinking. Then he'd come home and expect me to feed him."

"Where's your Da now?" Gustav asked.

"Don't know," she replied. "And don't care as long as he leaves me alone."

"And are you?" he asked. "Alone?"

Her eyes narrowed. "I have a patron so don't go getting any ideas," she said. "He's got more money and power than you."

"I didn't mean anything by it," Gustav said. He smiled. "I just wanted to make sure that you are making your way all right. On account of your Da and all." He was quite certain that she did have a patron, but how to get her to tell him who it was?

"Do you want to help me look for anything worthwhile that was left behind?" Gustav asked. "I was planning on looking for goods to sell on my cart, but I didn't want to run into anyone who might have a prior claim."

"Or was bigger than you," the girl said with a laugh.

"Well, sure," Gustav tried to sound embarrassed. "I never want trouble."

"I'll help," the girl said. "But we split anything we find."

"That sounds fair." Gustav crossed the floor to the bar, the girl following him. He stepped behind it and looked around. The owner would have wanted anything important to him in sight, wouldn't he? A man like that, if he really was holding information that allowed him to threaten someone powerful, would want to assure himself that it was safe at all times.

And the presence of this girl with her mysterious patron—he was pretty sure that wasn't a word or concept she came across living in these streets—suggested that there was something here.

She joined him and half-heartedly opened a cupboard while he tried to lift up the top of the bar. It didn't budge. He ducked down and peered up at the underside but there was nothing hidden there.

Gustav took a step back to allow the girl to slide past him to the counter where the taps had once been. He was watching her feet and noticed a single board spring back into place once she'd stepped off it.

He put the toe of one boot on the board and pushed down. It gave a little, just enough to make him think that there was a hollow space under it.

He pulled his foot back and watched the girl pound on the wall above the counter. She was definitely looking for something hidden.

He didn't see anything around that he could use to pry up the floorboard with, so he pulled out his knife and flipped it open. The girl must have heard it because she spun to face him, fists up.

"Think there's something down here," Gustav said, trying to seem harmless. He knelt down and pressed down on the floorboard, dug the knife blade into the crack that appeared, and pried the board out.

The girl was beside him, reaching into the cavity before he could flip the board aside.

"Hey, we are splitting everything, remember?" He grabbed her arm before she could snatch the wrapped package away from him.

"This is mine," she said. "Let go."

"You lied to me," Gustav said. She jerked her arm, trying to get away from him, but he kept his grip on her. Dust from the package in her hand rose up in a cloud and she sneezed. Gustav pulled her off balance and she fell to the floor, her shoulder wedging into the opening.

"*Skit!*" she yelled, struggling to her hands and knees.

Gustav grabbed the package and stood up; his knife held out towards her. "I was willing to share," he said. "Until you got greedy."

"That's mine!" she called, getting to her feet. "I'm willing to kill you for it. Are you willing to die for it?"

Gustav readied for her charge but instead, she started to laugh. "You won't get away," she said. "I have someone waiting outside. If I don't come out, they'll come in. And they won't let you out without me."

Gustav sighed. "I *was* willing to share." His shoulders slumped as he pretended to give up. It didn't look like he was going to be able to take this to Nadez. He raised his knife and sliced the twine that was wrapped around the package and shook it.

Coins fell to the floor, along with a couple of pieces of paper.

The girl dropped to the floor and ignoring the coins, grabbed the papers. Gustav stuffed the wrapping along with one remaining paper into his shirt before slowly backing out from behind the bar.

"My friend will still kill you," the girl called to him.

Instead of replying, Gustav crept towards a set of crumbling stairs. The girl didn't even spare him a glance when they creaked and groaned as he climbed them.

A landing led to three dismal sleeping chambers. None of the rooms had doors, and he guessed that this was where the earlier scavengers had gotten them. He entered the only room with a window and looked out it onto a roof that was patched and crumbling in places.

He pulled the paper out from his shirt and studied it for a moment before setting it down on the floor. He didn't have Kaja's memory, but he'd be able to remember this, especially since he'd seen something similar.

It was a promise to pay note much like the ones for the stores Tarmo Holt had opened. Only this had been signed by Holt as security to Clan Freeholder Henrik Ottosen. And the amount surprised Gustav. If the other papers contained similar sums, it looked like Tarmo Holt owed his fellow Swyfordian Clan Freeholder a lot of money. And this was just what the barkeep had. It was likely that there were many more notes than what had been hidden here.

He left the paper on the floor hoping that once it was found the girl and whoever she had with her wouldn't bother chasing him.

He eased out of the window and lowered himself gently to the roof below. Hugging the outside wall of the tavern he carefully edged towards the building next door. Just past that building was an alley. He had just dropped to the ground when a head appeared at the window he'd escaped through. The man stared out it for a moment before retreating back inside.

Gustav turned a corner and jogged through laneways that led away from the tavern.

It took him two hours and he crossed the river three times before he felt safe enough to return to the Hall. He felt a brief pang of regret for his cart, but it was outside the tavern and he had to assume that it would be watched.

CHAPTER 6

CALDER STARED AT the map hoping that Luck would tell him which destination to choose, but nothing triggered his Trait. He sighed and stepped away from the table and stared out the portal.

It would take another four days to get to the Sapphire Sea, lots of time for his Trait to give him a sign.

The door to the sleeping chamber of the Captain's cabin opened, and Dag, towel wrapped around her, strode through it. She dumped her sodden clothes on a chair and dragged fingers through her wet hair.

"Clean, finally," she said. "The perks of sharing a cabin with the Captain are considerable. Your own shower and head as well as special meals from Cook." She walked to him, slid under his arm, and wrapped her own around him.

"What about the Captain?" he asked as he leaned his cheek against her head.

"Oh, he gets perks too," she replied.

"Does he? What perks, exactly?"

Dag turned to face him and kissed him. He closed his eyes, enjoying the soft warmth of her lips, the scent of her freshly washed hair. She grabbed his hands and pulled him towards the sleeping chamber.

Her hands pulled at his shirt, tugging it over his head. When his head emerged, his breath caught in his throat. She'd dropped her towel and stood naked in front of him. He pulled her to him and kissed her, feeling the heat where their bodies touched.

"You have too many clothes," she said as she climbed onto the bed.

"I do," he agreed. His trousers dropped to the floor, and he joined her. Gently, she pushed him onto his back and straddled him.

He gasped when her hand found him and guided him into her. She leaned over him, her damp hair brushing across his chest as she kissed him. She rocked her hips into him and lifted her eyes to meet his. A slow smile spread across her lips as she increased the tempo. He thrust up to meet her, and she stilled and tensed. His hands found her breasts, and he lifted his head and sucked one nipple into his mouth as he pushed his hardness into her. She gasped, and a second later he thrust urgently with his own release. Their foreheads met as their breathing returned to normal.

They shared a shy smile before Dag laid one cheek on his chest and draped one leg across his waist.

He sighed, enjoying the feel and weight of her for a few moments before turning to look into her eyes.

"I didn't assume this," he said. "When I brought you to this cabin. I meant to ask you if you wanted your own space." He shrugged. "But then things happened and, well, here we are."

"Yes," Dag replied. "And where we are, where *I* am is my choice. If I didn't want this," she leaned over and kissed him, "I would have told you." She paused. "But I can move to another cabin if you want me to."

"No," he said and smiled. "I didn't assume this because I didn't dare expect it, not because I didn't hope for it."

"Good." She sighed into his shoulder. "I would miss the perks if I moved."

"So would I," he said. Calder brushed the hair from her face before he sighed too.

"There's work to be done," he said as he moved out from under her and swung his legs over the side of the bed. Dag ran a hand down his spine, and he shivered and closed his eyes. He wanted nothing more than to turn to her and lose himself in her again, but there really was much to do. There was always too much to do.

He found his clothes and pulled them on before stepping back into the other room.

"I'll go find us some tea and something light to eat," Dag said. He heard the sounds of her feet hitting the floor and smiled.

Then his attention focused on the map on the table. He walked over to it and stared down. It seemed that Luck was working after all.

"What is it?" Dag asked. She stepped to his side, pulling her shirt on.

"My Trait," he said. "It was just triggered. I know where we have to go." He jabbed a figure down on the map. "Here. To Arressa."

"That's where Holt has taken Inger?" Dag asked.

"That's where my Trait is telling me we should go," he replied. He hoped that meant they'd find Holt and Inger, but as usual, he just didn't know.

NADEZ RUBBED HER eyes before looking back down at the paper on her desk. She added one final sentence before handing the sheet over to Kaja, who was sitting across from her.

The younger woman studied the sheet before handing it back to her.

"Yes, every word is just as I was told," she said.

"Good." Nadez blew on the paper to make sure the ink was dry before setting it onto the stack in front of her. She and Lauma had decided that some things were too dangerous to send to each other in written form: there were far too many people they weren't sure they could trust, including Lauma's assistant Mykol, so they'd taken to using Kaja and her Memory Trait. They still needed written records, just not ones that could be intercepted while being delivered.

There was a sound outside her office and then a knock on the door.

"It's Gustav." The door opened and he poked his head in. "I have news."

"Come in," Nadez waved him to the seat beside Kaja. "Your timing is good. Kaja should hear this too, in case we want Lauma to know."

"I could have used her Trait today," Gustav said as he sat down. "I couldn't bring anything to show you, but I did look at a document. A promise to pay note."

"Found at the tavern?" Nadez asked, scowling. The tavern owner and the man who had been working with him to drug Jarri and coerce Janni were in the jail. She'd questioned them and they'd both claimed they were working alone. And they might have been, although *someone* had told them about Janni's Trait. The Breck twins were recovering, thankfully. Janni was already in the process of Making herself another chair with wheels and Jarri was eating solid food.

"Yes," Gustav replied. "I watched as the neighbours stripped the place of everything they could and then someone new came to investigate." He paused. "A girl of about fifteen who was pretending to be the daughter of a tavern customer."

"How do you know she was pretending?" Nadez asked. She knew how to tell, but she wanted to make sure Gustav did too.

"She was clean," Gustav replied. "Even though her clothes weren't. And she moved like someone who has been trained to fight but not trained to disguise that fact."

"Could she be one of ours?" Kaja asked. "There are a few students who would fit that description."

"Let me find the list," Nadez replied, worried now. The students rarely knew much about those not in their own training groups, so it was entirely possible that Gustav wouldn't recognize a fellow Intelligencer student. She pulled out the list and ran a finger down it.

"Kaja, who do you think it could be?" Kaja had memorized the list, but as with all the students, Nadez wanted to make sure they could interpret the information they gathered.

"Pia Engen," Kaja said. "Her family is from Nordmere and she's been a student for almost three years."

"And her Trait?" Nadez asked.

"Concentration," Kaja said. "But I'm not sure what that does, exactly."

"I'm not sure either," Nadez replied. "I assume that she is able to block everything else out and focus on her objective." Which might be helpful, but only if what you are blocking out isn't a danger to you. "When exactly did she arrive at the Hall?"

"Oh," Kaja said. "She arrived shortly after Tarmo Holt became Grand Freeholder."

"I see," Nadez said, turning to Gustav. "Does this make sense with regards to what you found?"

"I'm not sure," Gustav replied. "The promise to pay note was from Tarmo Holt to Henrik Ottosen. There were only three, but if there are more, then I would say that Holt owes him a lot of coin."

"What did Holt use the coin for?" Nadez asked. This time it wasn't a test. Tarmo Holt was a wealthy Freeholder; why did he have to borrow from a potential enemy?

"He owned quite a few ships," Kaja said. "And was keeping that fact hidden. Perhaps that's how he paid for them."

"Yes, that makes sense," she replied. "But it doesn't explain why an Intelligencer student is working for Ottosen."

"Holt has been after his own Intelligencers for a while now," Gustav said. "Maybe he was trying to buy one from Ottosen?"

"Hmm," Nadez said. "We assumed Holt wanted Intelligencers in order for him to remain Grand Freeholder, but what if it was because Henrik Ottosen already had his own?"

"Maybe Holt would have been content to wait six years for his chance to be Grand Freeholder again," Gustav said. "But once he found out that Ottosen has Intelligencers, he wasn't sure he would be elected."

Nadez sighed. "We need to identify every student and Intelligencer from Nordmere who might be in the service of Henrik Ottosen."

"I don't think we can assume it's just the Nordmerians," Gustav said. "Vilis wasn't from Nordmere and he was compromised."

Nadez sighed again. "You're right. We can't trust anyone, not even Intelligencers and students. We need to stop looking for them. If any Intelligencers or students do return to Tarklee, we need to be very cautious."

"You think Intelligencers working for someone else would be the most likely to return to the Hall," Kaja said.

"Yes," Nadez agreed. "That would be my direction if I was building my own team of Intelligencers. Kaja, repeat this conversation to Lauma Strauskas. In private, of course. Gustav, get some rest. As soon as the Breck twins are ready, you are to travel with them to Lavais Island."

Once they'd left, Nadez dropped her head into her hands. She already had so few trustworthy resources at her disposal, and now that she could no longer trust Intelligencers, she didn't know how she would find more.

DAG STARED OUT across the endless expanse of the sea. There was nothing in front of them except for clear blue sky and waves. Even the birds had turned back to land.

She tipped her hat back and stared up at the sails. The wind was blowing from directly behind them and the sails bulged out towards the bow.

"I see you found a hat," Darya said as she joined her in the shadow of the main sail.

"Rafael loaned it to me." Dag ran a hand across the rim. Between the sun, the wind, and the sea, her cheeks were red. And this was only the first of what Calder said would be a four-day journey. "I'm not sure how the sailors from the Fair Seas Treaty Alliance manage it."

"They often burn too," Darya said. "But then they darken. Not as dark as me or even the captain," she said, referring to Calder. "But enough that they don't blister again. Most of them anyway; I have come across two sailors who never did get used to the sun."

"I'll do my best to keep to the shade," Dag said. Her fair skin had suffered recently when escaping Strongrock with Calder, although her arms were more golden than pink now. And it wasn't as though she was planning a life at sea. Was she? Was Calder going to stay at sea as an Intelligencer? Unless he was the ship's captain, he probably wouldn't be able to bring her along. And what about her own career as an Intelligencer?

"Captain asked if you could join us in his cabin," Darya said. "No rush, he said. Rafael has the ship while we try to figure out where the *Neas* will land. Captain said he needed your abilities." She nodded. "I'll fetch tea and meet you there."

"All right," Dag said, but Darya had already gone.

She stared out at the horizon again. Where would Holt land? She wasn't sure she had enough information for her Trait to be useful, but she was happy to have the chance to try to do anything. It turned out that sailing while not a sailor was boring.

Calder was staring at the map when she entered the cabin. She joined him at the table and met his brief smile with one of her own.

"My Trait is quiet," he said. "I was hoping that yours wouldn't be."

"Luck already told you Holt was sailing to Arressa," she said. "How many places are there for him to land?"

"Two main ports," Calder said. He leaned over the map and pointed at two places along the coastline of Arressa. "There is only one major river in the south and it's far too marshy for a town, and there are no villages along the coast this far north, but there are a few olive groves."

"It would help if we knew why he's going to Arressa," Dag said.

There was a knock on the door.

"Come in," Calder called, and Darya entered, followed by a youth carrying a tray. He put the tray on a side table and left.

"Who knows the most about Tarmo Holt's businesses?" Calder asked Darya.

"Not his business," Dag said, the spot between her shoulder blades itching. "He has his family on board: he'll want to take them somewhere safe."

"So why Arressa?" Calder asked. "Who does he know there?"

"Where was Ansdottir from?" Dag asked. "Does anyone know?"

"She was from the Pale Sea," Darya said. "At least that's what everyone said."

"She had the colouring," Dag agreed. "But that could just mean her parents were from there. Who does Holt know from Arressa?"

"Charis," Calder said. "He's Arressan."

"We know he's on the *Neas*," Dag said. "I saw him just before they set sail, and Teacher said the pirates were going to fetch him to speak to her. Holt did trust Charis when he vouched for Inger."

"Charis didn't ship out with Ansdottir until the *Bright Breeze* was taken," Calder said. "Then suddenly he was a trusted officer. I assumed he'd been a pirate all along, but what if he had been sent by Holt?" He turned to Darya. "Ask the crew and see if anyone has shipped out with an Arressan named Charis."

"Yes, sir," Darya said and turned and left.

Once the door was closed, Dag poured tea for her and Calder.

"I don't have enough information for my Trait to work out the connection between Charis and Holt," she said, setting Calder's cup down on top of the map. She took a sip of her tea and stared at the coastline of Arressa. It was nestled in between Pilalia and Tobei, but other than the lines indicating the borders, there was nothing that set it apart from the other two countries.

"When I first met him," Calder said. "Charis told me that he'd studied navigation at the best schools in Arressa. At the best schools on any sea." He leaned over the map and jabbed a finger midway along the coast of Arressa. "That would be here, in Messanos."

Dag stared at the spot on the map for a moment. "I don't think they're in the city," she said. "My guess is that they went a little north. This spot." She moved Calder's finger slightly up to what looked like a small cove.

She stepped back and shrugged. "That's not something my Trait is telling me," she said. "I just think Holt would try to safeguard his family outside of a city."

"Navigation schools are expensive," Calder said. "I wonder if Charis is from a well-off family?" He frowned. "It's possible Charis and Holt are somehow connected. Charis was never a typical pirate."

"Neither were you," Dag said and was rewarded with a laugh.

"You're right," Calder replied. "Come on, I need to update the course logs." He grabbed her hand and pulled her towards the door.

Nadez strode down the street and onto the pier, her heart sinking. She could only think of bad reasons for this ship to be back in the harbour so soon.

It wasn't Calder and Dagrun; she knew enough about ships to know that. She heard her name being called and turned to see Lauma Strauskas running towards her.

"What's happened?" Lauma called. "Where is my son?"

"I don't know," Nadez replied. "I was notified a few minutes ago that a ship, one of our two ships, was back." She turned and continued along the pier, Lauma at her side. "The ship does not look damaged, so that's a good thing." She thought; she hoped.

They waited while two dinghies from the ship were lowered and people climbed into them.

"Are those children?" Lauma asked.

"I think so," Nadez said. "But from where?" She relaxed. Children were a mystery, but what she didn't see—injured people—would have been worse.

She recognized Captain Eklund when the lead dinghy was

closer to shore. And there were indeed children; about a dozen of them, all different ages, filled the two small boats.

"Captain," Lauma said as the dinghy reached the pier. "Is my son safe?"

"Yes, he's fine," Eklund said. He stepped onto the pier and joined them. "Everyone is fine. The *Atlaine* went on ahead in pursuit of Holt. Captain Rahmson asked us to bring these children here to Tarklee. He said that you would look after them."

"Did he?" Lauma said.

"Where did these children come from?" Nadez asked. The small occupants of the dinghies crowded around a single adult on the pier.

"They are Fair Seas Treaty Alliance orphans that the pirates took to Strongrock," Eklund said. "Captain Rahmson and Dagrun Lund worried that they would be abandoned by the pirates now that Ansdottir is dead. That," he pointed to the woman the children were huddled around, "is Teacher, their caretaker."

"Teacher," Nadez called. "Can you come here and talk to us?"

"Yes, ma'am," the woman replied. She crouched down to speak to the children before she rose and stepped away from them.

"How long have you been looking after these orphan children?" Nadez asked.

"Fifteen years," Teacher replied. "On Strongrock. I wasn't much older than some of these when Captain Ansdottir found me. She knew right away that I wasn't going to be any good at sea, so she had me look after the younger ones."

"Where did she find these orphans?" Lauma asked.

"Here," Teacher replied. "In the city. There's a woman who looks for lost and orphaned children on the streets. They're usually starving, so she takes them in and feeds them until the captain came and picked them up and took them to Strongrock, where it was safe."

"We have orphanages, why weren't the children taken to one of them?" Lauma asked.

Teacher shrugged and Nadez left Lauma to deal with the children. She pulled Captain Eklund to one side.

"You saw Tarmo Holt?" she asked.

"The *Atlaine* caught up to him," he replied. "They had landed at the beach on Strongrock Island where these children lived. The

Neas was surprised and fled, although there was an exchange of gunfire. No casualties on our ship, I'm happy to say."

"And Calder and Dagrun went after Holt while you looked after the children?"

"They didn't leave until they'd found what Holt was after." Eklund grinned. "Real pirate treasure. We divided it and will use it to buy food to ship back here."

"Excellent," she said. And it was. Not only would it help get them through the winter, it meant that Holt had fewer funds than he'd been counting on. "If you see Calder and Dagrun tell them that Holt is indebted to Clan Freeholder Henrik Ottosen. Also tell him that we would like Holt and most especially his daughter, returned to Tarklee."

"I will tell them if I see them," Eklund said. "Do you need more time with me? I can spare an hour, but we've already lost four days with this," he gestured to the children. "And I would get on with my mission."

"Lauma," Nadez said, interrupting the Grand Freeholder's conversation. "Captain Eklund has updated me and would like to get back to his ship."

"I will not hold you," Lauma said. "When you see my son, tell him it will be a long time before I forgive him."

Eklund raised his eyebrows.

"She's been named Interim Grand Freeholder," Nadez explained. "And as you can tell, she's not happy about it."

"I think I will leave now," Eklund said. "I prefer not to get involved in politics." He turned and waved at his sailors, who were ready in the dinghies.

"As do I," Nadez said as she watched Eklund step into a dinghy and row away.

"We've settled it all," Lauma said. "Teacher will continue to care for these children. I'll have Mykol find them a place to live. And I'm going to investigate why the children were not taken to existing Nordmere or Swyford orphanages in the city. Every Fair Seas Treaty Alliance country is supposed to care for their people. Starving, orphaned children should never have to fend for themselves."

"I agree," Nadez said.

CHAPTER 7

"Is THERE A way to lock the wheels?" Gustav asked Janni. She was showing him how her wheeled chair worked. He'd told her it was because he needed to know about it before they travelled to Lavais Island, but mostly he was curious. It was an ingenious piece of equipment with a seat and three wheels that could be taken apart and assembled very quickly, an update Janni Made when told that she and her brother were travelling by sea.

"I'll Make one," Janni said. She spun the chair by twisting the handles on the two largest wheels. "If you think it will help on the ship."

"And docks," Gustav replied. "You don't want to wheel right off one."

"Gustav."

He turned to see Mykol heading towards them.

"Gustav, the Grand Freeholder would like to see you." Mykol didn't wait for an answer, instead he turned and walked back the way he'd come.

"He doesn't like you very much," Janni said.

"You don't need to be a trained Intelligencer to figure that out," Gustav replied, and Janni laughed.

"Your Trait doesn't work on everyone?" she asked.

"So it seems," Gustav replied. "I have to go. Say goodbye to Jarri for me."

"I will," Janni said, but she already sounded distracted.

Gustav walked away, shaking his head. When Janni was working on Making something, she retreated into her own world. Jarri was another matter. He was still weak, but his dependence on Kalvia, the drug he'd been force fed, was gone. Almost. Four days after they'd been rescued, Janni said her brother's cravings hardly bothered him.

Thank Nyorden Nadez had found them when she did; Kalvia addiction was harder to overcome the longer a person was on it.

He knocked on the outer office door and entered without waiting for Mykol to invite him in.

"As requested, I'm here to see Lauma," he said, knowing that using her name instead of her title irked Mykol.

"I'll see if she's available," Mykol sniffed, and instead of seeing if Lauma was ready for him, he went back to what he was doing. He finished writing and carefully blotted the paper before setting it in a stack.

Then he rose and went to the door to the inner office, knocked twice, and opened it.

"Gustav Gunnarson is here," he said, sticking his head inside.

"About time, send him in."

Gustav repressed the urge to snicker at Mykol as he squeezed past him into the office. He did turn and face him as he closed the door.

"I wish you would stop annoying him," Lauma said from her desk. "I need his trust and loyalty."

Gustav sat down in a chair in front of the desk and sighed. "I don't mean to but it's just . . ." he waved a hand around. "He doesn't respond to my Trait and that annoys *me*."

"Yes, but I expect more from you," Lauma said. "*You* are the trained Intelligencer."

"Half-trained," Gustav said before he could stop himself. "Sorry, I didn't mean that. I am grateful to be of service, and I will try to do better."

Lauma's face softened into a smile. "No, you are right to remind me. I'm afraid I compare you to Calder, who was fully trained at your age. And I don't think Mykol is immune to your Trait. I rather think that he is so afraid of it that he fiercely guards against it. He is never relaxed around you."

"Oh," Gustav replied. "I didn't think of that. So my Trait does work on him. That's a relief." And it was. He'd been poisoned by someone immune to his Trait: Joosep had suspected it was done by someone with the opposite Trait, but that was a guess. Who knew how many people were immune to Charisma?

"So," Lauma said. "How ready are you and the Breck twins to travel to Lavais?"

"Janni is ready," Gustav said. "She can't wait to start Making and Remaking the shipyards. It's the biggest project she's ever been assigned. Jarri." He sighed. "He's well enough to travel, and Janni can manage him, but when she's busy, he's sad."

"Won't he be busy as well?"

"Yes, sure, but it's a different kind of busy." Gustav had thought about this a lot in the past few days, what it must be like to have a negative Trait. "His Trait is to Unmake—destroy— things. I don't think he gets much joy in that, and certainly not the joy Janni gets from Making and Remaking."

"But this Unmaking will be critical," Lauma said. "The pieces of what he Unmakes will be used by Janni to Remake the shipyards."

"I know," Gustav said. "I'm hopeful that once we're there and he sees how important it is, that he'll feel better about it. It would be hard to Unmake things all the time. Especially after what . . . happened with his sister."

"It was tragic," Lauma said. "But she seems to have moved on from it. She doesn't blame him that I've heard."

"No, but he blames himself enough for the two of them."

"I'll talk to him," Lauma said. "I know far too much about Traits and blame and how they can poison your most precious relationships." She smiled sadly. "Calder had a twin with Bad Luck."

"Oh, I'm sorry," Gustav said. He knew what Calder's Trait was and that it was strong, but he hadn't thought about what that meant. "That might help Jarri. To talk to someone who knows about opposite Traits."

"I'll go see him when I have a few minutes," Lauma said. "Today or tonight since I hope the three of you can set sail tomorrow. Captain Sorensen and the *Oakhaven* have returned from taking my other son home."

"We'll be ready," Gustav said. "I didn't have a chance to send a message to my Da, but I'm sure he'll be as glad to see me as I will be to see him." He'd had word right after the shipyards had been destroyed that his family was safe. As a Journeyman Shipbuilder, his Da wouldn't be building ships, but no doubt everyone was clearing out the damage to the shipyard. Gustav was proud that he was going to be a part of the rebuilding effort.

"Good. One more thing," Lauma said as Gustav rose to leave. "My daughter Berna arrived on the *Oakhaven*: she will be joining you. If the local Freeholders have any concerns, she will deal with them as the representative of the Interim Grand Freeholder. She'll meet you on board at dawn."

"All right," Gustav said and left. He grinned as soon as he exited Lauma's office. He was going home!

DAG WATCHED CALDER talk to Belmina. She wasn't close enough to hear what was being said: both Calder and she had already spoken to Belmina and the rest of the pirates. Belmina claimed to know very little about Charis, just a last name: Diakos. She said that she didn't meet him until the *Bright Breeze* had been turned into the ghost ship.

None of the other pirates remembered meeting him before that, and Dag believed them: the problem was she didn't believe Belmina.

Her Trait had been triggered when Belmina had claimed no knowledge of Charis other than his last name. But the pirate had been tight-lipped ever since and now, three days later, Dag was still no closer to the truth.

Calder signalled that he was done talking about the weather with the pirate, and Dag squinted and concentrated on her.

There; her Trait had been triggered when Belmina glanced away. Dag signalled Calder, asking him to repeat what he'd just said. Yes, Belmina had reacted to that. She asked Calder to take note of Belmina's answers.

A few minutes later Belmina nodded to Calder and walked away. Calder headed her way.

"What was it?" Dag asked when he reached the shadow she was standing in. "My Trait was triggered twice. What did she say?"

"That she'd spent time sailing between Pilalia and Arressa," Calder said. "On short trips aboard ships that carried spices from Pilalia to Arressa and before picking up olive oil—"

"That," Dag said, interrupting him. "Olive oil. That's how she knows who Charis is. She may not have met him before the *Bright Breeze*, but she knows of him."

"Olive oil," Calder said. "It seems rather innocuous. There are a handful of olive groves in Arressa."

"And one of them has a connection to Charis," Dag said. "I'll talk to more people and see if I can uncover anything else."

"All right," Calder replied. "I'll be up on the bridge with Darya if you need me."

Dag watched Calder as he strode to the stern of the ship before she turned back to face the bow. She couldn't talk to Belmina, not so soon after Calder's conversation with the pirate. Calder might be her captain, but Dag didn't think the pirate trusted him. Not with her secrets, anyway.

When she entered the mess, she saw Rafael and made her way to his table.

"How much do you know about trade between Pilalia and Arressa?" she asked as she sat down. Rafael had given them some information about the navigation school in Messanos, but he hadn't studied there himself and had never heard of Charis Diakos.

"Quite a lot," he said. "My uncle owns a few ships that transport goods along that coast." He shrugged. "You asked before whether I attended navigation school in Messanos, and I told you no. What I didn't say was that I learned from my uncle, who did train there. I spent three years shipping along that coast before I signed up for the Merchant Adventurers."

"Why did you join them?"

"I wanted to see the world," Rafael replied. "And my uncle has no desire to acquire a ship that can sail to the Pale Sea. Besides, I wanted to earn my rank through skill, not through being the nephew of the ship's owner."

"And you have," Dag replied. "Will we be able to use your uncle's good name to get preferential treatment when we go to buy goods?" As much as Dag wanted to catch Tarmo Holt, she couldn't forget that the more pressing goal was to get supplies to help the Three through winter.

"I'd like to say yes," Rafael said. "But my uncle guards his reputation fiercely. If he's not in port then there will be no chance to ask him, and I would not trade on his good name without his consent."

"That's fair," she said before turning back to the map. "Calder showed you where on the map we think they're going?" she asked, and he nodded. "Do you know how many olive groves with sizeable estates ship out of that stretch of coast?"

"I can think of three that I've personally dealt with," he said.

"We need to talk to Calder," she said. "Can you fetch him? We'll meet in our cabin."

"I will ask him politely to join us," Rafael said. "I'm afraid that only you can *fetch* the captain."

"Oh, sure," Dag replied. "Just get him downstairs."

"I'll do my best," Rafael said.

"Thank you." Dag left for the cabin, where she spent the next ten minutes waiting for Calder and Rafael and staring at the map of Arressa.

"I'm here," Calder said when he arrived. "What is it?" He joined her at the table.

"Rafael is familiar with some of the olive groves along here," she jabbed her finger at the map. "I think one of them is the one we want."

"None bear the name Diakos," Rafael said. "I already told you that I don't recognize that name."

"We don't know if it's his real name," Dag replied. "Belmina isn't lying about that, but I wouldn't know if Charis lied to her."

"Here's what I remember." Rafael leaned over the map. "This land," he pointed just north of the area on the map, "has been in the same family for five generations. They own everything between the coast and the mountains from this point to half way to the border with Pilalia. It's the richest family in that part of Arressa and my uncle trusts them."

"I think we can rule them out," Calder said. "Even if a son from such a wealthy family became a pirate, why would they help Tarmo Holt?"

"Maybe he's helping them," Rafael said. "For the past few years a Pilalian named Pinho has been very active in shipping, and not everyone likes the way he conducts business."

"Fihaldo Pinho," Calder replied. "He has quickly become the richest and most powerful man in all of Pilalia."

The itch started between her shoulder blades. "There's something there," Dag said. "About this Pinho, but I don't think

Holt is helping someone else hide from him.”

“You think Holt is hiding from Pinho?” Calder asked. She nodded, and he looked down at the map. “In that case, no one would be willing to help Holt, not along this coast. I’ve crewed on one of Pinho’s ships before, and he has a reputation for being ruthless. And vindictive.”

“All right,” Rafael said. “Then what you want is this.” He pointed to a spot on the map just outside of that large estate. “This grove fell to blight about twenty years ago and the family has been struggling ever since. I have never dealt with them: their yield was too poor even when I sailed with my uncle. The family name is Pannos, I think.”

Dag felt the itch between her shoulder blades. “That’s it,” she said. “That’s where Holt is going.”

She turned her head at the sound of running in the hall. Someone banged on the door.

“Captain Rahmson,” a voice called from outside. “First Mate Demer asks for your presence on the bridge. A sail has been spotted.”

“Rafael,” Calder said. “With me.”

“Is it Holt?” Dag asked as Calder went to the door. “Is it him?”

Calder turned to her. “It could be.”

NADEZ STOOD AND stretched. It had been another long day at her desk, and her body just wasn’t used to sitting in one place for so many hours.

And her day wasn’t yet over. She left her office and locked the door behind her.

The corridors of the Hall were quiet, as they usually were these days. The only students around were Gustav and Kaja, who were so busy they barely had time to sleep.

She took a direct route to the infirmary. Jarri was finally well enough that he didn’t need to be here, but since he and his sister were leaving at dawn, they’d opted to stay in the infirmary rather than returning to their rooms in the Hall.

It made sense, but Nadez worried that part of the reason was that they feared being on their own; feared that someone else would find them and hold them hostage.

She sighed as she pushed open the door to the infirmary. Hopefully some meaningful work away from Tarklee would help them learn to trust themselves, especially Jarri.

There was a light shining near the back of the infirmary, and she made her way past a dozen empty beds to it.

"I hope I'm not visiting too late," she said even as she could see that she was not.

Janni was on the floor, hunched over her wheeled chair, and Jarri was sprawled on a bed, staring at the ceiling.

Jarri sat up quickly, but Janni ignored her.

"Not at all, Master Intelligencer," Jarri said. "Janni's just making sure she can lock the wheels in place so she doesn't roll all over the ship."

"Or roll off a dock," Janni said. "Gustav said that could be a problem."

"It would be," Nadez replied. "I just wanted to wish you well and see if there's anything you need before you leave."

"I think we have everything," Jarri said. "Janni?"

"I'm ready to go too," Janni said without looking up.

"How are you feeling?" Nadez asked Jarri softly. "The healer said that you are mostly recovered but that you still experience cravings."

"Not very often," Jarri said. "Not anymore. I hope that being at sea will help."

"And I hope that the extremely important work you both will be doing will help," Nadez said. Jarri frowned, and she shook her head. "*Both* of you are needed for this. The shipyards must be re-opened as soon as possible. For that, we need to make use of every single scrap that is salvageable. That's you, Jarri. Your Trait will save us time we don't have."

"You said that before," Jarri replied. "Gustav said it too, but I've never done anything like this before."

"None of us have," Nadez said. "We're all just doing the best we can. That's all anyone can do. Their best." She shrugged. Even though he was younger by a decade, she'd already asked Gustav to try to encourage Jarri. It seemed she was always putting too much on the youth's shoulders, but she had too few people she could trust the way she trusted him.

"I'll let you two get some sleep," she said. "Safe travels to you."

"Thank you," Jarri said. "We *will* do our best."

"I know you will," Nadez said. She turned and walked back through the infirmary and out into the hall.

This time she took a roundabout route as she made her way to Lauma Strauskas' apartment. It was on the upper floor, along a corridor with a half wall that looked out over the harbour. She waited in a shadow until she was certain that she hadn't been followed before she knocked on the door.

A young woman with Pilalian colouring let her in.

"You must be the Master Intelligencer," she said once the door was closed. "I'm Berna Strauskas. Mother is expecting you. Will you join us for a late supper?"

"I'd be grateful, thank you," Nadez replied. She hadn't eaten since this morning, and it was late enough that she hadn't expected to eat now. "I'm Nadez Norup, and I am very pleased to meet you." She followed Berna to a dining room. Lauma was already sitting at the table but not at one of the three place settings. She put the papers she was studying aside and stood up.

"I'll fetch supper," Berna said and left through another door.

"Strauskas?" Nadez asked. "When Calder is Rahmson?"

"Calder took his father's name when he came to the Hall," Lauma said. "Perhaps I should have argued with him, but I didn't. My other children stayed with me and took my name. Come sit down." Lauma sat at the seat at the end of the table, and Nadez took a chair to one side of her.

Berna came back with platters and set them down on the table before leaving again. She came back twice more until the table was laden with food.

Lauma picked up a plate of sliced smoked salmon and held it out to her. Nadez grabbed the tongs and slid a few pieces onto the plate in front of her.

"I hope you don't mind a cold supper," Lauma said. "We sent our staff home."

A tureen of cold beet soup sat in the middle of the table, along with a plate of sliced, pickled beets and onions and a bowl of dilled potatoes.

"Thank you for feeding me," Nadez said. "And although our meeting isn't exactly a secret, I made sure that no one saw me arrive so we can have some privacy."

"Gustav and the Breck twins are ready?" Lauma asked.

"Yes. They will meet Berna at dawn on the *Oakhaven*." Nadez turned to the younger woman. "I would appreciate it if you would treat Jarri with care. He is recovering from being forced into a

Kalvia addiction, and he is still fragile."

"Mother told me," Berna said. "After she talked to him."

"You saw him?" Jarri hadn't mentioned it, but then, why would he?

"Gustav suggested it," Lauma said. "At least I thought about it when I spoke to him. Gustav mentioned that it must be difficult to have a negative Trait, and I have some experience with that." She shrugged. "As does Berna. And we need Jarri's negative Trait almost as much as we need his sister's positive one."

"So I have told him," Nadez said. "Though I'm sure he doesn't believe me." She ladled some soup into her bowl and spooned it up.

"I have the pirate orphans settled," Lauma said. "As well as their Teacher. I don't think we need to worry about her: as long as the children are safe and fed, she's happy. But those children ended up on Strongrock because of deliberate actions by Nordmerian and Swyfordian Clan Freeholders." Lauma scowled. "They dismantled all of the Tarklee orphanages over the past dozen years. The pirate captain is the only reason why starving children didn't die in the streets of Tarklee. It will take some time, but I've already started setting up homes and caretakers. Including the woman the pirate captain employed. She and others like her will be given a monthly stipend to keep their doors open, and if a child does arrive, they will be reimbursed for all expenses. Which will be paid for by the Clan Freeholders. It is their duty, and I intend to make them fulfil it."

"What about adults?" Nadez asked. "We'll need to figure out food distribution long before winter sets in." It would be especially important if the ships could only buy limited supplies. Equal distribution might make the difference between hunger and misery and outright starvation and the riots that would result from that.

"I'm already working on that," Lauma said. "Mykol has his uses."

"I don't like him," Berna said. "Or trust him."

"Of course, I don't trust him," Lauma said. "But he does know how everything works. Everything proper, at least."

"I'm sure he knows plenty of improper ways things work too," Berna said. "I don't like him sitting outside of your office every day. I think he's planning something."

"He works very hard at not liking Gustav," Nadez said. "There must be a reason behind that."

"Tarmo Holt's daughter," Lauma said. "Saulia. Gustav befriended her at Joosep's request in order to spy on her father. Mykol is besotted with Saulia and blames himself for not protecting her from Gustav."

"How do you know?" Nadez asked.

"Mother knows everyone's secret loves," Berna said. "Sometimes even before they know themselves."

"I get a sense," Lauma agreed. "I always have. Calder thinks it's a Trait."

"Did Joosep ever talk to you about it?" Nadez asked.

"You think this *is* a Trait?" Lauma asked.

"Your son has one," Nadez replied. "Did he inherit that from his father?"

"Rahm? Have a Trait?" Lauma laughed. "If he had one, it wasn't very useful. Much like my insights into people's loves isn't useful."

"It uncovered Mykol's reason for disliking Gustav," Nadez replied. "And I can think of a way to use that knowledge to make sure Mykol does not betray us."

"Really?" Berna asked. "How?"

"Talk to him," Nadez replied. "Lauma, you should tell him that you wish to safeguard Saulia and her inheritance if anything should happen to her father. It's very likely that someone from Nordmere knows that Mykol would be willing to betray us in order to help her."

"But if I convince him that I am trying to help her he might choose to trust me," Lauma finished.

"Yes," Nadez agreed. "Or at the very least not work against you."

"I'll have to tell him the truth," Lauma said. "He'll understand the politics; he's been close enough to them for years now." She smiled. "I'll do it. Who knows, maybe Mykol will trust me with other things he's learned during his time with Tarmo Holt."

CALDER STARED OUT across the moonlit sea, searching for any sign of a light or a sail.

They'd been chasing a ship for hours but had only sighted it a few times. It was enough to confirm there was a ship but not enough to identify it as the *Neas*. Now that night had fallen, Calder had hoped that the ship they were following would light lamps, but they hadn't. Like the *Atlaine*, the other ship had chosen to sail dark tonight.

The deck in front of him slipped into a shadow, and he looked up to see clouds rolling in across the moon.

Suddenly the wind picked up, and the sails strained as they filled, the lines flapping against the mast.

He continued to stare out to sea while Darya had the sailors take in all but the mainsail. The ship continued to rush across the water, staying just ahead of the gathering clouds.

Thunder cracked and a sheet of lightning flashed across the sky. Calder thought he saw a sail off to their starboard, then the rain hit, and his vision was reduced to a few feet in front of him.

He made his way to the bridge and Darya, who stood with her feet planted wide as she studied the weather.

"I've ordered the lights to be lit, sir," Darya said.

"Good," Calder replied. "I thought I saw a sail about three degrees off starboard just before the rain started."

"I'd prefer to stay on course," Darya said. "I wouldn't want to come across another ship in this weather. We'd be on top of them before we had any warning."

"I agree," Calder said. "I'll be in the mess if you need me or you want a break and something warm to drink."

"I'll let you know."

Calder nodded and went inside. He pulled off his dripping oilskin coat and hung it on a peg before heading down to the mess. On a normal night it would be empty, but during a storm, hot tea was always available for the sailors who were on duty or those who just couldn't sleep.

He spotted Dag sitting at a table with Rafael, and after grabbing a mug of tea, he joined them.

"It's raining now," he said swiping at his wet hair. "It came a little later than expected." A sailor with weather sense, possibly even a Trait, had been predicting this storm for the past few hours.

"So there's no chance of finding Holt now," Dag said. The ship pitched, and she grabbed the table. "And he's going through this too."

"He is," Calder replied. "We need to weather the storm and

worry about Holt later."

"How long will the storm last?" Dag asked.

"It's moving in the same direction we're travelling," Calder said. "And will push us along with it so we could be in it for hours." He finished his tea and stood up. "I'm going to walk the holds and make sure we're not taking on water anywhere. Rafael, you should check on Darya every half hour and see if she needs anything."

"Yes, sir," Rafael said.

"Can I come with you?" Dag asked. "I've never seen a ship's hold before."

"Sure," Calder replied. "They're not very exciting, at least not unless there's a leak. Which we don't want to find."

He led the way out of the mess and back onto the deck. Wind whipped rain sideways, and Dag huddled against him as they made their way to the hold.

Once inside, he headed down a set of narrow steps. A few sailors looked up from a game of ludus.

"We're doing a walk through," Calder said as Dag joined him at the bottom of the stairs. "Have any leaks been discovered that I need to know about?"

"There's a damp spot near the bow," a woman said. "I checked it an hour ago, and it didn't look any different on account of the storm, but we need to keep an eye on it."

"I'll take a look," he replied. "Thank you."

He gestured for Dag to precede him as they walked across the wooden deck. A few crates of supplies were stacked along the edges and nothing looked wet. Hammocks were strung above them but only a few were occupied: the rest of the crew was on duty or holed up in the mess in case they were needed.

"Shouldn't this be full?" Dag asked.

"If this was a normal trading venture, yes," Calder replied. "Usually we'd be shipping dried fish and dressed timber, among other things. But we're not trading, we're buying food."

"So, this hold will be full on our way back," Dag said. "It doesn't seem like it will be enough to keep the Three from starving."

"No, it doesn't," he agreed. "That's why we need to make more than one trip. The pirate coin would usually be enough to hire ships to deliver goods to Tarklee, but this late in the season, with no guarantee they can get back home before the pass freezes over, I doubt we'd find any willing captains."

"Do you think that was Luck? Finding the treasure?"

"I think it was both of our Traits working together," he replied. "You discovered where it had been hidden, but Luck might have allowed us to arrive in time to know the pirates were searching for something and get there before they'd found it."

He stepped through a narrow door that led to the bow. "There's our damp spot," he said. He ran his hand across it: damp but not wet. "That sailor was right; this shouldn't be a problem." He turned to Dag. "Our inspection is done," he said. "And we have nothing to worry about."

"So now it's back on deck?" she asked.

"Yes. I want to check in with Darya," he replied. "Then we can get ourselves more tea."

Darya had things well in hand, so Calder and Dag spent the hours until dawn in the mess with some of the crew. Just after dawn, the storm broke and the ship settled back into an easy motion.

On deck, Calder breathed in the salty air.

"The sunrise is going to be beautiful," he said to Dag. "I've never seen one on land come even close to the sunrise after a storm at sea."

Pinks and reds and oranges stole across the sky, and Dag took a sharp breath. Smiling, he turned to her, expecting to see a smile. Instead she was staring out across the port rail.

"There's something in the water," she said. "Over there."

"A ship?" he asked just as a cry came from the rigging.

"Ship!" came the call. "Eight degrees to port!"

"Is it the *Neas*?" Calder asked. He couldn't quite see it.

"I don't know," Dag replied. "But something's wrong. I think it's sinking."

CHAPTER 8

As the *Oakhaven* passed out of the harbour, Gustav stared back at Tarklee. It was just after dawn and the city was not yet awake. It looked peaceful. He hoped it stayed that way.

"Does Janni need help?" Berna asked. She'd accompanied him to the stern as the ship got under sail. It was a cloudy, grey day, and the wind was cold.

"She'll ask if she does," he replied. "Or she'll get Jarri to help her. She prefers to do things on her own."

"She won't be able to navigate the stairs."

"Not in her chair," Gustav agreed. "So she might need some help with that. Or she'll just Make something that works for her."

"Nadez seems to think she and her brother will save the shipyards," Berna said. "You know what goes into building ships; do you think they can?"

"They'll do something," he replied. "Whether it's enough depends on what's left. And how much of it can be saved. Life on the island depends on the shipyards: they will already have every able-bodied person working on it." His father included. No doubt Gunnar Falk was working as long and as hard as anyone else. "They'll be grateful for the timber we're bringing, along with the Byholt woodcutters."

The woodcutters would dress this timber on site, to the specifications of those rebuilding the shipyards. Captain Sorensen would return to Cutterstown for more timber as soon as the *Oakhaven* was offloaded. How many more trips were required depended on how much the Breck twins could salvage and reuse. And the weather.

"I need some tea," Berna said. "And I need you to tell me everything you know about who's in charge on Lavais."

"I left when I was eleven," Gustav warned. "I'm not sure I can be of much help."

"You know more than you think you do," Berna said. "I guarantee it."

A few hours later, Gustav had to agree: he did know more than he'd thought. Berna's insightful questions had coaxed out small memories that he'd forgotten that now, even as a half-trained Intelligencer, he understood gave insights into how things were done on Lavais.

"I didn't realize just how much authority the shipyards had over everything," he said.

"You said it yourself," Berna replied. "*Life on the island depends on the shipyards.* It's the key economic concern for the Clan Freeholders and the reason why the pirates attacked the island. And the reason why we are heading there. It makes sense that those who make it successful have influence. And that includes your father. Does my mother know he's a Journeyman Shipbuilder?"

"I'm not sure," Gustav said. "Joosep knew, but Nadez might not." Nadez Norup knew he was from Lavais, but he couldn't remember telling her about his father.

"Well, it's a bit of good luck, as far as I'm concerned," Berna said. "We northerners wouldn't like some southerner coming in and telling us what to do. I expect Lavaisians will be much the same."

"We aren't here to tell them anything," Gustav said. "We're here to help."

"Yes, in *our* way with *our* people." She shook her head. "And we have no time to talk them into anything. They will feel like we're taking over, and we are."

Gustav frowned and then sighed. "I guess we are."

"Yes, and I'm counting on your Trait and your ties to the island to help us take control of the rebuilding effort with the least amount of bad feelings. Nyorden knows we don't need a revolt on our hands."

"As soon as we drop anchor, I'll have someone fetch my mother," Gustav said. "I suggest we talk to her while the timber is being unloaded."

"All right," Berna agreed. "The timber is the proof that we are here to help." She pursed her lips. "But why your mother and not your father?"

"My father has the skills and the trade," he said. "But my mother organizes him. She's the one we need to convince. She should meet Janni and Jarri too."

"Why?"

"Because she'll immediately understand that Jarri is frail and that if we're using him, we are desperate."

DAG POINTED AT the horizon. She was certain it was a ship, but she didn't see a sail.

"I see it now," Calder said. He passed the spy glass to Darya. "She looks like she took damage from the storm. The main mast is gone and she's listing to starboard. Probably taking on water."

"Is it Tarmo Holt?" Dag asked.

"No," he replied. "It looks like a Pilalian kog. It's a long way from the coast if it is."

"They only sail along the coast?" she asked. "And right now it has no sails?"

"It's missing its mast and sail," he replied. "Kogs are slow but wide and stable, which makes them good for navigating shallow harbours and the surf, but not very good at long distances."

"We've been spotted," Darya said. "They're waving at us."

"I'll hand out some pistols," Calder said. "Just in case."

Darya called an order that was belayed across the ship.

"In case of what?" Dag asked as she followed Calder to the gun locker.

"In case they're pretending to be disabled in order to lure us in."

Sailors hurriedly lined up in front of Calder, and he handed them guns along with packets of powder and shot.

"More pirates?" Dag asked softly when the armed sailors had gone. "Like the ones from Strongrock?"

"They're not as organized," Calder said. "They don't call themselves privateers, and there's no safe port for them. But they will kill you for what you have, the same as the Strongrock pirates. Come on, let's go to the bow in case either of our Traits wants to show us something."

Dag followed him to the bow where they stood near the railing. She stared out at the smaller ship, trying to see if there was anything that triggered her Trait.

"*Skit*," Calder muttered.

"What is it?"

"I know the man who's at the helm." He turned to her and grimaced. "You've met my mother. Now it seems that you are about to meet my father."

The *Atlaine* slowed as it went past the other ship. Calder called out something in Pilalian. Dag wasn't completely sure what he said, but she didn't think it included a greeting to his father.

The man at the helm, a middle-aged Pilalian, looked surprised for a moment before he smiled and replied.

Calder continued to speak to him, and the itch started between her shoulder blades.

"My Trait is telling me he's hiding something," she said when she got Calder's attention.

"We're both hiding that we're father and son," he replied. "Is it that?"

"I don't think so, but why is he hiding that?" She stared out at the other ship. It looked like there was a crew of less than a dozen: all men, all Pilalians. "Why are there no women on board?"

"That's not a good sign."

Dag looked over to see that Belmina had joined them.

"More Pilalian men than women take to the sea," she said. "But to not have any in your crew? That's either deliberate or because women won't ship out with that crew. I don't like either one of those reasons."

The *Atlaine* was now past the other ship, and in response to a flurry of orders the ship slowed and made a wide turn.

Dag followed Calder to the other side of the ship. She stared at the bow of the smaller ship as they approached it again. "They're pretending to be in trouble," she said, scratching between her shoulder blades. "They've *taken* their mast down. It's lying on the deck under that sail."

Calder sighed and shook his head. "We know you've taken your mast down," he called out in Nordmerian. "Tell us why or we will leave."

"The storm threatened it," Calder's father replied in the same language. "And pushed us out to sea. We realized that we were taking on water before we could get the mast back up."

"Can you pretend to take on water?" Dag asked. "Nothing he said was true: they aren't taking on water, and the storm didn't push them out to sea."

"*Skit*," Calder swore under his breath. "What is he up to?"

"Can you invite just him on board?" Dag replied. "I think we ran across him because of your Trait, and mine is telling me that he's hiding something we need to know."

"If you come aboard, we can discuss how we can help," Calder said.

There was a huddle around Calder's father for a few minutes, and then the suspected pirates parted, and he grinned. "I would be honoured," he said. "Can you launch a dinghy?"

"Of course," Calder replied. "Rafael," he called. The younger man stepped to his side. "Launch a dinghy with you and one person to row. Do not tie up to that ship. I don't care if that means he has to jump into the sea and then swim to you, your orders are to not get too close. We will have guns trained on each and every person on that kog until you are safely back on board."

"Yes, sir." Rafael hurried away.

Dag continued to stare at the smaller ship, trying to figure out what other secrets were being hidden on board.

"A dinghy is being launched," Calder called out. "We will allow your captain to board us, but that is all."

A few minutes later, Rafael and the dinghy rowed into view. Dag was interested to see that Belmina was at the oars.

"Should Rafael have taken a pirate with him?" she asked Calder. Although, when she stared at the woman, her Trait didn't activate. Belmina wasn't hiding anything.

"Belmina was a Pilalian sailor before she became a pirate," he replied. "I think she is deeply offended that there are no women on board that kog. So, she's making a point."

The dinghy stopped a few yards from the other ship, and Calder's father looked at his son and gave an exaggerated shrug.

"You'll have to jump," Calder said. "I don't trust you."

"What if I don't trust you?" was the reply.

"Then we don't talk. We'll pull our dinghy back and be on our way. It's your choice."

Calder's father shrugged again, and with a grin, he climbed over the rail and jumped into the sea. It took him only a moment to reach the dinghy. Rafael watched while Belmina helped their guest into the boat.

A few minutes later they were on their way back to the *Atlaine*.

"Keep your pistols trained on their crew," Calder said to a sailor standing at the rail. "Dag? I'll get him and meet you in the captain's cabin."

Dag nodded and headed below deck. Once in the cabin, she put away notes and charts and rolled up the map that had been laid out on the table.

When she was done, she stood in front of the door and looked around. Satisfied that she hadn't missed anything that could give away their secrets, she sat down at the table.

The door opened a few moments later.

"In here," Calder said and stood aside to let his father pass him. "Rafael, keep anyone else out."

Calder closed the door behind him as his father prowled over to her.

"What have we here?" he asked. "Such a lovely, fair-haired beauty." He smiled at her and sat down.

"I know who you are," Dag said. "What I don't know is why you didn't acknowledge your own son."

"Is she in charge here, Calder?"

"Dagrun, meet my father, Rahm," Calder said as he joined them. "Rahm, this is Dagrun. I suggest you answer her question."

"But you're not going to answer mine?" Rahm pouted but Dag knew he was pretending to be upset. "Oh, all right. I felt that it might put him in danger," he said. "It's a rough crew I'm with."

Dag met Calder's eyes and she shrugged. "Someone would be in danger if your relationship was known," she said. "But you or him?" She turned back to Rahm, whose eyes had narrowed as he looked at her. She resisted the urge to scratch between her shoulders: Rahm had secrets upon secrets.

"How is your mother?" Rahm asked Calder. "I hope she is getting the help she needs to take care of her lands." He turned to Dag. "She's delicate, my Lauma. I worry about her when I'm away."

Dag laughed. "I've met Lauma Strauskas. Delicate is not a word I would use to describe her. And if I'm not mistaken, she's the one who told you to stay away."

"Rahm," Calder said. "Why are you lying to us?"

"He's using small lies to cover up the big ones," Dag said. "Aren't you? Who were you waiting for? You are out in the middle of the sea, pretending to be in trouble. Who were you hoping to find?"

"Anyone," Rahm replied. "And everyone. Except maybe my son?"

"I think you are waiting for someone specific," Dag replied. "Who will be carrying something that has value. And it's not someone who knows you."

"I am simply waiting for anyone carrying anything," Rahm replied.

"Since when are you a common pirate?" Calder asked. "Since when are you a common anything?"

"I'm an uncommon pirate," Rahm replied. "I think it's time I returned to my ship."

"He only came aboard to make sure we didn't have the person he's looking for," Dag said. "Now that he's sure, he's ready to leave."

There was a knock on the door. Calder rose to answer it, leaving Dag staring at his father.

"So many secrets," she said softly. "Do you even know who you are? Who you can trust?"

Before he could say anything, Calder returned.

"The Pilalian who rowed the dinghy I sent to fetch you has confirmed with some of her fellow sailors," Calder said, "that the ship you are on, whatever name it might bear, belongs to Fihaldo Pinho."

"I am a pirate," Rahm said.

Dag was so itchy that she couldn't stop herself from rolling her shoulders. Calder raised an eyebrow at her.

"You are playing at being a pirate," Calder said. "But you aren't one."

"I never have asked you about your various disguises," Rahm replied, looking at Calder. "And you've never before asked about mine." He leaned across the table. "What's different this time?"

Dag stared at her hands. When she thought Calder had followed her gaze to them, she signalled. *He's a spy.*

Calder looked up from Dag's hands into his father's eyes,

doing his best to hide his surprise. Of course, his father was a spy: how had he not seen it before?

He nodded as if to himself, but in reality, he was telling Dag that he agreed. Rahm's eyes narrowed; one of the few reactions he'd never seemed able to control.

So, Luck had brought him to this truth.

"Why are you looking for Tarmo Holt?" he asked abruptly. Rahm's eyes narrowed again, and Calder smiled. *This* was why Luck had brought them together.

Rahm sighed. "I gave it away just now, I know." He shrugged. "Tarmo Holt owes something to someone I am beholden to. I am trying to collect for him."

"Why did you expect Holt?" Dag asked. "Did he send you a message? Is he meeting you?"

"I am the last person Tarmo Holt wants to see." Rahm laughed. "Except perhaps for Intelligencers." He grinned. "A woman spy, although you're not a real spy since you rely on a Trait."

"I can see why Lauma wants you to stay away," Dag replied. "If you think so little of women, why did you give Lauma so much money?"

"She's my wife," Rahm said. "And children of mine will never starve while I have breath in my body."

Calder sighed. "What does Tarmo Holt owe Fihaldo Pinho?" His father smirked, but Calder refused to rise to the bait: instead he looked at Dag. "What do you think we should do?" He was pretty sure they had to return Rahm to his ship, but it wouldn't hurt to make him sweat a little.

"I think he's been spying on the Three for a very long time," Dag said. "We could return him to face the Grand Freeholder's justice."

Calder laughed out loud. "That would be fitting."

"By now Tarmo Holt is no longer Grand Freeholder," Rahm said. "And the person I suspect holds that position now will let me go free."

Calder laughed again. "Your confidence is misplaced," he said. "I'm pretty sure you *don't* know who has taken over for Holt."

"Timonis is the logical choice," Rahm said. "He will be the next Grand Freeholder anyway."

"Except they didn't choose him," Dag said. "They didn't want to hold an early election until they had a chance to learn more about what Holt had done."

"And they didn't choose anyone from Nordmere," Calder said. "Holt tainted them all, at least for finishing this term." He thought his father was beginning to put it together. "They chose someone from Byholt. Who do you think is the largest landowner in Byholt? Thanks to the coin that has been sent to her by her rarely-present husband."

"Lauma? Don't tell me Lauma is Grand Freeholder. She can't be."

Calder stared at his father, confused. Instead of being angry at the realization that his estranged wife might hold power over him, he was afraid; horrified even.

"Tell us," Dag asked. "Tell us why she can't be Grand Freeholder."

"*Skit*," Rahm said. "*Skit, skit, skit.* The plans are already in place. It's already too late."

"Too late?" Calder asked. "Too late for what?"

"To save your mother," Rahm said. "To stop the assassination of the Grand Freeholder selected once Holt had fled."

NADEZ OPENED HER door to Kaja. It was the middle of the night and she'd thrown on yesterday's clothes when she'd heard someone frantically knocking at her door. Being accessible was why she'd finally given in and started spending her nights at her apartment in the Hall, but right now her stomach was in knots.

"What's happened?" she asked. She left the door ajar as she hurried back to her bedchamber and shoved her boots on, grabbed a coat, and returned to the main room. Kaja had closed the door and was pacing the width of the room.

"It's Lauma," Kaja replied, stopping to turn to her and meet her eyes. "She's safe for now, but she's gone into hiding."

"What? Why?"

"Mykol sent her a message," Kaja said. "She received it just after midnight and immediately came to see me. I . . . ." Kaja paused. "I know where the secret hiding places are. I told her about a few of them, and she said she'd stay safe. Then I came here."

"She told Mykol about her plans to safeguard Saulia?" The last time they'd spoken Lauma had agreed that it would be a good idea to talk to Mykol. Had she?

"I'm not sure," Kaja replied. "She seemed to trust Mykol's message; his warning."

"What did he tell her? And why didn't he tell her in person?"

Kaja took a deep breath. "*The Grand Freeholder is in immediate danger.* That's it; that's all that the message said. Nothing about why he didn't come himself. Lauma said it was delivered by a young lad she didn't recognize."

"Did she destroy the message?" If they wanted to keep Mykol safe, and maybe even get more information from him, they couldn't leave evidence of his betrayal.

"I destroyed it," Kaja said. "I burned it as soon as I'd read it."

"Good. Let's go." She headed for the door, Kaja right behind her. Lauma Strauskas was as safe as she could be, for now. It was up to Nadez to find out who the threat was from and stop it.

Moonlight spilled in over the half wall, illuminating the floor of the hallway that led to Lauma's apartment. Nadez signalled Kaja to remain where she was before she stepped into a shadow. Had someone already been sent to hurt Lauma, or had she and Kaja arrived first?

In a few quiet minutes she was half a dozen paces away from the door. Her next step would take her out of shadow and into a patch of moonlight that shone in over the half wall.

Just as she was about to take that step into the light, she heard a faint click. A thin line of shadow outlined one side of the door to Lauma's apartment. The door eased open a fraction more, and she thought she saw a glint of an eye looking out onto the corridor.

She and Kaja had arrived *after* the intruder. She thanked Nyorden that Lauma was already somewhere else, safe.

Nadez waited, hardly daring to breathe in case the sound of it gave her away. Five minutes later the door opened wider, and someone swathed in a black cloak crouched low as they exited. Nadez didn't see a weapon but there was plenty of room to hide one beneath their cloak. Had they been sent to hurt Lauma or to kill her?

As soon as the intruder eased the door shut, Nadez stepped out of the shadow.

"Did you find what you were looking for?" she asked.

The intruder bolted. As they ran past Nadez, she grabbed their cloak. The intruder spun, trying to twist their way out of the garment.

The smooth fabric slipped from Nadez's hand, and her opponent spiralled away from her, tripping on the tangled cloak. They fell hard against the half wall. Nadez clutched at the cloak, ready to grab the intruder again as they struggled to their feet.

But instead of retreating down the hallway in the opposite direction, away from Nadez, the intruder launched themselves over the half wall.

Her hands on top of the wall, Nadez looked down in shock. She heard a thud, but that was all she heard: no scream, no cry for help as the intruder plunged to their death. Just the thud of a body hitting the ground.

Kaja joined her. "They jumped," she said. "Why did they jump?"

"A suicide assassin," Nadez said, stepping away from the opening. "It must be. An assassin who is hired to kill someone and take their own life if they can't escape capture."

"In this case they didn't kill their target," Kaja said.

"No," Nadez said. She headed to the door to Lauma's apartments. "But that doesn't mean they didn't kill someone. We need to make sure no servants were here. And we need to recover that body."

And she'd have to talk to Mykol about how it was that he knew there would be an attempt on Lauma's life tonight.

GUSTAV STARED OUT at the Lavais harbour and the ruined shipyards in dismay.

The *Oakhaven* had dropped anchor an hour ago, but he'd stayed below while Captain Sorenson went ashore to meet with officials and send a message to his mother.

He'd been sent for a few minutes ago; a dinghy was approaching, and he was asked to come on deck and confirm that it was his mother. And it was. He'd recognize the way Venne Falk carried herself anywhere.

Then he'd turned his gaze to the ruin that used to be the source of pride and work for so many on Lavais Island.

The main huts had all been destroyed: there were only a few blackened timbers still pointing skyward, and the cradle was currently being taken apart by hand by a dozen workers. Which meant the winch must not be operational.

"We'll need someone to tell us what everything is for," Janni said from his side. She'd had her brother bring her chair up to the deck, and the twins had been whispering to each other as they stared out at the ruined shipyards.

"I'm sure that can be arranged," Gustav replied. "There are more than a few Shipbuilders out of work."

"They're all busy."

Gustav turned to see his mother staring at him.

"Mother." He hurried over to her and hugged her. "I'm very glad to see you."

"I am glad to see you too." She held him at arm's length and smiled at him. "You've grown so much. Your father will be happy too." Her smile turned to a frown. "But you cannot take him away from the work that has to be done."

"We won't," Gustav said. "Because we're here to help. Mother, this is Janni and Jarri Breck. This is my mother, Venne Falk. They have Traits that will help."

"Traits," she scoffed. "You are a likeable lad, always have been, but that's not going to help us rebuild. Although the timber and woodcutters you brought will."

"You don't understand," Gustav said. "Janni can Make anything and Jarri Unmakes. He'll break down anything that's left into usable pieces and Janni will reuse them to help rebuild the shipyards."

"It's true," Janni said. "Let us prove ourselves."

"It's not up to me," his mother said.

"No, you're right," Berna said as she joined them. "The Interim Grand Freeholder has sent these two, along with timber and woodcutters, as the very best resources available to get the shipyards building ships again. Which is crucial to the safety and security of the Fair Seas Treaty Alliance countries. Berna Strauskas," she said. "Daughter and representative of Interim Grand Freeholder Lauma Strauskas."

"I heard that Tarmo Holt was replaced," his mother said. "But I didn't hear why."

"He was plotting against the Fair Seas Treaty Alliance." Berna gestured to the shipyards. "Lavais was attacked on his orders."

"It was pirates," his mother said. "In a ship painted white."

"Working for Tarmo Holt," Berna replied.

"It's true," Gustav said. "I saw the pirate captain set many ships on fire in Tarklee Harbour. Just after that, Holt fled on his ship with his family."

"Clan Freeholder Timonis said nothing about that," his mother said. "Just that there was an Interim Grand Freeholder and that his turn at the position would come in the fall, as scheduled."

"Is he here?" Berna asked. "Clan Freeholder Timonis?"

"He's not here," his mother said. "He's keeping close to home these days. He did send out an order for anyone not involved in rebuilding the shipyards to take up fishing. Most folks thought it strange, and only a few people complied."

"I'll organize that," Gustav said to Berna. "I'll make sure that people with skills for fishing and drying are paired up with those without."

"Thank you," Berna replied. "I'll send a message to Clan Freeholder Timonis that I'm here in Lavais Port. I understand that his village was also attacked by the pirates, so perhaps he felt he needed to be there." She sighed. "I suppose it's time for me to join Captain Eklund on land." She left in search of the captain.

"You need to help us, Mother," Gustav said to her. "Getting Janni and Jarri working in the shipyards is critical."

"I suppose it can't hurt," she said. "Especially since it's an order from the Interim Grand Freeholder. No one can blame me for that." She frowned and leaned close. "Are these two up to task? Neither one of them looks very sturdy."

"They'll need help with the manual work," Gustav replied, loud enough for the Brecks to hear. He looked at the twins and shrugged. "But that's what everyone is already doing. Janni and Jarri will direct them so their labour makes more progress."

"All right," his mother said. "But getting folk out fishing? That'll be harder. Shipbuilders are not fishermen."

"Some of them will have to be," Gustav said. "If people want to eat this winter."

"Surely it's not that bad," his mother said. "Gustav, it can't be that bad."

"Tarmo Holt had been planning this for a long time," Gustav replied. "Food stores were destroyed along with most of the ships that could bring in more supplies in the few weeks we have before winter sets in and closes the Frozen Gap." He sighed. "We are doing whatever we can to ensure that this does not become a disaster: that includes trying to find and store more food as well as getting the shipyards back to building ships as soon as possible. But we all understand that new ships might not be ready until late summer or early fall. We need to do everything possible to survive until then."

CHAPTER 9

Dag rubbed a hand across her eyes. She and Calder were in the mess, drinking tea. And they had still not decided what to do with Rahm. Every time she looked at him her Trait activated. And it was intense. Calder's father had the most secrets of anyone she'd ever come across.

"We need to send him back to his crew," Calder said. "We've already kept him longer than we should have. If we detain him much longer, we'll need to take him with us."

"No," she said. "We do not want him on this ship. I'll talk to him one last time." She met his gaze. "Alone. Then we'll send him back."

Dag drained her mug and put it on the table before rising and heading down to the cabin where they'd locked Rahm up.

She nodded to Belmina and Rafael, who pulled a key from his pocket and unlocked the door.

"Get up," she said to Rahm, who was lying on the floor. They'd removed all the furniture from the small cabin, not wanting to give him anything he might be able to use as a weapon.

"Are you here to let me go?"

Dag was certain that that type of comment would usually be said smugly, but since he'd told them that Lauma was the target of an apparent assassination, he'd been subdued. Her Trait was on high alert, but she didn't think he was pretending this. He loved his former wife and did not want her dead.

"Yes," she replied once he was standing. "But not until we have a talk." She took a step towards him. "Whatever it is you are up to, you started long before you met Lauma Strauskas and had children with her. I need you to tell me what you know." She paused. "Let's start with Fihaldo Pinho."

"You know I can't tell you anything," Rahm drawled.

"I already know that someone, possibly the person you work for, is trying to kill the woman I believe you truly care for," Dag said. He didn't reply, but his eyes narrowed for just a second. "I also know that whoever you work for has no idea how compromised you are. No one knows you have a family in Byholt; no one knows that Calder is your son. What would happen if they found out that you are married to the Interim Grand Freeholder? Would they make you use that relationship against your family? Would you do it?"

Rahm sighed. "I would not harm my family."

"Except you already have," Dag said. "Lauma might already be dead." Her voice caught; she didn't believe that, *couldn't* believe that. Nadez would keep her safe. She had to. "Your *wife* might already be dead."

"I can't help her," Rahm replied softly. "As you said, plans have long been in place. I can't help Lauma no matter how much I might want to."

"What about Calder?" Dag asked. "The people you work for would probably prefer him dead too. Are you willing to help him? Or will you stand by and allow them to kill him too."

"He's got you," Rahm said. "And his Trait. He'll be fine."

"Berna might not be," Dag said. "Not when the plan is to starve the Three into submission this winter." He flinched at that. "You didn't know? That's how Tarmo Holt was planning on delivering the Three to your employer. We tracked Holt here to the Sapphire Sea, but we're not leaving until this ship's hold is full of food." She was looking for Inger too, but Rahm didn't need to know that.

"Starvation is a terrible way to die," Rahm said. "Even Holt wouldn't do that."

"Are you sure? He brought his family with him. I saw them on board his ship myself; his wife and daughter. A daughter the same age as Berna."

"He brought his family?" Rahm asked. "Thank you for that information. But I don't believe the Three will starve. You'll just send more ships like this one."

"Two," Dag said. "There are two ships left that can travel safely to the Sapphire Sea. The rest, along with the Lavais Shipyards, were destroyed on Holt's orders."

"I doubt Tarmo Holt would ever destroy so much property."

"Then Margit Ansdottir did it whether Holt wanted her to or not," Dag said.

"Ansdottir? I wouldn't have expected her to work against Holt like that." Rahm raised his eyebrows as if he was surprised, but Dag's Trait activated.

"You're lying," she said. "You knew that Ansdottir was going to betray Holt."

His eyes narrowed, and suddenly *she knew*.

"You're the one who told her to betray him," she said, nodding to herself. "Pinho must have threatened Ansdottir, and you were the one who delivered the threat."

"I admit I have crossed paths with the pirate captain," Rahm said. "But only because we are both in the same line of work."

"You're not a pirate." She stared at him. "I don't think you're a spy either. At least, you're not *just* a spy. By the way, she's dead now. Ansdottir."

"How?" Rahm seemed genuinely surprised and not unhappy about it. Was it because he would have needed to manage her?

"After Ansdottir and her pirates destroyed almost all of the ships in Tarklee Harbour, she went down with a stolen ship. Calder rammed her with a log hauler, and Ansdottir was trapped on board."

"My son did that?" Rahm sounded proud. "But it is too bad for Tarmo Holt that so many ships were destroyed."

Dag's Trait, already heightened, made her shoulder muscles twitch. There was something critical here.

"Why are you the last person Tarmo Holt would want to see?" she asked. "That's what you said earlier. Why?"

"Coin," Rahm said. "With Holt, it's always about coin."

"He owes the man you work for." It was starting to make sense. "Holt borrowed coin in order to buy so many ships."

"Ships that you say have been destroyed," Rahm replied. "Tarmo Holt is in a great deal of debt."

"I'm more concerned about the danger he's put the Three in," she said. "We're trying to keep people from starving this winter."

"I suppose you'll need to hire ships in the Sapphire Sea," Rahm replied, and her Trait activated again.

"From the man you work for?" she asked.

"I wouldn't advise it," Rahm said.

"Then why do you do his bidding?"

Rahm's eyes narrowed, but he didn't reply.

"What else do you know about Margit Ansdottir?" she asked abruptly and was rewarded when Rahm tried to hide his surprise.

"She is, or was, a fierce pirate," he said and smirked. "A legend. She could navigate the Teeth. So I've heard."

Something about the way he said that made Dag's Trait react. He'd seen her do it; Rahm had been on board Ansdottir's ship while she went through the Teeth.

"A legend," she repeated. Who, according to what she'd overheard at the Merchant Adventurers, had been robbing and destroying ships from the Sapphire Sea. She had to talk to Calder. She had an idea of what had happened. If she was correct, Tarmo Holt was no longer a threat. It didn't mean she was going to abandon Inger, but it did mean that she might not able to search for her right now.

"One last question," she said. "Are you going to tell Calder that you've been lying to him his whole life; that you used your own son to glean intelligence to use against the organization he works for, or shall I?"

THERE WAS A light on in the office. Nadez tiptoed over to the door. She was hoping it was Mykol, here as usual, pretending it was a day like any other. But it could also be someone else.

Probably not an assassin: why would they light a lamp? But someone could be looking for something.

She pushed the door open a crack and pressed her eye against it. Nothing in the outer office looked disturbed. Someone moved, and she relaxed when she saw Mykol sit down, a worried look on his face.

Nadez slipped into the office. The door to Lauma's office was closed, and no light shone from underneath the door.

"Are you alone?" she asked. A startled Mykol looked over at her. When he saw who it was, he nodded.

"The Interim Grand Freeholder has not yet arrived," he said. "Is she safe?" he asked in a whisper.

Nadez nodded and crossed the room to him. "She's in hiding. Even I don't know where she is." She pulled a chair up close to Mykol. "But you know I need to ask questions. I surprised a suicide assassin coming out of her apartment last night. They killed themselves before they had a chance to report back to whoever commissioned them."

She'd done her best to keep it quiet: she'd told the guard truthfully that it had been a suicide, someone jumping from above. She didn't say where they'd jumped from, but there were only a few floors with hallways that opened to the outside.

"But she's safe?" Mykol asked again.

"Yes, but in order to keep her that way, I need to know how you knew," Nadez said. "How did you know to warn her last night?"

"I can't tell you," Mykol said softly. "They'll kill me."

Nadez nodded. She'd expected this. It also meant that Mykol thought it likely he was being watched. "I'm not sure whoever is behind this knows what happened," she said. "I need you to pretend that I've given you the terrible news that Lauma has been attacked. Her apartment is already being guarded, and I've sent someone to the infirmary, also under guard, pretending to be her. If you hear of another attempt, can you let Kaja know?" She didn't want people to think Lauma was dead. Not only was she hoping to catch someone making a second assassination attempt, but the reported death of the Interim Grand Freeholder, even if a deception, would create a political situation she wasn't willing to deal with.

"Lauma Strauskas' promise about Saulia," Mykol said. "You will honour that as well?"

"Yes. Saulia Holt will be supported by Lauma Strauskas and I." She paused. "I promise you that I will do everything in my power to keep her safe."

"All right," Mykol said. "As long as it does not compromise either me or Saulia, I will contact Kaja if I hear of another attack."

"Thank you," Nadez said. "Now I ask that you keep Lauma's office locked. If there is anything official that must be dealt with, send for me."

She nodded and left for her own office, where she found Kaja waiting for her.

"Where is the body?" she asked her.

"I've had it taken to a jail cell," Kaja replied. "And put it under guard. Should we go look now?"

"Yes."

Nadez led the way out of the office and through the corridors of the Hall. At the jail, two guards wearing the colours of the Grand Freeholder flanked a wooden door.

"Cell twelve," Kaja said. One guard unlocked the door, and they both stepped aside.

"No one else accesses this cell," Nadez said.

"Yes, Master Intelligencer," the guard replied.

Nadez went through the doorway, followed by Kaja.

Cell twelve was in a secluded area of the jail. The door to the cell was open since this prisoner was never going to try to escape.

A grey cloth covered the face, blood seeping through it.

"They hit headfirst," Kaja said. "There is no chance to identify them."

"It's a woman," Nadez said. "And from the skin colour I would guess that they are from Pilalia, or maybe Arressa." She picked up a cold, stiff hand and turned it over. "I don't see any tattoos." She walked to the feet. A single doeskin slipper was crusted in blood. "Did we find the other slipper?"

"I didn't realize anything was missing," Kaja said. "Should I send someone for it?"

"No." Nadez leaned over to stare at the feet. "It will be proof of her suicide if her employers find it. There are callouses," she said. "On her hands as well. I think she was a trained assassin." She straightened. "Someone went to a lot of trouble and expense to bring in a professional killer from the Sapphire Sea."

She went back to the head and lifted the cloth. A single blue eye peered out from a face that was a pulpy mess.

"The blue eyes of an Arressan," Nadez said. She dropped the cloth. "And not very old. But who hired her?"

She sighed and turned to Kaja. "Lauma is not safe, so it's up to us to figure out who's behind this."

IT WAS MID-AFTERNOON before Gustav had a chance to eat. He entered the shipyard's dining hall and scanned the tables. He spotted Berna and steered towards her.

"You're telling me that Clan Freeholder Timonis's response is that he will not return to Lavais?" Berna asked. "Even though his presence is requested by the Interim Grand Freeholder's representative?" She looked up at Gustav and nodded, but her frown didn't waver.

Gustav sat down beside Berna, across from the two men she was speaking to. He recognized one of them: Leif Stendhal was a minor Swyfordian Clan Freeholder.

"I do not have any power over Clan Freeholder Timonis," Stendhal said. He sat up straight and smirked at Berna.

"You make your living off of shipbuilding," Berna said. "It would be very hard to do that without timber from my mother's holdings." Berna stared at Stendhal until his smirk faltered. "I may not have *power* over my mother," she said. "But I do have influence. I suggest you contact Timonis and let him know that anything other than his full co-operation may be considered an act of treason against the Three. That charge would make for a very different election process come the fall."

"Yes, Freeholder," Stendhal said. He seemed subdued as he and his companion hurried away.

"*Skit karl*," Berna swore. "And so is Timonis." She turned to Gustav. "I'm certain that he is fortifying his home and hoarding his food, and I *will* tell my mother. Timonis is expected to be the next Grand Freeholder, and this behaviour is reprehensible."

"What would happen if the election wasn't held?" Gustav asked.

"It has to be held," Berna replied. "It's one of the key agreements of the Fair Seas Treaty Alliance. A Grand Freeholder must be chosen every three years, and each country elects theirs during their turn in the cycle. In over fifty years it's never *not* happened."

"But what if it doesn't happen?" he asked again. "Or if whoever Swyford elects isn't trusted by Nordmere and Byholt? What then?"

"I don't know." She stared at him. "I don't know," she repeated. "Do you think this was planned?"

"Holt has been working on this for years; most likely even before he was elected Grand Freeholder. What if chaos resulting from divisive fighting between the Fair Seas Treaty Alliance countries is the goal? What would happen if the Three didn't trust each other?"

"Trade might be disrupted," Berna said. "My mother controls

most of the timber trade in Byholt. Currently, the Treaty regulates how much must be sold within the Three. But if she felt that Swyford and Nordmere were trying to take advantage of her, she could ignore the Treaty rules and sell to anyone, anywhere, at any price."

"Who would win?" Gustav asked. "In that scenario, who would benefit?"

"Besides her? Whoever owned ships," Berna replied. "Ship owners could charge any price they wanted to ship timber. Pilalia and Arressa would also benefit. Their forests don't produce the quality trees that are required for building ships, and not having access to timber limits the number of ships they can build."

"Which limits the amount of wealth and power they can accumulate," Gustav replied. "The Lavais shipyards could be put out of business if all of the timber was sold to the Sapphire Sea."

"Those who don't know her might think my mother would love to benefit from that," Berna said. "She would certainly be able to earn more coin from her timber. But money isn't what motivates her: making sure that the people who depend on her are safe, is."

"We can't assume the rest of the Clan Freeholders feel the same way," Gustav said.

"I think we can assume they *do not*," Berna replied. "But are any of them actively working towards the breakdown of the Treaty? Next time a shipment of timber arrives, I'll send a message to my mother. I will also complain about Timonis. If he expects to become the next Grand Freeholder, he can't want the Treaty countries to be mired in chaos or worse, for the Treaty rules to be ignored. But his current behaviour will not endear him to my mother."

CALDER STARED OUT at his father: a man who had been lying to him, and worse, using him, all his life. Rahm had returned to his ship, and now the mast was being set into place.

"Are you all right?" Dag asked.

He gave her a sad smile. "I will be. I'm angry and disappointed, but I'm not furious. I think I always knew that he couldn't be trusted." He sighed. "Now I know for certain."

"There's more," Dag said. "I'm sure Rahm thinks he gave nothing away, but he'd be wrong."

Calder laughed: he couldn't help it. "That definitely makes me feel better. What did my father the spy let slip?"

"He told me that Tarmo Holt is in a great deal of debt," Dag said. "I think that's how he was able to own so many ships. I believe that debt is owed to the man your father is working for."

"Fihaldo Pinho," Calder replied. "So now that Holt's ships have been either destroyed or confiscated by us, Holt is on the run from Pinho."

"Yes," Dag said. "Tarmo Holt's plans never included his ships being destroyed: the shipyards and food stores, yes, but not the ships. Not *his* ships. They were going to be his way to hold the Three hostage over the winter."

"He'd send them for food, and when they returned, he could charge starving people whatever he wanted to." The more he understood of Holt's plans, the more detestable he realized the man was.

"Yes, but Ansdottir betrayed him," Dag said. "She destroyed all of the ships, not just the ones that didn't belong to Holt. I think it was because Pinho had threatened her; your *father* threatened her in Pinho's name because Ansdottir had been robbing and destroying Pinho's ships."

"Ansdottir betrays Holt in order to put him at Pinho's mercy," Calder said.

"Yes," Dag said. "I think that's why Holt was looking for the treasure: I think he was hoping to use it to pay off his debt to Pinho."

"Or maybe he'd buy another ship or two and pay the debt off over time," Calder replied. "The Three still need food for the winter. A few shipments this fall at inflated prices would probably tempt him." He shook his head. He had always hated politics; now he despised them. "It means that we are probably right about Holt being in Arressa. If Pinho is his enemy, then there is no way he's in Pilalia."

"Now the question becomes, what do we do?" Dag asked. "Do we search for Holt, or do we buy supplies and go home?"

"We do both," Calder said. "It's not just Holt we're looking for. It's Inger too."

"Yes," Dag replied. "But she can't be the priority."

"And it's Lucky that we know it's not safe to land in Pilalia," Calder said. "Not when Pinho controls much of the coast. We'll head for Messanos and buy food there. And while we're there, we can see where our Traits take us."

"DID YOU FIND what you were looking for, Master Intelligencer?"

Nadez looked up from the papers she was studying to find Captain Winther, the leader of the Merchant Adventurers, standing in the doorway, looking at her.

"Yes," she replied. "Do you need your office back?" She was only halfway through her search, but it was his place of business.

"No, no," he said and then seemed to deflate. "With no ships, there is no work for me to do. I was just trying to be useful." He turned to leave.

"And you have been," Nadez said. "By allowing me access to your records."

"If you told me what you were looking for, I might be able to help," Captain Winther said, turning back to her.

Nadez eyed him. Should she trust him? Could she? He'd only recently been put in charge of the Merchant Adventurers. The previous person, the one who had helped Tarmo Holt hide the many ships he owned, had abandoned the post and returned to Nordmere under the protection of Henrik Ottosen. Winther, a Swyfordian, had replaced him, but he was a captain without a ship, and his heart wasn't in running the organization.

"I'm looking for the arrival of any young, Arressan women," she said. "A well-dressed traveller, not part of a ship's crew."

"There was a young woman I heard about," Winther said. He stepped into the room and stared around. "Arrived alone, she did, which is quite unusual." He walked over to a shelf and studied the spines of books. "It was right after midsummer, and I'd just returned from a trip to the Sapphire Sea when I heard about her." He pulled a book from the shelf and brought it over to the desk. Flipping it open, he leafed through the pages.

"Here," he pointed to a paragraph of writing. "That's the list of goods from my ship: any other ships in the harbour at that time will be recorded before or after mine."

Nadez peered down at the section of the ledger he was pointing to. It was a list of trade items: barrels of wine, spices, sacks of dried peas.

The entries above and below were for different ships, but the goods listed were much the same.

"This one," she pointed to a ship listed two above Winther's.

"The *Fair Winds*. Who owns this ship?"

Winther leaned over the ledger. "That's a Pilalian vessel," he said. "I don't know it myself, but most Pilalian ships are connected to Fihaldo Pinho in one way or another."

"Thank you, Captain Winther," Nadez said. "That has been very helpful."

"Glad to help," Winther said. He closed the book and returned it to the shelf. "Let me know if there's anything else I can do."

"I will." Nadez sat back in the chair as Winther left. She'd recognized the signature of the person who had bought the goods from the Pilalian ship. It was the very same man who was now protecting the former leader of the Merchant Adventurers: Henrik Ottosen.

Why had a Pilalian ship delivered an Arressan woman to him? It had to be the assassin. But what was the connection between Ottosen and Arressa? And where had she been since arriving at midsummer?

GUSTAV TIED THE small sailboat up to the dock and stepped out onto the wooden planks. A couple of fishermen nodded to him before they went back to folding their nets.

The warehouse took up the bulk of the shoreline, although he could see a few huts in the background.

Dag had told him about her and Calder's stay here, and Gustav had immediately recognized the old-time Lavaisian in Solvig Madsen. She and people like her lived a more hardscrabble life than shipbuilders, who for generations had relied on wages earned from shipbuilding to pay for everything they needed.

Now that no ships were being built and no one was earning coin, people like Solvig would help the islanders survive the winter. That was his hope, anyway. First, he had to convince her.

"Hello?'" he called as he approached the warehouse. "Solvig Madsen, are you at home?"

The warehouse door slid open, and a grey-haired woman peered out at him.

"Who's asking?"

"My name is Gustav Gunnarson," he said pulling out his patch. "I'm a friend of Dagrun Lund and Calder Rahmson. They told me you were helpful. I was hoping you would help me."

"I know 'em," Solvig said and smiled. "Told them the pirates needed to be dealt with. They did that, didn't they?"

"They did," Gustav said. "Calder rammed a log hauler into the pirate captain's ship, and she went down with it. I heard it from Calder himself."

"Gunnarson, is it?" Solvig asked. "There's a Gunnar over to the shipyards. That your family?"

"My Da. He's working at repairing the shipyards."

"Heard they have to start over." Solvig shook her head. "Won't be any new ships until next fall."

"We hope it's sooner," Gustav said. "Spring, if all goes well." He paused. "But we need to get to spring. Your warehouse, is it empty?"

"Aye, and this late in the season it should be half full with more food stores due in. You here about the Clan Freeholder's request to double up on fishing?" She nodded towards the fishermen.

"Yes," he replied. "We need to catch and dry as much fish as we can."

"Over here we already catch and dry as much as we can." She squinted at him. "You said you needed help. What do you need help with?"

"I need your help to convince the fisherman here to take on two or three people who can help them. Then the dried fish could be stored in your warehouse until it's needed." He paused. "The people who will be coming to help will be inexperienced, and there is no coin in this for you."

"Aright," Solvig said. "We don't need to be paid; this is for Lavais. We'll do it. I don't even have to ask anyone else. We've been worried ever since we heard about that request."

"Thank you," Gustav replied.

"We'll make sure there are beds for everyone you send," Solvig said. "They'll get plain food and shelter, but we'll take care of them."

"Again, thank you. I'll send half a dozen in the next few days."

"We'll be ready," Solvig said.

Gustav said his goodbyes and made his way to the sailboat. By the time he had cast off from the dock, Solvig was already talking to the fishermen. All three of them waved at him, and he waved back.

Relieved, he unfurled the sail and headed back to the

shipyards.

With his task accomplished, he was able to enjoy being on the water on a clear and sunny day.

He'd fumbled a bit sorting out the sail at first; it had been years since he'd sailed a boat, but he'd practically grown up on the sea, so it had quickly come back to him.

He grinned as he manoeuvred the small boat to the undamaged bit of pier. He tied up next to another sailboat and spent a few minutes taking the sails down and packing them away before walking over to the work area where the ship cradle was being rebuilt.

A dozen people were standing around, staring into the damaged shipyard. He spotted his father in the middle of the crowd.

"What's going on?" he asked when he reached Gunnar Falk.

His father turned to him. "Gustav. Come see." He stepped aside to allow Gustav a clear view of the worksite. Damaged and burned timber and equipment was scattered across the whole floor of the work area. Jarri stood in the middle of it, his sister beside him in her chair. Near them were two piles of neatly stacked debris.

"They've already taken apart the cradle," his father said. "And in such a way that more than half of it can be reused. Just that will save us a month." His father slapped his shoulder. "I wouldn't have believed it if I hadn't seen it with my own eyes."

"That's great news," Gustav replied. "I knew they could help, but I'm glad they're proving to be useful. Make sure you tell them they're helping." Jarri especially would appreciate knowing he and his Trait were valued.

"I will," his father said. "Between these two and the woodcutters who are working on the timber, most of us here will be watching instead of doing."

"Then convince them to learn how to fish," Gustav said. "We need to store as much food as we can before winter sets in, and I have some fishermen ready to train people willing to learn."

"You and your mother both talk as though the world is ending." His father sighed. "But I suppose it won't hurt to keep a few of these workers busy for a couple of weeks."

"Good. Have them come see me or Berna." He nodded to his father and eased away from the crowd.

His stomach grumbled. He'd let Berna know that he'd been successful once he'd eaten.

Chapter 10

Excited, Dag watched as they approached the harbour, doing her best to get a good view while staying out of the way as Calder and the crew prepared to anchor the *Atlaine*.

They were off the shore of Messanos, Arressa, and Dag was eager to get a closer look. She'd never been to a port along the Sapphire Sea, and even from here she could see that the city was built very differently from anything in the Three.

The buildings all shone white in the late morning sun, and instead of familiar pitched roofs, many of them had domes. The whole city seemed to march uphill away from the sea towards a ridge of mountains.

Screeching seagulls had chased them all the way to the harbour. Three other ships lay at anchor, and the *Atlaine* was sailing towards them.

Sailors scurried across the deck while others clambered above, rolling up the sails and tying off ropes. Eventually, the call came to drop anchor, and the ship slowed and then finally stopped.

"Captain would like to talk to you on the bridge," Rafael said to her, and Dag nodded. With one last look at the shining city, she followed him to the stern.

"We're sending a party ashore," Calder said when she reached him. "I'd like you to come."

"Yes!" she grinned, not hiding her pleasure. Calder returned her smile for a moment.

"It might be dangerous," he said in a serious tone, "and I need you and your Trait to be on high alert."

"Of course." It was a foreign port, and they didn't expect Tarmo Holt to be here, but that didn't mean someone from the *Neas* wasn't. In fact, she was hoping Inger was here. "Holt's ship isn't here."

Calder's smile returned. "You're right. Are you learning how to recognize ships?"

"His," she agreed. "I was on it, so I'm pretty sure I would recognize it." She'd watched Joosep jump into the sea while on that ship.

"The dinghy will be ready in a few minutes," Calder said. "It will be me, Rafael, and the pirates. We don't plan on stopping any closer to Pilalia, so they'll be leaving us here."

"I'll get a chance to say goodbye to Belmina." Despite the other woman's past as a pirate, Dag had grown to like her sharp wit.

As promised, in a few minutes the dinghy was in the water, and Dag climbed over the gunwale, down the rope ladder, and settled into the prow. She stared at the port city, trying to force her Trait to search out secrets and Unseen dangers, but if there were any, she wasn't finding them.

The eight Pilalian pirates manned the oars, and soon the little dinghy was skimming past the other ships that were at anchor as it made its way to the pier.

Calder called out directions as they jockeyed with a dozen other small boats to find space to land along the pier. Eventually, the dinghy wedged into an empty section, and the pirate closest to the pier jumped out. Dag tossed him the rope, and he pulled them in and tied them up.

The pier was busier than anything Dag had seen in Tarklee; small boats of every shape were squeezed in along its length: some were being unloaded, and the crates and barrels were piled high along the dock, forcing people to step around them.

"Rafael will stay with the boat," Calder said when he joined her. "Anything?"

She shook her head.

"Good," Calder replied. "Let's go."

"Belmina," Dag called. The Pilalian stepped over to her. "I just wanted to wish you luck and say that I am glad I met you."

"And I you," Belmina replied. "Though at one time we were

enemies." She held out her hand, and Dag grasped it. "If I find out anything about your sister, I will do my best for her."

"Thank you." Dag nodded, and Belmina smiled before turning and hurrying to catch up to the rest of her crewmates.

"Let's go," Calder said. "The Merchant Adventurers have an agent here. They should be able to tell me who has food for sale."

Dag fell in beside Calder as he led them along the pier towards a nearby street that was lined with a handful of wooden buildings.

Gulls screeched overhead and waves lapped against the many boats tied up at the pier, but all of that was drowned out by the murmur of dozens of voices. She caught snatches of Pilalian and Yedrissian, although she wasn't fluent enough in either to decipher what was being discussed. She heard other languages that were spoken too fast for her to recognize, along with a smattering of Nordmerian.

And the people! Everyone she passed was darker than Calder. There were Yedrissians with skin as dark as charcoal and Tobeians, who were just slightly lighter. She caught a glimpse of a head of pale hair, but when they got closer it wasn't someone from the Pale Sea. An older Yedrissian, with long white hair, was selling fish off the pier.

She followed Calder along the street and into a small building.

A Nordmerian sat behind a desk, and Calder went over to him while Dag wandered around the small room. She paused for a moment to study a map of the Sapphire Sea that hung on one wall before joining Calder.

"Can I help you?" the Nordmerian said, looking up at Calder. His gaze travelled to Dag, and his eyes lit up.

"You're from the Pale Sea?" he asked.

"We both are," Calder said. He pulled his patch out and handed it to the man. "We are here on official Fair Seas Treaty business and would like your help."

The man handed the patch back to Calder and sat back in his chair. "I don't work for the Three," he said.

"We know," Dag said. "But we were hoping you might help us anyway." She smiled at him. "This is my first time on the Sapphire Sea, and I'm finding it overwhelming." She pulled out her own patch, to make sure he knew that she was also an official. Calder didn't actually step back, but somehow, he seemed to withdraw from the conversation.

"Of course, I didn't mean to imply that I wouldn't help." He stood up. "Aki Thorsen, Administrator for the Merchant Adventurers for Messanos."

"Dagrun Lund," Dag said. "And this is Calder Rahmson. We are both agents for the Fair Seas Treaty Alliance based out of North Tarklee. We have news, and we need help."

"News is always welcome," Aki said. "Come, sit, and we can talk." He gestured to the chairs that were in front of the desk. Dag sat down, followed by Calder.

"So, what news from the Pale Sea?" Aki asked as he sat down behind the desk.

Dag felt the itch grow between her shoulder blades as she watched him shove a paper under a stack of others. She gestured to Calder to let her talk, and he leaned back in his chair.

"There is terrible news, I'm afraid," Dag said. "Most of the ships belonging to Merchant Adventurers have been destroyed by pirates." Aki looked up quickly, but she wasn't certain his surprise was genuine.

"*Nyorden!*" Aki said. "That explains why I've not been visited in weeks. When are they expected to be replaced? Trade cannot be disrupted for too long. Think of the fortunes that are being lost."

"The Lavais shipyards are being asked to work miracles," Dag said. "In the meantime, we have one of the few ships that survived and are looking to continue to trade, although at a much-reduced level."

"Of course," Aki replied. "Which ship are you on?"

"The *Atlaine*," Dag replied. Aki blinked, and her itch increased. "Do you know it?"

"I know every ship," Aki said. "What kind of trade are you looking for?"

"Food," Dag replied. "Basics for the winter: grain and dried berries and ale, of course."

The door to outside opened, and a gust of wind blew in. The papers on Aki's desk scattered, but he ignored them as he frantically waved away the person who stood in the open doorway.

Dag turned in time to see a blond man retreat and close the door.

"Who was that, and why didn't you want us to meet them?"

she asked Aki.

Calder was on the floor, scooping up the papers that had blown off the desk. Aki tried to get past Dag to stop him, but she blocked him.

"Who was that, and why did you make them leave?" she asked again.

Calder stood up. He placed a stack of papers on the desk and held one up.

"It might have something to do with this," he said. "It has the seal of the Merchant Adventurers on it, and it tells every office to deny goods to a list of ships. The *Atlaine* is on this list."

"You have no right to that," Aki said.

"Did Holt deliver it?" Dag asked Calder. "Or is it older?"

"It's older," Calder said.

Dag met Calder's eyes and nodded. This meant that someone else in the Three was working against Holt. And possibly working with Pinho.

She looked at the now closed door. That didn't mean whoever had opened it didn't know where Tarmo Holt and her sister were.

NADEZ HURRIED DOWN the hallway towards the infirmary. For days they'd kept up the pretence that Lauma Strauskas was recovering from an attack, and it seemed that someone had finally decided to visit her.

"What do we have?" she asked the two guards who were stationed outside the door to the infirmary.

"An unauthorized visitor," one of the guards said as she opened the door for Nadez.

Three more guards were at the far end of the infirmary. When Nadez reached them, she saw that they'd strapped someone to one of the beds.

"Report," she said, staring down at a girl who didn't look older than about fourteen or fifteen.

"She snuck in through a window," a guard said. He gestured to an open window across from the bed. "She didn't see us until it was too late for her to run." He showed her a long, thin dagger. "Had this on her, and it looked like she knew how to use it."

"Who are you?" Nadez asked as she leaned over the girl. She stared up at Nadez with a blank expression. "So, they sent someone with even less experience this time." She stepped back and studied the girl. Was she the one Gustav had run into in the tavern where Janni had been imprisoned? The former Intelligencer student? It would make sense to send someone who knew the Hall.

"Ottosen can't help you, Pia Engen," she said and was rewarded when the girl's eyes widened. "Lauma Strauskas is alive and in excellent health. Shall we put you in the cell with the other failed assassin?"

"She's dead."

"That she is," Nadez replied. She stepped away from the bed and lowered her voice to talk to the guard she'd spoken to before. "Take her to a jail cell. And be very careful. She's a partly trained Intelligencer student."

"Yes, Master Intelligencer," the guard replied.

"I'll want to talk to her later," Nadez said. "She has answers to my questions." She didn't bother looking at the girl again.

Nadez walked over to the open window and looked out. This girl was not a suicide assassin but someone, most likely Ottosen, had sent her. Now that she'd been caught, would Ottosen send someone else to either free her or kill her so she couldn't give away his secrets?

She didn't think her young captive realized that the second option was as likely as the first.

She would talk to her at some point, but she'd leave her locked up for a day in the hopes that she'd realize that she wasn't going to be rescued.

CALDER YAWNED AS he stared at the Merchant Adventurers office. No one had entered or exited since he and Dag had left over an hour ago. As the sun tracked through the afternoon sky, he shifted over a step in order to stay in the shadow of the building he was leaning against.

Dag had gone in search of the man who had almost entered the office in the hopes that he knew where Holt and Inger were. But that had been a while ago, and he expected her to return soon.

Half an hour later, he was starting to get worried. She'd never been in a foreign port, and there was so much that could go wrong. He never should have let her go by herself.

He sighed. Dag would not appreciate him interfering with her duties even if he was trying to keep her safe. She was a trained Intelligencer; less experienced than he was, but the past month had shown that she was smart and capable. And more importantly, he trusted her to know when she was out of her depth. If she hadn't felt confident and safe doing whatever she was doing, she would have returned already.

Besides, her Trait would keep her from walking into any hidden danger or traps.

The door to the Merchant Adventurers office opened, and Aki poked his head out. Calder froze while the other man looked up and down the street. He made a hand gesture and closed the door again.

Calder grinned. Unless whoever was watching for that signal had seen *him*, he was about to see the person Aki hadn't wanted him to.

Yes, there he was. A man crawled out from under a wagon and hurried to the door. His hat was pulled down, covering his head, but the hand that reached out to open the door was light skinned. He had the colouring of someone from the Pale Sea, so it was probably the one who had interrupted their meeting with Aki.

Calder frowned. Where was Dag? This was the person she'd followed, so why hadn't she found him? He looked past the handful of wooden buildings to the narrow lane that stretched deeper into the city. Where was she?

The door to the Merchant Adventurers office opened again, and the man exited. Calder's focus narrowed as the man paused to scan the surrounding streets. After a moment, he hurried away.

Calder hesitated, but because his Trait had activated, he slipped out from shadow and into sunlight to follow the man. He kept expecting Dag to step out from some hiding spot and join him, but she didn't. He had to assume that she was following her Trait just as he was following his.

The man travelled deeper into the city before circling back towards the harbour. He ducked down a narrow lane, and Calder peered around the corner of a building.

He was gone. There was no trace of the man he'd been following. Had he realized that he was being followed?

There were a couple of fishing huts he might have been able to reach before Calder reached the corner, but that was it. The lane ended a few paces past the huts, and he didn't see anyone there, let alone the man he'd been following.

He stepped out into the street and headed down it, hoping that something triggered his Trait.

The lane ended at a set of wooden stairs. At the bottom, a dock jutted out into a narrow channel. Calder stared down at it. He'd been to Messanos many times before, and he'd never seen this little dock. He looked up at sheer cliffs that rose above him. Dozens of birds swirled above the channel that stretched past rows of fishing huts.

His focus narrowed on a small sailboat that was tied up at the very end of the dock. He started down the stairs towards the boat.

The man he'd been following was not here, but now he had to wonder if this little sailboat was what his Trait wanted him to find. He slowed as he approached the sailboat. He couldn't see anything unusual about it.

"Who are you?"

Calder turned to find a young woman glaring at him.

"Lost is what I am," he said, smiling. "I got turned around up there, and then when I saw this little dock, I couldn't resist taking a closer look." He gestured to the sailboat. "Is that yours?"

"My father's," she said. She crossed her arms. "What's so interesting about this dock?"

"I've spent a fair amount of time shipping in and out of Messanos," he said. "And I've never seen or heard of this dock. I figured it must be special."

He took another step towards the boat, wondering if she would try to stop him.

"It's private," she said, matching his steps. "That's probably why you've never heard of it."

"Mind if I take a look at your father's boat?" he asked. "I've spent more time than I wanted recently sailing boats this size in the Pale Sea, and I was wondering if there was something different about it that might make for a more pleasant experience."

She laughed and seemed to relax. "I don't think anything will make sailing one of these a more pleasant experience. Go ahead."

As Calder walked the last few steps to the boat, his companion kept pace with him. His focus narrowed on the stern, and he leaned over to try to see what Luck wanted him to find.

He covered his gasp with a cough as he straightened. "Your father's boat, you said. Most of these little boats aren't named."

"Someone he was fond of once," she replied. "And wanted to remember."

"So, he's sentimental," Calder replied, wondering if it was really true.

He looked again at the sailboat. *Hakon* was painted on the bow: this boat was named after his dead twin. He turned to study his companion's face, trying to see if he recognized anything about it, trying to see if there was anything of Rahm in her, this young woman he suspected was his half-sister.

DAG BRUSHED HER hair from her eyes and stared out at the pier. She'd expected it to be easy to find the blond man who'd almost entered the Merchant Adventurers office, but for some reason, her Trait hadn't led her to him. Instead it had brought her here, to a small, white house only a few streets away from where she'd left Calder.

Would Calder come looking for her, or would he wait at the Merchant Adventurers office? She'd been gone far longer than she'd expected and was starting to worry about what he'd do.

Her Trait had activated the moment she'd seen this Arressan man, and she'd followed him here. He'd gone inside the house an hour ago, and she hadn't seen him come out. At some point, she'd have to give up waiting for him to emerge.

"I thought you left," someone said in Nordmerian.

Dag looked over her shoulder. The Arressan she'd followed squinted down at her. She slowly rose, wondering how he'd seen her when she'd thought she was well Hidden. And how he'd left the house undetected.

"I should have," she replied, stalling for time. He seemed to recognize her, but since she'd never seen him before, she assumed he'd met with Inger.

He tsked and shook his head. "Nothing good gonna come from you still being here. Told you I couldn't help you, and I meant it."

"I thought I'd ask one more time," Dag replied. "Just in case you changed your mind." It sounded like Inger had left the city. This man might know where she'd gone.

"Foolish girl. I know that Holt thinks Pinho will be lenient with him, but he won't. And I'm not chancing getting myself noticed by the likes of him."

"Pinho or Holt?" Dag asked. She sidled close to him. "Tell me when you last spoke to me." She grabbed his arm with both hands.

"What? What are you talking about?" He tried to get away, but she held him firmly. "You're not Inger? Who are you?"

"I'm her twin sister," Dag said. "And I'm looking for her. Can you please tell me when and where you saw her? Was she all right? Was she hurt?"

"Hurt? No," the man replied. "Twin, huh? She never said anyone was coming after her, let alone a twin. I might have had a different answer seeing as twins be so charmed."

"Charmed?" she asked. "As in Lucky?" Was Calder's Luck part of his Pilalian heritage?

"In my experience, things work out when twins are involved is all," the man said. "You gonna let go of me?"

"If you tell me when you saw my sister," Dag replied. "And what she wanted help with." Maybe Luck wasn't a Pilalian characteristic after all: things *hadn't* worked out for Calder's twin.

"Two days ago," he said. Dag released his arm, and he rubbed it. "She wanted help finding a place."

"A place, what do you mean, a place? A place to hide?"

"Nah. She was looking for a place. You know, a place to live and some work she could get paid for. Told her she could teach folks to speak Nordmerian if she spoke better Arressan."

"Was she still travelling with Tarmo Holt?" Dag asked. Inger must realize that she couldn't return home: why else was she looking for work and a place to live and not a ship back to the Three?

"Yep," he replied. "Apparently, she was welcome to go up the coast a ways with him, but she was hoping to stay here. Told her if Pinho found out about her, he'd use her to find Holt, or he'd make some of Holt's debts stick to her."

"He can't do that," Dag said, then stopped. Maybe he could. This wasn't the Three, and she had no idea how much power a wealthy man like Pinho might have.

The man chuckled. "More than that pale skin and blonde hair tells me you're not from here. Pinho can do whatever he says he can."

"Do you know where my sister went?" Dag asked. "North or south along the coast?"

"Dunno, and I'm not interested in speculating." He looked around. "Don't need to go looking for trouble." He nodded and hurried away.

She watched him turn a corner and disappear from view. At least she had proof that Inger had made it to Messanos safe and sound. And that Holt seemed willing to extend what little aid he could to her. Not that his help might not put her in danger.

She turned to leave. It was time to look for Calder.

She made her way back to the Merchant Adventurers office, but he wasn't there. With no clues about where he'd gone, she decided to return to Rafael and the dinghy. He'd show up at some point.

CHAPTER 11

"THEY'RE IMPRESSIVE," BERNA said, and Gustav tore his gaze from Janni and Jarri to look at her.

"Yes," he agreed. The Breck twins were getting an incredible amount of work done now that they each had a team of Lavaisians working with them. Despite their opposite Traits, their methods were surprisingly similar. A twin would point at something, give instructions, and others would perform the tasks of taking something apart or putting something together.

Jarri's work of tearing down the ruined structures was almost complete, and because Janni had been working beside him, they already had teams of woodcutters and ship builders making replacement parts for components that were beyond salvaging.

As well, Janni had made some updates that his father said would make the shipyards more productive than before.

"Were they ever put to use as Intelligencers?" Berna asked.

"I don't think so," Gustav replied. "And certainly not for anything this important. I think that Joosep should never have taken them to the Hall. Who knows what they might have created if they'd stayed in their village?"

"I don't know," Berna replied. "If they'd stayed in their village, they might not have done anything this important either. They're only *here* because we know about their Traits. And that's due to Joosep." She shrugged. "I think we should just be grateful that they are here."

"You're right," Gustav said. He didn't really want to think badly of Joosep: he'd probably done his best. Everyone made mistakes, even the people in charge. And Joosep's last mistake of leaving the safe apartment and seeking out Holt had been fatal.

"Clan Freeholder Strauskas?" It was Eryk, the man who'd been assigned as Berna's assistant. "Clan Freeholder Timonis has arrived."

"Thank you, Eryk," Berna said. "Gustav, I'd like you to come with me."

Gustav nodded and followed her and Eryk along the narrow street to the shipbuilding office.

Gustav recognized Clan Freeholder Timonis as soon as he entered the building. Timonis watched Gustav and Berna arrive, but he didn't get up from the bench he was sitting on.

"Clan Freeholder Timonis?" Berna asked, and he nodded. "I appreciate you coming. I am Berna Strauskas, and I am the representative of Interim Grand Freeholder Lauma Strauskas." She indicated Gustav. "This is Gustav Gunnarson. He is representing Master Intelligencer Nadez Norup."

"I hope you are well," Gustav said. Timonis was his Clan Freeholder, but he'd never actually spoken to him before. Berna hadn't offered Timonis her hand to shake so neither did Gustav.

He waited silently beside Berna, but Timonis did not stand up to greet them. The longer it went on the more insulting it became. Gustav kept his face blank, but he knew he and Berna would laugh about this later. They'd both had people underestimate them because of their age, and as frustrating as it was, most people came to realize they wielded real power. Eventually.

"Is this it?" Timonis finally said. "Am I to deal with children? Where are the adults with experience? Where are the people with authority?"

"I assure you that *we are* the people with authority," Berna said. "And we are both highly trained and in the past month we have both acquired a great deal of experience."

"Some of the *adults with experience* did not live through what we have," Gustav said.

"When you are over your petulance you may join us in my office," Berna said. She turned and winked at Gustav. He quickly pivoted to follow her before his grin escaped.

They were already seated, Berna behind the desk and Gustav

in one of the chairs in front of it, by the time Timonis paused in the doorway to the office. A spiteful person would have made him wait, but Gustav had never seen Berna be spiteful. And she wasn't this time either.

"Please sit, Clan Freeholder," she said. "You will tell us how your efforts for provisioning for the winter are proceeding, and we will tell you how the shipyard rebuilding is going."

Timonis glared at Berna, but he did sit in the empty chair beside Gustav. He sat with his back rigid and his head high.

"What I will do," he said, "is ask why you felt it appropriate to summon me without regard to my status? Not only am I a Clan Freeholder, but I expect to become the next Grand Freeholder."

"Yes, that," Berna replied. "It makes it all the more disappointing that you had to be summoned; that you weren't already here overseeing the most important task in the Three: rebuilding the shipyards."

"Perhaps you've been overseeing the second most important task?" Gustav asked even though he knew the answer was no. "Ensuring that there is enough food for your people to survive the winter?"

"How dare you speak to me like that," Timonis replied. "When I become Grand Freeholder, you will both regret insulting me this way."

"Whenever that may be," Berna said. "It would be unheard of to not have a vote, but I believe that since the Three are facing famine and my mother is the one doing all she can to prevent that, she would have enough support to continue as Interim Grand Freeholder until the emergency is over." She frowned. "Even your fellow Swyfordian Clan Freeholders might wonder why not only did you not try to manage your country's problems but you ignored very clear direction, thereby hampering my mother's efforts to save Swyfordians."

"She can't postpone it," Timonis said. "She wouldn't dare. There are rules around when voting is required."

Berna frowned. "Yes, but these are extraordinary circumstances. My mother has never wanted to be Grand Freeholder, but she knew that someone had to fix the mess Tarmo Holt dragged the Three into. She also knew that you wouldn't do what was needed."

Gustav nodded. "She would delay the vote, and I am certain

that the Master Intelligencer would support her."

Timonis frowned but didn't say anything else. Gustav looked over at Berna, who nodded at him.

"I'll start with an update on food stores," Gustav said into the silence. "I've organized extra fishing: half a dozen people not busy at the shipyard have been sent to other parts of the island to help fishermen double or hopefully triple their catch. There's an empty warehouse big enough to store it all in once it's been dried or pickled." He paused. "Although the pickling ingredients will be used for vegetables first. The woodcutters organized themselves and have begun foraging for mushrooms, wild leeks, and beets as well as tree nuts. Once their work in the shipyards is done, some of them have offered to go to the mainland and see what they can find there before they return to the north. They are understandably worried about their own families and villages." He turned to Timonis. "What progress have you made?"

"The people are doing what they always do," he said. "I expect the ships will arrive from the Sapphire Sea well before winter."

"Then your people will starve," Berna said. "We have two ships and given the little we know about who Holt was working with, we don't expect anyone to come to our rescue. Not even if we had double or triple the coin to spend." She shook her head. "I will be contacting the other Swyfordian Clan Freeholders. They will have a chance to save their people in spite of you."

"They won't believe children either," Timonis said. He rose and looked down on them. "I will be at my estate when the food shipments arrive. And I will send a formal complaint to your mother." He turned and left. Gustav heard the door slam shut.

Berna shook her head. "My mother would have given him a piece of her mind. That *skit* is willing to let his people starve. The worst is that even if they do, *he* won't."

"I'll ask Solvig Madsen if she or her fisherman can get the word out to Timonis's people," Gustav said. "They are practical; they'll know who to reach out to. I'll let you know if they need any people or resources."

"Thank you."

Gustav nodded and left. He didn't blame Lauma Strauskas for not wanting to be Grand Freeholder; despite how well she was coping, it seemed a thankless job. The wonder was that ambitious but uncaring people like Timonis felt that a position like that was their right. He sighed. One Grand Freeholder had caused the dire situation they were facing, and the man who was expected to become the next one seemed indifferent to any danger.

NADEZ SIGHED AS she opened the door to her apartment. Pia Engen, the would-be assassin, still wasn't talking, but at least there had been no attempts on the girl's life. Nadez hadn't been able to find out much about her: her training mates and instructors had all fled the Hall and anyway, there was no way to be sure if any of them could be trusted. Perhaps they too had been compromised by Ottosen.

She froze. Someone was here. Carefully, she turned to close the door, pulling the small knife from her belt. It wouldn't do much against a real weapon, but it might buy her time. She closed the door and then stood with her back against it, ready to fight.

"It's just me."

Nadez blew out the breath she'd been holding. "Lauma." She turned to see the Interim Grand Freeholder hovering near the door to her sleeping chamber. "Are you all right?"

"I'm fine," Lauma replied. "I heard from Kaja that a second assassin was captured. I thought I might speak to them."

Nadez made sure the door was closed and locked before crossing the room and sitting down at the table.

Lauma joined her. "You didn't say no, so I assume that you think it's a good idea."

"Time will tell if it's a good idea," Nadez replied. "But I haven't had any luck with her. I think she's the same person Gustav met after we rescued Janni and Jarri. Pia Engen."

"Engen? So Ottosen is behind this?" Lauma replied. "Shall we go now?"

"Why not?" Nadez had just come from the jail, so returning so soon might even unnerve their prisoner.

The girl looked up from the cot she was sitting on when she and Lauma arrived. Nadez nodded to the guard, who let them into the cell. Nadez leaned against the bars, out of the way but close enough to help if the girl attacked Lauma.

"Pia Engen," Lauma said as she took two steps closer. She stopped and stared down at the girl, who glared up at her.

"I recognize that look," Lauma said. "Mad at the world. My own son wore it for years after his twin died. Pertu, wasn't it?

Don't look so surprised. I take note of every twin who dies at the age of five. That's when Traits manifest." She shook her head. "Ottosen didn't mention that, did he? That the woman he sent you to kill had something in common with you. We've both lost a twin to a Trait. You a brother and me a son." She crouched down beside the bed. "What was his Trait? My son, my living son, says his Trait is his to disclose, but my other son's Trait? That's mine. Hakon was Unlucky. I suspect poor Pertu's Trait was something similar." She sighed and stood up.

Pia stiffened when Lauma said her brother's name, and Nadez prepared for an attack that never came. Instead the girl sat very still for a minute.

Suddenly, she seemed to collapse in on herself, hugging her knees to her chest. Lauma was about to reach out to comfort her when Nadez grabbed her arm and pulled her away.

"You learned well," Nadez said, stepping in between Pia and Lauma. "But I was the one who designed that very strategy for getting your enemy to let down their guard." She paused. "I know that your Trait is Concentration, so I'm going to assume that no matter what you are feeling, you can set your emotions aside in order to complete your task."

"Concentration," Lauma said. "The opposite would be Distraction. That's why your brother is dead."

"Leave him out of this!" Pia said. "He has nothing to do with anything."

"I think he has everything to do with everything," Lauma replied. "He's the reason why Ottosen found you; why you were sent here to be trained and why you are so angry at the Intelligencers, and by extension the Grand Freeholder, that you agreed to try to kill me."

"You don't know anything," the girl said.

"I know an angry child when I see one," Lauma said. "One who's been hurt and can't see her way out of it." She turned to Nadez. "Ottosen could very well send someone to kill her, but this child is so broken that I'm not sure she cares."

"We'll do our best to keep her alive," Nadez replied. She followed Lauma out of the cell. "Do you really think she doesn't care if she lives?"

"She likes to think she doesn't," Lauma replied. "From what I remember of the family, her parents are both dead, but I'll see if

I can find any living kin. Maybe they can change her mind."

"Thank you," Nadez replied. "She didn't deny that she was working for Ottosen."

"She also didn't deny that she was sent to kill me," Lauma replied. "Both of those together should give me some political leverage to use against Henrik Ottosen."

CALDER PAUSED AND looked back at the sailboat that carried his twin's name and the woman who was probably his sister.

She didn't look up: he'd said his goodbyes without asking her for her father's name or telling her his own. He wasn't sure if it was because he didn't want to know or he was worried about her reaction.

If she was Rahm's daughter, it seemed that she didn't know he had another family.

Could it be a coincidence? Hakon wasn't a common name even in Byholt. It was his mother's grandfather's name, and he'd never met anyone else with it.

He sighed and continued walking away. Whatever this mystery might be, it wasn't his priority. It *couldn't* be his priority. Buying food for the Three was.

But right now, he needed to find Dag.

He retraced his path back to the office of the Merchant Adventurers. When Dag didn't come out of a hiding spot and join him in the street, he made his way back to the dinghy.

"There you are," Dag called when he stepped onto the pier.

He relaxed and waved at her and Rafael. This late in the afternoon the fishing boats had all docked. Men, women, and children clambered over the boats, cleaning up and fixing nets as they readied their boats for tomorrow.

"Did you find anything?" he asked when he reached Dag and Rafael.

"Inger was here," Dag said. "I met a man who had spoken to her two days ago. He said she was trying to find a place to live and paid work." She grinned. "She's trying to leave Holt."

"Did she?" Calder asked. If Inger wanted to get away from Tarmo Holt, they needed to help her. "Leave him and find a place to live and work?"

"Not yet," Dag replied. Her smile slipped. "The man I spoke to said he couldn't help her, so she left with Holt. They were headed to a place along the coast. This man I spoke to seemed afraid of angering Pinho.”

“He's a man to be feared,” Rafael said. “From what folk around here say. Fihaldo Pinho controls ever single shipment that goes in or out of every port along the coasts of both Pilalia and Arressa.”

“Rafael thinks we might have trouble buying goods,” Dag said. “That we may need to go to Tobei or even Yedris in order to get beyond Pinho's influence.”

Calder sighed. “I knew he controlled Pilalia but full control of Arressa is recent. And moving south will add extra days to our travel time,” he said.

“Which means the *Tazeyar* won't be able to make more than a single trip before the Frozen Pass is closed,” Dag said.

“Is she here?” Calder stared out towards the ships that lay at anchor. “She is here! They made excellent time.”

Dag grinned. “I saw the ship as soon as I got back here. We should get out there.”

“Yes,” Calder replied. “We should.”

He and Rafael got the little dinghy ready to launch and Dag climbed into the bow. It took them a dozen minutes to reach the *Tazeyar*.

“Grab the line,” a familiar voice called from above, and Calder looked up and over his shoulder to see Jaak above them, a line in his hand. He tossed it down and Dag caught it.

Calder pulled in his oars, turned around in this seat, and took the line from Dag, pulling on it until they were directly beneath the gunwale. A rope ladder dropped down, and after tying it to the dinghy, Calder followed Dag up to the ship's deck, Rafael behind him.

“Captain Eklund,” Calder said. “Permission to come aboard.”

“Permission granted,” Eklund said. Then he grinned. “I've never had an easier trip through the Frozen Pass: the winds were with us the whole way. I was hoping we'd find you here rather than in Pilalia. We'll get a better price with two holds to fill.”

“We need to talk about that,” Calder said. “In your cabin, if we can.”

“Of course.” Eklund turned to Jaak. “See if you can find us some tea and something to eat then join us.”

Jaak hurried away and Eklund led the way to his cabin. Calder and Dag sat at the table while Eklund rolled up a couple of charts and maps to get them out of the way.

"We just now heard that Fihaldo Pinho controls all the shipping along this coast as well as Pilalia," Calder said. "Do you know him?"

Eklund frowned. "In the spring he controlled Pilalia's coast and only a section of Arressa's. How has he managed to expand his reach so quickly?" He shook his head. "And I do know him. He has no qualms about charging exorbitant prices for anything. Worse, he will strike deals that put you at his mercy."

"Is that what happened to Holt?" Dag asked. "What does Pinho do to people who don't repay him?"

Calder heard the note of fear in her voice: not for Holt, but for Inger.

"He cuts them off," Eklund said. "And demands everything they have."

"Pinho has already demanded everything from Holt," Calder said. "That's probably why he betrayed the Three. The question is, what does he do to someone who has already lost everything?"

"He hasn't," Dag said. "Not yet. Tarmo Holt has a wife and daughter. As well as land in Nordmere." She turned to Eklund. "Does Pinho have a son in need of a wife?"

"I'm not sure," Eklund replied. "But it's possible."

"A son, a nephew, a brother," Calder said. "Pinho will find someone he trusts who is willing to marry Saulia. Holt might have played right into Pinho's hand. He's practically delivered his daughter to him."

"If that's Pinho's goal, then Holt has also sealed his own fate," Dag said. "Saulia can only inherit if there is proof that her father is dead."

"The Interim Grand Freeholder and the Master Intelligencer are also interested in Saulia Holt," Eklund said. "They asked me to task you with finding her and bringing her home so that she can inherit the Holt Freeholdings."

"*Skit*," Calder swore. Purchasing food just became one of two competing priorities. They needed to find Saulia Holt and make sure Pinho couldn't use her to gain control of the Holt Freeholdings and threaten the Three.

THERE WAS A knock on Captain Eklund's door, and Jaak entered carrying a tray with a teapot and mugs. Dag barely noticed when he joined them at the table. She was preoccupied by worry about Calder. Her Trait had been triggered the moment she'd seen him on the dock. He had a secret that he didn't have before. What had he found in Messanos?

He met her eyes and she raised her eyebrows; he nodded sadly.

"I'll go after Saulia," Dag said. "Inger's been travelling with Holt, so I'll find her too. Hopefully between us we'll be able to convince Saulia to leave with us."

"You think Inger will help?" Calder asked.

"Yes. Ansdottir's control over her died when she did, and I truly believe what that man who talked to Inger told me," Dag replied. "My Trait would have sensed a lie or secret. Inger doesn't want to be with Holt and is trying to figure out how to make a life here."

"Why wouldn't she go home?" Jaak asked.

"She can't," Eklund said. "She was an active participant when the shipyards and ships were destroyed and will be considered an enemy of the Three."

"Yes," Dag agreed. "Unless we can convince the Fair Seas Treaty Alliance that she was an unwilling participant because of a Trait."

"I doubt Nordmere will agree even if they believe it," Calder said.

"I know," Dag said and sighed. "It's highly unlikely Inger will be allowed to return home, and if she does, she'll be charged with treason. Unless," she paused, hardly daring to speak it out loud in case no one agreed with her. "Unless she can somehow do something that benefits the Three and proves that she is loyal."

"If she helps save Saulia from Pinho," Calder said. "Her uncle and Saulia herself if she inherits, may agree to forgive the charges." He met her gaze, and Dag was grateful to see true hope in his eyes. "It could work," he continued. "And it won't hurt. Take Jaak. You'll need someone to help you find Holt. There's no way to travel by land, so you'll need to go by sea."

"We'll need a sailboat," Dag said. "I can't see making poor Jaak row me up and down the coast in a dinghy while I search for Holt's hiding place."

"I know where we might be able to borrow one," Calder said,

and Dag's itch intensified.

Calder sighed. "We ran across my father, Rahm, on the way here," he said to Eklund and Jaak. "It seems he is a spy for Fihaldo Pinho. I think I need to ask my father for help buying food. As well," he looked at Dag. "Today while in town I stumbled across a sailboat that I think belongs to him."

"How do you know?" Dag asked.

"Because it was named the *Hakon*," he replied. "My twin's name. The woman I spoke to said it was someone the man who owned the sailboat had cared about." He turned to Dag. "She also said that man was her father."

"Oh, yes," Dag replied, looking for signs that Calder was hurt by this. "That seems more than possible. Rahm has more secrets than anyone I've ever met. A second family makes sense."

"That's what I think," Calder said. "I'm actually surprised I didn't wonder about it before now. And because he has done this one small thing that unites his two families, I believe he will help me."

"If it helps us fill the holds of both ships, then you need to try," Eklund said. "If it doesn't work, we won't be much worse off."

"I know," Calder said. "I'll need to search out my father."

"I'll come with you," Dag replied. "As soon as we have the use of that sailboat, I can look for my sister."

GUSTAV STARED OUT at the *Oakhaven*. The log hauler had arrived yesterday with more timber and woodcutters. Some of the woodcutters already here were leaving on the ship later today, sailing back home to Byholt to help their own families and communities prepare for winter.

He shook his head. Despite the logging camps that dotted the coast of Swyford, none of the Clan Freeholders had sent any woodcutters to Lavais to help.

"I'll leave on the ship," he said to Berna. "And let your mother know that Swyford won't even help their own." He also wanted to talk to Nadez and make sure she understood that Clan Freeholder Timonis could not be counted on to put the Three above his own interests.

"I still can't believe that not a single Swyfordian Clan Freeholder is willing to help us save their own people," Berna said.

"Maybe they just haven't replied yet," Gustav said, even though he didn't believe that. Berna had sent messages to every Clan Freeholder in Swyford: every single messenger had returned without a response.

"More likely they have already been told by Timonis not to co-operate," she said. "Make sure my mother understands that."

"I will," Gustav said. "Should I tell her to send someone older?" He gave her a sly smile.

Berna laughed. "My mother would come herself," she said. "Timonis will not like what she says if she has to travel here. He thinks he will be Grand Freeholder in a few months, but given the way he is acting, my mother will never allow it."

"What can she do about it?" Gustav asked. Lauma Strauskas was the largest landowner in Byholt, but that gave her no input into Swyford's choice for Grand Freeholder.

"I've been thinking about this since we talked," Berna said. "And my mother could pull Byholt out of the Treaty."

Gustav was shocked. "Would she do that? Could she?" What would happen to Swyford, his home country, if Byholt pulled out of the Fair Seas Treaty?

"I'm sure she would discuss it with the other Byholt Freeholders," Berna replied. "But she owns enough land to make that decision on her own."

"Even if it would hurt all three countries?" Gustav asked.

"Maybe," Berna replied. "My mother would hate to pull out of the Treaty, but she would hate it even more if Byholt was governed by someone willing to put the safety and security of Byholters at risk in a never-ending search for power and coin."

Gustav sighed. "I couldn't even blame her."

"She controls the majority of Byholt," Berna said. "Which means she has the ability to withdraw the country from the Treaty. Given what we know about the politics in Nordmere, I think it safe to say that they would also leave rather than be under Timonis's control." She shrugged. "That's if the Fair Seas Treaty is even valid if one country withdraws."

Gustav stared out at the *Oakhaven*. "Would Swyford and Clan Freeholder Timonis still receive the shipments of food he's counting on?"

"My mother would not deliberately allow people to starve, so shipments would not be interrupted before more ships have been built," Berna said. "But I will start organizing a system for food distribution that bypasses the Clan Freeholders."

"That's a good idea," Gustav said. "Solvig Madsen's warehouse will need to be safeguarded by us. Timonis is her Clan Freeholder."

"I'll send some of the newly arrived woodcutters," Berna said. "They can do double duty: help fill the warehouse by fishing and foraging and guard it for the Three."

"Will they?" Going against a Clan Freeholder on their own land would normally be considered a crime.

"They log for my mother," Berna said. "And I've known some of them all my life. They will follow my orders on behalf of the Interim Grand Freeholder. If Timonis doesn't like it, he can lodge a formal complaint."

"To your mother." Gustav grinned. "I'll warn her about that."

"Thank you," Berna said.

"I'll say my goodbyes, then," Gustav said. "I'll be back as soon as I can, but if no ships stop in Tarklee on their way south, I'll have to take the coastal road."

"I don't think there's any need to rush back," Berna said. "Other than the Swyford Clan Freeholders, no one is contesting my authority. Besides, the repairs are moving along quickly, and none of the shipbuilders want to jeopardize that."

Gustav left to find his bunk and pack up his few belongings. As he waited amongst the woodcutters for a seat in a dinghy, he couldn't stop thinking about what Berna had said about her mother's ability to end the Fair Seas Treaty Alliance.

He didn't think a single person should have that type of power, but neither did he think it wise to have a man like Clan Freeholder Timonis become Grand Freeholder.

Just as it hadn't been a good idea to have a Grand Freeholder like Tarmo Holt.

He'd ask Nadez for her perspective. He had to talk to her about it anyway: Intelligencers worked for the Fair Seas Treaty Alliance. What would happen to them if the Alliance no longer existed?

Chapter 12

Nadez stared at her closed office door. She was expecting Clan Freeholder Ottosen, but he was late. Or perhaps he'd changed his mind and wasn't coming to see her after all.

He didn't have to meet with her; although, he could not ignore the Interim Grand Freeholder's request for a meeting. Nadez would ask Ottosen her questions in front of Lauma if she had to.

There was a commotion in the outer office, and a moment later, a knock on her office door. Kaja poked her head in.

"Clan Freeholder Ottosen to see you, Master Intelligencer."

"Please send him in," Nadez said. She didn't rise when Ottosen entered her office. Instead, she gestured to the single chair placed directly in front of her desk. As she'd expected, the Clan Freeholder had brought someone with him, but she wasn't planning on letting Henrik Ottosen control anything about this meeting.

"Have a seat, Clan Freeholder," she said. She flicked a hand signal to Kaja, who took the arm of the second man and steered him back through the doorway.

"We have a very comfortable guest chair where you can wait," Kaja said. She nodded at Nadez as she closed the door.

"I would prefer to have my assistant attend this meeting," Ottosen said.

"Would you?" Nadez replied. "Does he know that you have sent assassins to kill the Interim Grand Freeholder?"

"Do you have proof that I did that?" Ottosen scowled, but he didn't repeat his request for his assistant to join them.

"Enough," Nadez said. "I have a dead suicide assassin who arrived by ship a few weeks ago. A ship carrying cargo that you personally signed for." She leaned forward. "And I have Pia Engen, a Nordmerian Intelligencer student. Not only was she trying to assassinate the Interim Grand Freeholder, but we can associate her to the kidnapping and torture of two of my Intelligencers."

"Signing for cargo is not proof," Ottosen replied. "And no one will believe whatever this child says."

"It's enough to worry Lauma Strauskas," Nadez replied. "The intended target of two assassination attempts."

"What is she going to do about it? Nothing." He smirked. "She can't do anything without more proof."

"You seem very certain that the girl won't betray you," Nadez said.

"I don't even know the girl you're talking about," Ottosen said.

"Oh, then I guess the girl's younger sibling isn't living in your household?" Lauma had ferreted out that information.

"I have no such girl in my household," Ottosen said.

"I thought you didn't know Pia Engen?" Nadez replied. Then she stood. "I never said the younger one was also a girl. Come, it's time to meet with Lauma Strauskas. I just wanted you to know what information we have before we meet with her."

"I'm having a confidential meeting with the Interim Grand Freeholder?" Ottosen asked.

"Yes," Nadez replied. "Come along." She didn't wait for him; instead she made him hurry to keep pace with her. By the time they were outside of Lauma's office, she liked to think that he was a little less composed and sure of himself.

Nadez smiled as she pushed the outer office door open and entered.

Mykol quickly rose to greet them.

"Clan Freeholder," he said. "Master Intelligencer. The Interim Grand Freeholder is ready for you. This way."

Nadez took a step back to allow Ottosen to enter Lauma's office first. She closed the door once she was inside and took the last empty chair.

"I don't see why the Master Intelligencer needs to be at this meeting," Ottosen said.

"You don't?" Lauma's eyebrows rose. "There have been attempts on my life, and we have information that points to you being behind it. Why should I feel comfortable being alone with you?"

"Information," he scoffed, "is not proof."

"No, but it is very telling that you have not denied it." Lauma held up a hand when he would have interrupted. "Don't bother. Besides, we have a witness."

"She's a child who would say anything," Ottosen said. "She was trained here to do just that."

"Your assertion that you don't know Pia Engen grows less and less believable," Nadez said.

"She's not the only witness we have," Lauma said. She paused and then smiled. "I can practically see you going through the list of people who know about this and trying to figure out which one has betrayed you."

Nadez suppressed her own grin when Lauma sat back and continued to watch Ottosen.

"You have no proof," Ottosen said finally.

"You've said that already," Lauma replied.

"As Interim Grand Freeholder you can't act on anything without proof."

"Is that what you think?" Lauma asked. "That I have no recourse?" She leaned over the desk. "Famine is around the corner, and I am doing everything in my power to keep it at bay, and that includes commandeering ships and supplies and any warehouses the supplies are currently in." She picked up a piece of paper and handed it to him. "This is my declaration of emergency measures on behalf of the Fair Seas Treaty Alliance. By now every single warehouse in Tarklee has been visited by Treaty Guards. They will remain in place until I say they are no longer required."

"You can't do that," Ottosen said. "I will lodge a formal complaint."

"Yes, of course," Lauma said. "That is your right. And I will make certain to read it and pass judgement on it as soon as more pressing matters do not require my attention. This meeting is over. Mykol is available to help you with your complaint."

Nadez stood up and stared at Ottosen until he rose. She

followed him out of the office, waiting while he spoke to Mykol about making a formal complaint. Once he was gone, she returned to Lauma's office.

"He put up less of a fight than I thought he would," she said. "I don't like it."

"He has something else planned," Lauma replied. "I just don't know what."

"Neither do I," Nadez said, wishing yet again that there were more Intelligencers that she could trust in the Hall. If Dagrun Lund was here her Trait would be able to uncover Ottosen's plans. As it was, she'd need to try to find out herself. If she could.

Unfortunately, her face was becoming recognizable in the city, and most people didn't willingly talk to the Master Intelligencer.

CALDER STARED AT the *Hakon*. There were a few dinghies tied up on the dock near the little sailboat, but he didn't see anyone nearby. He hand-signalled Dag, indicating that he was going to get closer.

"I thought it was you."

He spun at the sound of the familiar voice.

Rahm peeled away from the side of a nearby building and stopped in front of him, his hands on his hips. "Esma said someone was skulking around here, asking about the name on the boat. Who else would it be?"

"Esma," Calder said. "My sister. Who knows nothing about me or Hakon."

"There was a time when I wanted to introduce my children to one another," Rahm said. "But at the time, your mother would never have forgiven me."

"So you risked your children never forgiving you," Calder said. "How many? How many children? How many sisters and brothers do I have that are strangers to one another?" His anger surprised himself. He'd thought he had accepted it but now, faced with siblings he'd missed knowing, he found himself furious.

Rahm sighed. "Even now, telling you could put them at risk," he said sadly. "That's why I've kept this secret for so many years."

Calder thought about his mother: about her gift, her Trait for knowing who people loved. "She knew," he replied. "She probably knew the minute she saw you after you'd found someone else." He nodded. Now it made sense. Her anger at Rahm wasn't because he was away at sea, it was because he'd met another woman while he was away.

"She didn't know," Rahm said. "No one did."

"She has a Trait," Calder said, and his father's face paled. "Or had one, if she's even still alive after the man you work for sent an assassin." He had to believe that she was alive; that his mother was more than a match for anyone sent to kill her. "She didn't need proof because she *knew*. All those lies you told her? She knew they were lies."

"The assassin was not sent on behalf of anyone from the Sapphire Sea," Rahm said. "You'll need to look closer to home to find them."

"Who is it?" Calder asked. "If you know, you have to tell me."

"I don't have a name," Rahm said. "I'd tell you if I knew."

Rahm looked sad and a little defeated when he met Calder's eyes. "You really don't know, do you?" Calder asked.

"I do not," Rahm replied. "But Lauma is resourceful, so I have hope she was able to survive."

"I do too," Calder said. His father's hope fuelled his own. His mother had to be alive.

"You're going to tell her about my other family," Rahm said.

"Of course, I am. She needs to know that she was right for all those years. Right not to trust you and right that you were lying to her." He paused. "And right to make you stay away, despite the fact it meant the three of us rarely saw our father. At least Yakop, Berna, and I don't have childhood memories of you lying to us." Although he now knew that Rahm had been lying to him for years.

Rahm shrugged. "I cannot go back and undo any harm I have inflicted on you. But perhaps you hope I can redeem myself, even a little. Why else are you here?"

"I do need help. We," Calder signalled to Dag, who stepped out of her hiding place and joined him, "need help. Your help."

"I would help my son," Rahm replied. "But I do not owe anything to anyone else."

"That's fine," Calder replied. "Since I am the one asking. You can help me, and I will help others."

Rahm sighed again. "What do you need help with?"

"I have two ships whose holds I need to fill with food," he said. "I have coin and expect to pay a high price this late in the season, but I understand that the man you work for controls the movement of goods along this coast."

"I can get you approved to buy goods," Rahm said. "If you are willing to pay a premium. What else?"

"These same two ships hope to return and buy more food before the winter. We are willing to pay an even higher price at that time, of course."

"I can't guarantee the goods you seek will be available," Rahm said. "But your coin will not be refused if there are things you want to buy and you can pay the price."

"Fair," Calder said. He looked over at Dag, who nodded. "And I want to borrow the *Hakon*." He gestured to the sailboat. "Dag is looking for her sister. She has an idea of where to find her, but she needs a boat."

"Can she sail?" Rahm asked. "I would hate to lose that little boat. Esma learned how to sail on it."

"I'll have someone else with me," Dag said.

Rahm looked from him to Dag and then back to him. "Then yes," he said. "I understand the need to make sure your family is safe. That's all I've ever tried to do for mine."

"Thank you," Dag said.

"Yes," Calder said. "Thank you. How much time do you need before we can start asking around at the market?"

"You can start tomorrow morning at first light," Rahm said. "And once you start, the less time you remain in the harbour the better."

"Understood." It would be expensive, but Calder knew that purchasing and loading the ships could be done in a day. With Luck, they would be on their way back to the Pale Sea by sunset.

"I'll be back here at the same time," Dag said.

"I'll make sure it's known that you have my permission to take the sailboat," Rahm said. He held out his hand and Calder clasped it. "I have people to see so I'll be off." He flashed a smile and left, but Calder thought the usual swagger in his father's step was subdued.

"His secrets are catching up with him," Dag said from his side. "I'm sorry they are causing you pain too."

Calder looped an arm around her shoulder and drew her to him. "I am too. But at least with his help, our path forward is clear. You and Jaak will need a secure place to wait for me once you find Inger. Where I can pick you up when I return for a second shipment of food. Probably not here in Messanos though." If Dag was able to persuade Saulia Holt to leave her parents, he didn't want his father to find out. He couldn't trust him not to tell Fihaldo Pinho.

GUSTAV TRIED TO stay out of the way as the crew of the *Oakhaven* readied the ship to drop anchor. The sun was coming up over the horizon, bathing the tallest buildings in Tarklee with sunlight.

"The dinghy will be ready in a few minutes," Captain Sorenson called to him. "We won't be staying longer than the time required to set you ashore."

"I appreciate you making the stop at all," Gustav replied. When he'd boarded in Lavais, he hadn't realized that the *Oakhaven* wasn't planning to stop in Tarklee on its way back north. Sorenson had quickly agreed to take him ashore, but Gustav was painfully aware that this was taking time away from a tight schedule.

A sailor waved. "That's your signal," Sorenson said. "I'm certain everyone will appreciate the good news about the shipyards."

"I'm sure they will," Gustav agreed. He was equally certain the Interim Grand Freeholder and the Master Intelligencer would be unhappy about the behaviour of the Swyfordian Clan Freeholders. "Thank you, Captain Sorenson, for bringing me home safe."

"And I thank you for helping the Three," Sorenson said.

Gustav nodded and turned toward the sailor who had waved at him. He climbed over the railing and down into the waiting dinghy.

He stared out at the city as the crew rowed towards it. Home. His mother and father were in Lavais, but while he'd been there, he'd realized that Tarklee and the Hall were home now. And he was happy to be back.

The corridors were empty as he made his way through them. He pushed open the door to the outer office of the Master Intelligencer. The room was dark and empty, but a light was on in the inner office. He knocked and smiled when Nadez called *enter*.

"I came here first," he said. "Thinking you are the one more likely to be up this early."

"Gustav!" Nadez jumped up and hugged him. "I am very glad to see you." She stepped back and looked him in the eyes. "But I do hope bad news does not bring you. Sit." She gestured to the chairs in front of her desk as she sat back down behind it. "Did you come by the road? I wasn't aware that any ships were due in."

"The *Oakhaven* made an unscheduled stop," Gustav replied. "And I have good news. And bad."

"Any good news is welcome," Nadez replied. "So start with that."

"Janni and Jarri are making so much progress on the shipyards that I've been told they will be ready to start building ships in two months," he said. "The *Oakhaven*'s next shipment will be lumber for ships, not just for repairs. They hope to build two ships by spring."

"Two! That is good news. You'll have to come with me and tell Lauma herself. Berna is doing well?"

"She's doing what she can," he said. "Lavais Island has risen to the occasion, but the Clan Freeholders have not. Fishing has been expanded, and woodcutters have been foraging as much food as they can, but only on the island. Clan Freeholder Timonis does not believe the situation is as desperate as it is, and the other Clan Freeholders are taking his lead."

"What doesn't he believe?" Nadez asked. "He's visited the shipyards since they were destroyed, hasn't he?"

"He has," Gustav said. "But no matter how much Charisma I tried to use when I spoke to him, he thinks that both Berna and I are too young to understand the situation."

"Is he being stupid, or does he have an ulterior reason?"

"Berna and I are not sure," Gustav said. "Timonis is likely to become the next Grand Freeholder, and neither of us believes he cares about the well-being of the Three. All he's interested in is being named Grand Freeholder and having authority over the other Clan Freeholders."

"Politicians," Nadez. "I hate them."

"The positions do seem to attract the worst people."

Gustav turned to see Lauma Strauskas standing in the doorway.

"It is good to see you, Gustav Gunnarson," she said. "I assume that since you did not come directly to me that my daughter is well?"

"Yes," Gustav replied, getting to his feet. "Berna is well. I'm sorry. It was early and I thought that the Master Intelligencer was more likely to be in her office."

"Don't be sorry," Lauma said. She sat down in the second chair and gestured to Gustav, who sat back down in the chair beside her. "I keep unpredictable hours on purpose these days. Ever since the attempts on my life."

"Are you all right?" Gustav asked, shocked. "I mean, of course they didn't succeed. Who was it?"

"The first was a suicide assassin who arrived here by ship at midsummer," Nadez said. "We believe that she was met by Clan Freeholder Ottosen."

"The first?" Gustav asked. "There was more than one?"

"Yes," Lauma said. "Nadez believes you have met the second would-be assassin. A former student named Pia."

"The girl from the tavern where Janni was being kept?" She'd had less training than him. "Why did they think she had the skills to kill you?"

"We assumed that it was because she knows the Hall," Nadez said. "But I would very much like to see if you can get more answers."

"Yes, of course." He paused. "But there is more I need to tell you."

There was a sound from the outer office.

"Ah, that will be Kaja," Lauma said. "She arrived just after I did, and I asked her to find us some tea and breakfast." She smiled. "I recognized Gustav's voice and had a feeling we would be here for a while."

The door opened, and Kaja entered. She nodded at Gustav and put the tray she was carrying on the desk. She turned to leave.

"Kaja," Lauma said. "Find a chair and join us." Lauma looked at Nadez. "I think it's important that we have no secrets among us," she said. "Secrets can be exploited by our enemies."

"I agree," Nadez said. "Gustav, can you pass out the plates?"

THEY ATE QUIETLY. Nadez took a last sip of tea and set her cup down. It was time to share Gustav's news.

"Lauma, Gustav has been telling me about the lack of co-operation from the Swyfordian Clan Freeholders. Gustav, why don't you tell Lauma what you told me? Start with the good news."

Nadez listened as Gustav repeated his news. He'd been taught well: his account varied only slightly from what he'd told her. Whatever Joosep Sepp's shortcomings had been, he had ensured excellent training for his Intelligencers.

Lauma asked much the same questions as she had, and eventually, Gustav's report was complete.

"Thank you, Gustav." Nadez said.

"I, um, there's more," Gustav said. "Berna gave me two messages for her mother." He turned to look at Lauma. "She is organizing food distribution and working around the Swyford Clan Freeholders. There's a warehouse on Lavais a short distance from the main harbour. A woman named Solvig Madsen owns it and has organized the local fishermen. They are teaching woodcutters from the north how to fish and preserve their catch. The woodcutters are also foraging to fill that warehouse. And they will guard it."

"Guard it against Clan Freeholder Timonis?" Lauma asked.

"Yes, if they have to. Berna assumes that Timonis will lodge a formal complaint and thought it best if you knew in advance."

"All right," Lauma said. "I'll add it to the complaint Ottosen is going to make. The complaint I have no plans on addressing until the crisis is over. That's one message, what's the other?"

"We," Gustav paused. "Berna and I, we met with Timonis, and neither of us thinks he should become Grand Freeholder."

"I'm not sure I can do anything about that," Lauma said. "I could perhaps delay it until the spring. Once the shipyards are producing ships, there will be no reason to not have the vote. It's a condition of the Treaty."

"Yes," Gustav replied. "But it would not be required if the Treaty no longer existed. And that could be done by you taking Byholt out of it."

Nadez looked at Gustav in shock. "Destroy the Treaty? Why? What would that accomplish?"

"It would ensure that I and all my fellow Byholters would not be governed by people who always put their own self-interests first," Lauma said. "Tarmo Holt wasn't the first, and from the sounds of Timonis, he won't be the last Grand Freeholder only interested in what they can extract from the Alliance for themselves." She chuckled. "Trust my daughter to find the perfect threat."

"Will it just be a threat?" Nadez asked.

"Well, a threat is only useful if you're prepared to go through with it." Lauma raised a single eyebrow. "When it works, the Fair Seas Treaty Alliance is good for every single person in all three countries. But when it doesn't? I haven't had a lot of opportunities to get out and really see North and South Tarklee, but what I *have* seen has shown me that the Treaty does not work for many of the people who live here. As a Clan Freeholder, I would be ashamed to have my people live with such despair and hardship. Nordmere and Swyford seem to accept it, but I will not allow them to do this to my country."

THE SKY WAS barely light when Dag stepped onto the little dock, Jaak right behind her.

She'd said a bittersweet goodbye to Calder on board the *Atlaine*. Neither of them had acknowledged that this could be goodbye for a long time or, if things went horribly wrong for either of them, forever.

There was no way to know for certain if the weather would allow Calder to return before the Frozen Pass closed. If he made it back here and they found each other, Dag would be able to take them through the Teeth on the return trip. But that was if they found each other.

Tarmo Holt might have made his peace with Inger, but there was no guarantee that he would listen to her twin. Unless his situation was so dire that he was willing to entrust his daughter to her. And if he did, then Dag and Inger might share Saulia's danger.

"This is the boat," Dag said when she reached the *Hakon*.

"I'll make sure the sail is there," Jaak said. He hopped into the boat and opened a compartment below the mast. He pulled out a neatly folded white cloth and shook it out. "It looks good." He quickly rigged the sail, rolling it up along the spar.

"I guess it's time to go," Dag said. She untied the line and stepped into the little boat and sat down in the bow.

Jaak grabbed one of the oars that lay in the bottom of the boat and shoved it against the pier, pushing them away from it.

Dag sighed and stared ahead as Jaak paddled them through a

narrow inlet. Buildings lined their path, and on one side a cliff rose up behind them.

Once they were out from between the buildings and on the open sea, Dag searched for the *Atlaine* and the *Tazeyar*. Even this early, small boats were on their way to the two ships: proof that Rahm had kept his promise to ensure that Calder could purchase supplies.

"Turning north now," Jaak called. He unrolled the sail and the wind caught it, and soon they were skimming across the water. When he sat down at the tiller, the boat veered to the left.

They'd mapped out their route last night with Rafael. Except for a few olive groves, the coast was rugged and mostly uninhabited. There were few rivers, and some of the ones that did reach the sea dried up during the hot summer months.

On the assumption that Charis was helping Tarmo Holt hide, Rafael had pointed out the olive groves he remembered, including the one that had been abandoned. Dag's Trait had reacted to more than one of them when she'd traced her finger along the line of the coast.

She and Jaak would follow the coast and visit each site to see what her Trait uncovered. It wasn't much of a plan, but it kept them away from the open sea and the most likely chance of being discovered by Pinho.

Up the coast just inside the Pilalia border was a small village where they would meet Calder when he returned from delivering goods to Tarklee.

Calder and Jaak estimated about a day to reach the first location along the coast. She and Jaak would land just south of the cove and do their best to determine if Holt was there. They only planned on landing and investigating on foot if Dag's Trait activated.

They were out of Messanos now. Cliffs rose up directly from the sea to hills covered in windswept pine trees. Black and white birds huddled beside the numerous holes that dotted the cliffs, their calls carried away on the wind.

An hour later, the cliffs sloped down to marshlands. The insects that lived there found them, forcing Dag to fan her hands in front of her face in an effort to keep the clouds of tiny bugs at bay.

"Forgot about this part of the coast," Jaak said. "I'm usually far enough out to sea that the insects aren't a problem. Want me to take us farther out?"

"No," Dag replied. "My Trait works better closer in." She didn't want to miss any secrets along this coast. Secrets, especially ones that were behind them, could be dangerous.

By the time they left the marsh, much of her exposed skin was covered in itchy red bumps. Dag was so focussed on ignoring the itchy insect bites that she almost missed it when the itch started between her shoulder blades.

"There's something around here," she said to Jaak. She leaned over the bow and stared at the coastline in front of her. "There." She pointed at a gap between two bushes.

The boat rocked as Jaak scrambled to roll the sail up. Dag kept her eyes on the spot on shore as Jaak paddled them closer.

"It's a path," she said. "And look, there's a place for a boat to tie up."

A small, dead tree had been stuck into the muddy shore. When they were close enough, she grabbed it. It held, and the right side of the boat swung toward the shore.

"I'll take a look," Jaak said.

"No," Dag said and put a hand on his arm. "I'll go. There's a secret here somewhere, which means someone might have guarded it with traps."

Jaak frowned, but he sat back down. Dag quickly tied the boat to the tree and stepped out into ankle-deep mud.

She followed the crude steps that had been dug into the side of the bank up to the small path.

Insects clouded around her, and she waved a hand, momentarily scattering them. With a glance back at Jaak, she entered the gloom of the forest.

Most of the forest along the shoreline seemed to be hemlock, a terrible wood to harvest, Calder had told her, and the reason there were no logging camps along this coast.

The path looked like it hadn't been used for a while, maybe not at all this summer. Fern fronds leaned out across it, and every few steps, Dag had to brush them aside.

A few minutes later, she came to an overgrown clearing. Two tree stumps had been left intact in the centre, and just past them was the remains of an old fire.

On the other side of the clearing, the path continued on.

A sentry post, she wondered. A place for guards to keep watch? She crossed the clearing and headed deeper into the forest.

She didn't have to go far. A cabin sat in the middle of a larger clearing. It was quiet and looked unlived in, but her Trait activated, and she knew there was at least one secret hidden here.

She walked around the cabin, passing a single empty window. At the back, her feet sunk into spongy earth, and at the edge of the clearing, there was a tiny stream.

The only path was the one she'd arrived on: the trail did not go any further into the woods. This cabin was the only reason anyone came this way.

The door opened easily, and she stepped inside, focussing her Trait to search for any hidden traps or dangers. But it was just a simple cabin.

The single room held a bed, a table, and four chairs along with a stove. A bucket sat by the stove, and wood was stacked beside the stone fireplace.

Dag ran a hand across the table, leaving a line in the dust.

Who did the cabin belong to? And why was it so deep in the forest?

She slowly walked around the room. Her Trait was quiet now, which made her wonder if the cabin was the only secret. She stepped back outside and immediately felt the itch between her shoulder blades.

She ran her hands across the flat plain of the door, but the planks were solid. She reached a hand up to touch the top of the door frame, and a block of wood shifted slightly under her fingers.

Dag wiggled the block loose and let it drop to the ground. Above the door was a hidden compartment. She felt inside the cavity, and for a moment, she thought it was empty. Then her fingers brushed against something made of cool metal.

She pulled the item out and swept her hand through the opening, but nothing else was inside it.

She brushed off what looked like some kind of coin; although, it was much larger than any she'd seen before. Symbols had been stamped on both sides.

Not a coin, a token. She ran a finger over one side of the token. She recognized the three wavy lines in a circle that Arressa used to identify their government agents. Much like she had a patch that identified her as an official for the Fair Seas Treaty Alliance.

But the other symbol was a mystery: two crossed swords or knives, she couldn't tell which, above a single open eye.

She pocketed the token and replaced the wood above the door and headed back to the path. There were no more secrets to be found here and no way to know why this token had been hidden or who owned this cabin.

Jaak was waiting for her when she returned to the shore.

"The path leads to a cabin," she said. "But it was empty." She held out the token. "Except for this."

"An Arressan token?" Fear flickered across his face. "You should have left it where it was," he said. "It's a dangerous thing to have."

"Why? It's just a token for an Arressan official."

"No," Jaak said. "It's a token for an Arressan Resolute."

"Oh." Dag stared at the token. She'd been taught about Resolutes, though even her instructor hadn't been certain they were real. They were rumoured to be the most dangerous and feared assassins. Tales said that not even death stopped them from completing their task. "How do you know?"

"I saw one once," Jaak said. "After I left the pirates, I shipped out on a vessel from Arressa. My bunk mate had a token like that. Won it in a game of ludus he said. Whoever held it could name a target, and the Resolute had to kill them in order to get the token back. But then we arrived in port, and my bunk mate left the ship and never came back. His friend said the Resolute found him. Turns out the sailor who lost the token in ludus had already named someone. The Resolute killed my bunk mate and took his token back."

"So, this token means that the Resolute hasn't finished the job?" she asked. The first clearing made more sense now. It *was* a guard post.

"Or he has and is now looking for his token. You don't want him coming after you." Jaak stared at her. "When he comes back and finds his token missing."

"But why hide it?" Dag asked. "It doesn't make sense for the Resolute to hide it." But it didn't make sense for anyone else to hide it either. Who gained from stealing and hiding a Resolute's token?

"No one knows why Resolutes do what they do," Jaak said. "You're going to keep it, aren't you?"

"I am," Dag replied. "My Trait showed it to me. I can't ignore that." She untied the line from the tree. "Let's go. We need to find a safe place to spend the night, and it's not here."

"I agree with you on that point," Jaak said. He didn't look happy, but he paddled them away from the shore and raised the sail.

CHAPTER 13

"We're ready set to sail, Captain," Rafael said. "The holds are secured, all the barges have returned to shore, and the *Tazeyar* signalled that they're ready to go."

Calder nodded. "Excellent. First Mate? Take us home."

"Aye, sir." Darya took a step forward and started calling out orders. All across the ship, sailors jumped into action.

"I'll take the midnight watch," Calder said. He wouldn't sleep anyway, not with Dag out there somewhere. "I'll be in my cabin until then." He turned and went below.

He sighed as he closed the door, shutting out all of the day's distractions.

Buying and loading the food had been remarkably easy. Merchants had approached *him* with offers, making him wonder at his father's influence. He seemed to have far more authority than a subordinate to Fihaldo Pinho, even one who was his top spy, would have, but why? What was his father to Pinho?

As Dag said, Rahm had more secrets than anyone she'd ever met.

He paced the cabin, too on edge to rest. If Luck held, along with the weather, they would reach Tarklee in less than a week, and now that he was on his way back home, his worry about his mother intensified.

He jammed his hands in his pockets, telling himself that she was alive. Lauma Strauskas was not a helpless woman and neither was Dagrun Lund. He had to trust that the most important women in his life had the skills and knowledge to keep themselves safe. He had to.

He sat down at the table and stared at the map of the Sapphire Sea. The place where he planned on meeting Dag, Inger, and Jaak was marked with an X. He wet his finger and carefully removed the mark. He didn't expect a spy to be on board his ship, but he couldn't assume there was no risk. For years his own father had been using him to gather information.

The ship settled into the steady rhythm of sailing on calm seas, and he rolled up the map of the Sapphire Sea, exposing the one for the Pale Sea.

It should take them four or five days to get to Strongrock, although they weren't planning on getting close enough to the island to be seen.

Then they had to go through the Frozen Pass, where they might be forced into a delay. If they arrived after dark, they would need to wait for daylight. The days were now much shorter that far north, which meant a tight window to get through the pass. The *Atlaine* would go first: Calder was counting on his Luck to find a safe passage that the *Tazeyar* could follow.

Once in Tarklee—his stomach clenched with worry for his mother—they would take as little time as possible to unload and set sail again. No matter what had happened to his mother, he was not going to strand Dag in the Sapphire Sea for the winter.

He sat staring at the map until there was a knock on his door.

"It's your watch, Captain," Rafael said from the other side.

"I'm on my way." Calder stood and stretched before leaving his cabin.

GUSTAV LOOKED ACROSS the street and grinned. His little cart appeared much the same as it had the last time he'd seen it, when he'd left it outside of the tavern where Janni and Jarri had been held. A young man in well-patched clothing carefully stacked the goods before he unfolded a tarp, covering them.

"I trust you had a good day?" Gustav asked when he approached. The youth looked up, and his welcoming smile turned to apprehension. "Ah, you know who I am," Gustav said. "Don't worry, I just wanted to know if my old cart was in good hands." He grabbed a corner of the tarp and tied it to the cart.

"I thought it had been abandoned," the lad said. "And, well, I thought I could make a living."

"And have you?" Gustav had never actually done much selling; his cart had only ever been a way to hide in plain sight. He patted the tarp. "You do seem to have a healthy amount of goods for sale."

"I can give you some coin," the youth said. "For the use of your cart."

"I'm going to assume that it does provide you a living," Gustav said. "That's good. And I don't want your coin. All I ask is that you don't take advantage of people with even less than you. That maybe you even help someone, if you can."

"Yes, I will," the youth replied. "I do that anyway. Someone has to."

"Exactly," Gustav said. "I would also ask that you don't acknowledge me if you see me in the streets. And if I need to borrow it for a few hours, you let me." The youth nodded, and Gustav patted the cart. It was good to know that his old disguise was available if he needed it. He nodded to the youth before crossing New Bridge.

Nadez had asked him to see the prisoner, Pia Engen, but he'd pleaded exhaustion and asked her to postpone that until tomorrow. He felt a little uncomfortable about lying to the Master Intelligencer, but he didn't want to offend her by telling her his real reason for the delay.

He wanted to take the pulse of the city and see if anything was better since Lauma Strauskas had become Interim Grand Freeholder and Nadez had been named Master Intelligencer.

Because whatever he found would help him decide on what he thought he should fight for. He couldn't blame Berna and her mother for being willing to dissolve the Treaty and safeguard their own people, but *his* people were on Lavais. His people were Swyfordians and would still be ruled by their Clan Freeholders.

If the Treaty was dissolved, his loyalty would be to Swyfordians, like the people here in South Tarklee. They might be miles from Lavais, but they were still governed by the same Clan Freeholders. Like Tavet Timonis.

Dusk had fallen by the time he arrived at the old warehouse. He hadn't planned on coming here, but he also wasn't surprised to find himself standing in front of it.

Light streamed out from the windows, and he headed to the door at the side. It wasn't locked, so he pushed it open.

"Hello?" he called as he stepped inside.

"Greetings." A woman came towards him, a smile on her face. "Are you looking for a meal? Supper has already been served, but we can always fill a plate for someone in need." She gestured to a long table that ran the length of the far wall. A few people sat at it, cradling mugs.

"Sorry, no," Gustav replied. "I thought this . . . I mean, this warehouse belongs to . . ." he trailed off. Should he mention Tarmo Holt?

"I know who it belongs to," the woman said with a frown. "But the Interim Grand Freeholder has declared that it can be used to feed those in need. The Alliance supplies the food we need to do that. It's simple fare: we serve more salt fish than people like, but it's filling."

"Do you feed a lot of people?" He'd given Lauma and Nadez his news: it looked like he should have asked them for theirs.

"We do," the woman answered. "Some people we cook for and feed here, but others get supplies to take home. The old, the very young, as well as the infirm can't always travel even somewhere close."

"This is a very good thing," Gustav said.

"Yes. After the riot," she leaned closer, "and the owner of this warehouse fled, we expected the worst. Food was scarce before, but at least it was available for those with coin. And then guards showed up here. But they didn't come to round up anyone, instead they were asking for volunteers. People willing to cook and clean and feed their fellow citizens." She beamed. "I stepped up right away. Once I was trained, they had me visit some of the other food halls and help them get organized too."

"There are other places that feed people?"

"Many," she replied. "I've been to four others myself." She mentioned some locations, and Gustav recognized them as warehouses he'd identified for Joosep and Dagrun.

Someone called out, and the woman turned. "I must be going," she said to Gustav. "If there's nothing you need."

"No, thank you." He watched her hurry off toward the small office. He took another look around before stepping outside.

Back in the streets, he realized that there was a difference he hadn't noticed before.

This part of the city was still poor. There was little work, and the places where people lived were crude. But the people he saw seemed less desperate, less angry.

He made his way to another warehouse and found the same situation: a warm welcome and the offer of food if he needed it. This warehouse had a half a dozen sleeping pallets lined up in a dark corner. Someone coughed, and a baby whimpered.

"Poor family was burned out of their home two nights ago," the man who greeted him said. "We'll try our best to find them another place, but in the meantime, they're warm and dry and fed."

"That's very kind of you," Gustav said. In all of the weeks he'd spent on the streets of Tarklee, he'd never seen anything like this.

"Directions from the Interim Grand Freeholder," the man replied. "She's the one who's kind. We're just following her lead."

"But you're still helping," Gustav replied, recalling Lauma's remarks that she would be ashamed to allow people to live in hardship and despair. He'd thought she was referring to Byholters; that she was declaring that her own people would never live in such dire circumstances, and she was. But she'd already started changing the lives of the people in Tarklee. She'd already taken steps to ensure that Swyfordians and Nordmerians would be aided using Alliance resources.

"It's easy to help when we have everything we need to do it."

"I see that." Gustav nodded and went back out into the city.

He had his answer. Lauma Strauskas could not be allowed to dissolve the Treaty. Nor could she hand over the office of Grand Freeholder to Timonis.

He sighed. One answer led to another question. How to accomplish that? How to keep Lauma Strauskas as Grand Freeholder?

GULLS SCREECHED OVERHEAD, and Dag rolled over to look up at them. The sky was just starting to brighten with dawn.

"Caught some fish," Jaak said from where he sat by the fire pit.

"I'll refill the waterskins." Dag stood up and brushed sand from her trousers, picked up the two waterskins, and went to the small stream.

They'd found this little inlet late last night. A clear stretch of beach gently sloped up to a line of trees, and at one end, a stream fed into the sea. Jaak estimated that they were still about an hour away from the next place marked on the map and declared it safe enough for a fire.

They'd passed the first marked spot late yesterday afternoon. Dag's Trait had activated when she'd first looked at the map, but there had been no reaction when she'd seen the place in real life, so they'd kept going. An hour after that, they'd stopped for the night.

They'd dragged the sailboat up onto the soft sand before eating some of their journey rations and enjoying a few hours of insect-free warmth around the fire before bedding down; Dag at the edge of the forest, and Jaak in the boat.

The water in the stream was clear and cool, and Dag scooped some up and rinsed her face. Once the water skins were full, she returned to the beach.

Two fileted fish were spread out on top of flat stones that Jaak had placed in the fire. Flames licked the edges of the fish, turning them brown.

"Calder cooked fish the same way," she said. "They were delicious."

Using sticks, Jaak dragged the stones out of the fire onto sand. "Fresh fish cooked simple," he said. "Not much better than that." He pushed one fish onto a fern frond and handed it to her.

Dag blew on it for a moment before taking a bite. The sweet flesh melted in her mouth, and she sighed. "Just as good as I remembered and much better than our travel rations. Did you learn how to cook this way as a sailor?"

"No," Jaak said around mouthfuls. "I learned how to do this on Strongrock: from Teacher."

"Of course," Dag replied. She'd forgotten that Jaak had been a pirate. "I didn't think to ask what happened to Teacher and the children." That was why the *Tazeyar* had returned to Tarklee: to make sure the Strongrock orphans were safe.

"They were set ashore safe and sound," Jaak said. "I think Calder's mother was taking charge of them, but the *Tazeyar* had to leave before I heard where they'd live." He looked over at her and shrugged. "Our arrival surprised them. And Teacher and the children were another surprise."

"I'm sure they'll all be looked after," Dag said.

"I think so. If it were me, I would have loved being taken back to the city. And they're better off there than staying on Strongrock now that Captain Ansdottir is dead." Jaak tossed his fern into the fire and wiped his hands on his trousers. "I'll get the boat ready."

Dag took a last bite of her fish before shoving sand onto the fire, smothering it. When she returned to the beach after a quick trip into the woods, Jaak was standing in the gentle surf, one hand holding the line as the sailboat floated beyond him.

Dag waded out and climbed in, taking her usual seat in the bow. Jaak followed her into the boat and quickly raised the sails.

The sun was rising when they rounded the point and headed north.

"WE'RE REALLY CLOSE," Jaak said, his voice a whisper. "Do you see anything?"

Dag peered out at the shore. They'd sailed in silence since leaving the little cove they'd overnighted in. Her Trait triggered, and she motioned to Jaak to slow down. The boat rocked when she pulled down the sail.

She looked back to find Jaak sitting with a single oar in his hands.

"Just past that stand of trees," she said softly.

Jaak nodded, and she turned to stare at the coastline as he paddled them towards the shore. When they were so close to shore that she thought they would run aground, the little boat swung north again. They hugged the shore as they passed the stand of trees.

If they hadn't been sailing so close to land, they might have missed the inlet. It was just on the other side of the trees, and from where Dag sat, it looked as though it ended at a beach. But her Trait activated, and she pointed forward.

The inlet didn't end at a beach; instead it led through a thick stand of trees. Dag reached out and scooped up some water. It was still salty, but not as salty as the sea.

The marsh they passed through had been cut back to provide a wide path through it. As soon as they exited the marsh, Dag saw the dock. A ship was there, one she recognized: the *Neas*.

"We found them," she said quietly.

A young woman stood on the dock, staring at them.

"Inger?" the young woman called. "Is that you? Where did you get that bo—" She didn't finish the sentence. Instead she turned and ran up a steep hill towards a wooden building.

"We'll wait," Jaak said. He paddled them over to the dock.

"Yes," Dag agreed and stepped out of the sailboat and tied it up. She turned and stared at the path that led up to the building. A moment later, someone ran down it, blonde hair streaming behind them.

"Dag!" Inger called out. "Dag!"

Then her sister was in her arms. Dag hugged her tight, her shoulders relaxing after so many weeks of tension.

Relieved, she leaned away from her twin and grinned.

"For someone with your Trait, you were awfully hard to find."

"Even for someone with your Trait?" Inger replied. "I'm *so* glad to see you." Her smile slipped. "Although, you might wish you hadn't come. We need to talk before anyone else knows that you're here." Inger looked over her shoulder at the path. "I know a place if you're all right taking your boat."

"Won't that girl tell Tarmo Holt we're here?"

"Saulia?" Inger shook her head. "She's furious with her parents for getting them all into this predicament. She'll tell them, but we'll have had our talk first."

"All right." Dag untied the boat. "Jaak, meet Inger. Inger, this is Jaak."

"I recognize you from the Broken Mast," Inger said. "You're a pirate. Dag?"

"Jaak has been a friend all along," Dag said. Well, he'd been a friend of Calder's anyway. "Come on."

Inger frowned but got into the boat, and Dag climbed in after her. Jaak used the oar to shove them away from the dock and then, following Inger's direction, paddled them back the way they'd come. After travelling a few minutes through the marsh, Inger pointed to a narrow channel on the right.

Tufts of tall grasses gave way to a small pond. The hill that rose above the pond was covered with dead trees, their dried limbs reaching into the sky.

"I've come out here in a dinghy a few times to be by myself," Inger said. "There's a rock over there that gets good sun. We can talk there."

"Good," Dag replied. "I want to know why you were asking for work in Arressa."

AT THE SOUND of a knock, Nadez looked up. Her office door opened, and Kaja peered in.

"Gustav is here to see you," Kaja said.

"Send him in." Nadez set aside the papers she was working on as Gustav entered her office. His usual carefree attitude was subdued.

"We aren't due to talk to Pia until this afternoon," Nadez said. "At your request."

"I'm not here about that," the youth replied. He paused and looked around the office. "You haven't changed much in here."

"Tidied up," she replied, wondering why Gustav was stalling. "And repaired anything that had been broken." In truth, both the inner and outer offices had been in a frightful condition. Joosep's assistant Arnor had been killed just outside her office door, and the poor man's blood had seeped so deep into the stone that no amount of scrubbing had been able to remove the stain. Now a carpet lay over the spot, hiding the evidence of his death from visitors but reminding Nadez every single time she walked over it of what could happen if she wasn't careful. And smart.

"Sit down, Gustav," she said. "And tell my why you're here."

He sat down but fidgeted, clenching and unclenching his hands. Finally, he looked up and met her gaze.

"I walked around the city last night," he said. "Visiting some of the poor neighbourhoods I used to frequent in disguise." He looked away. "So much has changed in such a short period of time." He swivelled his head to look at her again. "We can't allow Timonis to make things worse again."

"Ahh, you saw the food halls." Nadez nodded. "Lauma set them up. They've been well received by everyone, even those who don't need them. Even I was surprised at how quickly the city calmed down after the riot, and that was due in great part because of the food halls."

"Good," Gustav said and sighed. "Then you agree that they must be continued."

"As long as Lauma is Interim Grand Freeholder," Nadez replied. "They will. But once Swyford elects Timonis, it will be his decision. The territory within the city belongs to Swyford and Nordmere, and even the Grand Freeholder does not interfere with how those countries manage their affairs. But Lauma rightly argued that we are dealing with extraordinary events, so I backed her use of coin."

"That's what I mean," Gustav said. "Neither Swyford nor Nordmere can be allowed to make things worse again. We are talking about citizens of the Three. How can we stand by and allow them to live in misery?

"It's not my decision," Nadez replied. "You know that. Intelligencers work for the Grand Freeholder, who is elected as the representative of the Three. We do not make policy decisions."

"Don't you think we should work for all of the citizens of the Three?" Gustav asked. "And not just the Grand Freeholder? Isn't that the mistake Joosep made? Trusting the Grand Freeholder to do what's best for the Fair Seas Treaty Alliance when all Holt wanted to do was use the position to consolidate his power and line his pockets?" He shook his head. "You and Lauma both know that Timonis will do exactly the same thing. Lauma's option is to dissolve the Treaty, but the people in Tarklee will still suffer. And what about us? What happens to Intelligencers when there is no Treaty? Do we all go back to our home countries and work for Clan Freeholders and spy on each other?"

"What's your suggestion?" Nadez asked.

"Make sure that Timonis doesn't become Grand Freeholder," he said. "And that Lauma remains in the position."

"What you are asking for is impossible," Nadez replied. "And if either of us did anything to try to make that happen, we would be considered traitors." The message Gustav had relayed from Berna to Lauma about dissolving the Treaty Alliance had startled her. Even more worrisome had been Lauma's real consideration of it as a solution. But as much as she hated that option, it was not her decision to make.

"Against whom?" Gustav asked. "Wouldn't knowingly working for a corrupt Grand Freeholder be treason against the people of the Three?" He paused. "Besides, Intelligencers don't swear to follow every order the Grand Freeholder gives them, we swear to uphold the laws of the Fair Seas Treaty Alliance."

"That's true," Nadez replied. "But I still don't see how I can arrange it so Lauma remains Grand Freeholder. I would need evidence that Timonis had broken a law before I could prevent him from becoming Grand Freeholder."

"So, do that," Gustav replied. "If he's as corrupt as Tarmo Holt, there should be plenty of proof." He stood up. "Perhaps it's time for me to return home and make sure my family survives this uncertain future."

"No," Nadez said. "Please don't leave yet." She flashed a hand signal: this was too dangerous for spoken words. Gustav's face lit up, and he grinned.

"We'll talk later," Nadez said. "You already agreed to speak to the would-be assassin this afternoon."

"Yes, Master Intelligencer," Gustav said. He got up, nodded, and left.

Nadez leaned back in her chair and stared at the closed door.

Gustav was right, of course. She had felt forced to accept the exact same restrictions that she'd blamed Joosep for tolerating; a key condition that had contributed to the dire circumstances the Three were currently facing.

She smiled. But Gustav had also provided a way to find a solution. All she needed was proof that Timonis was breaking a law.

With a sigh, she pulled out the papers she had been working on before Gustav's arrival. It was a report about Clan Freeholder Timonis. Written in Joosep's hand, it was obviously a preliminary report. Unfortunately, she wasn't able to find the full report, and she couldn't ask the Intelligencer who completed the mission about it. This had been Dagrun Lund's assignment.

DAG LOOKED OVER at her sister and sighed. After fearing for her life for so long, to finally see her, touch her, it almost didn't seem real.

And Inger seemed different, as though the weeks they'd spent apart had made them strangers.

"So, you and Calder, huh?" Inger said.

"That's the first question you ask me?" Dag replied and laughed. "About a man?"

"Not just a man," Inger said. "A man you care a lot about." Her smile faded. "A man I expected to talk you out of coming after me. I am awfully glad that he didn't."

"Of course he didn't talk me out of it," Dag replied. "He didn't even try. In fact, I wouldn't be here if Calder hadn't helped me."

She leaned back on the rock, enjoying the breeze that kept the insects away. Jaak was a few feet away, lying in the bottom of the boat.

"I ruined everything," Inger said. She grabbed one of Dag's hands. "For both of us."

"It wasn't all your fault," Dag replied. "Ansdottir had one or more Traits that kept people loyal to her no matter what." She nodded to Jaak. "He was one of Ansdottir's orphans on Strongrock. I once heard him say that what was the Captain's stayed hers, including people. Whatever hold she had on people died when she did." She shook her head. "From what we could tell, Strongrock and the Broken Mast became unruly once she was gone."

"They were always good to me," Inger said. "Even though Ansdottir and Ursa tried to kill you. Right after you told me you thought she had some kind of hold on me. By the time I saw Calder up north, I knew the Captain had a Trait, but it was too late for me to escape the influence she had over me. I wish I'd listened to you sooner."

"I'm not sure you could have done anything differently," Dag replied. "Calder and I think her Trait made people loyal to her, over anything or anyone else in their lives." She sighed. "Enough about the past, we need to discuss the future. Were you truly trying to find work and a place in Arressa?"

"Yes, although it turns out I don't have the skills to do that." Inger shook her head. "Since my Arressan is so poor, I can't even get work as a server. I should have spent more time helping you with your language lessons than being mad that my Trait was useless." She frowned. "Except someone found a way to use my Trait to do terrible things, and now I can't go home."

"No, you can't," Dag replied. "Believe me, I will do everything in my power to change that, but it will take time."

"Don't spend too much time on it," Inger said. "I know it's impossible."

"Difficult, but not impossible," Dag replied. She grinned. "I am very well connected these days. Calder's mother is the Interim Grand Freeholder."

"What! Why is he an Intelligencer and not a Clan Freeholder?"

"That's a long story for another day," Dag said. "Just trust me that people with power know about you and that I haven't given up. What about Holt? What is he planning?"

"I'm not sure he's planning anything," Inger said. "He seemed to have lost all hope after we stopped at Strongrock. Now I think he's simply trying to stay alive."

"After Strongrock?" Dag asked. "He was looking for pirate treasure, but we scared him off."

"That's why he was so intent on stopping there even though we all knew Captain Ansdottir was dead," Inger said. "You found it, didn't you? The treasure."

"That is my Trait," Dag replied. "What about this place?"

"It belongs to Charis's family," Inger said. "An old olive grove." She gestured to the dead trees on the slope above them. "Apparently disease killed off the trees, and most people have forgotten about it. At first, Holt and his wife were grateful to Charis for bringing us here, but it does not have the amenities they are used to. Fear coupled with not being comfortable means that there are a lot of arguments. I should have stayed in Arressa even without work or a place to live."

"Fihaldo Pinho is after him," Dag said. "And it does not look good for Holt. He owes Pinho a lot of coin, and since Ansdottir destroyed his ships, he has no way to repay him."

"That must be why he was so desperate for the treasure," Inger said. "Do you know that because of your Trait?"

Dag nodded. "In part. I think I know what Pinho wants and how to stop him from getting it. It involves saving Saulia Holt. And you."

"But not Tarmo or Asla?" Inger asked quietly.

"No. Like you, they will be considered traitors to the Three. I think there's a good chance that their daughter will not be. We think Pinho plans to kill Holt and his wife and force Saulia to marry someone of his choosing. That way he acquires Holt's Clan holdings."

"Tarmo Holt will help," Inger said. "To keep his daughter safe. We need to go talk to him."

"Then let's go," Dag said.

CHAPTER 14

GUSTAV SQUARED HIS shoulders as he waited for the door to the jail to be opened. Nadez stood beside him, and Lauma Strauskas hovered behind her.

The guard pointed to a corridor, and once through the door, Gustav headed down it. Aware that the two powerful women were a few paces behind him, out of sight, he approached the jail cell.

It was her; the girl he'd met outside of the tavern where Janni and Jarri had been imprisoned.

The girl's expression changed from wariness to surprise when she recognized him.

"We meet again," Gustav said. He stopped in front of her cell and stared at her. "This time it seems I have the advantage."

"I don't care," the girl replied.

"I think you do," Gustav said. "You might not care much about what happens to you, Pia Engen, but I'm pretty sure there are others who you do care about." He smiled, trying to put all of his Charisma into his next words. "I can help you save them."

"You don't know anything about me or what I want."

"You were an Intelligencer student," Gustav replied. "So I do know some things about you. For instance, I know you had a twin, Pertu, who died at five, most likely when his negative Trait manifested. Your Trait is Concentration, so his would have been something like Distraction."

"Why do you care?" Pia asked. "Why would you want to help me after I . . ."

"After you set those thugs on me at the tavern and then attempted to assassinate the Interim Grand Freeholder?" Gustav asked. "Because you are an Intelligencer. No matter why you came to the Hall, the fact is that you did, and were accepted. So, like it or not, you are one of us." He might have emphasized Nadez's point a little more than she had, but he felt it. Pia *was* one of them. Theirs to help or to keep from doing harm.

"Is that it?" she asked. "That doesn't even make sense. I was sent here to do precisely what I was doing: infiltrate and spy on the Three and report back."

"But you did none of that by choice," Gustav said. "I can tell by the bitterness I hear in your voice. I think it's because you truly did find a home here in the Hall. I know I did," he finished softly.

Pia looked up at him, and he could see belligerence warring with hope on her face.

"Is it your sister?" he asked. "Has Ottosen promised to hurt her if you betray him?"

"He'll kill her," Pia said. She turned her head away. "Leave me alone."

Gustav backed away from the cell. When he was certain that Pia wasn't going to look at him again, he turned and went back down the hallway. Nadez and Lauma were already outside of the jail when he caught up with them.

"Ottosen has threatened to harm a girl," Nadez said. "That's worse than trying to assassinate the Grand Freeholder. But it's good that you had her confirm it. That's more than we've been able to get out of her."

"My Trait didn't seem to work on her," he said, almost to himself. "But it often doesn't when people are terrified. Can we help her?"

"I'll find out more about the sister," Lauma said. "And where she is. In Ottosen's household would be my guess. He'll want her close to make sure Pia understands the threat." She turned and left, leaving Gustav with Nadez.

"You think that she is terrified?" Nadez asked. "Why? She just seems angry to me."

"She Concentrates on her anger to mask her fear," Gustav replied. "Using her Trait to make us believe she is more in control than she really is. I think she must use the same tactic with Ottosen. Otherwise, why would he ever think she was capable of carrying out an assassination?"

"You don't think she was ever a threat?"

Gustav sighed. "I wouldn't say that. A cornered animal is dangerous, and she feels cornered. But her Trait is Concentration. I would think that would have allowed her to find out that Lauma was not in the infirmary."

"You think she wanted to be caught?"

"Maybe," Gustav replied. "If it means that both she and whoever she is trying to protect are safe. If she thought we would do what we are planning on doing: helping her and the sister she's trying to keep safe."

"And she can't just tell us who it is and where to find her," Nadez said.

"Not when she doesn't trust anyone, especially not the people she is working for," Gustav finished.

"So she says nothing so she can't be blamed if we *do* find out," Nadez replied. "And if we don't, she and her sister are no worse off."

"I'd also suggest that she's been training as an Intelligencer long enough to realize that if we can't help her, then no one can."

"So, she's basically given up," Nadez said and sighed. "The poor thing is far too young to be trying to best Henrik Ottosen." She clapped a hand on his shoulder. "But I'm confident that the rest of us are more than capable and that we'll save Pia Engen's sister."

I hope so, Gustav thought as he followed Nadez back to the Hall.

IF ANYTHING, THE insects and humidity were worse when Jaak took them back through the marsh to the dock.

"Are you sure he won't try to hurt me?" Dag asked as Inger led the way up the hill.

"He has no reason to," Inger said. "Look, Saulia told them. They're waiting."

At least that was true: a dozen people were at the top of the hill.

Hoping that her sister hadn't led her into a trap, Dag sent a worried look over her shoulder at Jaak, who had opted to wait in the boat. He gave a slight wave, and with a deep breath, she turned and followed Inger up the hill.

She recognized Tarmo Holt and Charis. Her Trait activated when her eyes fell on him.

The tired-looking woman beside Holt must be his wife Asla, and the young woman, the one who'd assumed she was Inger, was their daughter Saulia. The person she had to convince to leave when she and Inger did.

"Tarmo Holt," Inger said. "May I present my sister, Dagrun Lund, Intelligencer for the Fair Seas Treaty Alliance."

"I know exactly who and what you are," Holt said. "I had many discussions with Joosep Sepp about your progress." He smiled but it didn't reach his eyes.

This man had lost much but hadn't quite given up, Dag thought, despite what Inger had said. So it was time to let him know that she knew who and what he was, too.

"Joosep Sepp," Dag said. "My boss, who worked for you. Who I saw lying in a pool of his own blood on the *Neas* just before you fled Tarklee. Who was bleeding because he'd been tortured by you."

"You have no proof," Holt said.

"No," Dag replied. "But because of my Trait, I *know*." He flinched but didn't back down. Dag didn't care because Tarmo Holt no longer mattered. She met Saulia's wide eyes.

"Your father had the Master Intelligencer tortured," she said.

"Don't listen to her," Holt said. "She's a trained liar."

"I was there," Dag said, still talking to Saulia. "On the *Neas*. You and your mother had already been sent below when Joosep was brought on board, bloody and broken." She looked at Holt. "He vouched for Inger and then threw himself overboard to cause a distraction to allow me to get off your ship Unseen."

"Papa?" Saulia asked.

"You have no proof of any of that," Holt said. "So, if you came for your sister, take her and leave."

"Inger will leave with me," Dag agreed. She paused. She was about to say that she wanted Saulia too, but Holt didn't seem desperate enough. Ahh, he still thought he had a way out.

"I found it," Dag said instead. "What you were looking for on Strongrock. So, if you are planning on sailing back there to look for the pirate treasure, you're too late."

"No," Holt said. "I don't believe you. You can't have found it." But his shoulders dropped, and Dag knew that's what he'd planned: he'd still hoped to buy his way out of the dangerous situation he'd created.

"You know what my Trait is," Dag said. "I did find it. So there is no chance of paying off your debt to Fihaldo Pinho. I know you owe him a great deal of money."

"It's Henrik Ottosen's fault," Holt said. "I borrowed from *him* and then he betrayed me by selling my debts to Pinho. I *need* that treasure. You have to give it to me."

"I don't have it," Dag said. "It is being used to buy food for the Fair Seas Treaty Alliance countries: countries that face starvation this winter because of you."

"Papa, is that true?" Saulia asked. "What have you done?"

"The ships, *my ships*, would have been enough to supply all the food that was required," Holt said. "Until Ansdottir betrayed me. She was only supposed to burn ships that didn't belong to me."

"Yes," Dag said. "So that you would have the only food available and could charge whatever you wanted. You created a food shortage so that you could profit. You were willing to let hundreds, thousands of people face starvation if they couldn't afford your inflated prices."

"Papa?" his daughter said, but he ignored her. "Mama? Did you know about this?"

Asla looked her daughter in the eyes. She didn't say anything, but by the look on Saulia's face, her mother had known.

"Get your sister and go," Holt said. "It will be one less mouth to feed, to be honest."

"I'll make it two less mouths to feed," Dag said. "I'll take Saulia as well."

"No," Asla said. "You are not taking my daughter." She gripped her daughter's shoulders, but Saulia shrugged and stepped away from her.

But Holt's head had snapped up, and he'd lost a little of his defeated look. "You have a proposal?"

"I am sorry, but I do not think I can save you," Dag replied. "But I can save your daughter from Fihaldo Pinho. I think I know what his plans for her are. I think you know too."

"He has a nephew," Holt said. "I found out that's why he bought my debt from Ottosen. He plans to have his nephew control Holt Freeholdings by marrying Saulia." His laugh was bitter. "Ottosen will eventually find out that Pinho has no intention of sharing Nordmere."

"Then let Saulia leave with me," Dag replied. "I will help her."

"Can you make sure she is allowed to keep the Holt Freeholdings?"

"I will do everything in my power," Dag said, "to help Saulia inherit all of your Freeholdings."

"No," Saulia said. "Papa, you are not dead, don't give up."

"I may not be dead yet," Holt replied, looking from her to his wife. "But without the pirate treasure, I have nothing to bargain with. When Pinho finds us, he will kill everyone else and take Saulia anyway. Returning to Tarklee will mean death for all of us, and the Holt Holdings will be divided up between Ottosen and the other Clan Freeholders. Even Seppa could be tainted by my actions and share our fate. There are no good choices, but this one keeps my daughter out of Pinho's hands."

"Tarmo?" Asla looked at her husband with horror. "You said you could resolve this; instead you've killed us all."

"Once Ottosen sold my debts to Pinho, I knew I was likely doomed," Holt said and sighed. "Because I know what he wants. Control over everything and everyone on both the Sapphire and Pale Seas." He looked at his wife. "And I suspected that he planned on using Saulia to get it. But he's not the only threat. I didn't dare leave the two of you in Tarklee because you would not be safe there either."

"Because of Ottosen," Asla said. "You think that once you'd fled, he would use us to consolidate his power."

"Not use you," Holt said. "Kill you. With me exiled, he would certainly replace me as Grand Freeholder. Once Saulia was dead and Seppa discredited, all of our Clan Freeholdings would be divided between the two remaining Nordmerian Clan Freeholders: Ottosen and Heikki." He sent a pained expression towards Dag. "With Joosep Sepp dead and the Intelligencers adrift, no one would be there to stop him."

"Ottosen is not Grand Freeholder," Dag said. "And the Intelligencers are not adrift."

"What? Who else could have possibly been voted in?" Holt asked.

"Lauma Strauskas," Dag said. "She's been appointed Interim Grand Freeholder until the Three are ready for the next elections.

Nadez Norup is in charge of the Intelligencers."

"Lauma Strauskas?" Holt started to laugh. "Lauma Strauskas? Ottosen will not like that. But she has always said she never wanted to be Grand Freeholder."

"She's prepared to clean up the mess you left," Dag said. "And that will include helping Saulia remain alive and in control of the Holt Holdings."

"I'll go," Saulia said. She stepped out of her mother's arms.

"Saulia," Asla said. "You can't. It's far too dangerous."

"It's dangerous to stay here, isn't that right, Papa?" Saulia looked at her father, who hung his head and nodded. "I'm not going to let others make my decisions for me or take away my choices."

"I have real hope that you will be safe," Holt said. "Despite all of my mistakes."

Dag looked from Holt to his wife Asla before meeting Saulia's eyes. "Then you and Inger should pack water skins and some food and meet me at the boat," Dag said. She nodded to Inger and walked back down the hill.

She'd done her part; she'd explained the situation, and Holt and Saulia had both seen it as the only way out. She'd leave it to Inger to make sure Asla Holt didn't get in the way.

"I think we'll be able to leave soon," she said to Jaak when she reached the boat.

"Good." He slapped at his neck. "I won't be sad to leave these insects behind. Oh, *skit*."

Dag followed his gaze to see Charis coming down the hill towards them. He had a sack slung over his shoulder, and the skin between her shoulders itched: her Trait telling her he was hiding something.

"Jaak!" he called. "Son of Jebris, I did not expect to see you here!"

"Charis," Jaak said. "Somehow, I'm not surprised to see you. What's in the sack?"

"Food for all of us for a few days," he said. He tossed the sack into the boat. "I'm coming with you."

He was about to step in when Dag stood up and pushed him back onto the dock. "I have not given you permission," she said. "And I'm not sure I'm going to."

Charis's expression changed to one of pleading. "You have to, please. If Pinho finds me, I'm a dead man."

"I'm not sure why that's any of my business," Dag replied. "Besides, I'm not even certain that this little sailboat can safely carry five people."

"It can," Charis replied. "I know this boat: it belongs to Rahm." He shook his head. "And just when I was sure he wasn't the Rahm I've been looking for, here you are, Jaak, in his boat."

"You've been looking for Rahm?" Dag asked. Then she understood: Charis knew Calder as Rahm. He must know something about Calder's father. "You'll need to tell me why you've been looking for Rahm," she said. "I need the truth if you want to leave with us."

"Honestly, Pinho will kill me if he finds me," Charis said.

"You told me that already," Dag replied. "Why? And don't tell me it's because of your ties to Holt. I know you were on his ship by accident. You were picked up after Ansdottir's ship was rammed."

"You said you were there," Charis said. "I wasn't quite sure before. And it was after Rahm sank Ansdottir and her ship: the same Rahm who owns this sailboat." He gestured to the little boat.

"I have the boat now," Dag said. "And you haven't answered my question." She narrowed her eyes. "If Tarmo Holt talked about me, then you know I have a Trait."

Charis sighed. "And it's the opposite of Inger's. I suppose I *will* have to tell you the truth. I work for the Arressan council."

Dag stared at him. He was telling the truth about this, but it wasn't the whole truth.

"I am not formally a spy," Charis said. "But I was assigned to keep an eye on Pinho's activities and report back with what I considered the threat he posed to Arressa. And I did." He looked away and his shoulders slumped. "But while I was at sea, trying to determine what Pinho was up to, he was in Arressa, taking control of the council. I was sending information about his activities to *him*." He shook his head. "Information that he wants kept secret."

"Why are you looking for Rahm?" she asked.

Charis shrugged. "Because I think he is the only one who can rid the world of Fihaldo Pinho."

"Why do you think that?"

"Because he was hired by the Arressan council to do exactly that a year ago. There was a signed contract and coin was paid, but Rahm has not yet fulfilled his part of the deal. I want to either make him fulfil his contract or learn why he hasn't."

"He's an assassin?" Dag was surprised but not shocked. Calder's father had many secrets. It would also explain how he knew that an assassin had been sent to kill the Grand Freeholder.

"More than an assassin," Charis said quietly. "He's a Resolute."

"We're here."

Dag looked up to see Inger, with Saulia in tow, standing on the dock.

"Jaak." Dag turned to him. "Can this boat really carry five?"

"It'll be slow," he said. "But she can do it."

"He," she replied absently. "The boat is named after a boy. Get in, all of you. We need to leave now." Inger and Saulia stepped in and sat near the bow with her while Charis took a spot near the mast. She didn't like having him on board; he was still hiding something, and until she knew what, she couldn't trust him. But she also felt that what he knew could help them all.

And if Rahm truly was a Resolute, did that mean the token she had in her pocket belonged to him? Had it been hidden at the cabin in the woods in order to keep it from him? To keep him from fulfilling his contract and killing Fihaldo Pinho?

She stared ahead, watching for hidden dangers as Jaak navigated them out through the marsh and back to sea. Hoping she hadn't welcomed any dangers onto this little boat by allowing Charis on board.

CALDER STARED UP at the sails. The wind was with them, pushing them homewards.

"We should be within range of Strongrock in a few hours," Darya said. "I can't remember ever making such good time. Jebris is smiling up at us."

"I didn't know you believed in the god of the sea," Calder said. To be honest, his lack of knowledge about his First Mate was his failing. He'd spent most of his time on this ship in his cabin: first planning with Dag and now worrying about his mother.

"Don't believe," she replied. "But don't disbelieve either. I will admit that wind like this pushes me onto the believing side."

"Me too," Calder said. "But we need to keep clear of Strongrock. There are still pirates there." And there was a ship as well, one they were probably using now that they'd learned of Ansdottir's death.

He wandered up to the top deck and stared out across the blue sea. A journey they expected would take five days had taken a little under three. As always, he worried that his Luck was trying to get him somewhere quickly.

"Sail ahead," came the call from above. A sailor pointed starboard towards the horizon, and Calder rushed over to the railing.

Yes, there was a sail: a ship. He made his way back to Darya.

"I signalled the *Tazeyar*, sir," she said when he joined her. "Telling them to circle around and keep out of sight for now."

"Good." He turned to Rafael, who had just come on duty. "See if anyone recognizes the ship. I suspect it's Ansdottir's *Vassan*, but we need to be certain." Rafael nodded and hurried off towards the main mast.

"If it is pirates?" Darya asked.

"Then they'll probably be undisciplined, drunk, or both," he replied. "But they have a cannon, so we'll want to steer clear of them."

"Who would it be if it's not pirates?"

"Who indeed," Calder replied. "Fihaldo Pinho would be my guess." Pinho might have already killed Holt and taken his daughter hostage. He could be ahead of them, instead of behind. His heart sank. And what had happened to Inger?

Rafael hurried back and handed him the spyglass. "It's the *Vassan*," he said.

Calder sighed in relief as he searched for the ship. It *was* the *Vassan*, and it was sailing towards Strongrock.

"I don't think they've seen us," he said. "Head due north and have the *Tazeyar* follow us." He watched the *Vassan* as the *Atlaine* turned and pointed north. The other ship didn't veer from its path. When it was barely a speck on the horizon, he lowered the spyglass.

"They're not coming after us," he said. He didn't know the pirates well enough to know who might be captaining that ship now that Ansdottir was dead and Charis had fled with Holt. As long as they didn't affect his mission, he didn't really care.

CHAPTER 15

NADEZ TUGGED HER formal tunic down before she knocked. The door opened and Kaja nodded, ushering her into the Interim Grand Freeholder's apartment.

She'd been inside just once before, when only Lauma and her daughter Berna had been home. Now the hallway was filled with light and music, and the hum of multiple conversations emanated from the main living area.

"Master Intelligencer Nadez Norup," Kaja announced.

A few people nearby looked up, but for the most part, the wealthy and powerful of Tarklee ignored her and concentrated on each other.

She spotted Lauma and nodded to herself when she saw who she was speaking with: Clan Freeholder Henrik Ottosen.

So, their plan had worked, at least so far.

Nadez wandered around the room, trying to see which members of his household Ottosen had brought to this party.

She picked up a plate and selected a few items from the laden food table: a couple of pickled herring and a sampling of cheese. Plate in hand, she walked over to the window and stood facing the room as she nibbled on her food.

She recognized many of the people in the room: Clan Freeholders and their families, mostly.

A few of the less wealthy Swyfordian Clan Freeholders were here, although Clan Freeholder Timonis was absent. Lauma had only given a day's notice for the gathering, so only those already in the city would be in attendance.

Lauma was the only Clan Freeholder from Byholt, but all of the Nordmerians were here. Except for Tarmo Holt, of course.

"May I take your empty plate?"

Kaja waited expectantly and Nadez leaned closer.

"The girl isn't here," Kaja said. Then she smiled and grabbed Nadez's now empty plate.

"Thank you," Nadez replied.

Kaja walked away, and Nadez slowly made her way towards Lauma.

"Grand Freeholder," she said when Lauma looked her way. "I thank you for your hospitality, but I'm afraid my duties beckon."

"Master Intelligencer," Lauma replied. "I appreciate that you were able to spare even a few minutes to join us. I know only too well how tasks seem to multiply when we are not in our offices." She nodded at Ottosen who smiled politely. "Despite the unending work, it seemed past time to gather all of the Clan Freeholders and their families and acknowledge the trials we have been through in the past weeks. Don't you agree, Clan Freeholder Ottosen?"

"Of course," Ottosen replied. "It is a very good idea for us to stand together in times of instability."

"Yes," Lauma said. "I only wish I had been able to give everyone enough time to travel here."

Nadez eased away from the conversation. Lauma knew what she had to do, just as she did. She let herself out of the apartment and hurried back to the Hall and her office.

"Was she there?" Gustav asked as soon as she closed the door.

"No." Nadez shook her head. "So it's up to us to go and fetch her."

"All right," Gustav said and then he grinned. "If she was at the party, it would have been too easy. Besides, since I dressed for the occasion, I would have been disappointed."

Gustav was wearing a uniform of a Fair Seas Treaty Alliance guard. Nadez didn't like misusing it even though Lauma insisted it was not a misuse, exactly. Since their actions tonight would help safeguard the Three, he *was* working on behalf of the Alliance.

Lauma had discovered that Pia Engen's younger sister was

being kept in Ottosen's apartment here in the city.

A former housekeeper of Ottosen's was the sister-in-law of one of Lauma's woodcutters. She said that the girl, named Frida, would be about seven years old now. The Engen girls had been taken into Henrik Ottosen's household when their mother died three years ago.

The woman claimed that his staff thought it generous of Ottosen to care for the orphans, although she herself thought it cruel to separate them when the older one was almost immediately sent away to school.

"Are you ready?" Nadez asked. Gustav nodded and stood up straighter. "Then let's go."

She led the way out of her office and through the hallways back towards the part of the city she'd just come from. Most of the wealthy Clan Freeholders had apartments near the Grand Freeholder's residence although a few also had estates in the city.

Their faint hope had been that Ottosen would bring Frida to the festivities, but even if he didn't, he and his family would not be at home. *That* was the reason Lauma was giving this party.

Nadez was going to demand access to Ottosen's apartment. Pia Engen was all the evidence she needed to conduct a search, and she was well within her rights as Master Intelligencer. In fact, she could have used actual guards, instead of Gustav. But not long ago, the guards had answered to Tarmo Holt, and neither she nor Lauma was quite willing to trust them with this task.

Besides, Gustav's Trait might be needed to convince the girl to come with them.

Nadez led them to an ornate door a floor above Lauma's apartment. She stepped back, and Gustav knocked on the door.

A woman opened the door, and Gustav put a hand on it.

"In the name of the Fair Seas Treaty Alliance, you will allow the Master Intelligencer to enter."

The woman attempted to close the door, but Gustav pushed it open another few inches.

"Do you mean to bar the Master Intelligencer from entering?" he asked.

"Clan Freeholder Ottosen is not at home."

"I'm not here to see him," Nadez said. She stepped past Gustav and crowded the woman until she backed up enough to allow Gustav to follow her inside. "No one is allowed to enter or leave until I have completed my search."

"My instructions are to not let anyone in when the family is not at home," the woman said.

"You're the housekeeper?" Nadez asked, and the woman nodded. "I'm the Master Intelligencer, and I have the authority to enter and search anywhere in the Three when I have evidence of a threat."

"I must let Clan Freeholder Ott—"

"You will *not* contact anyone," Nadez said, cutting the other woman off. "Unless you want to be charged with crimes against the Three."

"No, Master Intelligencer, please. But Clan Freeholder—"

"Secure the door," Nadez said to Gustav. She turned to the housekeeper. "I'm looking for the girl named Frida: take me to her."

"There's no one here by that name."

The housekeeper was clearly afraid, but her obvious lie tempered any compassion Nadez might have felt for her.

"You won't like what happens when I find her myself," she said. It was possible the girl really wasn't here, but highly unlikely. "Are you certain your Clan Freeholder will help you after you've been charged with treason for lying to the Master Intelligencer? I will say this one last time. Take me to the girl named Frida."

The woman hesitated for a moment before she frowned and headed down the hall, away from the door. After a quick nod at Gustav, Nadez followed her.

At the very back of the apartment, close to the kitchen, the housekeeper stopped in front of a narrow door.

"Open it," Nadez said.

A set of keys rattled as the woman searched for the correct one. She finally found it and unlocked the door.

Nadez pushed the housekeeper into the room first. Anyone willing to lock a child into her room at night would probably be willing to lock the Master Intelligencer in with her.

"Frida Engen?" Nadez asked. The room was small. She and the housekeeper took up all of the floor space not covered by the narrow bed.

A head poked out from under the covers, and the wide eyes of a child looked up at her.

"Come, child," Nadez said, her voice softening. "I'm going to take you away from here."

"You can't," the housekeeper said.

The girl had already crawled to the end of the bed and now stood up beside Nadez. She wrapped an arm under the girl's arms and lifted her up. Bare legs wrapped around her waist, and small hands clung to her neck.

Nadez sent a withering look towards the housekeeper. "Did I not tell you who I was?" she asked. The housekeeper nodded. "Then you know that I can. I have the right to remove this child from this house. If your Clan Freeholder wishes to lodge a complaint against the Master Intelligencer, then he may do so. I'm quite certain Grand Freeholder Strauskas would welcome a discussion about this child and her sister." Nadez turned and left, retracing her path to the front door and Gustav.

Gustav stepped out of the open doorway, letting her leave first.

"That was fast," Gustav said once the door was closed. "You lead in case they send anyone."

"She won't send anyone after us," Nadez said. "No one will do anything without Ottosen's direct orders." She headed off down the corridor, the girl still clasped against her side.

That was what had made Nadez almost wish the housekeeper had tried to detain her and give her an excuse to arrest her.

The child hadn't said a single word, nor had she been afraid of the strange woman coming in the night and offering to take her away. She'd simply moved close enough to be picked up and had hung on tight ever since. This child had so little trust in the people who were responsible for her care that she was willing to take any offered hand instead.

Once they reached the Hall, Kaja caught up with them.

"Clan Freeholder Ottosen received an urgent message and had to leave the Grand Freeholder's party," Kaja said. "So, we don't have a lot of time."

"We have enough," Nadez replied. "Is the other one ready?"

"Yes," Kaja replied. "I didn't explain very much. Only that if all goes well, she will be traveling far away from the city."

"Good." Nadez led the way to her office, nodding to the guard on duty. "You are dismissed," she said. The guard nodded and left.

Nadez pushed open the door to her outer office and set Frida down.

"Pia?" the younger girl said softly. "Pia?"

Pia Engen's surly look turned to one of joy when she saw her sister. "Frida!" She wrapped her sister in her arms. A moment later, the wariness returned.

"What do I need to do for you?" she asked. "Now that I know you have my sister."

"You need to help us all leave the city," Kaja said. "In case Ottosen sends someone after you. I'm not going to tell you where we're going, not until we're safely out of Tarklee, but then I'll tell you everything."

"That's it?" Pia asked. "We're just leaving? Why?"

Nadez sighed. "Gustav, you're the one who convinced me. You explain it to her."

"Because you're an Intelligencer," Gustav said. "You may not be fully trained." He grinned. "Neither are Kaja and I. But you are one of us. We owe it to you to make sure that you and your sister are safe."

"But I worked against the Three," Pia said.

"Against your will," Nadez said. "As Master Intelligencer, I cannot blame a barely-trained recruit for the terrible position an adult put her in. Now, you have a fair distance to go before dawn. Gustav will take you to the edge of the city. After that, you will need to find your own way. Kaja will explain where you are going then."

"IT SEEMS ODD that an Arressan would have a safe haven in Pilalia." Dag stared at Charis, but her Trait remained quiet. Again. She'd been trying to find a reason not to trust him ever since he'd joined them, but it seemed that he was telling the truth. At least, he wasn't hiding anything that triggered her Trait, which wasn't the same thing.

"Messanos is not safe," Charis said. "I know you think Rahm is your friend." The look he sent Dag made it clear that he knew Calder, who he thought was Rahm, was her lover. "But he will kill you if you get in his way."

"So you've said," Dag replied. "I promised to return this boat to him." If Rahm truly was a Resolute, then not returning the boat could be dangerous. Once they met up with Calder and the ship, the *Atlaine* would tow the boat back to Messanos.

"Jaak," she turned to the ex-pirate. "Do you have any objection to Charis's preferred destination?"

"We need to go somewhere," Jaak said. "And it's close enough."

"All right," Dag said assuming that what Jaak meant was that Charis's safe haven was close enough to the village where they were meeting Calder. "Charis, tell Jaak where it is and how to get there."

"I can take us there myself," Charis said.

"I'm sure you can, but I say that you will tell Jaak and he will take us," Dag replied. "The rest of us will do our best to stay out of the way. Once we reach safety, you and I will have a longer conversation about Rahm."

Dag closed her eyes and did her best to ignore Charis as he whispered to Jaak. She heard the directions anyway; her Trait didn't like secrets.

She opened her eyes and smiled at Inger. At least they were together. Her smile faded when she saw the sad look on her twin's face.

"What's wrong?" she asked.

"For one, I can't go home because I committed treason against my own country, and two, I have no way to make a living anywhere. Finally," she looked at Saulia, who was curled up in the bow. "People who helped me when they had no reason to are in danger."

"I can't help with the last issue," Dag replied. "Other than what we're already doing: getting Saulia to safety and back to her inheritance in Nordmere. As to the first, I have some ideas, but I need to discuss them, *we* need to discuss them with Calder."

"Hush," Jaak said. "Get the sail down and everyone stay low."

Charis quickly pulled in the sail, and Dag and Inger lay flat in the bottom of the boat. The tide tugged their little craft in towards shore, and Dag worried that they would hit a rock or a submerged tree and damage the boat and become stranded.

She lifted her head and peered over the gunwale. A ship was off to their right, its sails billowing, sailing in the direction they'd just come from.

Holding her breath, Dag watched it sail out of sight.

"Was that Pinho?" she asked softly.

"Him or someone working for him," Charis said. "That ship

was flying his colours."

"Are they going to find my parents?" Saulia said. "I know that's what they expected, Mama and Papa. That Pinho will find them and do something terrible to Papa, maybe even kill him."

"We need to get some distance between us and that ship," Jaak said. He clambered over to the mast, and he and Charis quickly raised the sail. Jaak sat back down at the tiller while Charis grabbed an oar and pushed them away from a downed tree. The wind caught the sail, and the little boat glided a dozen feet away from the shore and headed north.

"We can't help your family," Charis said, sitting back down. "If we'd stayed, we would have shared their fate. They knew that."

"How much longer?" Dag asked.

"Another two hours if the wind holds," Charis replied, looking up at the sky. "The days are shorter now, so we should arrive right around dusk."

"I'll watch behind us," Dag said. "In case that ship returns." There was no reason to think anyone on the ship had noticed them, but that didn't mean someone hadn't. When Pinho's crew discovered that Saulia was missing, they could come back this way, either by chance or because the little boat had been spotted.

They sailed in silence, Dag staring past Jaak's head and Inger and Saulia sleeping. She tried to ignore Charis, who sat with his back against the mast.

When she thought an hour had passed, she crawled past Charis and wedged herself into the bow between Inger and Saulia. They both had hollows beneath their eyes, signs of the worry and stress and fear they'd been living with.

Dag hoped that she could deliver on her promise to Saulia's parents to keep their daughter safe when even returning her to Nordmere didn't guarantee safety.

And she needed to find a solution for her sister, too. She stared out at the passing shoreline. She'd worry about that later. They needed to find refuge now, before Pinho discovered that the prize, Saulia Holt, had fled.

"There," Dag pointed. She recognized the spot from Charis's description.

"That's it," Charis agreed. "Jaak, the channel on the far side of that sand bar is deep enough for this little boat."

Jaak steered them closer into shore. Once the sandbar was

between them and the sea, the waves were weak enough that they no longer pushed the boat around. They sailed between the two trees towards a bend that took them farther inland. The bottom of the boat scraped sand, and they slowed for a moment before they cleared it.

"Just up here," Charis said. "I'll drop the sail," he said. Jaak nodded, and Charis untied a few lines and rolled up the canvas. Once he'd secured the sail, he picked up an oar and helped steer them into a narrow passage that ended a few feet away at a grassy bank.

Charis set the oar down and jumped out into hip deep water. With one hand on the bow, he pulled the boat up onto land.

"Welcome," he said and held out a hand to help Inger out. Saulia followed. Dag ignored his hand and stepped out onto dry land.

"Welcome to what?" she asked. "Oh." She saw it. At the top of a slope, there was a hut. Every part of it except the wooden door was covered in green grass.

"There should be wood, as well as blankets and fishing gear," Charis said. "The cabin tends to be damp and it might take a day to air it out, but we should be safe." He grinned. "There's a trail out back that leads to the nearest town, so even if a ship does find us, we can still get away."

"It will do," Dag replied. She hung back while Inger and Saulia followed Charis up to the hut.

"We should make sure he can't steal away in this boat," she said, although she wasn't sure Charis would dare to steal Rahm's boat. Unless he thought returning it to him would help him find answers.

"I'll dry the sail up close to the hut," Jaak said. "Then I'll pack it and keep it close."

"Thank you. How far do you think we are from the village Calder said he'd meet us in?"

"I'd be surprised if that's not where the trail Charis mentioned ends up," Jaak said.

"Good. Let's join them." Dag started up the hill. It seemed too much of a coincidence that Charis's safe haven had a land route to Calder's meeting point. More likely Luck had caused him to select that village as the place to meet.

GUSTAV PUSHED THE cart along the road while Kaja trailed a few feet behind him.

The girls, Pia and Frida, were hidden amongst the goods in the cart, the faded tarp covering them. He'd heard the odd whisper from them, but they hadn't moved in the hour since they'd climbed into the cart.

He'd promised the lad who now owned the cart that he'd bring it back as soon as he could. He put his head down and grinned. Two disguises in one night: first as a guard and now the familiar one of a cart merchant.

"We're almost at the edge of the city," Kaja said, catching up to him. "I'll look up ahead while you find a safe place to stop and unload."

"All right," Gustav said. He leaned over the cart and tapped on the tarp. "It's almost time."

He pushed the cart into a shadow and stopped, staring up at the sky. The nights were getting longer, and the sun wouldn't rise for a couple of hours yet.

Kaja returned and slid into the shadow beside him.

"It's clear in front of us," she said. "I didn't see anyone on the road."

"Then it's time to say goodbye." Gustav untied the corner of tarp and dragged it open. Pia sat up, pulling Frida with her. "I'll help you down," Gustav said, holding a hand out to her. He couldn't see her face in the shadows, but he imagined a frown since she ignored his hand and jumped down from the cart by herself. She turned and helped Frida down.

Gustav rummaged around in the back of the cart until he found the two carry sacks.

"Food and water for three or four days," he said, handing them to Pia. "Kaja has the coin safely hidden in case you were planning on running away."

"I thought we weren't prisoners," Pia said.

"You're not," Kaja replied. "So, if you do run away, I won't come looking for you. But it would be silly for you to do that before I tell you what we have planned." She leaned in close to Gustav. "I'll look for the man along the road you told me about. The one who helped Dagrun and Calder."

"Pavel Barda," Gustav replied. "He'll help you. I'll let them both know that you got off safely," he said referring to Lauma and

Nadez.

"Thanks." Kaja turned to Pia. "Let's go."

Pia slung both packs Gustav had given her over a shoulder and, hand in hand with her younger sister, followed Kaja out of the shadow and into the road. She looked back at Gustav once before they all turned a corner and were out of his sight.

Pulling the cart back into the middle of the road, Gustav headed back to the centre of Tarklee. It was just after dawn by the time he parked the cart beside the relieved youth he'd borrowed it from.

He stopped at one of Nadez's hiding spots and changed back into his normal clothes before taking the narrow alley and the small hidden door that led into Nadez's office.

She was at her desk.

"Delivered safely to the south end of the city," Gustav said. "They should be in Lavais within a few days."

"Good," she said. "You get some rest. Lauma promised she would keep Ottosen occupied until this afternoon."

"Thank you." Gustav left by the door that led into the outer office.

In a few minutes, he was in his own room. He peeled off the clothes he'd so recently changed into and crawled into bed.

Someone was knocking on his door. Gustav blinked his eyes open. There was another flurry of knocking. He rolled out of bed and quickly donned the clothes he'd taken off a few hours ago. Was it already afternoon?

"Who is it?" he called from his side of the door.

"It's Lauma."

He opened the door and Lauma Strauskas quickly stepped inside. He peered out into the empty hallway before shutting the door.

"I apologize for disturbing you," the Grand Freeholder said, pulling down the hood that covered her head. "I'd normally have Nadez come and tell you, but I don't want to be seen going to her office right now."

"Tell me what?" Gustav pushed a pile of worn clothes off a chair and onto the floor and gestured to Lauma, who sat down. "Sorry for the mess." He pulled the covers up a little and sat down on the edge of the bed.

"I know young men are not the best housekeepers," she said with a smile. "I raised two sons. Well," her smile faded. "I raised one and the other lived in a room much like yours."

"I imagine Calder cleaned his room when he knew you were coming," Gustav said. "The same as I do when my parents visit."

"I only visited him here once," she said. "I always hated the city, and Calder seemed more than happy to come home whenever he had time off." She looked around the small room. "He had less space at home than he did here. Now," she turned to him. "You need to know that Henrik Ottosen is furious that Nadez took Frida from his household. He didn't quite walk into the trap we set; he did not acknowledge that Pia was also under his care, but he knows that we know. He can't hurt Nadez or I, but if he realizes that you were with Nadez, he might come after you." She sighed. "I should have insisted that you go south with the rest of them. I'm afraid we've put you in danger."

"I'll go into hiding," Gustav replied. "Out in the city."

"I thought you might say that." Lauma pulled a small purse from a pocket. "Here's some coin. Stay safe." She sighed. "We are running out of people we can trust." She stood up and went to the door. "Don't take too long before you leave. And don't visit Nadez. Her office is being watched."

"I'll leave right away," Gustav said.

Lauma nodded, flipped her hood up to cover her hair, and left.

Gustav pulled on his boots and grabbed a coat from the peg beside the door and slipped out into the hallway, not even pausing to lock his door.

He was halfway to the intersecting corridor when he heard the sound of boots on the flagstones up ahead. The sound had barely registered before he turned and sprinted back the way he'd come, past his room, travelling deeper into the Hall.

He rounded a corner and stopped, pressing his back against the corridor wall. The footsteps stopped, and someone said something too quietly for him to hear.

Gustav peered around the corner: three men wearing the colours of Nordmere stood in front of the door to his room. Without waiting to see more, he jogged along the corridor, through the dining hall, and into the kitchen. A door led into a small alley, and once outside, he took a roundabout path to the harbour.

He had to do something no one would expect him to, not even Nadez. That meant he had to stay away from the poorer sections of town, and he certainly would not try to hide with his old cart.

At the harbour, a cool breeze blew in off the water, and Gustav slipped on his jacket. He found an out-of-the-way place to sit and stare out at the sea. He'd spend the day out in the open and watch for Ottosen's men.

CHAPTER 16

CALDER PULLED THE collar of his coat up in an effort to keep the bitter wind off his neck.

The day was deceptively sunny with clear skies and a good, steady wind filling the sails of both ships, but those winds were cold, bringing with them more than a hint of winter.

The *Atlaine* was in the lead, a half-dozen boat lengths ahead of the *Tazeyar* as they approached the Frozen Pass.

Looking through the spyglass, he was grateful to see that the ice hadn't yet formed along the edges of the pass, but with this weather, that would soon change. The wind coming down from the northwest was taking them through the pass quickly, but the air was cold.

"It looks safe," he said to Darya. "Take us through."

"Aye, Captain," she said. "Rafael, signal the *Tazeyar* that we're going through the Pass."

Calder stepped away as Rafael and then Darya called out commands. The top two sails were lowered, and the ship slowed. To counter the wind that was blowing them towards the port shoreline, the *Atlaine* turned slightly to starboard. He looked aft to see that the *Tazeyar* had also lowered all but the mainsail.

Gulls drifted above them, circling the ship. Every so often one would dive into the water, searching for a fish disturbed by the *Atlaine*'s passing.

Time seemed to slow as the ship crawled between the two

shores. Calder stared northward. The rocky shoreline gave way to scraggly pines that were permanently bent by the wind.

The trees here didn't grow tall enough to be harvested, and the wildlife was elusive, except for the gulls and the eagles.

Calder shaded his eyes against the glare of the sun off the sea. The Frozen Pass was as calm as he'd ever seen it. He looked over his shoulder, worried that it was the calm before the storm.

In the distance, a bank of clouds was building. Snow was probably on its way. He didn't think it would hit until they were through the pass, but it might make the return journey dangerous.

Half an hour later, the Pass widened, and they were out. Moments after that, the *Tazeyar* emerged and signalled them that all was clear.

Calder returned to Darya.

"Weather is coming in quick," she said. "I'm going to head us south and then west."

"You have the ship," Calder said. He eyed the storm clouds behind them. They were an angry grey now and higher than before. If the storm was as bad as it looked, then getting back through the pass would be a challenge. "Do you think this will close the Pass for the season?" he asked. He'd sailed through the Frozen Pass more often than she had, but she had more trips through it at the wheel of a ship.

"For all but the most skilled sailors," she replied.

Or the Luckiest, he thought. "That's what I think too," Calder said. He watched the storm until it hit, sending swirling snow their way.

He'd hoped that both ships would be able to make two trips to the Sapphire Sea, but even if the *Tazeyar* made it there safely, there was very little chance she would make it home.

So he'd take the *Atlaine* and the very best of both crews and count on Luck to get him to the Sapphire Sea. And count on Dag to get them back home through the Teeth.

"The winds might be cold, but they're strong enough to get us home before nightfall," Darya said.

"Good to hear," Calder replied, and then his stomach clenched. He would know the fate of his mother by the end of the day. He'd tried to put it out of his mind by telling himself that he couldn't do anything about it, but soon he would know.

He huddled against the wind instead of going below. By the end of the day, he'd know if his mother was alive.

DAG WALKED AROUND to the back of the little cabin. There was indeed a trail leading off through the woods. Later, she'd follow it and see if her Trait uncovered anything.

They'd spent yesterday cleaning out the cabin and airing out the two sleeping mats. Mice had nibbled a few holes in the cloth of the mats, but thankfully the food stores hadn't been disturbed. They had the food Charis had brought, but that would be gone soon.

Filets of dried fish were stacked in a metal box alongside two crocks of fermented cabbage. Dag had immediately set some fish to soak while Charis and Jaak built a fire.

The fire chased away the damp, unused feel of the cabin, and after a meal of their rations and some of the pickled cabbage, they'd all gone to sleep. Dag, Inger, and Saulia had pushed the two sleeping mats together and shared them while Jaak and Charis bedded down on blankets laid out on the floor.

Dag had woken up before the others and had decided to take a quick look at the area immediately surrounding the cabin.

"Find anything dangerous?"

She turned to find Charis watching her. She shrugged. "Not yet. You'd look too if our positions were reversed."

"I would," he agreed. "And since I know what your Trait is, I am genuinely interested to know if there is anything dangerous here."

"Who supplies the food?" Dag asked. "The cabbage hasn't been here more than a few months."

"Someone from the village comes along the trail three times a year," Charis said. "At least that was the arrangement a former Arressan Council member made."

"Aren't you worried that Pinho knows about this cabin?"

"Of course, I am," Charis replied. "But it seemed safer than where we were, waiting for him to come find us and kill us all."

"That *was* Pinho," she said. "In the ship. You said it was him or someone working with him, but I think you know that it was Fihaldo Pinho."

"I recognized his ship." He smiled sadly. "I didn't want to confirm that it was him in case Saulia became distraught."

"And gave us away when she realized that Pinho was on his way to kill her parents." Dag nodded. She stared at Charis, but her Trait was still quiet.

"You are looking at me very intently," he said. "Deciding if I can be trusted?"

"Yes," she said, coming to a decision. "I'll trust you with something, but only because I need information from you. Will you tell me what you know?"

"As long as it doesn't put me in more danger than I'm already in," Charis said.

"That's fair." Dag looked around. She didn't want anyone else overhearing them. "This way," she took a step towards the path. "I wanted to explore the trail anyway." She plunged into the woods, her boots sinking into damp earth.

"There's a clearing up ahead," Charis said from behind her. "It should be far enough."

She nodded. She assumed that far enough meant far enough that they wouldn't be overheard by anyone at the cabin. As she walked, she scanned the trail for any dangers or secrets.

The clearing was small, just a break in the trees really, and her Trait didn't trigger and warn her about any dangers. She stopped in the middle of the clearing and turned to face Charis.

"Rahm is not Rahm," she said abruptly.

"What? I've been searching for Rahm for months. It has to be him. That's his boat."

"The boat belongs to Rahm," Dag said. "But the man you think is Rahm is his son, Calder."

"Calder," Charis said. "Inger kept talking about someone named Calder. He's an Intelligencer for the Fair Seas Treaty Alliance. Like you."

"Like me," she agreed. "Rahm is his father. And he really did lend me his boat."

"So you know what he looks like?" Charis asked. "Do you know where to find him?"

"I know what he looks like, and I know where he keeps his sailboat, and I will tell you that I have never met anyone with more secrets than he has." She paused. "Now I need to know about Resolutes. Jaak says that they carry tokens."

"They do," Charis said. "Some people say the tokens are magic that help the Resolute track down their target."

"Do they do anything else?" Dag asked. "These tokens?"

"There are rumours that whoever holds a Resolute's token cannot be killed by that Resolute even if they are their target for assassination."

"So, if you knew a Resolute had been contracted to assassinate you and you had their token, they couldn't kill you?" Dag asked. She resisted the urge to put her hand in her pocket and finger the token she'd found at that other cabin in the other woods.

"You think that's what happened with Pinho?" Charis asked. "You think he has Rahm's token and that's why the contract hasn't been fulfilled?"

"If that's how things work with Resolutes, then yes. What power would someone who held the token have over the Resolute?"

Charis blew out a breath and paced the small area. "I'm not sure, but from what I know, a Resolute without his token would no longer be a Resolute. They couldn't accept any more contracts. And they might do almost anything to get that token back."

"I see." Dag stared at him again. "Someone did tell me that returning a token to a Resolute could be dangerous."

"Everything about a Resolute is dangerous," he said. "I'm actually surprised Rahm has a son."

"He does," she said. Should she tell him about the token?

"You have that look on your face again," Charis said. "Wondering if you can trust me. All I will say is that I helped your sister. I was hoping that somehow that would help me, but I did help her."

"I know." Dag closed her eyes. Her Trait wasn't warning her about Charis, but did that mean she could trust him? She hoped her Trait didn't trigger once she showed him the token. He didn't say anything while she was making her decision, which helped her make it.

"Why were you with the pirates?" she asked. "Sailing with Margit Ansdottir?"

Charis shrugged. "It was part of my attempt to find out who Rahm was. I had heard a rumour that Ansdottir had been approached by Pinho's agent. I was hoping that it was Rahm and that at some point, he would return to see her." He looked out into the forest. "When she started destroying ships that I knew belonged to Holt, I figured the rumours were true and that she was working against Holt for Pinho. After she went down with the ship, I was just trying to get home to safety." He sighed and looked at her. "But once back in the Sapphire Sea, I realized that there was no safety for me now that Pinho controls the Arressan Council. So, I stayed with Tarmo Holt."

Dag studied him. Nothing he'd said had triggered her Trait. And it fit with what she and Calder had discussed. Pinho had delivered a threat to Ansdottir, most likely by Rahm, and she'd betrayed Holt.

She put her hand in her pocket and felt the smooth metal of the token. She pulled her hand out in a fist and held it out towards Charis. Slowly she opened her fist, the token lying flat on her palm.

"I believe that this is Rahm's token," she said. "It was very well hidden."

"*Skit.*" Charis leaned over her hand. "I've never actually seen a token, but someone I know has. This is exactly how they described it." He straightened. "I don't suppose you would give that to me?"

"No," she replied. "But I will give it to Rahm. Will you help me do that?"

"Of course," Charis said. "That's even better than you giving it to me. You know who he is and where to find him."

"I do," she agreed. She didn't like murder, and liked even less that Calder's father would carry it out, but it would be the safest way to stop Pinho. Because even without Saulia, she didn't think Fihaldo Pinho would stop trying to take control over the Three. And with Rahm forced to work for him, Pinho might be able to.

NADEZ LOOKED UP from where she sat at her desk. Through the open door, she saw Lauma enter the outer office, Henrik Ottosen trailing her. It was late morning which meant that Lauma hadn't been able to forestall Ottosen as long as she'd hoped to.

"Grand Freeholder, Clan Freeholder Ottosen," Nadez called out. "Come in. I have a very good idea why you are both here."

"You came into my private apartment without notice and stole a child out of my household," Ottosen said, glaring at her from the doorway to her office. "Did you really think that you would be able to get away with that? I have asked the Grand Freeholder to ensure that you are punished."

"Did she mention what punishment that might be?" Nadez asked. "For carrying out my duties as I saw fit in order to protect the Treaty Alliance?"

"I would know your reasons," Ottosen replied. "The Grand Freeholder has promised that you will be dealt with harshly."

"Clan Freeholder," Lauma said. "I did *not* promise to punish the Master Intelligencer, *nor* did I promise that she would tell you her reasons. All I promised was to bring you to her so that we can all have a discussion."

"Please, sit down," Nadez said. "And we can talk."

The other two sat across from Nadez, and she stifled a smile. If he didn't realize it already, Ottosen was about to discover that it was two against one. He looked like he was about to speak, but Nadez held up her hand.

"We know about Pia Engen," she said. "And the suicide assassin."

"About what? About who?" Ottosen replied. "I have no knowledge of these people."

"Come now, Clan Freeholder," Lauma said. "It's very easy to verify that you are the one who sent Pia here to start her Intelligencer training."

"I don't know every child in my freeholdings," Ottosen said. "No one can."

"I do," Lauma said. "Helping every single child is part of my duties. And even if I didn't know every single one, I *would* know the sister of a child in my household."

"Prove that I knew they were sisters," Ottosen said. He sat back in his chair.

"We have proof that the suicide assassin came here by ship," Nadez said. "And that she was collected by someone in your household."

"That doesn't prove that I had anything to do with that." Ottosen smirked and crossed his arms over his chest.

Nadez didn't actually care about proof. Ottosen was on the defensive, which was what she had planned on. Besides, he was right, they had no proof that he was complicit in anything. "We have enough suspicions to make my entry into your home and the removal of the child valid under the Treaty," Nadez said. "And unless and until there is a formal enquiry, I am not *permitted* to share any evidence I have with you."

Ottosen turned to Lauma. "I wish to make a formal complaint against the Master Intelligencer."

"Denied," Lauma said, and Nadez concentrated on her hands in order to suppress her smile.

"Denied? On what grounds?"

"On the grounds that I am currently dealing with an emergency situation," Lauma replied calmly, "and taking scarce resources away from that to deal with a non-urgent complaint is not possible at this time." She stood up, forcing Ottosen to look up at her. "I suggest you wait until our current crisis has passed and resubmit in the spring, or whenever the election has occurred. Your choice."

"You will regret this," Ottosen said. "I promise. Neither Nordmere nor Swyford will tolerate you using a made up crisis to make a mockery of the Treaty complaint process."

"Clan Freeholder," Lauma said, her voice icy. "This is not a made up crisis, and I do not need your permission to act as I see fit to safeguard the Three. You've had your say, and I've given you my decision. I suggest you leave and let the Master Intelligencer get back to untangling the plot to kill me."

He glared at her and stood up.

"I will see that you *both* regret this," he said as he left the office.

He slammed the outer door shut on his way out. Nadez rose to make sure he wasn't hiding in the outer office, waiting to hear what they said after he'd gone.

"He seemed very sure that the suicide assassin can't be tracked to him," Lauma said. "He was very smug when you brought that up."

"There must be evidence somewhere," Nadez said. "I'm convinced that he knew she was here and that her target was you. And who else could have sent Pia to the infirmary when word was out that you were recuperating there?"

"He's certainly involved," Lauma agreed. "But with the girl now out of the city, we have no witnesses. And I wouldn't force her to speak against him anyway."

"If you dissolve the Treaty Alliance, you won't have to deal with him," Nadez replied. She hated that option and hated even more that if she was Lauma, she would think it the easiest and safest way out of all of this.

GUSTAV CROWDED INTO the narrow space between an abandoned fishing boat and the wall it long ago had been propped up against. He peered out past the bow to see if anyone had noticed him before stretching out in the shadow of the boat.

He'd been up since yesterday and was hoping to get a few hours of sleep before midnight, when he felt it would be safe enough for him to wander the streets and alleys near the harbour. He wanted to get a sense of who might be asking about him, in case Ottosen was trying to track him down.

He was just drifting off to sleep when a shout came from nearby. "Ships! Ships in the harbour!"

Someone ran past his hiding spot, and Gustav rolled onto his stomach to look out at the harbour. A dozen people were down on the pier, excitedly gesturing at the ships. A couple of fishing boats looked like they were getting ready to launch.

And sailing into the harbour were two ships.

It had to be Calder Rahmson and Dagrun Lund, back from the Sapphire Sea.

And if it wasn't, if somehow it was a ship from beyond the Pale Sea, he needed to find out who it was and what they wanted.

He scrambled out of his hiding place and ran down to the pier. The first boat had already left and was being rowed out towards the ships. Gustav hurried over to a second boat and wriggled his way through the crush of men and women until he was right beside the boat.

"Is it the *Atlaine*?" he asked. "I've kin on that ship."

"Aye," a man standing in the fishing boat said. "I recognize her. It's the *Atlaine*."

"Great news!" Gustav grinned, calling on his Trait. "Can I come with you?" He didn't bother waiting for permission and stepped into the boat. "I don't take up much room," he said as he edged past the man who'd spoken and wedged himself into a seat.

"All right," the man laughed. "It's my boat, so welcome aboard. That's it," he called out to the rest of the crowd. "Any more and we'll sink before we get out there."

The boat cast off, and soon the eight people manning the oars had it skimming across the harbour towards the ships.

The owner of the boat made his way to the stern, and Gustav, keeping the grin on his face, followed.

"It's a welcome sight," Gustav said. "After so long without seeing a ship in the harbour."

"A log hauler anchored not long ago," the man replied. "But I know what you mean. These ships will be carrying more than logs and dried fish."

"Friends and family for one," Gustav replied. "Home safe."

"Aye, home safe for the winter, most likely."

"You don't think they can make another trip?" He knew that Lauma and Nadez had assumed the ships could make a second trip; that they'd receive more than just two cargo holds of food. How would that affect their ability to feed people over the winter?

"They might make it out through the Frozen Pass this late in the year," the man said. "But chances are they wouldn't be able to return without taking a huge gamble. These are the only two ships in all of the Three. I can't see anyone risking losing them and the people on board."

"You're probably right," Gustav replied, hoping that he wasn't. They were now close enough to the ship for him to see people lining the railings above him. He recognized Calder Rahmson.

Gustav stood up and raised his hands high, signalling that he wanted to talk. Calder signalled back furiously, asking about Lauma. Gustav replied with the all-clear signal and even from this distance, he could see Calder's relief. Somehow Calder knew about the attempts on his mother's life.

A rope was tossed down, and the fishing boat was tugged in close. When a rope ladder was dropped, a sailor above pointed at him.

"You, come aboard."

A few of the men in the fishing boat grumbled as Gustav made his way to the ladder.

"Told you I had kin on this ship," he said and grinned as he passed the owner of the boat. "I'll put in a good word for you."

"I'd appreciate that," he replied.

Gustav climbed up, and at the top of the ladder, he leaned toward a sailor. "Can you let the boat owner aboard too? I owe him a favour."

The sailor looked over his shoulder, and Gustav followed his gaze to Calder Rahmson, who nodded.

"You, sir," the sailor called down. "The one who owns that boat. You have permission to come aboard along with two friends."

"Thanks," Gustav said when he reached Calder.

"You gave me good news," he replied. "Come, I assume that you have more to tell." He turned and headed towards the stern, and Gustav followed him. Instead of going directly below, Calder stopped beside a woman who stood behind the wheel of the ship.

"First Mate, the ship is yours."

"Aye, Captain," she replied.

Calder turned to him. "Come on. We have a lot to discuss."

It wasn't until Gustav had followed Calder into a large cabin that he realized that someone was missing.

"Where is Dagrun Lund?" he asked as soon as the door was closed. "Is she safe?"

"I am counting on it," Calder replied. "She went in search of her sister. My mother?"

"She's well," Gustav said. "Despite two attempts on her life."

"Two! I was told that there was a single assassin."

"There was," Gustav said, wondering who he'd met that knew that. "The first assassin committed suicide when they failed. A second attempt was rather clumsy and certainly not a professional. A former Intelligencer student forced to act by Henrik Ottosen." He grinned. "We've managed to rescue her and her younger sister from him and have sent them south."

"And my mother is safe?"

"Yes," Gustav replied. "Although Clan Freeholder Ottosen is angry with her and Nadez."

"Nothing I wouldn't expect," Calder replied. "I plan to stay only as long as it takes to unload. I promised Dag that I would return for her."

"Is her sister with Tarmo Holt?" Gustav asked. "And his family?"

"Yes. Dag is hoping that once she finds Inger the two of them can convince his daughter Saulia to leave Holt to and return here. We believe that if she doesn't, she will be used by Fihaldo Pinho to gain access to her father's holdings."

"Poor Saulia," Gustav said. "It seems that everyone wants to use her. Your mother and Nadez think that if Saulia survives and inherits that she can prevent Nordmere from falling under Ottosen's control."

"Poor Saulia indeed," Calder said. "Let's hope she survives. I am doubtful that her father will." He sighed. "I need to meet with my mother. Do you want to come with me? We can take a dinghy from the ship."

"No," Gustav replied. "I'd better go back the way I came." He grinned. "I'm hiding from Ottosen, and your mother might have already told him that I have left the city. Oh," he said as another thought struck him. "I went to Lavais with Berna. The Breck twins almost have the shipyards up and running, and your sister has everyone else organized. I thought you might want to know."

"That is excellent news," Calder said. "In case you didn't notice, my sister takes after our mother."

"I noticed," Gustav said and grinned. "I'll just sneak back up on deck and find the fishing boat." He nodded and left Calder standing in his cabin.

The little boat was still tethered to the ship, and Gustav quickly climbed down the ladder. A few minutes later, the owner of the small boat and the two men who had gone on board with him also returned.

The boat owner grinned and slapped Gustav on the back.

"Who do you know?" he asked. "That you were allowed on and got me on as well?"

"The most important person aboard," Gustav said.

"You know the Captain?"

"Maybe the second most important," Gustav replied. "I know the ship's cook. He's been sweet on my sister for years." He grinned. "Told him I'd put in a good word with her for him. Did they tell you what they have in the hold?"

"Saw it myself. Come on, let's get this boat back to shore. I have people to talk to and boats to get ready for the offloading."

Gustav climbed to the prow and let the boat owner answer questions from the rest of the people in the boat. If anyone here knew the ship's cook, they didn't mention it.

As soon as they reached the pier, Gustav jumped out and disappeared into the lanes and alleys nearby. He found a secluded spot where he could safely sleep until dawn.

CHAPTER 17

CALDER STARED OUT at the city as the dinghy headed toward it.

His mother was alive. He was grateful to Gustav for telling him that good news. His dread and worry had been increasing the closer they got to Tarklee.

As soon as the dinghy reached the pier, he stepped out and hurried through the crowds.

He'd assigned Darya the task of consulting with Captain Eklund about delivering the cargo and securing both ships overnight. Unloading wouldn't start until the morning, after he'd discussed where the goods should be stored with his mother.

Then he had to sort out a crew in order to set sail again as soon as possible. Now that he knew his mother was safe, he had no time to waste returning for Dag.

At this late hour, he decided to look for his mother at her apartment. She most likely had heard that the ships had arrived; she might even have sent someone to fetch him, but he was confident she would want their conversation to be private. So did he.

"Welcome back!" Lauma Strauskas said. She stood in the open door to her apartment. "It took you long enough to get here." She stepped back and let him slip past her. Once he was inside, she closed the door and enveloped him in a hug.

"Where's Dagrun?" she asked. "Is she all right?"

"She was the last time I saw her," he replied. "We separated.

She went to search for Inger while I arranged to buy food for both ships." His mother looped an arm through his and herded him down the hall. "I'm grateful for everyone's concern for her."

"Everyone?" his mother asked.

"Gustav came out to the ship just as we arrived in the harbour," Calder said. "He told me that you were fine, which was a huge relief. I know an assassin was sent after you."

She guided him into a sitting room. Nadez Norup rose from one of the sofas.

"How do you know? Nadez," his mother said. "Calder is here and Dagrun is not."

Nadez Norup clasped his hand. "I am glad to see you safe."

"Gustav told me about some of the progress," Calder said. "That the shipyards are almost operational, and Berna has Lavais mostly organized as far as foraging and storing food for the winter."

"Yes," his mother said. She sat down and patted the seat beside her. "How do you know about the assassin?"

"Father," Calder said. "He is working with Fihaldo Pinho, a Pilalian who is connected to Tarmo Holt and his plan to control all the shipping out of the Pale Sea."

"Leave it to Rahm to be working against the Three," his mother said. "I have never heard of Pinho. Is he a threat?"

"Yes. Dag and I think that Pinho threatened Margit Ansdottir into betraying Holt by destroying his ships. And that Holt somehow owes Pinho for the ships." He frowned. "Holt is now in debt to Pinho, and without ships, he has no way of repaying him."

"But the promise to pay note Gustav found was from Holt to Ottosen," Nadez said. "We assumed that's how he financed the purchase of those ships."

"Holt borrowed from Ottosen?" Calder asked. "Father said Holt owed *Pinho*. Do you think Ottosen could have sold the debt to Pinho?"

"Oh yes," his mother replied. "Ottosen would get his money back *and* he would leave Holt at the mercy of Pinho. He could rid himself of a rival at no cost to himself. It doesn't explain the suicide assassin though."

"I assume Pinho has a goal?" Nadez asked. "He wants some land in Nordmere? Perhaps this Pinho sent her?"

"Maybe," Calder said, but he wasn't sure. "I don't see how

killing the Grand Freeholder helps him. And Father said I needed to look closer to home for the person who hired the assassin, although he said he didn't know who it was."

"Closer to home," Nadez said. "That brings us back to Ottosen. He did sign for the goods delivered by the ship we think she arrived on."

"Do you believe he truly doesn't know?" his mother asked.

"I'm not sure I can believe anything Father says," Calder said. He shrugged. "Dag and I are confident that Pinho plans to use Saulia Holt, that he plans to marry her to someone of his choosing in order to gain a foothold here."

"The daughter," his mother said. "Everything comes back to her."

"Dag is searching for her," Calder said. "And Inger. Dag's hope is that she and Inger can convince the Holts that Saulia's best chance of survival is with us."

"Good." Nadez said. "It seems that Saulia is crucial to keeping Nordmere out of both Ottosen's and Pinho's grasp. You're planning on returning for them?"

"I am," he agreed. "I'll take one ship and hope that Luck will see us through the Frozen Pass. Dag will have to bring us through the Teeth on the return trip."

"I'll oversea the unloading," Nadez said. "In the morning."

"Thank you." Calder rubbed his eyes. Now that the stress and worry over his mother was gone, he was exhausted.

"I'll make up a room for you," his mother said. "Unless there is anything that can't wait?"

"You're safe," he said. "That's the most important thing." His mother patted his hand and followed Nadez out of the room.

He must have fallen asleep because the next thing he knew his mother was urging him to get up and leading him to a bedroom. He was just able to strip off his clothes and climb into the bed before sleep caught up with him again.

THE FISH STEW was bland, but at least there was a lot of it. They'd finished most of their other rations and didn't have any other options. Dag scooped a second helping into her mug and took a sip.

"Always hated dried fish," Jaak said. "But one of the few things I remember about my Ma was that she loved it."

"It's pretty rare around the Sapphire Sea," Charis said. "Fresh fish is usually easy enough to find."

"As long as you feel safe enough to fish," Dag said. She and Charis had been arguing for two days about what to do next. They agreed that Rahm should be given the token, but Charis wanted to head out right away in the sailboat and find him. For Dag, keeping Saulia and Inger safe from Pinho was her priority no matter what Charis wanted. But she knew that every day they stayed at the cabin meant it was more likely that Pinho would find them.

"I'll do the cleanup," Inger said. She took her mug along with Saulia's to the small counter before going outside with the bucket. Inger returned a few minutes later with water.

Dag joined her at the counter and set her mug on it. "Thanks," she said. "I can't tell you how much I appreciate doing small things like sharing a meal. Even if it is dried fish."

"Especially since we won't be together much longer," Inger said.

Dag sighed. "Once you've finished cleaning up, we all need to have a discussion. There are decisions to be made."

"Does this have anything to do with the quiet argument you and Charis have been having?"

"You noticed?" Dag was surprised. Inger's Trait had always meant that she missed anything below the surface.

"Sure," Inger said. "It's pretty obvious. I'll be done here in a few minutes. Then we can have that discussion."

"Yes," Dag replied, distracted. Inger had just said that something that definitely should not have been obvious was obvious to *her*. Was this proof that her sister's Trait had really changed?

She sat back down at the table and nodded at Charis.

"Let's talk," Dag said. Saulia looked worried, but Jaak stared at his hands. Inger pulled up a chair and sat down.

"Calder is returning for us," she said. "We have a pickup point and it is very close by, but he won't be there for almost a week."

"Can't we stay here?" Saulia asked.

"There isn't enough food for all of us to wait here for a week," Dag said. "We do have coin but sending someone along the forest trail to the village to buy food reveals our presence far too soon to people we don't know and therefore can't trust."

"Pinho could find out that we're here," Charis said. "Since he controls trade along the coasts of both Arressa and Pilalia. I have no doubt that he is looking for Saulia."

"We could fish, but that means risking being seen on the coast," Jaak said.

"Yes," Dag said and sighed. "Both of those options leave us here, waiting for Pinho to find us."

"You're going after him," Inger said. "That's what you've been arguing about. You're going after Pinho."

"Yes." Surprised again, Dag looked over at her twin. Inger should never have been able to figure that out. "We are going after Fihaldo Pinho. Not directly." She pulled the token from her pocket and put in on the table. "We are using this and the person it belongs to."

"I want no part of any Resolute," Jaak said. He pushed his chair away from the table and got up and paced the small room. "They're dangerous."

"They are," Charis said. "But Pinho is even more dangerous. The Arressan Council contracted a Resolute to eliminate Pinho over a year ago. I was sent to find out why the contract had not been fulfilled. Dagrun and I both believe it's because somehow Pinho acquired the Resolute's token and hid it. We think that the Resolute is now working for Pinho in order to earn back his token."

"That's why it was hidden in the . . ." Jaak paused. "Where it was hidden and even you had trouble finding it." He looked at Dag.

"I think so," she said.

"If you knew that this Resolute will kill Pinho," Saulia said. "Why didn't you say anything earlier? This might save my parents."

"Unfortunately," Dag said. "I—we—didn't put the pieces together until now. I thought Resolutes were a myth until I found this token. And I certainly didn't realize the significance until Charis told me that the Arressan Council had hired one who hadn't fulfilled their contract." Dag didn't tell Saulia that she would never have risked everyone's safety to try to save her parents. No one wanted to hear that their family was not the priority.

"You need to know who the Resolute is in order to return the token," Inger said, again surprising Dag with her ability to grasp what she *hadn't* said. "So, who is it?"

"It's Rahm," Dag said. "The man I borrowed the sailboat from. Calder's father."

"*Skit*," Jaak said. "A Resolute knows who you are?"

"And helped us," Dag replied. "Not only did he loan me the boat, he's the one who made it possible for Calder to buy supplies in Messanos."

"Where do we find him?" Saulia asked. "We need to leave right now."

"And some of us will," Dag replied. "But not all of us. The sailboat is slow carrying all five of us. We need to split up." She'd been worried about this, but the way Inger's Trait seemed to have changed was making her feel more confident. She didn't think Inger's Trait would risk exposing them, of making them Seen, the way it would have in the past.

"I don't want to go in search of the Resolute," Jaak said.

"Good." Jaak relaxed at her reply. "Charis can sail the boat," Dag continued. "Jaak, I need you to stay here with Saulia and, in five days, take the forest trail to the village to meet Calder. If all goes well, he'll be there soon after you arrive. You tell him the plan and he can meet Charis, Inger, and me in Messanos. After we've returned the sailboat to Rahm and given him his token." She was betting all of their lives that Rahm was the Resolute and that this was his token. If she was wrong, she could be putting them all in even more danger than they already were in.

"You'll check on my parents on your way along the coast?" Saulia asked. "And make sure that they are safe?"

"That's why I want Inger with us," Dag lied. She wanted Inger with her because she didn't want her sister out of her sight. And she couldn't trust that Inger's Trait had changed, that sending her with Jaak and Saulia wouldn't get them all Seen by the wrong people. At least she had a chance of shielding Inger's Trait with her own.

"I like this plan," Jaak said.

"I do too," Charis said.

"Then it's settled," Dag said. It was the best course of action that she could think of. It also left room, if all went well, for her to pressure Charis into helping her with a second plan she had. If all went well.

She sighed. There were so many things that could go wrong.

NADEZ STOOD ON the pier, watching as a dozen barges and small boats were unloaded. Goods were stacked up, lining the shore.

"It doesn't look like enough," Gustav said from her side.

"It's not," she said. "Which is why Lauma sent messages to every Clan Freeholder to have their people put up as much food for winter as they could." She shrugged. "And part of the reason why Calder is leaving as soon as the *Atlaine* is unloaded and the crew is ready."

"I thought he was returning to pick up Dagrun Lund and her sister?"

Nadez looked over at Gustav. He'd shown up a few minutes after she'd arrived: apparently, he'd been hiding out in the harbour rather than in his usual haunts. That was why he'd been the first to greet Calder.

"Inger Lund can't return to Tarklee," she said. "Or any one of the Three. Not after her part in the destruction of the ships and the shipbuilding facilities in Lavais."

"Oh. Will Dagrun leave her behind?"

"We have to hope so," Nadez said. "Calder won't be able to return to Tarklee without Dagrun." She was actually hoping that Calder and Dagrun could be persuaded to make a few more excursions to the Sapphire Sea over the winter. They could sail through the Teeth, which as far as she knew never froze, so there was no reason to stop trying to buy more food.

"First Mate Demer," Nadez called when she spotted the woman stepping out of a boat. "Are you here with an update?"

Darya Demer waved and headed her way. Nadez smiled when she realized that Gustav had slipped away.

"This is the last of it," Darya said when she reached Nadez. "I've paid the people for the use of their boats and their labour."

"You have?" Nadez was surprised. "I thought you would need to save your coin for your next trip."

Darya laughed. "You heard about the pirate treasure? There's still plenty to pay for more provisions."

"I didn't realize you'd found quite so much." She grinned. "That is good news. Are you ready to set sail?"

"We are," Darya said. "There are a few crew members from the *Atlaine* who are going home, but there are more than enough from the *Tazeyar* willing to take their places." She shook her head. "We all understand that the Frozen Pass will be tricky, but we trust the captain." Someone called her name and Darya looked over her shoulder. "I'm needed," she said to Nadez. "Tell the captain that the *Atlaine* will be provisioned and ready to sail by nightfall."

"I will," Nadez said, but the woman had already left.

Nadez walked along the pier to the shore. The fleet of boats and barges were scattering to the smaller docks, and the last of the goods had been unloaded.

Lauma was up ahead, speaking to a group of people, and Nadez made her way over to her.

"You'll only get in her way."

Nadez looked over her shoulder. Calder was leaning against a building. He joined her. "My mother has already assigned people to take the goods to warehouses," he said. "Now she's making sure that there are two guards for each warehouse: one local person and one Fair Seas Treaty Guard."

The people Lauma was talking to paired off and went in different directions, and just as Calder had said, each pair contained as least one uniformed guard.

"There you are," Lauma called and joined them. "I think that's it. The food is all being distributed and placed under guard. Shall we dine together?"

"I need to return to the *Atlaine*," Calder said.

"Then that's where we will go," Lauma replied. "I assume that the crew must eat, so we can too."

"Darya said that the ship will be provisioned and ready to sail by nightfall," Nadez said. "That should give us time to eat and talk."

"The *Atlaine* will be ready to leave?" Calder asked. "With a crew?"

"That's what she told me," Nadez replied. "There are a few crew additions from the *Tazeyar* to replace sailors who wanted to go home. Everyone knows that as welcome as these shipments are, they are not enough."

"Then let's get ourselves aboard," Calder replied.

Back on the pier, they found a dinghy from the *Tazeyar*. A couple of sailors readily agreed to take them out and return them to shore whenever they were ready.

Nadez stared back at the city as they were rowed away from the pier. It wasn't a view she'd seen in years, and the setting sun bathed the upper floors of the Hall with a golden light. The city looked peaceful. She hoped they were able to do enough to make sure it stayed that way all winter.

"I'LL HAVE COOK send your meal to your cabin," Rafael said when Calder stepped on board.

"Thank you," Calder replied. "When the First Mate has a moment, can you ask her to join us?"

"Aye, sir," Rafael said. He nodded and turned towards the bridge.

"This way," Calder said to his mother and Nadez. He led them down to his cabin. Someone had made sure that his cabin was clean. Every surface was spotless, and all of the charts and maps had been tucked away.

"Earlier, Darya reminded me of the pirate treasure," Nadez said. "You found it on Strongrock?"

"Dag did." He grinned. "After we surprised Tarmo Holt. We got there quickly by sailing through the Teeth, thanks to Dag. Holt stranded some sailors on land, and we figured that they had been looking for something."

"And Dagrun found the treasure?" Lauma asked. "Using her Trait?"

"Yes. That's where we picked up the children too, the ones we sent back here on the *Tazeyar*."

"I'm disgusted that children were left to fend for themselves in this city," Lauma said with a frown. "Both Nordmere and Swyford failed horribly. All orphaned children are being looked after properly now," she continued. "And I've made arrangements for families to get help before things get so bad that children are left to fend for themselves."

There was a knock on the door, and Calder opened it to a couple of sailors carrying serving dishes and tableware. They quickly laid everything out onto the table and left.

Nadez, Calder, and his mother sat down and helped themselves to cold beet soup and a savoury stew.

"You're certain that you can get back out through the Frozen Pass?" his mother asked. "That your Trait will keep you safe?"

"Yes," he replied, trying to sound more confident than he was.

"I hope you find the Holt girl," his mother said. "We need her in order to keep either Pinho or Ottosen from controlling Nordmere."

"I don't like that Ottosen can't be accused of trying to kill you," Calder said.

"If we have Saulia Holt on our side, we can make him pay in other ways," his mother said calmly. "The second attempt was clumsy. I don't think he'll try again."

"Two attempts on the life of the Grand Freeholder should be enough to put him in jail for treason," Calder said.

"There's no real evidence," Nadez said. "The assassin arrived on a ship along with goods being delivered to Ottosen, but there's nothing to say that Ottosen knew she was coming."

"Or that he was the person she met," his mother replied.

"I don't like it. The Grand Freeholder was the target, not you specifically. Rahm was horrified when he learned that you were the Grand Freeholder." Calder finished his meal and pushed his plate away. His mother was still in danger; he didn't like that he had to leave.

"I can't imagine Rahm being horrified about anything," his mother said. "Let alone about my safety. That man stopped caring about me a long time ago."

"Why do you think that?" Calder asked. He'd spent the day with his mother but had yet to broach the subject of his father's other family.

"I just knew," his mother said. "One time he returned from the Sapphire Sea and I knew. He'd found someone else or decided I wasn't the one to make him happy. I have never been sure what happened, but I knew something had."

"Would you want to be certain?" Calder asked.

His mother clutched his hand. "You know! Yes, I want the truth. I could never get that from your father. I want to know that a major decision I made was based on more than a hunch."

"More than a hunch," Calder said. "I think it was your Trait." He smiled sadly. "Dag said that Rahm has the most secrets of anyone she has ever met." He looked at his mother. "He found someone else. He has another family, one that does not know about us. I met a half-sister who was looking after a boat named *Hakon*."

"Hakon." His mother closed her eyes. "Yes, it was around that time when things really changed, although it was years before I stopped believing what he told me and listened to what my heart was saying." She sighed. "I am sorry that you have a sibling that is a stranger. I know growing up without being close to Yakop and Berna was hard on you."

"My expectations of my father were always very low," he said. "But I was the one who made the choice to leave home at a young age and stay away."

There was a knock on the door, and Calder rose to answer it. Darya entered, followed by two crew members. They placed a pot and some cups on the table before retrieving the plates and serving dishes.

"I hope you don't mind if I join you for tea?" Darya asked.

"Please sit," Calder said. She pulled up a chair, and he sat back down. "I owe you thanks for making the ship ready as well as retaining the crew."

"I know that time is not our friend," she said.

"You met the Master Intelligencer, Nadez Norup, earlier, I think." Darya nodded. "And this is Interim Grand Freeholder Lauma Strauskas, my mother. Meet First Mate Darya Demer."

"Did you meet my former husband as well?" Lauma asked. "Rahm?"

"Yes." Darya's eyes flicked from his mother to Calder and back to his mother. "I did. He was pretending to be a pirate."

"I suppose he is a pirate of sorts," Lauma said.

"He's a spy," Calder said. "And was one when he met you."

"I can't say that I'm surprised," Lauma said. "I always wondered where all the coin came from, and he never gave me a good answer. Well, we will not solve the problem of Rahm, but I would like some of that tea."

The rest of the conversation was light and soon word came that the *Atlaine* was ready to sail.

Calder helped his mother climb over the gunwale and down into the *Tazeyar*'s dinghy. He watched until the small boat was almost at the pier before heading to the bridge.

"Haul anchor!" he called. His order was relayed across the ship, and a moment later, he heard the sounds of the anchor being pulled in. As soon as he heard the all-clear, he turned his gaze to the path out of the harbour.

A couple of orders later and the *Atlaine* was sailing back

towards the Frozen Pass. If they made good time, if Luck was with him, he'd reach the meeting location, and Dag, in five or six days.

CHAPTER 18

DAG LOOKED BACK at Jaak and Saulia, who stood in front of the grass-covered cabin. No one waved; it wasn't a fond farewell. They were separating to go on dangerous journeys. Dag only hoped that hers, Inger's and Charis's was the more dangerous one and that Jaak and Saulia stayed safe.

Charis steered the little boat around the bend and then Jaak and Saulia were out of sight.

Now that there were only three of them, the sailboat skimmed across the shallow water. A few minutes later, they were sailing alongside the sandbar that hid this little cove. Dag stood up and, with one hand on the mast, scanned the path ahead.

Her Trait was quiet; no twinges or itchiness, nothing to indicate that there were any hidden dangers nearby.

"I don't see anything," she said to Charis.

"Good. I'll keep us close to the coast anyway," he said. "At least until we reach the old olive grove."

"All right." Dag remained where she was, staring out at the sea. After an hour, her eyes were tired, and she sat in the bow beside Inger.

"Did I ever tell you that I was sorry?" Inger asked. "For running away when you were on your first assignment? I had very good reasons for not wanting to be caught up in Joosep and Holt's schemes." Her sister sighed and reached for one of her hands. "But I didn't really consider how worried you would be, and I should have been *way* more grateful that you came after me." She looked away. "And I should have listened to you when you warned me about Ansdottir and Ursa."

"A Trait was being used on you," Dag said.

"And I knew that!" Inger met her eyes. "You told me you thought that was what was happening. And I ignored you."

"You still helped Calder and I escape," Dag said. "Despite being under Ansdottir's influence."

"I suppose so." Inger sighed and dropped her hand. "I just wish I hadn't made so many mistakes. And listen, I am not your problem to solve. I know I can't return to Tarklee or the Three. Once we make it to Messanos, I'll get off this boat and walk away."

"No," Dag said. "You're my sister. Whatever part you played in burning the shipyards and the ships, I know that Ansdottir was the one making the decisions. And that because of her Trait you had very little choice." She paused. How much of an unclear plan should she tell Inger? All of it, she decided. So her sister didn't do something rash or dangerous like walk away from her as soon as they reached Messanos.

She leaned close. "I have an idea," she said. "Charis doesn't know it yet, but he's going to help, as will Calder's father. I think you could manage the Merchant Adventurers office. And while you're doing that, you could spy for the Three."

"The Merchant Adventurers sounds good, but Dag, you know my Trait won't allow me to spy." Inger shook her head. "I'm far too literal for anything like that."

"You were," Dag agreed. "But I think that somehow Ansdottir's Trait changed yours. I think you see and understand underlying motives and issues in a way you never have before."

"You're wrong," Inger said. "My Trait works the same as it always has."

"Then how come you realized that I knew who the Resolute was?" she asked. "You never would have figured that out before."

"It was pretty obvious," Inger said. She paused and frowned. "You're saying that it wasn't at all obvious."

"That's exactly what I'm saying," Dag agreed. "And the fact that it was obvious to you means that somehow your Trait has changed. Perhaps as a result of being influenced by Ansdottir's, but I really don't care how it changed only that it has. Because it means there might be a place for you in Messanos." She didn't say she hoped that as an agent for the Three and that by working in service to the Fair Seas Treaty Alliance, Inger might prove her loyalty and eventually be allowed to return home. Too many other things depended on that.

"All right," Inger said. "I won't do anything until you have a chance to work out this plan of yours." She shrugged. "It's not as though I have anything else in mind."

"Good." Dag leaned over and hugged her twin. "This will work, I know it." She'd make it happen.

"We need to survive the next few days first," Inger said. She leaned away and smiled ruefully. "Something else that is obvious to me that might not have been before."

"Yes." Dag sighed. "We need to survive."

It was almost dusk by the time Charis steered them toward the inlet that led to the old olive grove. Once they were behind the stand of trees, he rolled the sail up and grabbed an oar and paddled them inland.

"Can we get to the dock by land and see if Pinho is there?" Dag asked.

"No." Charis shook his head. "That's one reason why I had Holt come here. Because of the marsh, the only access is by water, and if you don't know the channel, a ship can easily run aground."

"Would Pinho know someone who had been here before?" Dag asked. "This belonged to your family, but other people must know about it."

"It was never a secret," Charis replied. "Just abandoned because the groves died."

"We'll need to go slow," Dag said. "And be quiet in case Pinho is already here. But I need to know for certain what's happened to Holt and his wife."

Charis paddled them through the marsh, and Dag stared ahead, waiting for her Trait to activate. In the end it didn't, and the little boat made it to the small dock.

There were no ships at anchor, not even the *Neas*, and there was a whiff of smoke in the air.

"I need to look," Dag said. "To be sure." She turned to Inger. "Charis and I will go. You stay here with the boat." Normally, her sister would have argued, but when Dag met her eyes, all she saw was understanding that Dag still didn't trust Charis enough to leave him alone with their only means of travel. More evidence that Inger's Trait had changed.

Charis led the way up the hill. The front of the house looked almost intact, but the roof was missing and the door was off its hinges. Through the open doorway they could see the damage the fire had caused.

Furniture was charred and blackened, and drapes had burned away.

"Any bodies?" Dag asked.

"Not yet." Charis took a tentative step forward, testing the floor. When his second step went through a floorboard, he backed out. "We'll have to go around."

They found them out behind the house: half a dozen sailors along with Tarmo Holt and his wife Asla. They'd been rounded up into a circle and shot at close range.

"The rest must have been taken," Charis said. "Some of them were probably used to sail the *Neas* to wherever Pinho wants it."

"At least we're sure," Dag said. She didn't have a lot of sympathy for Tarmo Holt: he had planned to starve the Three for his own profit. His wife might not have had much say in her husband's actions, but she certainly had enjoyed the benefits of his underhanded dealings. And if these were his most loyal sailors, they too had probably been complicit.

"A small thing to be thankful for," Charis said. "And we know that Pinho is ahead of us."

"We hope," Dag said. "Let's go." She turned and went back to the boat.

"Did you find them?" Inger asked.

"Yes," Dag replied. "Holt and his wife and a few sailors. It looked like a quick death." She climbed into the boat and sat down. Charis got in after her, and she felt him push them away from the dock.

"It would have been me," Inger said quietly. "If you hadn't come to find me, it would have been me."

"Maybe," Dag said. "They would have taken Saulia alive, so they might have kept you alive too."

"I doubt it."

Dag nodded and stared at the bottom of the boat. She doubted it too.

NADEZ HURRIED DOWN the hallway towards the office of the

Grand Freeholder. She didn't bother knocking before sweeping through the half-open door.

Lauma Strauskas and Mykol both looked up at her.

"I'm glad you're here," Lauma said. "Mykol has some worrying news." She ushered them both into her inner office. Lauma didn't sit, instead she started pacing the small space, which worried Nadez even more than the cryptic message to come right away had.

"It's Ottosen," Lauma said. "Mykol, tell the Master Intelligencer what you told me."

"Clan Freeholder Ottosen has sent messages to all the Nordmere and Swyford Clan Freeholders," Mykol said. "Asking for their support to remove Lauma Strauskas from the Interim Grand Freeholder position and appoint him instead."

"I sent word to Byholt, of course," Lauma said. "With Captain Eklund and the *Tazeyar*. It will take a day or so to get there and the same for the ship to return with the Clan Freeholders."

"Does Ottosen have enough votes to remove you from office?" Nadez asked. "Nothing has changed since you were first appointed."

"He plans on using the Holt vote for himself," Lauma said. "Mykol heard that from someone within Ottosen's household."

Mykol nodded. "It's a trustworthy source," he said. "One who also wishes Saulia to inherit her father's freeholdings."

"Can Ottosen do that?" Nadez asked. "Holt has fled, but there are no formal accusations of treason against him." Lauma had deliberately not filed a charge against Holt; without Saulia as the heir, it would leave the Holt freeholdings at risk.

"He can if he has proof that Holt conspired against Nordmere," Lauma said. "The Nordmere Clan Freeholders can declare Holt a traitor to Nordmere and revoke his voting rights. The Alliance still must agree to allow someone else to vote in Holt's place. If Ottosen gets enough support from Swyford, they might be able to do it."

"Could they vote to hold the election right away?" Nadez asked. She didn't see anything else Swyford might get in return for supporting Ottosen.

"That's what I think they want," Lauma said. "But for that vote, I can insist that all Clan Freeholders are present."

"Will the Nordmerians try to permanently strip Holt's

freeholdings from him and his heir?” Nadez asked.

“No,” Lauma said. “There is a process that includes efforts to find the Clan Freeholder and their heir or proof that they are dead. Since there are very real reasons why we cannot officially send a ship to the Sapphire Sea in search of Holt and his family, they can’t do that at least until spring.”

“Officially,” Nadez said. She’d been watching Mykol, who had looked crestfallen when Lauma said there would be no search for Holt. “Then it’s a very good thing that we already have an unofficial search in progress.”

“Do you?” Mykol asked.

Lauma looked at Nadez and she nodded.

“We do,” Lauma said. “One of Nadez’s Intelligencers is already in the Sapphire Sea searching for Saulia and her family. My son is on his way to meet them and return them here before winter.”

“Will they find Saulia?” Mykol asked. “They have to find her.”

“My Intelligencer is the very best at finding anything,” Nadez replied. “I am certain Saulia will be found.” And she was: Dagrun Lund could find anything. But that didn’t mean Saulia would be found alive or that she could be convinced to return home. Although, based on Calder’s report, the dangers of home paled in comparison to the dangers Saulia and her family faced in the Sapphire Sea.

A relieved Mykol left, and Lauma finally relaxed enough to sit.

“You’ve made a decision,” Nadez said. “About how to stop this.”

“Yes,” Lauma said. “I do think that Ottosen plans to use Swyford’s desire—Clan Freeholder Timonis’s desire—to become Grand Freeholder to gain their votes.” She shrugged. “I will tell Timonis that if that happens, he will *never* be Grand Freeholder. The position he has been chasing for most of his adult life will be forever out of reach.”

“You’ll threaten to dissolve the Alliance.”

“Yes,” Lauma said. “I will threaten to dissolve the Fair Seas Treaty Alliance.”

Nadez blew out a breath. “If that’s the only way to ensure its continuance, then I guess you have to.”

“I would prefer the Alliance to survive,” Lauma said. “But I would rather dissolve it than have Byholt governed by Ottosen.”

“I’m certain that Timonis will see that in your face,” Nadez said. She could see it. She just hoped it didn't come to that. People would suffer if the Alliance was dissolved. And since she worked for the Alliance, she would no longer be in a position to help many of them.

DESPITE THE COLD air, the sea was calm when Calder stared out at the Frozen Pass. They'd made excellent time overnight and had reached the Pass far sooner than expected, just after dawn. Then the strong winds that had propelled them here had suddenly died, making the journey through the Frozen Pass as safe as it could be now that ice had started stretching out from the shore.

His Luck seemed to be helping them, and he'd given the order to head straight into the narrow gap between the Frozen North and the rocky shore of Ostland.

Now they were nearing the halfway point. A fine mist drifted up off the water into the colder air, and the ropes were accumulating a thin coating of ice.

"Keep those lines clear!" he called.

Sailors rapped on the lines, and ice cracked and showered onto the deck.

The single sail puffed out as wind caught it, pushing them forward. Calder looked off the starboard railing and recognized a rocky outcrop. They were two thirds of the way through now.

"I'll be glad to come back through the Teeth," Rafael said from his side. He blew on his hands before shoving them under his arms. "It's just as harrowing, but at least it's warm."

"It is that," Calder replied. He would be happy to come back through the Teeth too. That would mean he'd found Dag safe and sound.

He tried not to worry about her. She was well-trained and had a formidable Trait but still, she was only a few months out of training. And he loved her. It was hard not to worry.

"Port three degrees," he said.

"Aye, sir." Darya moved the wheel slightly, and the ship pointed towards port.

He requested a few more minor direction changes as they crawled their way past ice on their port side. Finally, the call came that they were out, and a cheer went up.

Calder relaxed and shared a smile with Darya and Rafael.

"You two go get warm and fed," he said. "I'll take the wheel."

"Yes, sir," Rafael replied. "I'll relieve you in an hour."

"Thank you."

The two had barely left before the wind suddenly picked up. He called for the sails and soon they were skimming south. He set a course to keep them well away from Strongrock. By the time Rafael returned to take the wheel, they'd left the Frozen Pass far behind them.

His Trait was definitely helping him get back to the Sapphire Sea. But as always, he wondered if it was a good thing.

"WE SHOULD STOP for the night," Charis said.

It was the first time any of them had spoken since leaving the old olive grove and the bodies of Tarmo Holt and his wife.

"I'll find us a safe place," Dag said. From the bow she'd been scanning for any hint of Pinho's ship. Now she moved over to the right gunwale so she could study the shore.

Half an hour later, she directed Charis towards a spot where rocks rose directly up to a stand of trees. In behind them, a narrow inlet led to a pebbled beach.

Inger helped Charis lower the sail while Dag kept watch, but she didn't see any ships or boats on the sea. Charis jumped out and waded to shore, pulling the little craft behind him. He tied them up to a tree.

"It's too rocky to pull the boat up on shore," he said as he waded back out to them. "I'll have to tie it up so it floats in one place." He went to the stern, grabbed a second rope, and headed back to shore.

"Come on," Inger said. She climbed out of the boat into knee-deep water, and Dag joined her.

"We need to find something to eat," Inger said, pulling her towards the beach. "Charis, do you think there are any fish here?"

Charis had tied the second rope to another tree, keeping the sailboat safely away from the rocks. "We're on water," Charis said. "I'll catch something."

"Thanks," Inger replied. "We'll get a fire ready."

Once they reached the trees, Inger stopped and faced her.

"I know you feel bad about Holt," she said. "I do too. I feel even worse for his wife."

"Me too," Dag replied. "Tarmo Holt did some terrible things." Dag sighed and looked over at Charis. He was using some rope and making what looked like a net. "Things that still might cause misery and illness and death for people whose wellbeing he should have been protecting. And he did it for coin and power. His wife might not have known the extent of his offences, but she probably knew enough. So, I'm not mourning them, not really." She looked at Charis again. He wanted the token to go to Rahm, but that didn't mean she trusted him with their only way to reach Messanos. "But I'm the one who will have to tell Saulia." She would also have to confirm their deaths in Tarklee so that Saulia could inherit her father's Clan Freehold.

"Saulia knows that her father did some horrible things," Inger said. "I can tell her he's dead if you want. She'll mourn her mother more, but I heard them argue. Asla Holt knew much of what her husband was doing and was more than willing to enjoy the riches his actions provided them. She blamed him because his plans didn't work out and they were all in danger, not for putting his profits and her family's comforts above other people's misery." Inger smiled sadly. "I guess my Trait really has changed. I didn't know I knew all of that, but it's true."

"Thanks," Dag said. "It's what I thought, but it was still hard to see them dead." She had never seen people killed for revenge, or because they were in the way or whatever reason Fihaldo Pinho had for killing the Holts.

"I saw far too many deaths when I was with the pirates," Inger said. "I was on board when we took a ship. I didn't kill anyone with my own hands or gun, but I was responsible for their deaths just the same. It's not something I'm proud of." She met Dag's eyes. "I saw you watching Charis," she said quietly. "Don't forget that he was with the pirates too. We're right not to trust him." Inger laughed. "My Trait really is different."

"I like it," Dag replied. "We don't argue nearly as much as we used to. And I don't trust Charis, nor does he trust me. We'll see what happens when I give the token to Rahm." She didn't need Charis's trust, but she would like his help to set Inger up with work and a life in Messanos. It was the least he could do for the people who helped restore the Arressan Council to power. As long as that was what happened.

"You collect stones for a fire pit, and I'll find something to burn," she said to Inger.

"All right," Inger agreed. "I'll keep an eye on Charis while you check for any Hidden dangers.”

“That’s what I said,” Dag replied and grinned. She was still grinning when she left the beach behind and entered the woods.

Nothing in the woods triggered her Trait, so with an armful of fallen tree limbs, Dag stepped back onto the beach. Inger waved to her from where she sat on a dead tree.

Dag dropped her burden beside a ring of rocks and sat down beside her twin.

“Has Charis had any luck? I’m hungry.” The moment she said the word Luck she thought about Calder. She hoped he was on his way back: hoped that Jaak and Saulia were able to meet him at the village in Pilalia.

“He caught two fish,” Inger said. “He tied them to the boat somehow and went back for more.”

“Good.” She spotted him wading through the surf, coming their way. “It looks like he did catch more.” She leaned over and pushed two flatter rocks into the middle of the circle and filled in the space between them and the rest of the rocks with kindling.

She dug a flint from her pocket, and by the time Charis arrived with the cleaned and fileted fish, the fire was burning steadily.

They cooked and ate quickly. Dag doused the fire with water from the sea almost as soon as they were finished. It was almost dark, and they had no way of knowing if Pinho was somewhere along the coast.

He would be searching for them; she was sure of that. His plans for taking control of land in Nordmere depended on him finding Saulia Holt. He would know that someone had come and taken her away: he might even know it was her. Holt and his wife knew her name, but his whole party knew Inger and would have recognized her as Inger’s twin.

“I’ll take first watch,” she said. Inger offered to take the second watch, leaving the last one to Charis.

Her watch was uneventful, and finally, it was time to wake Inger.

“Wake me just before you wake Charis,” she said. Inger nodded, and Dag lay down for a few hours of sleep.

After Inger woke her, Dag pretended to be asleep while her sister roused Charis for his turn at watch. It took all of her effort, but she stayed awake throughout his watch. He didn’t try to steal away in the night and strand them without a boat, but that didn’t mean she trusted him.

The birds were singing when she finally sat up and stretched, ready for a day that should see them in Messanos. Meeting with Rahm the Resolute.

CHAPTER 19

GUSTAV WANDERED PAST the alley for a second time, just to be sure. The second plank from the left on the fence at the end of the alley was out of place. It was the signal.

He kept on the path he was on but turned left at the next street. A few steps later, he slipped between two ramshackle buildings. He paused for a moment to make sure no one was following him before edging between the buildings. He slid the door aside and crawled inside.

"Over here."

He followed the voice to the corner, where slivers of light filtered in through gaps up near the roofline.

Nadez Norup sat with her back to the wall. She rose and stretched.

"I'm glad you came," she said.

"I check each signal every day," Gustav replied. "Just like you told me to."

"I appreciate it." Nadez pulled a small, flat pouch from beneath her shirt. "I need you to take this to Clan Freeholder Timonis. It's from Lauma Strauskas, warning that if he follows Ottosen's lead and votes to remove her from the position of Grand Freeholder, she will dissolve the Fair Seas Treaty Alliance."

Gustav stared at the pouch. "We can't let her do that," he said. "It will be bad for everyone if the Treaty is destroyed."

"I know," Nadez replied. "Lauma would prefer to remain in the Three, but she's not willing to let Ottosen harm her people." Nadez sighed. "She hopes that by threatening to take away Timonis's chance to be Grand Freeholder, he will allow her to serve until the crisis is resolved."

"She's buying time," Gustav said. "Waiting for Saulia Holt to arrive?" Nadez stared at him, and he shrugged. "Calder told me that Dagrun was looking for both Saulia and her sister Inger. It sounded as though whoever had Saulia would control her father's freeholdings."

"Yes. For Saulia's sake, let's hope we find her first." She pushed the pouch against his chest so that he was forced to grab it. "If we don't, then this will not be an idle threat. Lauma is even less willing to have a Pilalian use a foothold in Nordmere to take over the Three."

"A Pilalian? Is that who is after Saulia?"

"Yes," Nadez said. "A Pilalian who we believe worked with Ottosen to manipulate Tarmo Holt. We think he's trying to gain control over Holt's freeholdings."

"Through Saulia." Gustav sighed. "Lauma must think this Pilalian is worse than dissolving the Treaty."

"As do I," Nadez said, and Gustav looked at her in surprise.

"But that would mean the end of the Intelligencers," he said. "How can you support that?"

"We Intelligencers let all of this happen right under our noses," she said. "If we can't fix it, then maybe we don't deserve to exist as an organization."

"But that was Joosep." Gustav hated to talk ill of the dead, but the more he learned, the more he realized how many mistakes Joosep had made.

"It was also me," Nadez replied. "I walked away even though I knew that Joosep's approach was wrong. What I failed to understand was that it was also dangerous. Joosep never questioned any of the Grand Freeholders he worked under. He simply followed their direction."

"Aren't you just following Lauma's directions?" He waved the pouch at her. "By going along with this?"

"I talked her out of dissolving the Treaty once," Nadez said. "But then we learned of a new threat from Ottosen and this Pilalian. You're the one who told me that Swyford is taking little to no action to ensure that their people are fed this winter. Should Lauma allow Timonis, once he's confirmed as Grand Freeholder, to appropriate the food that she and her people have been diligently stockpiling and distribute it to save his own people?"

"He wouldn't—" Gustav stopped. "Of course, he would. All right. I will deliver your message. I assume that I need to take the road."

"Yes. If Timonis happens to arrive by ship, Lauma will give him his message in person." Nadez gave him a sad smile. "For all our sakes, let's hope he listens. Safe travels." She placed a hand on his shoulder and squeezed as she went past him and out the door.

Gustav stared at the pouch before tucking it inside his coat. If Clan Freeholder Timonis was elected Grand Freeholder and Lauma Strauskas withdrew Byholt and all of their resources from the Alliance, Tarklee would be a terrible place this winter.

People in the city were already at the edge of starvation; when they were pushed over the edge there would be riots and fights over the little food that was here. How could the Clan Freeholders not know that? They probably assumed that they and their households would be safe, but they were wrong.

All it would take was a single rumour, true or not, that they had food and starving and desperate people would leave the city and descend on the Clan Freeholders. So no, none of them would be safe.

He waited a few more minutes before leaving to find some travel rations and then go south, to the road that led to Timonis's freehold.

THEY PASSED THE hidden inlet that led to the secret cabin in the woods just after noon. Dag marked it to herself but didn't mention it to Inger or Charis.

She'd been worried that Pinho might have assigned guards, or worse, that he himself was there making sure the token was still safe.

But if the disappearance of the Resolute's token had been discovered, there was no sign of it. No guards, no ship, no dinghies or smaller boats.

Now the sun was starting to set, and she thought she saw lights far ahead.

"I think we're almost there," she said to Charis.

Inger looked up from where she'd been dozing against the mast.

"That's Messanos," Charis agreed. "I'll need you to navigate when we get closer."

Dag nodded. No doubt the route that led to where Rahm kept his boat was hard to see from here, but she trusted that her Trait would show her the way.

And it did. She pointed, and Charis sailed the little boat between two long docks. The docks ended at land, but a narrow slice of water led deeper into the city. Charis rolled up the sail and slowly paddled them through the channel.

Finally, Dag recognized the dock she and Jaak had left from.

"There," she said. As soon as the sailboat was close enough, she hopped out onto the dock. She held onto the boat while Inger and Charis got out. Charis tied the boat up before stepping back into it.

"Leave it," a woman said as she walked up to them. "I'll look after the sail myself."

Charis jumped back onto the dock, and by the time the woman stopped a few feet away, Dag, Inger, and Charis were facing her.

"I'd like to see Rahm," Dag said. "And thank him for the use of the *Hakon*."

"He's busy," the young woman said. "I will convey your thanks to him. I'm grateful that you returned the sailboat. I really didn't expect to see it again." She turned to leave.

"I know who Hakon was," Dag said. "Even though you don't. I must see Rahm. Tell him that the sailboat isn't the only thing I wish to return to him."

The woman turned back and frowned. "Why should I believe that you know who Hakon was?"

"Because you know Rahm has secrets," Dag replied. "Secrets he doesn't even tell his daughter. Rahm knows I'm very good at uncovering secrets. He'll want to see me."

The woman shrugged. "I will tell him. If you're wrong, you'll regret it, not me." She turned and walked away from them.

"Should we wait here?" Inger asked. She looked around. "What if Pinho has people watching this dock?"

"Rahm can find us," Dag said. "Charis? Do you know somewhere close where we can wait?"

"Yes, it's safe and we can get a meal." He led the way off the dock and into the town.

Charis stopped in front of a dingy hut that Dag was certain was much closer to the dock than the route he'd taken them would have her think.

He knocked on the door, and it opened a crack.

"Get in," a grizzled man said. He pulled Charis forward and wrapped him in a hug. Dag edged past the two men into a dimly lit room. It was a tavern of sorts, but more subdued than any tavern she'd been in before. The half dozen patrons sat quietly around three tables, tankards or mugs in front of them. A few grunted or nodded at Charis, but no one spoke.

"We'll be safe enough here," Charis said. He ushered them to the only unoccupied table and sat down. "It's a sanctuary house: a place where anyone can eat and drink without fear. I spent some time here since," he lowered his voice. "Since Pinho took control of the council."

The man who had greeted Charis returned with a tray laden with food and a pot of tea.

"Thank you," Dag said. He nodded and left without saying a word. "Who is he?"

"Names are not used here," Charis said. "He provides sanctuary, and anyone who comes here pays a high price for it." He pushed a plate of smoked salmon toward her. "Let's eat, and then if your friend does not find us, at least we'll be fed when we look for a place to spend the night."

The platters were almost empty when the door opened. Even though no one had been speaking, the room became even quieter.

Dag looked up to see Rahm standing in the doorway.

"He's here," she whispered to Inger and Charis, but Rahm had already taken the two steps to their table. He dragged a chair from another table and sat down. He ignored Inger and Charis and instead focussed his gaze on Dag.

"Being important to my son will not save you from my anger," he said to her. "No one talks about Hakon, ever."

"I needed your attention," Dag said with a calmness that she didn't feel. "I have something that I believe belongs to you." She leaned closer to him. "Resolute."

His eyes narrowed, and she knew she was right. Calder's father was a high-level assassin.

"I know what you have," he said. "I knew the minute it arrived in the city. It's how I tracked you here. Where did you find it?"

"In a cabin in the woods," she said. "It was very well hidden. Even with my Trait, I had some difficulty uncovering it." She sat back. "I am quite certain it was put there by Fihaldo Pinho. And you just confirmed that it belongs to you."

Rahm laughed, and the rest of the people in the room seemed to shrink in on themselves. Two men near the door scurried out it, and everyone else stared down at their drinks.

"You'll be forgiven for threatening to tell my daughter about Hakon," he said. "If you return to me what is mine."

"We want you to fulfil the original contract," Charis said, and Rahm looked at him for the first time. "The agreement you struck with the Arressan Council."

"Does he hold what is mine?" Rahm asked, turning back to Dag. "Should I be dealing with him?"

"I have it," Dag said. "But his request is also my request." She reached into her pocket and grabbed the token. She put her hand flat on the table, the token under it, and slid it across the table. She lifted one side of her hand, and Rahm slid his hand under hers, taking the token away. He slipped his hand below the table.

"I will do what you ask," he said and sighed. The smile he gave her had no humour in it. "Your request will be fulfilled as soon as possible." He stood up then paused to look at her. "My son has found himself a formidable woman. May he have more fortune with you than I had with his mother."

He left, and Dag let out a big breath.

"Out. Now." The man who ran the sanctuary stood over them, glaring. "None of you are welcome here ever again. Out."

Dag rose and followed Charis out the door, Inger right behind her.

"I thought it was a sanctuary?" Inger asked. "Why did he kick us out?"

"I didn't expect that," Charis said. "But Rahm does not look like a man who would observe the rules of a sanctuary."

"Or any rules at all," Dag replied. How would Calder take it when she told him that his father was an assassin?

"He's practically family," Inger said. "Now that you and Calder are so close." She linked her arm. "But I don't think he should be invited to any family gatherings."

"Are you going to tell him he can't attend?" Dag asked. She shook her head. "Come on. We need to find a safe place to wait for Calder. He should be here in a few days."

Chapter 20

NADEZ WATCHED A couple of merchants close up their shops and hurry away before she stepped into the street.

In the days since she'd sent Gustav off to Swyford, she'd taken to wandering the streets and alleys of the city, looking for signs of unrest or anger or anything that might give her warning that Ottosen intended to use the citizens of the city in a plan or diversion that would somehow allow him to seize control.

At least that's what she tried to tell herself she was doing.

In reality, now that she was the only Intelligencer in all of Tarklee, she felt ineffective and defenceless. So, she wandered the city making sure that all her old safe hiding places were secure in case . . . she wasn't sure what she expected to happen. That was one of the problems.

The Fair Seas Treaty Alliance seemed to be in peril on so many different fronts that she had no idea what might happen. And no real way to counter any of the threats.

After making sure she wasn't being watched, she rounded the corner to the small stable that was her first and most personal hideout.

She slid the wooden plank aside and entered the dark space. But she was so restless that no sooner had she entered, she turned and left.

Her path through the streets eventually took her to the

harbour. Fishing boats and barges were tied up along the docks close to shore, quiet at this time of the day.

Not that the barges were busy even in daylight. There had been a flurry of activity when the *Atlaine* and *Tazeyar* had arrived with full holds, but those goods had already been dispatched to warehouses throughout the city.

Farther out, the harbour was empty. Lauma had sent the *Tazeyar* north to collect the Byholter Clan Freeholders. If they made good time, they would be here tomorrow. Only after the Byholters had been delivered would the *Tazeyar* go south for the Swyfordians: and Clan Freeholder Timonis.

Nadez hoped Gustav was able to deliver his message to Timonis first. He was Swyfordian and had been part of the successful rebuilding of the shipyards, an enterprise that Timonis received much of his wealth and power from. Timonis might actually listen to him. And she knew that Gustav took Lauma's threat to dissolve the Alliance seriously.

When all of the Clan Freeholders were in Tarklee, the full council would meet.

And either Lauma would remain Interim Grand Freeholder or the Fair Seas Treaty Alliance would be broken.

Nadez sighed as she looked out at the far too empty harbour. She knew it was days and days too soon to expect Calder to return with Saulia Holt, but she wished to see him sail into view all the same.

She turned and headed away from the harbour. It was time to visit Lauma.

Even this late at night, the lights glowed in the Grand Freeholder's office.

"Mykol," she said when she entered the outer office. "I am surprised to see you here this late. I assume the Grand Freeholder is still here as well?"

"Yes, Master Intelligencer," Mykol said. "I'm sure she will appreciate the interruption." He gestured to the closed door. "I feel that we're both just waiting for something to happen."

"As am I," Nadez replied. But were they all hoping for the same thing?

She knocked on the door and opened it, and Lauma glanced up at her. Papers covered the desk in front of her, and she looked tired.

"Come in," Lauma said. "And join me in my futile search for anything that might help me delay Ottosen from convening a partial council meeting." She gestured to the papers on her desk. "Notes from every single Treaty Alliance council meeting since its inception. I have not been able to find anything to help me, but perhaps you will see something I have missed."

"That seems a better use of my time than what I've been doing," Nadez said. She shut the door and pulled up a chair.

"Which is what?" Lauma asked.

"Wandering through the city and hoping to stumble across anything that might cause us trouble," Nadez said. "Like you, I had no luck."

"Not finding trouble is preferable to finding it." Lauma reached behind her and pulled a stack of documents from a shelf. "Here, you look through these older notes while I finish up with the records from the last twenty years."

Nadez took the stack of papers from her. "What am I looking for?"

"Anything that might set a precedent for requiring a full council to make certain decisions," Lauma replied. "I know that the Treaty stipulates that partial council decisions are binding as long as every Clan Freeholder has been notified of the meeting. Ottosen is trying to say that the notification is enough: that we do not have to allow time for a response."

"That's why you sent the *Tazeyar* to Byholt first," Nadez said. "Ottosen cannot call a meeting until we can reasonably assume Swyford has been notified."

"Yes," Lauma agreed. "It buys us a few days at most. I fear that one day after the *Tazeyar* leaves for Swyford, Ottosen will insist on holding the meeting. With Holt missing and all but two of the Swyfordians absent, all he needs is a single Swyfordian Clan Freeholder to side with him and he will have enough votes to remove me."

"I assume you have spoken to the Swyfordians in the city," Nadez said.

"Yes. Clan Freeholder Skala has been reasonable. He lives in the city and was here when the riots started. The other," Lauma paused. "Clan Freeholder Nowak is angry that I have not yet called for an election. I fear that I need to have Timonis's backing before she will vote in my favour."

"Let's assume that Timonis is convinced to back you," Nadez said. "I have great faith in Gustav's ability to plead your case."

"I do too," Lauma said. "I just hope we can find some way to make sure the meeting doesn't happen until all council members are present."

"Then let's look," Nadez said. She pulled the stack of papers closer. The top one was dated just over twenty years ago. She recognized a few of the names of the council members in attendance, including Henrik Ottosen. Briefly, she wished that Dagrun Lund was here. No doubt her Trait would uncover a handful of things that could be helpful.

Nadez finished searching through her stack of papers and set them aside.

"Here," Lauma said. "Take these. I have the ones from the inception of the Alliance through the first twenty years. These are from the meetings that led to the agreement."

Nadez took the stack of notes. The papers were brittle, and the ink had faded. Some of the Clan Freeholder last names were familiar but more were not; evidence that fortunes had been lost by some and gained by others since the Treaty had been signed.

She rubbed her eyes as she peered down at the faded script. It was late and she was tired, but something about this tugged at her.

She brought the document closer to the lamp. She could hardly make out the words but— "I think I found something," she said. "I can't make out every word." She handed the page to Lauma. "You try."

Lauma peered down at the text, frowning. Suddenly, she smiled. "Yes, this will do it. *"Only a meeting that includes every single council member,"* she read out loud. *"Either in person or by proxy, will be considered valid in the event that one or more members of the Alliance wishes to make a change to this agreement and a majority of each country must agree to any such change. In the event that a member country wishes to withdraw from the Treaty, the majority of the withdrawing country is all that is required."*

Lauma blew out a breath. "Through Gustav I am already informing Swyford of my potential decision," she said. "I will discuss this with my son and the rest of the Byholters once they arrive. If Ottosen threatens to hold the meeting, I will tell him and his fellow Nordmerians that I want to discuss dissolving the treaty." She smoothed a hand across the paper in front of her and grinned. "Thank you for finding this, Nadez." She rose with the paper in hand. "Now I suggest we both get some sleep."

"I am more than willing to find my bed," Nadez said. As she followed Lauma out of her office, she hoped that she hadn't just helped her end the Fair Seas Treaty Alliance.

CHAPTER 21

CALDER LOOKED THROUGH the spyglass. The small village seemed quiet. Was that because there was nothing to worry about or because enemies were hiding, waiting for them to land?

If Dag was here, and able to, she would have signalled him by now. Something was wrong.

"Rafael," he said. "You're with me. First Mate, you have the ship." He nodded to Darya and headed to starboard, where the ship hid the fact that a dinghy had already been lowered into the sea.

"You said that you know this village?" he asked Rafael when he joined him in the dinghy.

"Yes," Rafael said. "It's called Redreef, after the red spice they harvest from plants that grow on the sand dunes farther inland."

"Will you be recognized as a friendly face?"

"I don't see why not," Rafael said. "It's been a few years since I was here trading with my uncle, but he still comes this way. He's known up and down the coast as a fair trader."

"Good. I'll row and you will ask around for Dag and Jaak." He sat down at the oars and Rafael sat in the stern, facing him.

In a few moments, Calder was rowing them towards shore.

"Tell me when someone comes to investigate," Calder said.

"There's a man on the beach," Rafael said. "He looks rather nervous. Oh, he has a pistol." Rafael raised his hands over his head.

"Hello," Rafael called out in Pilalian. "We have no weapons and mean you no harm. We were separated from some friends and are hoping to reunite with them here. Can we come ashore?"

"State your name," the man called out. "Or go back to your ship."

"Rafael Machado," he called out. "I used to sail with my uncle Adao Machado, and we often stopped here to trade for spices."

"Adao Machado? I know him as a fair man. Come closer."

"He's lowered his weapon," Rafael said to Calder. "I think that is a good sign."

"He recognized your uncle's name," Calder said. "I take *that* as a good sign." The pistol was not. Had they used weapons against Dag? Her Trait wouldn't let her walk into danger. At least he hoped it wouldn't. But she was travelling with her sister: it was possible their Traits cancelled each other out.

"Stand up," the man on shore called out.

Rafael stood up, balancing as the dinghy was rocked by a gentle surf. "If there is anyone here who was selling spices four years ago, I urge you to fetch them to verify me," Rafael said.

"No need," the man on shore said. "I recognize you. You are who you say you are: the nephew of Adao Machado." He gave a sharp whistle. "You may land on the beach."

"Thank you," Rafael said and sat down.

Calder took three more strokes and then the bottom of the dinghy scraped sand. He pulled the oars in and jumped into knee-deep water, and Rafael followed him. Together, they pulled the dinghy up onto the beach.

"We have what you are looking for," the man said. "I ask that you take it and leave immediately."

"Yes," Rafael said.

Calder stepped past the man, searching for . . . there. "Jaak!" he called out. Jaak had just stepped out from behind a house. A young woman he assumed was Saulia Holt was at his side. Calder's smile faded when he saw the pistol pointed at Jaak's back.

His heart clenched. There was no sign of Dag or Inger. Where were they? Jaak nodded at him and then shook his head, leaving Calder to wonder what he was trying to tell him.

"Back in your boat," the man on shore said. "All of you."

Calder ignored him; all of his attention focussed on Jaak.

"Where is she?"

"She's not here," Jaak said. "But she was fine when we parted ways."

"Stop talking and get off our beach," the man said. He pointed his pistol at Calder, who stared back at him.

For a moment Calder was tempted to force the man to make a decision. He'd been fired on at close range more than once before. Each time something had gone wrong and he hadn't been hit, but Luck was such a chancy thing to trust in. One time he'd been so certain of his Trait that he'd forced a man to shoot at him. The bullet hadn't struck him, but an innocent bystander hadn't been so Lucky.

"She's not here," Jaak said when he reached him. "But I know where she went."

"All right." Calder walked backwards, keeping the pistol between him and Jaak, Rafael, and Saulia.

"We're in," Rafael called.

"We will return to my ship and do as you ask," Calder said. "And leave."

"Go now before I change my mind," the man said.

Calder waded out to the dinghy and pushed it out past the surf. Rafael already had the oars in the water and was turning the dinghy around. Calder hoisted himself into the stern. He sat facing land while Rafael rowed them towards the *Atlaine*.

"Can't tell you how glad I am to be back at sea," Jaak said. The smile dropped from his face when Calder turned and glared at him.

"It was her idea," Jaak said. "Splitting up. We found her sister and Holt. This here's Saulia Holt." He gestured to her. "She found something else too, something she wanted to return to its owner. So she went back to Messanos. Said she was planning on returning your Da's boat to him."

"She can't sail," Calder said.

"Oh right, you don't know," Jaak said. "We met up with Charis too. He went with them."

"Charis?" Calder had forgotten that Dag had seen him on the *Neas*. "And she trusted him?"

"Enough," Jaak said. He looked up, and Calder followed his eyes. They'd reached the *Atlaine*. "The rest of the tale would be better told in private," he said. "And I'm sure Saulia and I wouldn't mind something other than dried fish to eat."

"We'll talk in my cabin," Calder said. "After I ask the First Mate to set sail for Messanos."

DAG SIGHED AND pulled a card. She was terrible at ludus, and Inger wasn't much better, but besides sleeping, there was nothing else to help the time pass.

After her talk with Rahm, Charis had led them to this small apartment. It was part of a network of safe places that the old Arressan Council had created. It reminded Dag of the apartment she'd shared with Joosep, Arnor, and Gustav. A small place with a water supply, a privy, and a stock of dried rations.

Sadly, it also reminded her that two of the people she'd shared that space with were dead.

"Ludus," she said softly, laying her cards down.

"I quit." Inger grabbed all the cards and stacked them before rolling over and stretching out on the floor. "When did Charis say he'd return? I'm almost hungry enough to eat the salt fish."

"He hoped to be back by midday," Dag said, pushing away her worry. He'd left yesterday evening, and it was now close to sunset. They'd slept all day yesterday, and after a meal of smoked fish, Charis had left to search out any of his contacts who might still be able to help him. Dag had also tasked him with finding out if a position at the Merchant Adventurers could be arranged for Inger. She hoped that task didn't prove too dangerous.

"He's asking about me too, isn't he?" Inger asked. "I know that he's looking for news of Pinho, but you also asked him to inquire about me."

Dag sighed. She was still getting used to Inger being able to recognize things that were Hidden. "I asked him to see what can be done at the Merchant Adventurers office," she said.

"Thank you." Inger was quiet for a moment. "Even if it doesn't happen, I can't tell you how much I appreciate you trying. I know I ruined my old life and part of yours along with it. And yet you came after me, saved me from death, and now you're still helping me. I'm not sure I deserve it but thank you."

"Of course, you deserve it," Dag said. "You're—" There was a noise at the door. She relaxed when she recognized the signal.

She hurried over and rapped the response. As soon as Charis replied, she unlatched the door and let him in.

"Fresh fish and some peaches," he said as he put a basket down on the table. "And news."

"Peaches first," Inger said. She tossed one to Dag and bit into a second.

"News first," Dag said.

"Pinho has fled the city," Charis said and grinned. "Yesterday, he left in a hurry with his family: his wife, brother and sister-in-law, and all of their children."

"You think he heard about Rahm?" Dag asked. "How is that possible?"

Charis shrugged. "Perhaps someone from the sanctuary saw a way to make some coin. Doing Pinho's bidding in an attempt to earn back his token must have been frustrating. Maybe Rahm wanted him to know? Maybe he wants Pinho to be afraid? But Pinho is gone. What remains of the Arressan council is meeting this evening. I've been asked to attend. I'd like the two of you there as well."

"Is this about me?" Inger asked. "At the council?"

"Yes," Charis said. "There will never be a better time to ask the council to reward those who helped rid Arressa of Pinho. Eat up, we'll need to leave soon."

It was dark by the time Charis led them to a sturdy stone building. A lamp hung over the door, and when Charis knocked, an Arressan woman answered.

"The council will be ready for you in a few minutes," she said as she ushered them into a waiting room. "I'll come and get you when it's time."

Dag wandered around the small room before stopping in front of Charis. "Does this mean that we can ask the council directly for a position for Inger at the Merchant Adventurers?"

"Yes," Charis replied. "As long as there is a position. The office was closed when I went there today."

"I think the position of Administrator is available," Dag said. "I have good reason to believe that the current Administrator, a man by the name of Aki Thorsen, has been working for Pinho. I think Inger would make a very good Administrator; one with the complete trust of the Fair Seas Treaty Alliance."

"I could do that," Inger said. "I wouldn't expect to be very busy until more ships are built. That would give me time to learn what's required and practice my Arressan."

A door opened, and the woman who had greeted them leaned through it. "The council will see you now."

Dag followed Charis through the door, Inger behind her.

Three men and a woman sat around a table that could accommodate three times that number. Charis stopped and gave a quick bow.

"Charis Diakos," one of the men said. "Thank you for your service."

"And for not giving up when all looked lost," the woman said. "You have been notified of your reward: Arressan lands Pinho had bought this past year. Are we to understand that this is not adequate?"

"I do not ask for me, esteemed Councillors. I ask for my friends from the Fair Seas Treaty Alliance. Without them, Pinho would not have been chased away."

"I would reward anyone who helped," the first man said. "But what can we do for them?"

"Inger Lund would like to be appointed Administrator for the Merchant Adventurers in Messanos," Charis said. "I am told she would have the trust of the Fair Seas Treaty Alliance."

"That can be done," the councillor said. "Does someone speak for the Three?"

"I do." Dag pulled out her patch. "I am an agent of the Fair Seas Treaty Alliance and speak for them in this matter."

"Done," the woman said. "And with our thanks. Charis Diakos, we will leave it to you to get this matter settled. I'm sure you realize that we have many other things to manage."

"Thank you," Charis said.

He turned and grinned at Dag while gesturing for them all to leave.

They were outside the building in moments.

"That's it?" Dag asked. "It's done?"

"There will be some details to sort out," Charis said.

"Like removing the current Administrator," Inger said.

"And the official notice will likely take a day or so," Charis continued. "But yes, that's it. Come on. We will have much better accommodations tonight."

CALDER STARED OUT at the city of Messanos, hoping with all his heart that Dag was there.

Was his father? The man Jaak claimed was one of the most dangerous assassins, a Resolute.

When Jaak explained that Dag thought his father was an elite assassin, he hadn't questioned it for a moment: that piece of information made everything else make sense.

His father's amusement at his role as an Intelligencer; his second family; his different roles every time Calder crossed paths with him, all those things now made sense.

Dag had warned him that Rahm had more secrets than anyone she'd ever met before. He trusted her and her Trait. So, he wasn't really surprised.

"Ready to go ashore," Darya said.

"Let's go. Second Mate," he said to Rafael. "The *Atlaine* is yours until we return."

Jaak looked up from one set of oars when he stepped into the dinghy. He nodded. Jaak was going to accompany him to the dock where his father kept the *Hakon*. Neither of them wanted to go alone, and Calder hadn't burdened Darya with the information about his father.

"Where to first, sir?" Darya asked.

"The Merchant Adventurer's office," he said. As much as he wanted—*needed*—to find Dag, his priority was still filling the hold so they could feed the people of the Three. Without his father's influence, Calder was hoping that the Administrator would help this time. If they couldn't find Dag; he closed his eyes. Without Dag they would have to trust his Luck to get them back through the Frozen Pass safely.

There was a different feel to the streets as he led the way to the Merchant Adventurers. There were more people on the docks and more smiles and jokes being called out.

He rapped on the door to the office and leaned inside, and his heart stuttered. Dag! No, it wasn't Dag, but it was almost as good.

"Inger!" He swept her into his arms. "I am very glad to see you."

"Dag said you might be here today." Inger stepped away from him. "I am so very sorry for all of the grief I caused you."

"I'll forgive you anything if you tell me that your sister is well."

"I'll tell you myself."

Calder turned to find Dag smiling at him. She stepped into his open arms, and he sighed into her hair.

"I am glad to see you," he said. "Jaak told me about my father."

"You met up with Jaak and Saulia?" Dag asked. "Are they well?"

"Yes. What about Saulia's parents?"

Dag shook her head sadly. "I will have to be witness to Tarmo Holt's death when we get back to Tarklee."

"We can leave as soon as we fill the hold," he said. "That's why we're here."

"The Administrator is newly installed," Dag said, "But I'm sure she'll do her best for you."

He looked over Dag's shoulder at her twin. "Truly?"

"Charis helped us get it approved by the council," Inger said. "As a reward for us helping rid Arressa of Pinho."

"Pinho fled the city," Dag said. "When it became known that he is being pursued by a Resolute, people who worked for him scattered. Including the former Merchant Adventurer Administrator."

"And Charis," Calder said. "Jaak told me that he's not a pirate after all."

"No," Dag said. "He was looking for a man named Rahm. To find out why he hadn't fulfilled a contract."

"And found me instead," Calder said. "I need to look for him. My father."

"I'll go with you," Dag said. "Inger can get started on securing our cargo."

"Good." He turned to see Darya and Jaak waiting just outside. "First Mate Darya Demer, meet Inger Lund. You two are in charge of filling the *Atlaine*'s hold. Jaak, you can stay here too."

"Good," Jaak said with evident relief. "Can't say I really wanted to see your Da."

"I know, and I appreciate that you were willing to." He turned to Dag and grabbed her hand. "Come on."

He sighed as they walked along the main docks to the small dock hidden at the north end of the city.

The *Hakon* was there, looking the same as it had before Dag and Jaak had sailed away on it.

"You again." The same woman he'd met before, the one he assumed was his half-sister, walked towards them. "My father said you might come by." She shaded her eyes against the sun as she stared at him. "He also said that you would tell me who

Hakon was."

"He was my brother," Calder said, surprised by her comment. "My twin. But he died young and our father left for the sea."

"My name is Esma," she said. "Brother."

"How long have you known?" Calder asked.

"You have the look of our father," Esma said. "But I didn't realize why you seemed familiar until you," she looked at Dag, "told me you knew who Hakon was and my father became dangerously angry." She shrugged. "That little sailboat always meant almost as much to him as his children, which only makes sense if it was named *for* one of his children."

"Is Rahm here?" Calder asked. "We do not have a lot of time before we set sail."

"He's gone," Esma said. "Something changed recently, and he left very suddenly. You might see him before I do."

"I'll come back to visit," he said. "When I can. Now that we know. You have another older brother and a younger sister as well."

"You beat me. There is just one younger brother here." She smiled. "That I know of. And I would like to see you again."

"I'm Dagrun Lund," Dag said. "My sister Inger has just become the new Administrator for the Merchant Adventurers. Perhaps you could stop and introduce yourself to her one day?"

"An appointment for services in aid of Arressa?" Esma asked, and Calder and Dag both nodded. "She sounds interesting."

"We should go," Calder said. "It has been very nice to meet you."

It was an odd feeling walking away from a sister that he hardly knew, but at least she knew they were family.

He sighed.

"What's wrong?" Dag asked.

"I will have to tell my mother about Esma. And Yakop and Berna, as well."

Only Jaak was at the office when they returned.

"Ship's being loaded," Jaak said. "Inger seems to have some influence around here. They said to feed yourselves and be ready to board at dusk."

"Come on," Dag said. She tugged him, and he followed her out of the office and through the city to a narrow lane.

Dag reached up and found the key and opened the door. "It's

one of Charis's hiding places," she said as she pulled him in and shut the door. "We should have it all—"

Her breath was taken away by his kiss. She pulled away and smiled as she led him to the bed.

CHAPTER 22

GUSTAV JUMPED OFF the wagon and waved to Pavil Barda. Clan Freeholder Timonis's estate was just up this road, according to Pavil.

Gustav had walked nonstop along the road from Tarklee to Pavil's house, where he'd been able to convince the older man to take him to Timonis's freehold. He'd also learned that Pavil had done the same for Kaja and Pia and Frida Engen, except he'd taken them to the coastal town nearest to Lavais Island.

Which was where he was going once he delivered Lauma's message.

Because no matter what Nadez thought, Gustav knew that the end of the Treaty Alliance meant hardship for many people. He wasn't about to let that happen.

Even if Saulia Holt was found and agreed to support Lauma Strauskas, that left people like Henrik Ottosen and Tavet Timonis making decisions based on what was good for them, not what was good for the people who depended on them.

That had to change, he just didn't know how. But he'd do his best to figure out a way.

A moment after he knocked on the door, a woman opened it.

"I have a message from Interim Grand Freeholder Lauma Strauskas for Clan Freeholder Timonis," he said, patting the pouch he held. "I have been instructed to deliver it to him in private."

CHAPTER 23

"Drop the topsail," Calder called, and the order was belayed across the ship. The sail was taken in, and the ship slowed. Tarklee harbour was straight ahead.

"I'm getting good at sailing through the Teeth," Dag said from his side. "I think we shaved off half a day."

"More than that," he agreed. "We made it home in record time. You'll get as much practise sailing through the Teeth as you want."

"I know." Her smile faded. Three shipments of food were not enough to feed all three countries even with the efforts to stockpile more food for the winter. As soon as they unloaded the ship and delivered Saulia Holt to Nadez and Calder's mother, they would be returning to Arressa. At least she would see Inger again.

"I hope you're ready," Dag said to Saulia when she joined them. Fishing boats and barges were launching from shore towards them, ready to unload the goods in the holds of the ship.

"Do I have a choice?" Saulia asked. "I know you trust Lauma Strauskas." She turned her head to look at Calder, who was calling out orders to sailors scurrying about the deck. "Because she's Calder's mother. You don't know the politics of the Clan Freeholders."

"You're right," Dag replied. "I don't. But you do. You were born into this, as was Lauma." As was Calder, although he'd not been raised in it the same way Saulia had. "There's Nadez and Lauma now." She waved at two people on the dock, and Nadez waved back.

NADEZ WAVED AND squinted at the ship. Even from here, she recognized Calder and Dagrun. Her breath caught as she tried to make out the smaller figure at their side.

"They're home safe," Lauma said. "I see my son. And thank Nyorden, I think they found Saulia Holt."

"Are you sure?" Nadez asked. She was afraid that wanting Saulia to be found would make her see something that wasn't there.

"I am." Nadez turned to see a grinning Mykol. "That's Saulia Holt." His grin slipped. "I don't see either Tarmo Holt or his wife Asla, and I doubt Saulia would be on deck without them."

"We knew this was a possibility," Lauma said to him. He nodded, and she turned to Nadez. "Let's go greet them, shall we?"

"Yes," Nadez replied. A dinghy had been launched from the *Atlaine*, and she and Lauma hurried towards the end of the dock, her steps lighter than they'd been in days.

The Fair Seas Treaty Alliance just might survive after all.

The End

Acknowledgements

As always, thanks to the crew at Tyche Books – especially my editor Karley Hauser and publisher Margaret Curelas.

BIOGRAPHY

Jane Glatt loves that along with creating original worlds, writing fantasy allows her to indulge her curiosity about an eclectic group of subjects. So far she's researched synaesthesia, medieval guilds, tidal rivers, cities atop bridges, pirates and privateers, plants used for healing, and the history of spying. For that last one she blames a visit to the International Spy Museum (yes, it's a real place), in Washington D.C.

For news on Jane's future releases visit her website http://janeglatt.com/index.html and sign up for her newsletter